DISCARD

THE BOYS FROM SANTA CRUZ

Also by Jonathan Nasaw

When She Was Bad
Twenty-Seven Bones
Fear Itself
The Girls He Adored
Shadows
The World on Blood
Shakedown Street
West of the Moon
Easy Walking

THE BOYS
FROM
SANTA CRUZ

Jonathan Nasaw

ATRIA BOOKS

New York London Toronto Sydney

ATRIA BOOKS
A Division of Simon & Schuster, Inc.
1230 Avenue of the Americas
New York, NY 10020

First Atria Books hardcover edition February 2010

ATRIA BOOKS and colophon are trademarks of Simon & Schuster, Inc.

For information about special discounts for bulk purchases, please contact Simon & Schuster Special Sales at 1-866-506-1949 or business@simonandschuster.com.

The Simon & Schuster Speakers Bureau can bring authors to your live event. For more information or to book an event, contact the Simon & Schuster Speakers Bureau at 1-866-248-3049 or visit our website at www.simonspeakers.com.

Manufactured in the United States of America

10 9 8 7 6 5 4 3 2 1

Library of Congress Cataloging-in-Publication Data is available.

ISBN 978-1-4165-9178-8
ISBN 978-1-4391-0072-1 (ebook)

For Luke Nasaw

(who has always been like a son to me)

Part one

CHAPTER ONE

1

On the morning my father telephoned from Marshall City to announce that the FBI was closing in, I was in the trailer watching Teddy, my stepmother, getting dressed.

Don't get me wrong, I wasn't there for the show. Teddy was a pre-op, post-implant trannie, built like a nose tackle with tits. But August can be brutal in the Sierras (the temperature was already ninety-two in the shade) and the trailer boasted the only air-conditioning on the property. I was fifteen, living alone in a nonair-conditioned school bus about a quarter mile up the hill from the trailer. No inside plumbing, but I had electricity and all the privacy I wanted. More important from their point of view, so did Big Luke and Teddy.

When my father called, I was sitting at the fold-down table in the kitchenette, working on my second cup of coffee. Teddy's reverse strip show was taking place at the other end of the trailer. She'd left the bedroom door open, and came out half-dressed to answer the phone. I was only wearing shorts and sandals myself. Not wanting her to get any ideas, I pretended to be real interested in looking out through the half-open louvers at the vegetable patch behind the kitchen, where the dusty tomato stalks were slumped against their stakes like soldiers tied up in front of a firing squad.

Somehow I could tell from the silence that it was bad news. I turned around. Teddy had collapsed into the recliner looking as though somebody had whacked her in the paunch with a baseball bat and she was still trying to draw her first breath.

"What?" I asked her.

She looked over at me, surprised, like she'd forgotten there was anybody else in the room, then nodded slowly, with the phone to her ear and her mouth hanging open. I couldn't tell whether she was nodding in response to me or to the phone. Finally, though, she pulled her shit together. She started saying stuff like "don't do anything stupid," and "I'll take of everything," and "nobody has to know anything." Then she looked up at me again. "You better tell him," she said into the phone, then held it out to me.

Ten years later, I can still remember the funky smell of the trailer, the rumble of the air conditioner, the way the dust motes danced in the stripes of sunlight knifing in through the louvers as I took the phone from my stepmother. "Hello?"

"Little Luke?"

"Dad?"

"Get out."

"What?"

"Haul ass. Some very bad shit is about to go down. You don't need to get messed up in it."

"Where should I go?"

"Your grandparents."

On my dead mother's side, he meant. He was an orphan. I was about to become one. "No way. Not happening."

"I don't have time to argue. Put Teddy back on."

That was it. No last fatherly advice, to your own self be true, don't piss into the wind. Not even a lousy good-bye, much less "I love you." I could hear the sirens in the background, so I understand the pressure the man was under. But would a kind word to me have fucking killed him?

Instead I got to hear Teddy's last words to him. "I love you, baby." Then a pause, long enough for an "I love you, too, baby." She must have known what was coming, because she held the phone away from her ear. We both heard the shot. "Fuck you," Teddy started screaming into the receiver. "Fuck you, you fuckers, just fuck you." Really stretching the old vocabulary there.

I pried the phone out of her hand, heard a man's voice, not Big Luke's, yelling something about a gutless son of a bitch, and hung it up. I don't know if I can explain what I was feeling. It was like I knew what had happened and I didn't know, all at the same time. Everything else was crystal clear, though, everything I could see and hear and touch. Teddy was collapsed in the armchair. She had panties on, no shirt. Her beefy arms were hanging straight down over the sides of the chair like they didn't belong to her. I put my hand on her bare shoulder. It was warm. She reached up and grabbed my wrist, leaned her wet cheek against my hand. Then she pulled my hand down and pressed it tight against her breast. I think for a second there she forgot who I was or thought I was my father or something. I took a good feel, more out of numb curiosity than anything else. It felt okay, but not like I thought it would. I could feel the implant squishing around.

Next thing I knew, I was on the floor with my ears ringing. My stepmother was heading for the bedroom. "If you're still here when I come out, I'll kill you," she said over her shoulder.

2

Ten o'clock Tuesday morning. A stakeout in the post office in Marshall City, California. Sweat stains in the shape of landmasses were already spreading across Pender's hula shirt from the armpits, the bulge of his belly, the small of his back, threatening to merge like the Pangaea hypothesis in reverse. Bill Izzo, his partner, sat in an air-conditioned car parked across the street, radioing a heads-up into Pender's flesh-colored earpiece whenever someone fitting the general description of the unknown subject, or Unsub—male Caucasian, dark hair, bodybuilder physique—entered the building.

The reason Special Agent William C. Izzo was cooling it in the car while Special Agent E. L. Pender sweltered in the post office was that no matter how they were dressed, Izzo always looked like an FBI man and Pender never did. Six-four, beefy, homely, and bald as a melon, dressed in that soggy Hawaiian shirt, Bermuda shorts, calf-high black socks, and open-toed sandals, he stood in the lobby, pretending to fill out an Express Mail form while stealthily eyeballing the fourth tiny door from the right, third row from the top, in the wall of brass-and-glass P.O. boxes. Because it might not be Unsub who picks up the mail, Pender had to keep reminding himself. Could be anybody: a brother, a girlfriend, a little old lady.

"Ed, this could be it." Izzo's voice crackled in Pender's ear. "Jeans, red tank top. Arms like Popeye. Could be strapped."

Pender acknowledged by twice tapping the miniaturized microphone under the collar of his shirt. The front door was to his right. As the man in the tank top passed him on his way to the P.O. boxes, Pender snuck a glance at the photo underneath the manila envelope he'd been pretending to mail. It was a grainy blowup of Unsub wearing the Lone Ranger mask he'd worn in the video. This looked like the same man; he reached for the right box, and he even twirled the dial of the combination lock with his knuckles, so as not to leave fingerprints.

"That's our guy," Pender whispered into his collar. But the post office was full of civilians, so he and Izzo agreed to take Unsub down outside, on the street. Izzo relayed the information to the deputy from the Marshall County Sheriff's Department, who was out back covering the loading dock.

Pender waited for Unsub to pass him, then followed two or three paces behind. But just as Unsub opened the front door, the deputy sheriff came charging around from behind the building brandishing a pump-action shotgun.

Aw, fuck, thought Pender, as Unsub turned around and headed back into the post office, nearly bumping into him. Their eyes locked; Pender knew he'd been made. Gunfight at the O.K. Corral time. Unsub reached for the .38 automatic in the waistband of his jeans, Pender for the Smith & Wesson Model 10 he was carrying in a behind-the-back kidney holster instead of his trusty calfskin shoulder holster, which would have required him to wear a jacket in the August heat.

Advantage Unsub, who drew first and pulled the trigger while Pender was still fumbling behind his back. Happily for Pender, either the gun misfired, or Unsub had neglected to chamber a round.

By then Pender had succeeded in drawing *his* gun, but the lobby was too crowded for him to fire. Unsub faked left and darted right, across the lobby, dodging panicked postal patrons, then vaulted over the counter, heading for the loading dock in back. Which was supposed to have been covered by the plainclothes who'd blown the stakeout in the first place, only he, of course, was around front now.

The year was 1985. Pender—forty years old, twenty pounds over fighting weight, and smoking a pack of Marlboros a day— hauled himself ingloriously over the counter and chased Unsub out the back door, across the loading dock, down the concrete ramp, across a dusty alley, and through the back door of a two-story wood-frame antiques store. Izzo charged through the front door of the shop as Pender burst in through the back. A woman who had taken cover behind a glass knickknack case pointed timorously to the staircase leading up to the second floor.

"Any way out from there?" whispered Izzo.

"Only through the window."

Izzo was wearing a Kevlar vest beneath a single-breasted gray suit tailored to fit it, so he took the point. Through the third of the three doors on the second floor, the agents could hear Unsub talking to someone on the telephone. The smaller Izzo gave Pender a little would-you-care-to-do-the-honors? wave in the direction of the door. Pender pointed down to his sandals. Izzo shrugged, splintered the door latch with his Florsheim. The door sprang open. Over Izzo's shoulder, Pender saw Unsub sitting behind an empty desk with the phone in one hand and the .38 in the other.

Izzo yelled, "Drop it! Put your hands up!"

Unsub said, "I love you, too, baby," into the phone, then put the muzzle of the .38 in his mouth, sucked in his cheeks, and pulled the trigger. This time the gun did not misfire.

3

I believed Teddy when she said she'd kill me. Up until then we'd maintained an uneasy truce, but with my father out of the picture, all bets were off. I didn't leave the property, though. I had no place to go. Instead I snuck around behind the trailer and peeked in through the louvers in time to see Teddy, now wearing a T-shirt and shorts, backing out of the bedroom dragging Big Luke's old green steamer trunk.

When she kept going, dragging the trunk out the door and down the cinder-block doorstep (which Big Luke had been meaning to replace with something permanent at least as long as I'd been there), I assumed she was going to haul ass like he'd told me to do. I peeked around the side of the trailer to see if she was gone yet, but she'd only dragged the trunk as far as the fire pit, a scooped-out circle of blackened ground with split logs around it to sit on. We hadn't used it all summer, because the surrounding woods were too dry for open fires.

Teddy knelt and opened the trunk with a key, then trotted into the shed at the end of the driveway and came out with a big red gasoline can. She didn't bother with the spout, just unscrewed the top and sloshed gas all over the trunk. She patted through her pockets looking for a lighter, but for once in her life (Big Luke and Teddy both smoked like chimneys) she didn't have one.

She started back for the trailer. I ducked out of sight again, but as soon as she went inside, I raced straight across the clearing for the fire pit. I had to know what was in that trunk, I just had to. And to be honest, what I thought I was going to find was dope. (Big Luke and Teddy were small-time dealers, weed and meth, mostly.) Instead the whole trunk was stuffed full of videocassettes. What the fuck? I reached down, picked up one that the gasoline had somehow missed, and was turning it around to read the label when I heard a popping sound. Simultaneously, the dirt kicked up a couple feet to my left. I looked up, saw Teddy standing in the doorway of the trailer holding her dainty little pearl-handled .22 pistol. She fired again, from the hip. The trunk took a little hop, then there was a *whomp* and a *whoosh,* and the next thing I knew I was flying backward through the air.

I landed about ten feet away, barefoot: the explosion had blown me right out of my sandals. Through the flames and the oily black smoke and the rippling heat waves, I saw Teddy walking slowly across the yard toward me, aiming the gun two-handed. Every couple of steps the gun jerked, but I must have been deaf from the explosion because I didn't hear any shots. It was like I was watching a movie, only somebody had turned off the sound.

But my nose still worked. I smelled the stench of gasoline and melting plastic and something even worse, that took me a second to identify. It was burning hair: I realized suddenly that my Mohawk was smoking. And Teddy was still coming. So now I was scrambling to my feet and slapping at my hair, while all around me bullets I couldn't hear were smacking into the dirt, kicking up silent puffs of dust.

Then a miracle happened. When she reached the burning trunk, Teddy stopped, raised the gun, put the barrel in her mouth, looked me right in the eye, smoke billowing around her, and pulled the trigger.

Another miracle: I could hear again. Not the shot, but the soft crackling of the flames and the bubbling of the melting plastic, and finally, after what seemed like an impossibly long time, a two-part thud as Teddy dropped to her knees, then pitched face forward into the trunk.

It was over then, except for one last spooky sound, a high-pitched, drawn-out *eeeeeeeeeeee,* like steam whistling through a teakettle. I don't know what it was exactly, whether it was Teddy screaming, which would have meant she was still alive somehow, or just something that happens when a body burns in that position, superheated air being forced through the vocal cords or something like that. But even after all these years, sometimes at night, when it's very quiet, I still hear it: *eeeeeeeeeeee . . .*

4

Before 1985, the snuff film was something of an urban legend. Everybody knew somebody who knew somebody whose cousin claimed to have seen a sex video that included an actual murder, but nobody claimed to have seen one personally until the FBI's Organized Crime division raided a warehouse in Paramus, New Jersey, in June of that year, and found a carton of identical videocassettes labeled *Principals of Accounting, Tape 3.*

Even then, the videos might have gone unnoticed if Special Agent William C. Izzo hadn't been the spelling bee champion of P.S. 139 in Queens in his youth. He not only knew the difference between principals and principles, he still remembered the mnemonic: the princiPAL is the student's PAL.

At first viewing, Izzo thought he'd uncovered some run-of-the-mill amateur porn: roly-poly, middle-aged woman having sex with a buff, dark-haired white guy wearing a white Lone Ranger mask. But in the last fifteen minutes of the half-hour video, the victim was throttled unconscious, then revived, throttled, revived, and ultimately strangled to death.

Watching it even once wasn't easy—poor Izzo had to view it repeatedly, first with his ASAC (Assistant Special Agent In Charge), then with the SAC, then with the AD (Assistant Director). And after the spin-off investigation had been green-lighted with Izzo as CA (Case Agent), he watched it over and over, frame by frame, with a technician, searching for clues to the identity and/or location of the videographers.

The big break in the investigation, however, was provided not by Izzo, but by a rookie agent sifting through the warehouse garbage on a barge moored off Perth Amboy. In early August, the rook discovered a stained and crumpled bill of lading for a carton of educational videocassettes shipped from a post office box in Marshall City, California.

When efforts to identify the box's leaseholder failed, Izzo proposed a potentially man-hour-eating stakeout. Figuring he'd need at least four agents to do the job right, he asked for eight and got one. Special Agent E. L. Pender from the Liaison Support Unit, who'd been working on a similar case in nearby Calaveras County, was dispatched to assist Izzo.

Pender had already been in California for nearly three weeks, helping the locals identify victims of the serial murderers Charles Mapes and Leonard Nguyen. Day after day, he studied the women in Mapes and Nguyen's videotaped torture-murders in an effort to match their descriptions and likenesses with those of missing women from all over the western United States. And night after night he drank himself into a near stupor in an effort to shut off the goddamn VCR in his head long enough to fall asleep.

The only good thing about the Mapes-Nguyen investigation, at least as far as Pender was concerned, was that it was over. Mapes was dead, Nguyen had fled, and one way or another, all the victims who could be identified, had been, leaving only a few charred bone fragments to be buried anonymously.

And now that Unsub was (a) dead, and (b) an unsub no longer, having been identified through fingerprint records as an ex-con named Luke Sweet—last known address, a trailer in the Sierra foothills—Pender was hoping that the Marshall County investigation was all but wrapped up as well. He was looking forward to getting home, putting in a little R & R.

"Going to eat some crab cakes, play a little golf, maybe get laid if the missus is in the mood," he told Izzo, as their Bu-car, a dark blue Crown Vic on loan from the Sacramento field office, hitched on to the tail end of a law enforcement convoy consisting of basically every vehicle in Marshall County with a dome light and a siren.

"You're married?" said Izzo. "We've been working together, what, almost a week—I had no idea you were married."

Pender shrugged. "Yeah, well, you may have put your finger on part of the problem there."

5

I suppose if I bothered to put myself in Teddy's place now, I could work up some sorry. Back then, I was too busy putting out the fire to be anything but glad she'd killed herself instead of me. My eyebrows were singed and my face was starting to sting, so first I hosed myself off and then I dragged the hose out from behind the trailer as far as it would reach. I was still about fifteen yards short, but by aiming high I was able to arc a stream of water down onto the trunk.

And onto Teddy, of course, who was still on her knees, but jackknifed over the trunk with her head and arms inside and her big ass sticking out. The fire hissed and steamed and bubbled, the smoke billowed out black, then white. I put the hose down and went over to take a closer look. Lucky for me I'm not squeamish, because not only was the smell completely toe-curling, but all that melted plastic and celluloid in the bottom of the trunk was hardening as it cooled. If they wanted to bury Teddy they were going to have to either cut off her head, or dig a T-shaped hole and bury the trunk with her.

So now I'm soaking wet, slightly singed, and newly orphaned. I suppose I must have been in shock, too, because despite Big Luke's warning, I still didn't haul ass. Instead I hiked back up to my bus, toweled off, smeared Neosporin on some minor burns, took a couple aspirin, pulled on a pair of cutoffs and a T-shirt with WHAT THE FUCK ARE YOU LOOKING AT? hand-stenciled on the back, and rolled a fatty. Then I put a Bob Marley record on the turntable, switched on the outside speakers, cranked up the volume, then climbed up onto the roof of the bus and sat down on my lawn chair to get stoned and think things over.

I didn't get much thinking done, though. When I saw the turkey vulture circling low in the sky over my dad's trailer, I could feel the anger boiling up inside me. Big Luke hated vultures. Sometimes he'd take me up into the hills and we'd use them for target practice. So I scrambled down the ladder, grabbed my thirty-ought-six and a box of shells, and crept down the path, barefooted and quiet as an Indian, with Bob Marley covering what little noise I did make.

As it turned out, I could have driven down there in a tank and the vulture perched on the edge of the trunk probably wouldn't have noticed. Hissing and grunting, its bald red head stabbing up and down, it tore off chunk after chunk of Teddy's ass with its curved ivory beak, leaving deep red gouges in the charred flesh.

I took cover behind the shed, then leaned out, took careful aim, and knocked the nasty old scavenger off the trunk with a single shot. Reloaded. Waited. Ten minutes, fifteen minutes . . . and here came another one. Gliding effortlessly, silhouetted black against the sky, it was an easy target. I led it a few inches, dropped it out of the sky. Reloaded. Waited. Half an hour later, a third vulture came soaring in from the north, but something, maybe the corpses of its buddies, alerted it, and it drifted away without ever coming into range.

And now I was alone again, except for what was left of Teddy, and I was feeling so empty I almost missed the vultures. But then I had to laugh. Because in the distance, up the hill, I could hear Bob Marley singing about how he was gonna chase dem dirty baldheads out of de town.

My next move was to drag a tarp out of the shed, drape it over Teddy and the trunk, then weigh the edges down with stones, not so much because I gave a shit about Teddy's corpse, but because I just didn't want to give the vultures the satisfaction. Then I searched the trailer. I didn't find what Big Luke and Teddy called the inventory, but their personal stash was impressive. Close to two thousand bucks in cash, a couple ounces of weed, and a few grams of ice. (If you don't know what ice is, that's crank in a smokable form. If you don't know what crank is, that's meth. If you don't know what meth is, consider yourself lucky.) I also found a bottle of Percodan in the medicine cabinet, along with all Teddy's hormones and whatever. Swantzer, Theodora: take one every six to eight hours as needed for pain.

I took the cash, the weed, and the pain pills, but left everything else. And now I had a hard decision to make. In the words of the Clash song, should I stay or should I go? I hadn't done anything wrong, but when you're fifteen, that doesn't matter. If I stayed, there's no way the cops would have just taken my statement and cut me loose. Instead they'd probably have put me in Juvie while they got things sorted out, then shipped me down to Santa Cruz in custody of my grandparents, Fred and Evelyn, who'd tell me what to eat, when to sleep, what to wear, and how to cut my hair.

Either that, or they'd ship me off to some kind of foster care, probably a group home, where they would also tell me what to eat, when to sleep, what to wear, and how to cut my hair. Either place they'd make me go to school until I was eighteen.

Of course, I could always just run away, but then I'd be homeless. Homeless with enough money and dope to make me the king of the runaways for a while, true, but then what?

In the end, I decided to give Fred and Evelyn one more chance to do right by me, but on three conditions. One, I would get down there on my own, rather than waiting around for the cops to arrive and possibly spending several nights in Juvie while they got the custody issues straightened out. Two, I would arrive with cash and stash sufficient to see myself through the next few months. Three, I would not call first. If my grandparents didn't want me, I decided, let them tell me to my face.

CHAPTER TWO

1

Due to the length of the convoy blocking the driveway leading up to Sweet's trailer, the two FBI agents had to hike the last few hundred yards. Pender had changed into a pre-rumpled blue-and-white-striped seersucker sport coat and peach-colored golf slacks before they left Marshall City. Izzo was wearing the same miraculously unwrinkled gray suit he'd worn throughout the stakeout and the chase, but had ditched the Kevlar vest.

They arrived just in time to see the sheriff's deputies pulling a tarpaulin off a bulky object in the middle of a clearing, unveiling a charred human body jackknifed over the side of a scorched metal steamer trunk. The upper half of the corpse was inside the trunk, which was filled with sooty, oily-black water. Chunks of flesh had been torn from the lower half, presumably by turkey vultures, two of which lay dead within a few yards of the trunk.

"And me without my spoon," Pender muttered, as the flash-bulbs began to pop.

Once the body had been photographed in situ from every imaginable angle, the deputies struggled in vain to remove it from the trunk. It wasn't until after they'd drained off the water that they realized the head was firmly encased in eight to ten inches of melted, rehardened plastic.

Yet another surprise was in order for the deputy who'd been assigned to free the body by chipping away at the plastic. Up close and personal, he announced, the corpse appeared to be female from the waist up and male from the waist down.

One more important discovery was made by one of the weaker-stomached deputies. After getting a good look at the star attraction, the man had staggered off into the bushes to launch his lunch and returned with a videocassette he'd found lying in the dirt. He handed it to Izzo, who showed it to Pender, who winced when he saw the label: *Principals of Accounting, Tape 4.*

"C'mon, there's bound to be a VCR in the trailer," Izzo said eagerly.

"Let me know how it comes out," said Pender.

Izzo thought Pender was kidding at first. He started toward the trailer, then turned back—Pender hadn't moved. "What's the problem, Ed?"

Pender shrugged. "I've been chasing serial killers going on ten years now. I've seen shit that'd turn Jack the Ripper's stomach. Half-eaten corpses, skulls stacked like cannonballs on the court-house lawn, you name it. But up until three weeks ago, I've never actually had to watch the victims suffering before they died. Now it seems like everybody and their brother's got a camcorder. Mapes and Nguyen, Sweet and Swantzer, it's like a fad or something, and lemme tell you, podner: it's getting real old, real fast."

Izzo, who'd taken a sudden interest in studying the dirt at

his feet, waited a few seconds, then asked Pender if he'd finished venting.

Pender nodded—a short, sharp nod, like a bull rider signaling for the chute to be opened.

"Good," said Izzo. "Because I'm at least as sick of this shit as you are, and I'll be goddamned if I'm going to watch this thing by myself."

2

Once I'd decided where I was going, my next problem was figuring out how to get there. After weighing all the options, I decided to take Teddy's Olds. It seemed like it would be more fun than taking the bus and less risky than hitchhiking with a backpack full of dope. And if I did get pulled over, not having a driver's license was going to be the least of my problems.

The car was a '77 Delta 88 with air-conditioning, a tape deck, and a V-8 engine that pressed you back against the bench seat when you floored the accelerator. I had all the weed I could smoke and enough money to buy all the fast food I could eat, so in spite of all the harsh things that had happened to me that day, once I got the hang of driving, I was almost happy.

The closest I came to getting arrested wasn't while I was driving, it was when I pulled in for gas at an ARCO mini-mart near Davis. By the time I saw the highway patrol car parked outside, I was already committed. I figured driving away without buying anything would have looked even more suspicious, so I pulled up to the pumps, got out of the car, went inside, gave the guy a twenty against a fill-up, went back out to the pump, pushed the button for the 87 octane, lifted the nozzle casually, turned around, and discovered there was no place to put it—the gas tank was not on that side of the car.

I was sure the cop was checking me out. The scorched Mohawk alone would have caught his attention. Not to mention my WHAT THE FUCK ARE YOU LOOKING AT? T-shirt. *Be cool,* I ordered myself. *Gas tank must be around the other side.* Fortunately, the hose reached. Unfortunately, the tank wasn't on that side, either. I nearly pissed my pants. *Where's the fucking gas cap? Is the cop getting suspicious? Don't look at him, don't look at him. But if he sees I don't know how to fill up the car, he's going to think I stole it.* To cover myself, I knelt down and pretended to check the right rear tire. *Think, dude, think! It's got to be someplace!*

So now I was walking around the stupid car, tugging the hose as far as it would stretch, pretending to check all the tires and the lights and shit. The cop's eyes were boring holes in me, and I was trying to act casual, but I was sweating bullets and my mind was racing a million miles a second by the time I noticed that the rear license plate was mounted on a spring. Suddenly it all came back to me. In the Olds, the rear license plate flipped down and the gas cap was hidden behind it. I must have seen Teddy do it a dozen times. End of crisis.

The rest of the ride was a piece of cake. It was dark by the time I reached my old hometown of Santa Cruz, where the palm trees meet the pines. I have to admit I got a little lump in my throat when the candy-colored lights of the Boardwalk came into view. We'd had some good times in this town, me and my mom. I used to have a season pass for the rides. Once I rode the Giant Dipper sixty-seven times in a row. I even had a little gang of friends. We were eleven, we had bicycles and boogie boards, and we owned that town from the university heights to the beachfront flats.

Then my mother died and I went to live with my grandparents, Fred and Evelyn Harris. That lasted about six months, until my grandfather slapped me for calling my grandmother a bitch (which I didn't, I only said she was *acting* like a bitch, which she was). Anyway, I punched him in his droopy nuts, and they sent me to live with my father.

But now my father was dead, too. I knew that for sure by this time: I'd heard it on the car radio. They said he'd shot himself to avoid being taken into custody, but they never said why he was being taken into custody in the first place.

I didn't know if Fred and Evelyn had also heard the news. They probably had, I thought, but since they hated my father more than they hated me, I hoped that would work in my favor. If they were willing to let bygones be bygones, I figured, so was I.

3

"Stop it there," said Izzo. He and Pender were sitting side by side on the narrow, scratchy sofa bed in the living room of the trailer, watching *Principals of Accounting, Tape 4* with the lights dimmed and the blinds drawn.

Pender hit the Pause button. The background rattle and hum of the air-conditioning swelled to fill the silence. "What?"

"You missed it. Run it back—there was a reflection in the window over the bed."

Pender reversed the tape, then ran it forward in slow motion, freezing the image when a figure wearing a backward-facing baseball cap and a San Francisco 49ers jersey appeared briefly in the dark glass of the horizontal window over the bed, peering into the viewfinder of the camcorder balanced on his shoulder. They couldn't quite make out the face behind the viewfinder. All they knew for sure was that it couldn't have been Luke Sweet or Theodora Swantzer, Sweet's transgendered, ex-con partner, because those two were both clearly visible on the bed. Butt-naked save for their Lone Ranger masks and Swantzer's genital-concealing panties, they were taking turns smacking around a skinny, teenage runaway who looked as if she were just beginning to realize how much trouble she was in.

The agents exchanged grim smiles. It had been doubly hard on them, watching the victims suffering, knowing that the killers were beyond the reach of earthly justice. It felt as if Sweet and Swantzer were taunting them—*look what we did,* they seemed to be saying with every thrust and blow, *look what we got away with—and you can't . . . fucking . . . touch us!*

So the discovery that the unspeakable pair had had an accomplice buoyed the agents' spirits a little. Izzo jotted down the time on the VCR counter—fourteen minutes into the tape—and made a note to have somebody blow up and tweak the frames in question. Then they settled back to watch the rest of the horror show, which ended shortly after the victim's death, with Luke Sweet delivering a chilling throwaway line—"You like apples? Well, how do you like them apples?"—as he climbed off the corpse.

The screen went dark. Over the hum of the air-conditioning, they heard the hackle-raising sound of a baying hound—the state police had brought in a cadaver-sniffing dog to search the property. "You look like you could use a drink," Pender told Izzo, thirstily eyeing the nearly full bottle of Jack Daniel's on the counter separating the living room from the kitchen area.

"Didn't anybody tell you FBI agents aren't supposed to drink alcohol, especially on the job?" Izzo asked him.

"Yeah, I think I heard something like that once," said Pender as he rinsed out two water glasses. "Ice?"

"Sure."

Pender was about to open the refrigerator door when one of the photographs affixed to it by magnet caught his eye. It was the former Unsub, standing in front of the trailer with his arm around a teenage boy. The boy was sporting a Mohawk hairdo and an adolescent scowl, and wearing a red 49ers jersey with the number 16 across the front. Pender took it down and turned it over—across the back of the snapshot, someone had written "Big Luke, Little Luke, Father's Day," with a felt-tipped pen.

"Oh jeez," he said, wincing.

"Beg pardon?" called Izzo.

"That 'accomplice' we were looking for, the one with the camera? It's Sweet's son. Little Luke. Looks like he's around fourteen, fifteen years old."

Izzo winced. "Man oh Manischewitz," he groaned. "Just when you think it can't get any sicker."

4

Not only had it been four years since I'd last been to Santa Cruz, but back then I'd been getting around on a bicycle. I didn't exactly get lost, but I must have made a wrong turn, because I found myself driving past the Boardwalk.

I pulled over to watch the people hanging out on the steps near the carousel, thinking I might see some of my old friends. I didn't, but I did see quite a few kids around my age, clusters of them laughing and acting goony, couples making out or strolling with their arms around each other's waists. Some of the white kids were punked out like me. Part of me despised them, but another part of me could imagine a different world, where if you were alone and there was a group of kids your age and style, you could just hook up with them. Of course, if they'd known I had all that dope and money, it would have been *them* trying to hook up with *me*.

It was around ten o'clock when I rang my grandparents' bell. Fred was already in his bathrobe and pajamas. Tall man, severe, always looked like he'd just finished shaving. I could tell by the look on his face that he knew what had happened.

"It's him," he called up the stairs to my grandmother. He didn't say hello, but he didn't slam the door in my face, either. A few seconds later Evelyn came bustling down the stairs in her nightgown and threw her arms around me. I was taller than she was, now. It was the first anybody had touched me since Teddy knocked me down this morning. For some reason I burst into tears. I didn't even know I had any tears in me.

I slept in my old bed in my old room that night. Clean sheets, cool ocean breeze, a long hot shower, salve for my burns, then one of Teddy's pain pills, and I was in dreamland. My dreams weren't as gory as you'd have expected, though. I didn't relive the events of the morning or anything like that. Instead, I dreamed that I'd driven Teddy's car someplace, only now I couldn't find it and I couldn't remember how to get home.

5

Early evening. Plenty of light, but the afternoon heat had largely dissipated by the time Pender and Izzo made it up to the derelict school bus where the boy in the photograph had been living.

"What a way to raise a kid." Izzo glanced around at the third-world squalor. Broken windows, bare, stained mattress, dirty clothes, empty Coke cans, potato chip bags, Twinkie wrappers, crumpled tissues. "You have to feel sorry for the little bastard. I wouldn't be surprised if they forced him to work the camera for them—maybe even molested him."

"That could explain why he shot Swantzer, first chance he got," said Pender. The deputies who'd discovered the bus earlier had already found the boy's thirty-ought-six hunting rifle and a box of cartridges identical to the ones found down by the clearing.

Pender and Izzo picked their way to the back of the bus, where the boy had carpeted the grimy, rust-pocked, ribbed metal floor with a fragment of Oriental rug, and fashioned a crude tent by hanging Indian bedspreads from the ceiling. A glass ashtray was filled with cigarette butts, and there was a well-worn copy of *The*

Catcher in the Rye on the rug, next to a black plastic film canister and a pack of rolling papers. Pender opened the little film can, shook a manicured green bud onto his palm. "Sinsemilla," he said. "No seeds. Ten times as strong as the old Mexican reefer—or so they say," he added quickly.

Izzo brushed a cobweb from the shoulder of his jacket and sniffed the air disapprovingly. "C'mon, let's get out of here before the smell starts to cling—I just had this suit dry-cleaned."

Pender followed Izzo back up the aisle and down the rubber-matted steps, feeling more than a little creeped out and claustro-phobic himself.

"Excuse me, are you done in there?" The deputy who'd lost his lunch and found Tape 4 was waiting outside the bus, along with an eleven-year-old female officer—that's how old she looked to Pender, anyway. "The sheriff wants us to toss the bus as soon as you're finished."

"Toss away," said Izzo.

"And while you're searching," added Pender, "if you turn up anything that might give us a hint as to where the kid's heading, an address book, something like that, let me know right away."

Meanwhile, out behind Big Luke's trailer, the cadaver dog, a lugubrious-looking bloodhound named Beano, had planted him-self on his haunches in the middle of the tomato patch and let out a bloodcurdling howl that echoed across the summer-gold hillside. By the time Pender and Izzo arrived, the deputies had pulled up the staked plants, roots and all, and begun to dig in earnest, their spades biting into the sun-baked earth with a meaty-sounding *ch-chunk, ch-chunk*.

From the pile of discarded plants, Pender selected a dusty, ripe-red, sun-warmed beefsteak tomato the size of a softball and was looking around for a hose or a spigot with which to rinse it off when one of the deputies' spades struck something hard.

"I think I hit bone," called the deputy, dropping to one knee and brushing away the loose dirt. "Yup, definitely hit . . . looks like . . . yup, it's a skull, all right. Who's got the camera, somebody got the camera?"

Pender's tomato didn't seem quite so appealing now. He reared back and tossed it as far as he could, heard it land far down the hill with a fat, wet *splat*.

"Good arm." A girlish voice behind him.

Pender turned—it was the little female deputy. "I think I pulled something," he said, gingerly rotating his shoulder. "What's up?"

She handed him a small address book, faux-leather cover, two inches wide, three inches high. On the first page, under "If found, please return to," the name Luke Sweet was written in a childish hand, with one Santa Cruz address crossed out and another penciled in. Pender flipped through the pages. The first entry was under *D,* for Dad. No phone number, just "Dad," a long, cryptic number, and an address that explained the cryptic number: San Quentin Prison, Marin County, CA.

Another half dozen entries—presumably Luke's buddies—were alphabetized by their first names—Joe, Kent, Larry, Michael, Micky—but on the *G* page was an entry for Grandpa Fred & Grandma Evelyn, with the same address as the one penciled in on the first page. At some point, obviously, Little Luke had moved in with his grandparents.

Which didn't mean that was where he'd gone now, but it was the closest thing to a lead they'd had since they learned of the boy's existence. Pender thanked the deputy, pocketed the book, and wandered off in search of a telephone.

CHAPTER THREE

I

It was still dark out when old Fred woke me up. "Get dressed, there's somebody downstairs who wants to talk with you."

I was pretty groggy. It took me a few seconds to remember why I was in my old room at my grandparents' house. Then everything snapped into place. Big Luke and Teddy were dead, and more than likely, the somebody downstairs who wanted to talk with me was wearing a badge and carrying a gun.

Climbing out the window was a tighter squeeze than it had been when I was eleven, but the drop to the lawn was easier now that I was taller. I lowered myself from the redwood gutter by my fingertips, dropped the last few feet, landed softly on my toes, and toppled over backward from the weight of my pack.

"Give you a hand there, son?" It was a huge fat guy wearing a loud sport coat and one of those stupid little checked hats with feathers in the brim. He had a cigarette in his mouth. When he reached down to help me up, his coat fell open and I saw the gun in his shoulder holster. I had the feeling he wanted me to see it, so I wouldn't try to run. I took his hand, which was the size of a first baseman's mitt, and he hauled me onto my feet easier than I could have lifted my backpack alone. "I'm guessing you're Luke."

"Who are you?" Through the open bedroom window, I could hear my grandfather pounding on the door and calling for me to hurry up.

"Pender. FBI. I was supposed to wait out here while you talked to your lawyer. Thought I might as well have a cigarette. You smoke?"

He shook a Marlboro out of the hard pack and gave me a light, but I only got a couple of puffs before I heard the bedroom door crashing open. Grandpa leaned out the dormer window calling my name. Pender stepped under the eaves with me, out of my grandfather's line of sight, and held a finger to his lips.

"We don't have much time," he whispered. "I'll make you a deal. You tell your lawyer you'll be happy to cooperate with the nice FBI man, and then you tell me everything you know about your father and Teddy."

"What's the deal part?" I whispered back.

"The deal part is, I don't search your pack."

I don't know if there's a word for what I experienced at that precise moment in time. Outside my head, everything seemed to stop. Even the smoke from our cigarettes seemed to hang in the air. But inside my head it was like a boatload of rats and the boat was sinking. Thoughts tearing around, scrambling up the walls, looking for a way out. I didn't even know I *had* a lawyer. I did know I was carrying a felony weight of weed. But could Pender do that anyway, just search my pack? And what did I know that he wanted to know? Big Luke's business? Who he bought from and sold to? Yeah, right, like

I'm gonna rat out the Indians my father bought his pot from. They'd cut my balls off and serve them to me for an appetizer.

But what choice did I have? I shrugged off the pack and stowed it behind a bush just as a guy in a light-colored suit and glasses came flying around the side of the house, his city slicker shoes skidding on the grass as he rounded the corner. "Did you see—" he started to call to Pender. Then he caught sight of me in the shadows. "It's okay, he's out here," he called up to my grandfather.

It was the lawyer I didn't know I had. He looked kind of young even to me, but he wasn't intimidated by Pender. "Shame on you," he told him. "You know better than that."

Pender looked around as though the lawyer must have been talking to somebody else, then spread his hands apart, palms up, and shrugged. "I'm minding my own business, enjoying a peaceful smoke, next thing I know your client almost lands on top of me."

I was just thinking about making a run for it when Pender edged over a couple of steps and put his hand on my shoulder, like he'd read my mind. His hand weighed a ton. "What do you say, son? You lawyering up?" Just in case I'd forgotten, he looked over my shoulder to where I'd stashed my backpack.

"I don't mind talking to him," I told the lawyer. "I haven't done anything wrong."

Famous last words.

My grandparents were waiting for us inside. Neither of them could look me in the eye, which pretty much told me what I wanted to know. But just to be sure, when the lawyer drew my grandparents over to the side of the room to confer with them, I asked Pender if it was Fred and Evelyn who'd ratted me out. "In a heartbeat, son," he said with a friendly wink. "In a goddamn heartbeat."

Although I'm mostly self-taught, I'm far from stupid. I'm also my father's son, so I should have known better than to trust a cop. But I was new at this and I was up against an expert.

In hindsight, I think Pender's talent wasn't so much getting you to like him as it was getting you to believe that he liked you. He told me he needed me to help him make some sense out of a few things, starting with the most bizarre crime scene he'd ever stumbled on. The way he said it almost made me feel honored to have been a part of it.

So I explained about Teddy and the phone call and the trunk and the explosion and how she tried to kill me. When I got to the part about shooting the vultures, the lawyer tried to stop me. I laughed at him. "Turkey vultures aren't exactly an endangered species," I told him.

"Besides, he needs the vultures," added Pender. He was sitting catty-corner to me, on my left, in Fred's master-of-the-house armchair. I'm on the sofa and my lawyer's sitting across from me on the other sofa, to Pender's left.

"What's that supposed to mean?" I asked Pender. "What would I need the vultures for?"

"To explain away the gunshot residue I'm sure we'll find on you." He still had that pleasant half smile, but there was a greedy glitter in his close-set, piggy little eyes as he lowered the boom. It reminded me of the expression that used to come over Teddy's face just before she fired up her first hit of the day. "Come on now, son, you don't really expect anybody to buy that ridiculous story, do you? For no particular reason, your stepmother decides to kill you. Then for no particular reason she changes her mind and decides to kill *herself*. Only instead of simply blowing her brains out like anybody else would, she decides first she's going to walk into the middle of a blazing fire, then she's going to kneel down and stick her head into a burning trunk, and *then* she's going to blow her brains out."

"That's not what I said. I said she shot herself *first,* then she—"

"Shut up," the lawyer said quietly but firmly. I shut up. "Agent Pender, this interview is over."

Pender ignored him. He leaned forward and put his huge hand on my knee. It made my skin crawl. "Son, I want to help you, but you have to give me something to work with. I don't care if you killed Teddy. Teddy was a monster, and believe me, I know, I've seen her rap sheet. So tell me you pulled the trigger in self-defense, I'll buy it. It's the victims I need to know about, so we can bring their families some peace."

"Victims? What victims?"

"The ones on those videos you and Teddy burned before you shot her."

"I told you, I *didn't* shoot Teddy, she shot herself." Scared, confused, close to tears, I turned to my lawyer. "You have to listen to me, he's making this stuff up, I don't know what he's talking about."

He tried to come to my rescue. "This is starting to sound like a fishing expedition, Agent Pender. Do you have any evidence to back up these charges?"

Pender turned to him. "So far, only the tape that survived the fire, and the two female bodies we found in the tomato patch," he said cheerfully. "But they were still digging when I left."

2

It was close to daylight by the time the Santa Cruz cops arrived to take me into custody. Pender had one more surprise for me: he called one of them into the backyard, and when they returned, the cop was carrying my backpack. Pender told me he was sorry, that the cop found it on his own, but I didn't believe him on account of his grin. By now it was practically splitting his big bald head in two. The man was just so *pleased* with himself he was starting to look like a Muppet.

I put up a hell of a fight trying to get to him. I wanted to tear that grin right off his face, just dig my fingers under his skin and rip, but I only made it about halfway across the room before the cops got me into a choke hold. Pender's laughter is the last thing I remember hearing before I lost consciousness.

I was only out a few seconds. Everybody was still there when I came to, but I had never felt so alone in my life. And I don't mean just friendless or nobody-loves-me alone. I was used to that. This was a different kind of alone, this was one of those science fiction deals where the hero finds himself in some other reality, in some other dimension or on some other planet, where everything looks the same as it did before but nothing is, and nobody seems to know it but him.

As for Fred and Evelyn, they acted like I had some kind of infectious disease, drawing themselves up against the wall so as not to have me brush against them while the cops were hustling me out of the house in handcuffs.

I spent the rest of that day in holding cells, courtrooms, and the backseats of cop cars. After I was arraigned for the dope in Santa Cruz (the kid lawyer pled me not guilty), they handed me over to a sheriff's deputy who'd driven all the way down from Marshall County to pick me up. Not looking real thrilled about his assignment, the deputy shoved me handcuffed into the back of his cruiser, where I sat or lay for the entire drive. Didn't talk to me except to bark orders, didn't give me anything to eat or drink, though he stopped once to feed his own face, and the only reason he let me get out to take a leak was because I warned him that otherwise I was going to piss all over the backseat.

We arrived in Marshall City early that evening. The courthouse had already shut down, so I was brought to the Marshall County Juvenile Facility for what they called processing, like I was lunch meat or something.

Thinking about lunch meat reminded me that I hadn't eaten anything all day except for a bologna sandwich in the holding cell in Santa Cruz while I was waiting to be arraigned. When I complained, the deputy who was conducting my second strip search of the day told me I had missed dinner, but said they would be serving cookies and milk before lights-out.

I spent the night in a tiny room with a bare cot, one blanket, no pillow. One-piece metal sink-toilet. Never saw any other kids, because they'd stuck me in something they called a segregation unit, where they put kids who break their rules, or are considered too dangerous to house with the other juveniles.

Me, I was so not dangerous, all I could think about was the cookies and milk. I constructed and reconstructed that snack over and over in my mind. What kind of cookies would there be? Would I get a choice? I was hoping for chocolate chip, but I was so hungry I'd have settled for oatmeal. And how many cookies would there be? If they said *cookies,* plural, that would imply more than one, wouldn't it? And what about the milk? I kept picturing a big frosty glass, but even I knew that was unrealistic. It would probably be one of those little waxy half-pint cartons like in a school cafeteria.

Pitiful, huh? Part of me aches for that poor naïve kid, but mostly I'm just embarrassed for him. That deputy was yanking your chain, I want to go back and tell him. No cookies and milk for you. Just heartbreak and betrayal. So the best thing you can do is toughen the fuck up as soon as possible, because as bad as things are in your life, they're about to get worse.

3

At forty, Pender discovered, he could no longer pull an all-nighter with impunity. His eyelids started closing on him a few hours into the drive back from Santa Cruz on Wednesday morning. He pulled over at a rest stop near Manteca and tilted the driver's seat of the Bu-car as far back as it would go—when you're six-four, you can forget about lying down in the backseat of anything smaller than a Greyhound bus. Then he tipped his tweed hat over his eyes and managed to catch an hour or two of fitful z's.

Pender reached the Marshall County sheriff's station, a low, adobe-style building attached by a covered walkway to the county jail, around two in the afternoon. He found Izzo packing up to fly back to New York. With Sweet and Swantzer both dead, Izzo told him, the Bureau had decided to pull the plug on this end of the operation.

"Marshall County gets jurisdiction over the snuff tape and the bodies in the tomato patch, so Little Luke's on his way back from Santa Cruz even as we speak."

"What about the Swantzer killing?"

"Looks like we were wrong on that one. Autopsy found a twenty-two slug in her head and a twenty-two pistol at the bottom of the trunk."

"So maybe the kid shot her with the twenty-two?"

Izzo shook his head. "The M.E. says it's a self-inflicted GSW."

"But—"

"Let it go, Ed."

"Let it go? How can you even say that? You saw that video he shot, what they did to that girl."

"He's only a kid. They probably forced him to hold the camera."

"I don't believe that for a second. I met him, Iz, I looked into his eyes, and lemme tell you, the hair on my arms stood up."

"I repeat: he's only a kid, Ed."

"So were Kemper, Mullin, and Frazier—they were all kids once," said Pender. Edmund Kemper, Herbert Mullin, and John Linley Frazier were the infamous trio of serial murderers who'd stalked Santa Cruz independently of each other in the early 1970s.

"So now he's a serial killer? I just finished telling you, he didn't even kill his step . . . his step-whatever. But don't worry," Izzo added, reluctantly. "It looks like the Marshall County DA agrees with you about the snuff tape. He says absent any evidence of coercion, he's going to try to get Little Luke tried as an adult."

Pender grinned. "I guess my work here is done, then, Nell," he announced, in a strangled Dudley Do-Right voice, then asked Izzo if he could catch a ride to the airport with him.

Izzo gave him a pitying look. "You want the good news first, or the bad news?"

"I always like to get the bad news out of the way."

"Your presence is requested back in Calaveras County. Somebody dug up another cache of videotapes buried out at Mapes and Nguyen's place, and they want you to take a look at them."

"What's the good news?" Pender asked warily.

"You get to keep the Bu-car."

After dropping Izzo off at the Sacramento airport, an exhausted Pender returned to the motel outside Marshall City where he'd been living for a week, fell asleep with his clothes on, and awoke a few hours later, still groggy, with his mind replaying the real-life horror videos he'd seen that summer.

Gallows humor helped a little. Thanks to Izzo, Pender's "And me without my spoon" remark the previous afternoon would eventually become part of Bureau folklore. What helped even more was the battered old pewter flask full of Jim Beam he always carried on road trips. He splashed a few inches of whiskey into a motel water glass from which he had removed the fluted paper colonial milk-maid's hat placed there for his sanitary protection, and tossed it back—no sipping tonight.

Then he took a long, hot shower, flouting the water conservation signs mounted all over the bathroom, with an explanatory card in the bedroom in case you'd forgotten since you left the bathroom. After patting himself dry, using every towel in the room, Pender donned a pair of beige slacks, a chocolate brown Hawaiian shirt with parrot green palm trees, and just to brighten things up a little, a pair of red socks under his brown Hush Puppies.

Behind the FBI's official ban on alcohol was a more reasonable de facto position: don't embarrass the Bureau. Get busted for drunk driving even once and you'd find yourself doing federal employment background checks in Bumfuck, Keokuk, or Cucamonga until you were old and gray—or in Pender's case, just old. So Pender's next move, after slipping off his wedding ring, was to call a taxi.

Following a free and frank discussion of local entertainment venues with the cabdriver, Pender wound up in a roadhouse called the Nugget, where a live band was playing Amazing Rhythm Aces covers to a surprisingly large and lively crowd, for a Wednesday night in the boondocks. He found a vacant stool at the bar, ordered a Jim Beam on the rocks, and sang along with the closing song of the set, "Third Rate Romance," in a pure, sweet tenor voice that sounded like it belonged to someone else, someone who looked more like Vic Damone than Killer Kowalski.

"I see you know all the words," said the woman on the next stool, in a husky voice steeped in cigarettes and Southern Comfort. Freckled redhead, roughly his age. Snug jeans and a faded denim jacket. Nice figure, as best he could tell without being too obvious about it. And he liked her eyes, he decided, especially the way they crinkled up when she laughed.

"It's a hobby."

"Third-rate romances?"

Pender laughed. "Song lyrics. Go ahead, try me—oldies are my specialty."

"Okay. How about 'What Becomes of the Broken Hearted?'"

"Jimmy Ruffin, 1966." He closed his eyes and ran through the first verse and the chorus, stretching out the concluding *baaaabeeee* while throwing in just a shimmer of tremolo. When he opened his eyes, he saw that she'd closed hers, and was swaying lightly on her stool. *Golden Tonsils strikes again,* thought Pender—the greatest tribute to his singing, he knew, was that, on a good night, it had been known to cause women to forget his looks. Of course, it also helped if they'd had a few drinks.

He could dance a little, too, for a white guy. But slow dancing was his specialty. Let's be honest, a gal's cheek is resting against your chest, she's not looking at your face. So while the band was on break, he fed a quarter into the jukebox and punched in "Sexual Healing," then led her out onto the dance floor.

By the time they returned to the bar, Pender had had ample opportunity to check out her figure, and concluded that while the rest of her might have been forty, the ass in those jeans couldn't have been a day over twenty-five. He'd also learned her name: it was Amy. As in the song by the Ozark Mountain Daredevils. Not that he'd had to ask: everybody in the place seemed to know her: the bartender, the band, the waitress, half the dancers. "Hey, Ameeey!" "How's it going, Amy?" "Freshen that up for you, Amy?"

That and another mystery—why the bartender wouldn't let him pay for their drinks—were cleared up during the inevitable what-do-you-do-for-a-living? conversation. "I work for the government," said Pender. "And you?"

She looked surprised. "I thought you knew."

Oh, fuck, he thought, *she's a pro.* Not that that would have changed his mind about leaving with her—but it would have taken a lot of the fun out of it. "What?"

"This is my place, the Nugget—I own it. Me and the bank, that is."

"I guess that seals the deal." Pender took her hand in both of his. "Congratulations, Amy: you are now officially the woman of my dreams."

CHAPTER FOUR

|

Not only weren't there any cookies or milk at lights-out in the segregation unit Wednesday night, it turned out there wasn't even any
lights-out. They dimmed them a little, I dozed a little, and the only
way I knew the long night was over was that somebody brought me
breakfast. Powdered scrambled eggs, burned toast, gristly mystery-
meat sausage patty, box of juice, and finally, too late to matter, that
long-promised carton of milk. No coffee: this was kiddie jail, after
all. Don't want to corrupt the youth of Marshall County with caf-
feine.

At least I didn't have to wear a jumpsuit. In Marshall Juvie, they
give you jeans with an elastic waistband so you can't hang yourself
with your belt, a T-shirt, and a denim shirt stenciled D.O.C. Depart-

ment Of Corrections. Rubber flip-flops so you can't hang yourself with your shoelaces.

After breakfast, my new lawyer came to see me. The kid yesterday, I learned, was like a junior junior associate of Wengert & Brobauer, the distinguished law firm where my grandfather was a major client. The new guy, though, wasn't even a member of the firm, but a hotshot defense attorney from Sacramento whom Wengert & Brobauer had recommended. Arnold Hobby, Esq. Short guy. Million-dollar suit, slicked-back hair, rimless glasses. He told me I was being accused of helping Big Luke and Teddy videotape themselves raping and killing some girl. What they call a snuff video.

Wow. You could have knocked me over with a toy balloon. I could hardly believe my ears, at least when it came to my dad being involved in something like that. Teddy, yeah: Who knows what weird shit went on inside that twisted brain? And of course there was that trunkful of cassettes she had been in such a hurry to torch. But Big Luke? Sure, he was an ex-con, but he'd done his time for peddling dope. And sure, he'd smack me around from time to time when he was tweaking, but he usually pulled his punches.

As for me being involved, that was ridiculous. Can you imagine a father getting his only son involved in something like that? So I started to tell Hobby the cops had probably made some kind of mistake about my dad, and that they were definitely wrong about me, but he raised his soft pink hand and stopped me. All he wanted to know, he said, looking hard into my eyes, was had I ever owned a red 49ers jersey with the number 16 on it?

"Sure," I told him, looking him right back in the eye. "But I haven't seen it in a long time. I think maybe my dad might have loaned it to somebody."

We were eyeball to eyeball for a couple seconds, then Hobby smiled. "Good lad," he said. "Now come watch me pull a rabbit out of my ass."

The hearing, I found out later, was meant to be just a formal-
ity, in which the State would lay out enough of its case to convince
the judge there was sufficient evidence to charge me. There wasn't
really supposed to be any cross-examination. But when the Marshall County detective testified that on the videotape they'd found
on the premises, which showed Big Luke and Teddy raping and
strangling a teenage girl, "the accused was clearly visible, reflected
in the window behind the bed, holding the camera," Arnold Hobby
jumped up from the table.

"Your honor, that's a gross, bordering on prejudicial, mischaracterization of the evidence."

The detective looked like he wanted to spit. "How would you
know? You haven't even seen it."

"Have *you*?" Hobby asked quietly. The detective went beet
red to the tips of his ears and clamped his lips together like somebody was trying to feed him a spoonful of buzzard puke. Hobby
gave him a few seconds, then prompted him again: "Well, have
you?"

He shook his head reluctantly. "Not *personally*. But I have it on
good authority from Special Agent William C. Izzo, of the Federal
Bureau of Investigation, that the accused comes into clear view
during the course of the tape."

Now Judge Higuera, a Mexican-looking woman with black hair
and bright red lipstick, looked over at the prosecutor, an assistant
DA. "Can you produce this Agent Izzo?"

The assistant DA conferred with his assistant. "Not at this
time, your honor. He's been called back to New York. But—"

"Have you watched the tape yourself?"

"I'm afraid not, your honor. I understand it was sent to the
crime lab in Sacramento last night for analysis. I was only assigned
the case a few hours ago."

"Can you produce anyone who *has* watched it?"

"Not at this time, your honor."

The prosecutor looked sick. The judge looked disgusted.

"Ball's in your court, Mr. Hobby. Have you seen the tape in question, or can you produce anyone who has?"

"No, ma'am."

"Then on what grounds are you challenging the characterization of the evidence?"

"Just this." Hobby reached into his briefcase, brought out a manila folder, opened it, and removed a single sheet of paper. "May I approach?"

The judge nodded. Hobby crossed the courtroom, followed quickly by the prosecutor, and handed the piece of paper up to the judge. Higuera read it, nodded again, then gave it to the prosecutor. He read it carefully and gave it back to her, then she gave it back to Hobby, who gave it to the detective.

"Would you please identify the document I've just handed you?" asked Hobby.

"It's a photostat of a standard form we have to fill out when we send a piece of evidence to the CDOJ crime lab."

"And this one is from your department, signed by yourself, referencing the videotape about which you've just testified?"

"Like I said, it's a photostat, but yes, it is—and I'd like to know how you got your hands on it."

"It was in with the copies of the search warrants I requested. I assumed you meant me to have it—you weren't trying to hide it from the defense, were you?"

"No, but—"

"Read the highlighted paragraph for us, would you please, Detective?"

The detective looked up at the judge, as if to say, Do I have to? and she gave him a sharp, kind of sarcastic little nod.

"It says: 'At apx minute fourteen, a figure wearing a red San Francisco 49ers jersey bearing the number 16 and holding a camcorder is reflected briefly in the window above the bed. Can you freeze-frame slash clean up slash blow up the image to clarify it for purposes of identification?'"

"To me, that doesn't sound like whoever was holding that camcorder was *clearly visible*," said Hobby. "Does it sound like that to you?"

Another pleading look/slap-down exchange between the cop and the judge. "No."

"So would you agree that your earlier testimony *was* in fact a grossly prejudicial mischaracterization of the evidence on this videotape?"

The detective didn't even bother answering.

"Chambers, gentlemen," said the judge. She and the lawyers were gone for ten minutes or so, and when they came back, Judge Higuera announced from the bench that not only would she not allow me to be tried as an adult, she wouldn't even indict me as a juvenile unless the DA came up with some admissible evidence, with a strong emphasis on the word *admissible*. I gave Hobby a low five under the table, so happy I wasn't going to be tried for murder that I clean forgot all about the drug charges down in Santa Cruz, at least until they slapped the cuffs on me again.

But Hobby told me not to worry about any of that, because of something called the fruit of the poisoned tree. If the arrest warrant had been obtained fraudulently, as the judge had just ruled, then the subsequent arrest would also be considered tainted, he told me. And so would any evidence obtained as a result of the search of my person and property during the course of the arrest.

While we were out in the corridor talking, the prosecutor came bustling up, grabbed Hobby by the lapels, and started swearing a blue streak. He told Hobby that he knew effing well that the effing evidence request form hadn't "inadvertently" been provided to him along with the effing search warrants, but had to have been given to him by one of his effing contacts in either the effing sheriff's department or the effing DOJ crime lab.

"Such language," said Hobby, gently prying the guy's fingers from the expensive-looking fabric. "And from an officer of the court." Then he turned to me and winked. "Don't worry about a thing, kid," he said, as the deputies led me away. "After we walk you on all charges, we'll sue the bastards for wrongful arrest."

Like an idiot, I believed him.

2

Lordy, I have died and woke up in heaven, thought Pender. Big old canopied feather bed, white curtains stirring lazily in the open window, sky the color of faded jeans, little birdies singing like they were having a contest—and he wasn't even hungover. Song lyrics jockeyed for position in his head, and "Oh, What a Beautiful Mornin'" triumphed—it may not have been original, but it was awfully goddamn apt.

All the while, though, there was something small and nasty scratching at the back door of Pender's consciousness. He tried to ignore it, but it slipped through while he and Amy were making sweet morning love, and he went embarrassingly limp.

"What is it?" Amy asked him, surfacing from under the covers.

"I just remembered where I'm supposed to be this morning."

"I knew it—I knew you were married."

"No, that's not it," he said miserably. "I mean, I am married, but that's not it."

Warily: "What, then?"

"I couldn't . . . I mean, you wouldn't want to— Aw, fuck it!" And suddenly, without any particular sense of having made up his mind, or even having thought it over, he knew what he was going to do. Or rather, not do.

3

The cop who drove me back down to Santa Cruz on Thursday afternoon made the one who'd driven me up to Marshall City seem like Mr. Rogers, but at least I got to sleep in my own bed that night. Seems that Fred and Evelyn had arranged for bail on the drug charges. But just in case you're thinking the old folks aren't so mean after all, here's the kicker. They'd nailed down the bedroom window and hired an off-duty cop to sit outside my door all night. Probably afraid I was going to slit their throats while they were sleeping.

I wouldn't have, though. I wouldn't even have run away. I had faith in Hobby and believed him when he said he was going to get me walked. But when I appeared in court Friday morning, instead of Hobby, a red-faced old man with a bow tie, double-breasted suit, and white hair swept up into a pompadour was sitting next to the kid attorney from the first night. It was Ellis Brobauer, managing partner of Wengert & Brobauer. Even the judge seemed impressed. The kid attorney looked absolutely terrified.

Brobauer never actually spoke to me. They went right into chambers, came out five minutes later, and he whispered something to my grandfather, who was sitting in the first row of the courtroom.

And yeah, in case you haven't guessed yet, they'd sold me out again. I was going into a private treatment program in Humboldt County, the judge informed me, and if I behaved myself, eventually the drug charges would be expunged.

So much for the fruit of the poisoned tree. So much for justice. "Thank you, your honor," Brobauer said smugly, earning him a coveted spot on my fantasy revenge list, along with Fred, Evelyn, and of course Agent Pender.

Things moved pretty quickly after that. I wasn't allowed to attend my father's funeral. I don't even know if he had one. Instead I was bundled into the back of a white van with THE MOUNTAIN PROJ-ECT stenciled on the doors. The driver, a thirtyish, sandy-haired psychologist called Dr. O, wore a corduroy jacket and a skinny tie. Kara, a relentlessly cheerful Viking with a long blond braid, rode shotgun. I wasn't allowed to talk, but there were sandwiches and bottles of juice, and at least this time I wasn't handcuffed. I couldn't help noticing, however, that there weren't any inside handles on the back doors of the van. I was still a prisoner, even though I'd never been convicted of any crimes.

On the drive north we stopped in San Francisco to pick up another prisoner at Juvenile Hall, high on a hill overlooking the city. The creepy Dr. O (his full name, I later learned, was Owen Oliver) stayed with me while Kara went inside with a paper bag full of clothes. Twenty minutes later an odd procession trooped out to the car. Behind Kara, there was a skinny little blond girl my own age, sandwiched between two uniformed deputies, each of whom had her by an elbow. Her feet were barely touching the ground.

I slid over, Kara opened the door, the deputies shoved her in. "Luke, this is Dusty. Dusty, that's Luke. You can say hello now, but after that, no talking for the rest of the ride."

I said hi, she mumbled something back, but in our mutual humiliation we could scarcely look at each other. An hour or so into the ride, however, I glanced over and saw tears running down Dusty's cheeks. As a show of solidarity I gave Dr. O and Kara both the finger, down low where Dusty could see it but they couldn't. She looked over at me, our eyes met for the first time, and then she flipped them the bird, too, but with an added feature I'd never seen before. She turned her left hand palm up on the seat between us, stuck her middle finger out, made an upward, jabbing motion, like she was sticking it right up their ass, and wiggled it obscenely. I had to bite my lip to keep from laughing out loud.

We arrived at the Mountain Project headquarters in the dark. It was one of those fishing-hunting lodge deals, a two-story cabin built of logs, with a big open central room, a high balcony on three sides, and the bedrooms on the second floor ringing the balcony. And you know those old World War II movies where the Nazi commandant tells the new prisoners that escape isss impossible? Well, I took one look at this place and told myself that escape isss very possible. But not just yet. Still queasy from the long car ride, I was so exhausted all I wanted was a nice soft bed to lie down on. I'd also have killed for a joint, but that obviously wasn't happening.

Neither was the bed, apparently, soft or otherwise. Instead, Dusty and I were led to a big storeroom filled with camping equipment, and they handed us checklists. Backpack, sleeping bag, thin foam pad, single-person shelter. Two pairs each trousers, hiking shorts, one pair boots. Three pairs thick socks, three T-shirts apiece, underwear. Sweatshirt, rain poncho. Saucepan, eating utensils, so many bags of trail mix, so many prepackaged freeze-dried meals, so many protein bars. Canteen, flashlight. Toothbrush, toothpaste, floss. Three packets biodegradable toilet tissue, female sanitary products if necessary, etc., etc.

"Get it all, get it right," we were told. Anything we failed to pack, we would have to do without, and anything extra was more weight we'd have to carry, in addition to the thirty-some pounds we'd already be packing. And of course: "No talking."

I had already figured out that the reason they were having us do this by ourselves was that they *wanted* us to fuck it up so they could give us a big lecture. So I made double sure to follow the checklist religiously. They also gave us a diagram of how to pack everything. That was complicated, but I managed pretty well. When I was finished I tried to give Dusty a hand, but Kara wouldn't let me.

Afterward I kept expecting an inspection of some kind, followed by a lecture, but all they checked was our boots, to make sure we'd picked out ones that fit. Then it was back outside and into a van. In the front of the van were two more counselors, which was what we were supposed to call them, like it was fucking summer camp or something. Gary and Diane looked fit and tanned and disgustingly full of energy for that time of night.

In the back of the van were three more kids, two boys and a girl, dressed like me and Dusty in Mountain Project T-shirts and khaki hiking pants. From the way they glared at us, I guessed they'd probably been waiting for us a long time. The fat white boy was Brent, the tall black kid was Stephen, and the girl's name was Cindra. Cindra's head was shaved, and if her boobs had been any bigger she'd have had a hard time standing up.

The van took off down a dirt trail. After that first exchange of glares, nobody made much eye contact. Mostly we looked out the windows, not that there was anything to see in the darkness. After a few minutes the trail started climbing and climbing. Halfway up the mountain it petered out at a small campground with a couple port-a-potties and a water fountain. When Dr. O ordered us to unpack the van, I assumed we were going to set up camp for the night. Wrong again.

"Drain your bladders over there, fill your canteens over there, and get your packs on your backs," called Gary. "For we have promises to keep, and miles to go before we sleep."

"It's cold," complained Brent.

"It'll warm up once we get going," Gary told him.

Brent sat down heavily on a log. "Fuck dat," he mumbled, trying to talk like a black kid, or what he thought a black kid talked like. "I didn't sign up to climb no fuckin' mountain in da middle of no fuckin' night."

"Suit yourself," said Kara cheerfully, and a few minutes later, we set off in a column. Dr. O was in the lead, followed by Stephen and me. Then came Kara, Cindra, and Dusty, with Diane and Gary bringing up the rear. The Death March had begun. A few minutes later we heard Brent crashing through the underbrush bellowing "fuck fuck fuck fuck fuck" as he blundered up the trail in the darkness. I have to admit, I thought that was so cold it was cool, leaving the fat slob behind like that, alone in the dark, to deal with the consequences of his stupidity. I didn't learn from Dusty until later, after we'd finally stopped to set up camp for the night, that right after we'd started out, Gary had peeled off and doubled back to keep an eye on Brent.

By the end of that first night's march, I had the game figured out. Bottom line: all this nature and survival crap aside, they meant to wear us down physically in order to break us down emotionally. So, exhausted as we were, once we had our tents set up (and what a drawn-out slapstick farce that was), they put us through a grueling group therapy session around the campfire.

Group whining session was more like it. Listening to my fellow campers bitching and moaning, I quickly lost what little sympathy I had for them. Their parents didn't understand them. Boo fucking hoo. Society was phony, everything was bullshit, and everybody but them was a hypocrite. Big fucking news, Holden fucking Caulfield. You want parents who don't understand you, I wanted to tell them, try asking Big Luke or Teddy for lunch money when they're tweaking. You'll get more than your feelings hurt.

I didn't say anything, though. When it came my turn to talk, I told the group that as far as I was concerned, I was still in jail, even if it was a jail without walls. And in jail, my father had taught me, you don't put your personal business out into the population, so I would pass on the soul baring.

"Passing is not an option," said Dr. O.

"You can't make me share," I replied. *Share* was their word for whine.

"No," he said. "But I can make sure nobody eats or sleeps until you do."

I looked around the campfire. Everybody was giving me dirty looks. Peer pressure: when you're a teenager they're always telling you not to give in to it, but then they use it against you whenever it suits their purposes. But I didn't give in because of the peer pressure, I gave in because I was hungry and tired. So hungry and tired that this time when I told the story, I left it all in, even Teddy's titties.

"Your stepmother had implants?" asked Dusty.

"My stepmother," I told her, "had a dick."

CHAPTER FIVE

1

In the old days, FBI special agents were required to be on call twenty-four hours a day, seven days a week, even when they were off duty, because, of course, special agents are never off duty. Until the advent of sky pagers, they were expected to leave one or more telephone numbers at which they could be reached, and/or call in their whereabouts at frequent intervals. You could always tell a G-man by the dimes jingling in his pocket, the in-joke ran, back when a phone call cost ten cents and there was a booth on every street corner.

Technically, then, Pender was already in violation of Bureau regulations when he left the motel Wednesday night without his newfangled sky pager. He only dug himself in deeper by not calling in Thursday morning, not to mention failing to report to work. But any residual guilt he might have experienced was more than trumped by the relief that came with realizing that he didn't have to watch any more goddamn snuff videos.

Thursday afternoon Amy dropped him off at his motel so he could check out. Just seeing the Bu-car parked outside the motel room was a material reminder of all the stuff he'd been putting off thinking about. Little stuff like turning in his resignation and telling his wife that he wouldn't be coming home. But he wasn't ready to deal with any of that just yet. Maybe Monday, he told himself, and quickly went back to *not* thinking about the stuff he wasn't thinking about.

A second night of free drinks, slow dancing, and vigorous sex, followed by a second day lazing around the farmhouse, left Pender feeling like a gigolo. So when one of the Nugget's two bouncers called in sick late Friday afternoon, he gladly offered to fill in. By then he'd met most of the full-timers—Steve, the head bartender; Barry, the head bouncer; Nestor, the cook; the waitresses, Karen and Mindy. And if their reception was a tad grudging at first, he understood they were only being protective of Amy.

Just in case he hadn't understood, Barry took him aside to let him know that he was one lucky son of a bitch and to warn him that if he mistreated Amy in any way, he'd find himself in a world of hurt.

"Now that that's behind us—Amy says you have some experience as a bouncer?" Barry was around Pender's size, but looked taller in his cowboy boots and high-crowned Stetson hat.

"It was a long time ago, but yeah." Like most of his colleagues in the Cortland County Sheriff's Department in the late sixties, he'd done his share of moonlighting in bars and at shows.

"'Cause no offense, hoss, but you look a little out of shape to me."

"Maybe, but I reckon I can still eighty-six a drunk with the best of 'em—hoss."

The first few hours, there wasn't much work for the bouncers. Pender helped Barry break up a fight, took the car keys from
a falling-down drunk, and called a cab for him. By the end of the
band's second set, when he did have to run a bottle-throwing
customer, the come-along hold he'd learned as a young deputy
sheriff in Cortland came in handier than anything he'd been
taught in the FBI Academy. What you want to do, Sheriff Hartung used to tell his men, is leverage the subject's wrist up past
his shoulder blade, so he's too busy treading air to put up a
fight.

When things heated up during the third set, Pender earned
even Barry's respect by smoothly disarming a drunken patron.
"You'll make a bouncer yet, hoss," he told Pender later, after
closing, when the crew and the band were unwinding with a few
drinks, swapping songs and shooting the bull. And with a few
slugs of Jim Beam under his belt, Pender discovered, it was almost possible, if not to actually forget the stuff he was trying not
to remember, then to pretend to forget, at least for a little while
longer.

2

Although I'd figured out the game the first night, it wasn't until
the next morning that Dr. O explained to us what the stakes were.
If you played it right, you got to go home (graduate, they called
it) and finish your treatment in the bosom of your familial unit. If
you played it wrong, you went from there into a residential program. And in case that sounds like bull sessions and pajama pizza
parties to you, you should know that in rehab language, *residential*
generally means "locked."

On the second day's hike, when we were finally allowed to talk to each other (the counselors sandwiched us in on the trail, two ahead and two behind), I learned that my revelations the night before had earned me some respect from my so-called peers. Brent was practically creaming. "Your own pad, your own gun, all da dope you cou' smoke, no muhfuggin' school. Muhfuh, dat musta been sweeeet!"

"Save your breath, wiggah," I told him, having just caught a glimpse of the next rise in the trail. "You're gonna need it."

It wasn't all work, though. After an especially hairy canyon descent, we broke for lunch at a secret swimming hole Gary claimed to have discovered—Lake Gary, he called it. Everybody changed into bathing suits, even the counselors, and we swam and splashed and frolicked around, happy as a bunch of otters for a couple hours.

The campfire group therapy that night was mostly about Dusty. Her deal was rough sex with older guys, we learned. It had started with her stepfather abusing her, of course, but by the time she was fifteen she had worked her way through a neighbor, two teachers, a minister, and the shrink who was supposed to be helping her with her problem in the first place.

Dr. O kept trying to get her to cop to having low self-esteem. He said that was why she liked it rough, and let the men use her. She made what I thought were a couple of very good arguments, such as that everything he was saying was based on the assumption that sex was bad. And even if that were true, she added, she was using the men as much as they were using her.

But after a while it appeared to me that she was starting to give in to him, to go along with all his bullshit. Dr. O would make some lame observation, and she would give him this wet-lipped, deer-eyed look, and say something like "You know, I never thought of it that way before."

I was probably the only one who noticed what was going on. "You planning to let Dr. O screw you?" I asked her that night. We'd set up our tents with the back walls touching so we could talk to each other through them.

"If I have to in order to graduate," she said. "I just can't face being locked up again."

They broke us up the third day. The girls hiked with Kara and Diane, the boys with Gary and Dr. O, and we had separate campfires that night. If anything, there was even more bullshit involved in the *boys only* therapy sessions, with everybody trying to outdo each other in acting tough.

Day four we marched in silence again, and instead of a campfire we had individual sessions, one of us at a time versus all four counselors. *Versus* is my word, of course, but it definitely describes my session. They started off by asking me to tell them in my own words why I was here, but without blaming anybody else. I said in that case it wouldn't be my own words, would it? Things went downhill from there.

The fifth day was the hardest climb of all, up a steep mountain trail in the broiling sun. By the time we set up camp in a boulder-strewn meadow with a view of forever, even my blisters had blisters. My feet hurt so bad I finally consented to let Dr. O (who was our medic despite the fact that he wasn't a real doctor) treat them. By then I hated him with a passion, having had all that time to obsess about him and Dusty having sex. It hadn't happened yet, but if it did, it would be soon. Tomorrow morning, we were told at campfire, our individual vision quests would begin.

These were to be like our final exams. We would be picking out our own campsites, isolated from each other, and making our own shelters, where we were supposed to spend twenty-four hours without eating or sleeping, and thereby obtain Wisdom with a capital Wiz.

There was more to it than that, of course. Among other things, we were supposed to find out what our so-called totem animal was. There was also this deal where we were each given what Dr.

O called a MacGuffin, a single candy bar that was supposed to represent our own particular addiction or barrier, sex in Dusty's case and drugs in my own. (But what if your addiction was candy bars? I joked to Dusty.) And although nobody came right out and said it, if you had half a brain, it was kind of obvious that you weren't supposed to actually *eat* the MacGuffin.

I wasn't buying any of it. All I could think about, that night before the vision quest, was Dr. O sneaking up to Dusty's campsite tomorrow night, and the two of them getting it on. Oh, god, how I hated that man. If he hadn't already been on it, I'd have added him to my fantasy revenge list. Instead I had to settle for mentally underlining his name.

Sleep was impossible. My tent was getting smaller and stuffier by the second. I opened the flap and stuck my head out to look at the stars. On the far side of the meadow, I could see all four counselors sitting around the campfire, having one of their endless gabfests, which meant nobody was watching us.

Figuring this might be my last chance to be alone with Dusty, I crawled around to her tent. She wasn't there. My first assumption was that she was off screwing somebody. But just before I went ballistic, I saw a small darting figure zigzagging across the meadow from more or less the direction of the campfire. I dove into Dusty's tent, and a second later she dove in on top of me. We exchanged *oof*s.

"What are you doing here?" she asked me.

"I was looking for you. Where were you?"

"Eavesdropping on the counselors. And guess what: it's all bullshit."

"Congratulations," I told her. "You just won the Academy Award for Duh!"

"No, I mean the whole graduation, no graduation thing." She grabbed my hand so tightly it hurt. "They already know who's going home and who's not."

I can't say I was surprised. "I'm guessing we're among the *nots*."

"We *are* the nots. Dr. O said I was 'continually displaying age-inappropriate seductive behavior' toward him. They're sending me to a residential in Orange County."

"What about me?"

"Military school in Arizona. They had a good laugh about that. Voted you most likely to make the Ten Most Wanted someday."

"Ten Most Unwanted, more likely."

She grabbed my hand in both of hers and pressed it flat against her chest. "Let's go, Luke. Let's run away, just you and me."

I could feel her heart thumping like a scared rabbit's through the thin fabric of her T-shirt and was acutely aware of the nearness of her little breasts on either side of my hand. *At least she won't be fucking Dr. O now,* I told myself. "Dusty, we're in the middle of nowhere."

"That's what you think!" Turns out we'd been hiking in a circle all this time. According to what Dusty had overheard, we were only a few miles from the little campground where we'd started out. "C'mon, what have we got to lose? At least let's make the assholes look for us."

I tried to tell her how dangerous it could be, tramping around unfamiliar mountains in the dark, but Dusty wouldn't listen. She kind of threw my hand away from her in disgust and said she was going with or without me. Then she reached up and ruffled the soft stubble where the hair was starting to grow in around my Mohawk, and said she'd much, much rather it was *with* me.

By now Dusty and I were both experts at packing for the trail. Our major problem was going to be food. What little we hadn't already eaten was supposed to be hanging in bear-proof bags twelve feet high in a tree at the edge of the meadow. I say supposed to be: Dusty and I each had a few protein bars and some trail mix stashed away, and of course our MacGuffins. Also we'd both filled our canteens before bedtime, and since the woods were full of raspberries, blackberries, and elderberries at that time of year, we decided to take our chances.

Our plan, such as it was, was to hike out to the road, then hitchhike to a phone. Dusty said she had a friend she could call in Arcata, but we hadn't really thought things out beyond that. Not that it would have mattered if we had, because within an hour, we were hopelessly lost.

It wasn't anybody's fault: we just guessed wrong. The trail forked, and the fork we chose began to climb and narrow and narrow and climb until it looked like it petered out at a crumbly shale ledge barely a foot wide. Sheer cliff to the right, sheer drop to the left. The moonlight had petered out, too, so I couldn't tell how far the fall would have been, but I could see with my flashlight that the path widened again on the other side of the ledge.

"I'm going to check it out," I told Dusty. "You wait here." Keeping my weight on my toes, I inched sideways out onto the ledge, hugging the cliff with my belly, and feeling as if my pack was going to pull me over backward at any second.

But it didn't. The path began a gradual descent, then widened to a grassy plateau. I put down my pack and went back for Dusty, took her pack from her, and helped her across the abyss. When we reached the plateau she threw herself into my arms and dragged me down onto the grass, laughing and crying and covering my face with wet kisses and salty tears.

"My hero," she said. It was the first time anybody had ever called me that.

Dusty and I zipped our sleeping bags together and made love under the stars that night. I didn't tell her I was a virgin, but I think she knew. She went gentle on me at first. I remember how her little breasts trembled and how my fingers trembled when I touched them. After I got the hang of it, though, things got rougher, which was how she liked it. She made me call her names and pinch her and slap her around, and when the names weren't dirty enough or the pinches and slaps hard enough, she'd call me names, names like *wussy* and *pussy* and *faggot*.

But no matter how hard I slapped her or how long I screwed

her, she couldn't come. The problem, she said, was that she usually did it drunk or stoned or with poppers. "I need something, or I just can't, you know, let go at the end." Then she gave me this sneaky little look. "Would you mind choking me?" she said.

"Choking you?"

"Yeah. It's something I learned from my minister. He used to make me strangle him with his tie just before he came."

"But I don't *want* to choke you."

"Wuss," she said.

So I did it. I slapped her and called her names, even though all I really wanted to do was kiss her and stroke her and whisper her name. At the end, when she was really squirming and thrashing and her nipples were like little pebbles, I put my hands around her throat and squeezed with my thumbs. She came so hard her eyes rolled back in her head and I could feel her belly rippling under me. Then I exploded inside her so hard I blacked out, too, for a microsecond.

When I came around I could still hear my own yell echoing back from the far side of the canyon we'd almost fallen into earlier. Dusty lay under me, unmoving, her head turned to the side and her eyes closed. She didn't seem to be breathing. *Oh, god, I killed her,* I thought.

Then her eyes fluttered open. "Oh, baby," she said hoarsely. "Where have you been all my life?"

Which sounded kind of funny, her still being a couple weeks shy of her sixteenth birthday.

3

We woke at dawn, our sleeping bags drenched with dew. We squeezed them out, packed up, then ate our MacGuffins, which we'd saved for last. Dusty's canteen was empty, so I gave her half of my water. In the daylight we could see the path we were on was a dead end, so we reversed course and started back up the trail in the direction we'd come.

We knew we'd have to hurry, because if the counselors hadn't missed us yet, they would soon. But there was no question of hurrying when we reached the narrow, crumbly ledge that had nearly stopped us last night. It looked even scarier in the daylight, with the cliff rising straight up on one side of the ledge, which was only a foot or so wide, and falling straight down on the other, a drop of at least thirty feet just to the *tops* of the pine trees—lord only knows how far it was to the ground.

I went first, slide-stepping sideways with my belly pressed against the cliff wall and my pack trying to tug me backward. I told Dusty to wait for me, that I would put down my pack where the ledge widened, then come back for her. But she didn't wait. I don't know why, I guess I'll never know why. All I know is, I had just dropped off my pack and was starting back for her when I heard the word *shit,* that's all, just *shit,* followed by another one of those screams that will be with me until the day I die. Not that eerie *eeeeeee* Teddy had made, but a sad, falling *ohhhhhhhh.*

After the scream came the sound of crackling, snapping branches as Dusty crashed into the evergreen canopy below. I thought, hoped, prayed to a God I didn't believe in, that she had survived, that the branches had broken her fall. But when I got down on my stomach and peered over the ledge, I saw her body lying spread-eagled in the trees, her head thrown back and her arms and legs splayed out, as if she were floating on her back, bobbing on the surface of a dark green sea.

"Hold on," I yelled. "I'm coming down, hold on." But then her body jerked a couple times, and the branches shifted and swayed, and I saw the dark stain spreading across her Mountain Project T-shirt, just above her heart. The branches had broken her fall all right: Dusty had been impaled before she reached the ground.

CHAPTER SIX

I

When Monday finally rolled around, Pender still wasn't ready to face the music. Instead he went camping with Amy and the crew down by the Kern River and found himself living through a two-day beer commercial. Daylight was for grilling burgers and franks over an open fire, drinking Bud out of the can, playing wiffle ball, and taking turns swinging out over the old swimming hole on a truck tire hanging by a thick rope from an overhanging tree branch. Evening was for sitting around the campfire toasting marshmallows, drinking Jim Beam out of his beat-up old pewter flask, and singing Merle Haggard songs. Nighttime was for making love under the stars, on a mattress in the back of Amy's pickup.

And whenever the stuff he wasn't thinking about showed signs of surfacing, he told himself a couple more days wouldn't make much difference in the long run. It was like hitting the snooze button on an alarm clock: it's not so much the extra ten minutes of sleep you're buying, it's the illusion of control.

But sooner or later the buzzer always goes off. Wednesday dawned clear and hot. One last pot of hobo coffee, one last plunge into the river, then they packed up, buried their garbage, and struck camp. It was in the cab of Amy's F-150, formerly white, now beige with Kern County dust, that Pender finally unburdened himself. He thought she'd be angry; instead she chuckled. "You? An FBI agent?" she said in her Southern Comfort–steeped voice, her eyes hidden behind mirrored glasses and a cigarette dangling from her lips. "Honey, you have *got* to be shitting me."

"I shitteth you not," said Pender, lighting up his first Marlboro of the day with his trusty Zippo. A legacy from his father, it had the letters *USMC* engraved on one side and the Marine Corps anchor on the other; the chrome finish was worn down to the brass. "The thing is"—he took a deep drag, blew it out the window into the slipstream—"I've gotten to the point where I don't think I can do it any more. Matter of fact . . ."

He took a sidewise glance toward Amy, who drove like a man, leaning back casually, one hand on the wheel, one elbow out the window. Unable to read her expression behind the shades, he blundered on. "I've been seriously thinking about eighty-sixing the whole goddamn enchilada, the Bureau, my fucked-up marriage . . . just giving it all up . . ." He paused again, to give her a chance to cut in, make this a little easier one way or the other; no such luck. " . . . and maybe moving out here for keeps."

He turned toward her, the seat belt tightening across his chest. The only sign that she'd heard him was that she'd gone perfectly still, except for her steering hand. Finally she blew a puff of smoke out of the side of her mouth and turned to face him. "You do what you got to do, honey," she told him, her cigarette bobbing. "Just don't do it for me."

They drove on through the August heat. Pender took a sudden interest in the landscape, the golden, rolling hills, the dusty green live oaks, a turkey vulture wheeling in the sky, a glowering, hunch-shouldered hawk perched atop a telephone pole. "I'm not sure what that means," he said eventually.

"It means, believe it or not, that I haven't been waiting around all those years for you, or anybody, to come along and rescue me. Not that I don't like you a lot, and not that it hasn't been fun."

When they got back to the farmhouse, Pender went in-side to pack, while Amy hosed down her truck barefooted, in a T-shirt and a pair of denim cutoffs. A few minutes later he came out carrying his suitcase and wearing his seersucker jacket, the houndstooth tweed hat with the little feathers in the brim, and a pasted-on grin.

"Have you made up your mind what you're going to do yet?" she asked him.

"Not precisely."

"That offer still holds good, you know." A weekend bouncer's job and the use of the vacant flat above the Nugget until he got himself settled.

"I'll keep it in mind," said Pender as he tossed the suitcase into the trunk of the Bu-car. But they both knew he didn't mean it. With the romantic future he'd been constructing in his mind un-masked as a daydream—and a rather immature, escapist daydream at that—Pender was having a hard time remembering why he'd decided to drop out in the first place. It wasn't that he'd forgotten about the videos—it was the depth of feeling, the utter despair, that he was unable to resurrect. *Hell, maybe a little R & R* was *all I needed,* he decided, slamming the trunk lid closed.

Amy turned the hose off at the nozzle and intercepted him as he opened the driver's door. She threw her arms around his neck and gave him a hug he wouldn't soon forget. Nor would he forget the last glimpse he caught of her in the rearview mirror, waving good-bye in a wet T-shirt and a pair of skintight Daisy Duke shorts.

2

Dusty dead. No food, scarcely any water. Only a vague idea where I was, and not a clue about where to go. I thought the shit was as deep as it could possibly be. Then the vulture showed up.

I couldn't yell or scream, in case the counselors were nearby, so I waved my arms, shook a stick, and chunked rocks at it to drive it away. But somehow the damn bird seemed to realize that I didn't pose any threat to it. So I had to stand there and watch as the vulture began to circle in deepening spirals, each pass bringing him closer to Dusty, spread-eagled and speared like a cocktail weiner in the top of the tree.

I decided there was no point sticking around to watch. I told Dusty I was sorry, turned my back, and walked away. It was early morning. Dew on the leaves, the western slope of the mountains still in blue-green shadow. For some reason I remembered a joke Big Luke used to tell, about what to do in the event you were attacked by a grizzly bear. Get to the center of the nearest large city as quickly as possible, was the punch line.

It sounded like a good idea to me, especially as staying put was not an option. I decided to head west, using the sun to orient myself until I struck the highway. But the same sun I had counted on to lead me out nearly did me in. After an hour or two, the heat was worse than anything I'd ever experienced in Marshall County. Or seemed worse, because at least at home there was water. Pepsi. Mountain Dew. Sprite. Cold beer when I could sneak one out of the trailer.

I did have a few sips of tepid water left in my canteen, but by midday even that was gone, and within a few hours I'd sweated myself dry. Everything was buzzing, my head, my eyeballs, the high blue sky, the heat waves shimmering off the rocks, the bleached white sunlight and the purple-edged shadows, and especially the insects, the gnats, blackflies, horseflies, bluebottles, mosquitoes, and god knows what else.

When I stopped and covered my ears, the buzzing only grew louder. I was on the verge of heatstroke, but I refused to quit. Scratched and scraped, mosquito-bit, sore-shouldered and leg-weary, I pushed myself until my legs started to cramp. The pain was excruciating. I managed to crawl off the trail and under the shade of a shale overhang, my thigh muscles twitching and jumping under the skin.

I massaged my legs until the cramps went away, then set off again. I found I could walk okay on the level, but uphill hurt like a bastard, and downhill the weakness in my thighs made my knees buckle. Which was a problem, because due west, the direction I needed to go, was all downhill, and getting steeper with every step.

What I needed was a decent walking staff. Just off the side of the trail I found a good straight stick, and had just finished stripping off the leaves and side branches when I heard somebody coming. I ducked down behind a bush and held my breath as Brent sauntered around the bend, sweating like a pig in a sauna. He had a blue bandanna tied around his forehead with three white feathers stuck into it, a walkie-talkie in a holster, and a canteen dangling from his belt. His nose was so buried in the map he was reading that he would have walked right by me if I hadn't stopped him.

"Dude," I whispered, still crouched behind the bush. I wasn't sure if he was alone, or how long it might be before somebody else came along.

Brent looked around. "Luke? Dat you?"

"Up here. Dude, am I glad to see you. I ran out of food and water hours ago."

He didn't have anything to eat, Brent said, but he unsnapped his canteen and handed it over. I took a healthy slug. Brent asked me where Dusty was. I told him we'd gotten separated. Which was true enough, as far as it went. But I knew if I told Brent what really happened, it was bound to hurt my chances of getting what I wanted out of him, namely his canteen, his map, and a head start.

When I asked him, though, Brent said no way. "This is a major deal, muhfuh," he said in his wiggah accent. "Dere's search parties all over da place, dey're bringin' in dogs and choppers. If dey find out I hepped you 'scape, Im'a be as fucked as you."

But I could tell from the way he said it that Brent wasn't all that eager to turn me in. Finally he agreed to give me the canteen and the map, but only if we made it look like I had somehow surprised and overpowered him.

If it had been up to me, I'd have given him a token tap. It was Brent who insisted I had to hit him at least hard enough to leave a mark in order to make it look good. He was also the one who pointed out that I should probably hit him from behind, because nobody would believe I could take him in a fair fight.

I didn't know about that. Though Brent was twice my size, he was also fat and slow. But I didn't want to argue the point. I told him okay, turn your back, then I let him have it with my new walking stick. Maybe a little too hard. He groaned and toppled over sideways in a seated position, like he was one of those G.I. Joe action figures that stays in the same position until you rearrange its limbs.

"Sorry," I told him. No answer. "You okay?" No answer. I rolled him over onto his back. The bandanna with the feathers had fallen off. One of his eyes was closed, the other was all pupil, and there was blood trickling out his ear. It occurred to me that Brent was going to be really pissed off when he came to. So just to make sure he wouldn't turn me in out of spite, I heaved the walkie-talkie halfway down the mountain.

Along with the map and the canteen, I also found a very cool compass and a big stash of trail mix and protein bars in Brent's day pack. Served the fat bastard right for holding out on me, I thought, wolfing down a Tiger's Milk bar while I consulted the compass and the map. It didn't take me long to get my bearings. Gary had thoughtfully taught us how to read topo maps earlier in the week, and Brent's search grid was clearly marked. As it turned out, I had come a lot closer to disaster than I could have known. Continuing due west would have led me down a deep ravine within a couple hours, and without food or water I might not have had the strength to climb up the other side.

No, west-northwest along the ridge I was on, though no picnic, was a much better route. I used the bandanna to tie Brent's feathers to the end of my walking staff, slung the canteen around my neck, and with map and compass in hand, off I went.

Hiking at a steady pace, stopping only when I absolutely had to rest my legs, I was off the mountain before sunset. Nightfall found me standing by the side of a dark two-lane road with my thumb out for a ride.

3

Although he'd been an agent since 1972, Pender had no idea how the Bureau was going to react to his having gone AWOL for six days—four if you didn't count the weekend. The range of possible responses ran from a slap on the wrist to dismissal, with the classic punitive stint running background employment checks as a likely median.

He knew better than to offer a mea culpa, though. The best

way to handle this sort of trouble was to brazen it out and hope that the prevailing confusion and inefficiency of the Bureaucracy would work in his favor. So instead of returning the Bu-car to the FBI field office in Sacramento, he drove to the Calaveras County Sheriff's Department and waltzed confidently into the office where the interagency task force working the Mapes-Nguyen investigation had been housed.

It was empty. Cleaned out—not even a desk or chair left. Pender tracked down one of the detectives he'd been working with and learned that Leonard Nguyen had been captured last Thursday morning after a shoplifting bust/shoot-out up in Canada. With both suspects now accounted for (it was Charles Mapes's suicide by cyanide, also after a shoplifting arrest, that had triggered the investigation in the first place), and Nguyen currently spilling his guts to the Mounties in hope of avoiding extradition, the task force had been disbanded.

"Nobody told *me*," said Pender, disingenuously. Not that he wasn't delighted to learn that Nguyen had been captured—serial killers rarely retired voluntarily. But at the moment, job one for Pender was finessing his career out of the hole he'd dug for it. He checked his watch: 5:00 P.M. California time meant 8:00 P.M. back east. An excellent hour for reporting in to the home office without actually having to talk to anybody. He found a pay phone in the lobby, used his phone card to call the Liaison Support Unit.

"This is Pender," he told the answering machine. "I just finished tying up a few loose ends out here in—"

"Ed? Hold on, let me turn this thing off." It was the LSU's formidable Miss Pool, one of a cabal of senior clerks who secretly ran the FBI. "Where on earth are you, Ed? I've been trying to get hold of you for hours."

For hours! Not, *all week,* or even *all day,* but *for hours*: two little words that meant Pender had almost certainly fallen through the cracks and landed on his feet. "Sorry, I guess the battery on that goddamn beeper thing must have run down. I'm still in Calaveras

County, home of the world-famous jumping frog. We just finished closing down the task force here. Now all I have to do is return the Bu-car to Sacramento, and with any luck I'll be on the next flight home."

"Not exactly," said Pool.

The good news was, he got to keep the Bu-car again.

4

By the time the Buzzard-mobile showed up, I'd been standing by the side of that dark country road for what felt like hours. I hadn't seen but three cars, all of which passed me by like I wasn't even there. I was tired, hungry, and sick at heart. I missed my bus, my music, my whole life before that one phone call from my dad busted it into a million little pieces. I also couldn't stop thinking about Dusty, and wondering if maybe I wasn't some kind of jinx. Seemed like everybody I'd ever loved died on me, starting with my mother.

So what's the use of all this struggling? I asked myself, and the answer was: ain't none, dude. I'd just about made up my mind to turn myself in (if I didn't starve first, that is) when I saw my shadow stretching out ahead of me and realized there were head-lights coming up behind me. I turned around and started walking backward with my thumb out as a big old flatbed truck material-ized out of the darkness. Its engine was coughing and farting, and its chassis and railed wooden bed were rattling and squeaking like the whole thing was about to shake itself apart, but at least it stopped for me.

The smell hit me as I was climbing in. Even though I knew it was bad manners, I couldn't help covering my nose and mouth with my cupped hands.

"Don't worry, you'll get used to it," said the driver, with a goony laugh. There weren't any dashboard lights, just the dim glow of the headlights reflecting off the windshield, but when he lit a cigarette, in the blue-white flare of the match I caught a glimpse of him from the neck up. He had one of those narrow, ax-shaped heads, with close-set eyes, a blade-thin nose, and no chin to speak of. His black hair was pulled straight back by a greasy-looking leather headband that matched his greasy-looking leather jacket.

"Here, this'll help." He handed me the lit cigarette, straight from his lips. The yuck factor was so high it was practically off the charts, but I took it anyway, and puffed at it until I had surrounded myself with a cloud of smoke that almost, but not quite, overpowered the stink.

"What *is* that smell?" I asked him, now that I knew he was aware of it, too. He jerked his thumb behind him, toward the flatbed. I turned and pressed my nose against the slider window in the back of the cab. At first I saw only a dark shape, then another car passed us in the opposite direction, and in the fast-moving sweep of the headlights, I saw a pair of huge, filmy brown eyes staring back at me. I was eyeball to eyeball with a dead horse.

"Christ on a crutch!" I jerked my head away so suddenly I got a crick in my neck.

"Welcome to the Buzzard-mobile," the driver said with a dim-watted grin. "Buzzard John, at your service."

"Luke Sweet, at yours." As I shook his hand, I noticed he was staring at the long white feathers I'd taken from Brent and stuck through the knot of the bandanna for luck.

"You know what kind of feathers those are you got there?" he asked me.

"No sir, I don't." I could tell he dug it when I called him sir.

"Them's eagle feathers. Bald eagle. Possession's a federal crime, unless you're a member of a recognized tribe. Like me."

"Then you take 'em." I untied the feathers and handed them over. "Last thing I need is a federal beef."

He chuckled as he reached into his pocket and handed me a neat little clasp knife with a cartoonish-looking buzzard's head carved into the wooden handle. "And you take this."

"What for?"

"I can't accept eagle feathers as a gift. It would put me too deep in your debt, spiritually. A trade is different."

"Fair enough," I said.

"Fair enough," Buzzard John agreed, arranging the feathers into his leather headband. "So where ya headed, Luke Sweet?"

That *was* the million-dollar question, wasn't it? By now I'd had plenty of time to think about it. The only person I knew in this part of the country was a guy named Rudy, a Hatchapec Indian pot grower my dad used to do business with. And while I couldn't be sure of an open-arms welcome from a pot rancher, Rudy had always acted friendly toward me. And one other thing I knew for sure. Welcoming or unwelcoming, there was no way he'd be calling the cops on me. "You know where the Hatchapec reservation is?" I asked him.

"I ought to," he said. "I am one."

Buzzard John was right. After a while, I kind of forgot about the smell in the truck. Especially after he fired up this humongous bomber of a joint. It was goofy fun at first, being stoned again after not smoking anything for over a week. We laughed and toked and made up jokey slogans for his business. "You Can't Beat Our Dead Horses," and "From Moo to Glue" were my two favorites.

A half hour or so later, the Buzzard-mobile dropped me off at the bottom of a long dirt driveway. "Those folks you're visiting, it's not such a good idea to drive up there unless they're expecting you. This late in the growing season, some folks bobby-trap their driveways. So if I was you, young Luke, I'd stick to walking in the ditches."

Right around then was when being stoned started to lose its attraction for me. And a few minutes after I started up the hill, it turned into a distinct liability. I was keeping to the gully like Buzzard John said, when I heard a truck coming up behind me. I turned around and was immediately blinded by the glare of a spotlight.

"Hands on your head!" Car doors slammed; footsteps pounded. Two guys jumped out. They slammed me against the side of a truck, then one guy held me while the other patted me down. I was expecting to be handcuffed and read my rights, but instead they lowered a sack over my head and shoved me into the back of their pickup. One of them must have climbed in with me, because when I started to reach for the hood, I felt a gun barrel prodding my chest. "Leave it on," was all he said.

The truck roared on up the hill. Jouncing around in back, I grabbed the side of the bed and held on for dear life, praying that the guy with the rifle had the safety on. The truck stopped, they hustled me out, took off the hood. I found myself standing at the edge of a cliff with the men flanking me, one at each elbow. The ravine below looked bottomless in the dark.

"Who are you spying for?" asked the guy at my right elbow. I saw he was wearing a straw cowboy hat, but I still hadn't seen either of their faces.

"Nobody. I swear on my mother's life, I'm not spying for anybody."

They leaned me out over the abyss. "I'm going to ask you one more time," said the man. "So unless you can fly, you'd better give me an answer. Who sent you?"

"Nobody sent me," I said again, wearily. "My name is Luke Sweet, Jr. I'm looking for a guy named Rudy. I don't know his last name. He's a Hatchapec, he's got kind of a hooked nose, you know, like . . ." I half-turned, drew a sharp angle in the air with my forefinger. The guy to my left kind of chuckled. The other guy, the one with the hat, yanked me back from the ledge and spun me around.

"Yeah, I thought I recognized you," he said. It was Rudy, of course, crooked schnoz and all. *Either he's gonna kill me here and now for making fun of his nose, or everything's finally gonna be okay,* I thought, sticking out my hand. Rudy ignored it. "Take him down to the house," he told the other man. "Keep an eye on him until I get there."

CHAPTER SEVEN

I

The epicenter of the search-and-rescue operation was the rustic, two-story former hunting lodge that served as the headquarters for the Mountain Project. In front of the lodge, jammed into the partial clearing and scattered among the fir trees, were sheriff's department and state police cruisers, ambulances, California Department of Forestry fire trucks and jeeps, pickups with light bars, and a variety of three- and four-wheeled off-road vehicles. CB radios and walkie-talkies spat and crackled, search dogs barked, and in the distance helicopter rotors beat the air with a percussive *whop-whop-whop* you could feel in your bones.

Night was just starting to close in by the time Pender arrived in the Bu-car. Searchers, including sheriff's deputies, park service rangers, and dozens upon dozens of volunteers, were being shuttled back to the lodge in canvas-covered, olive green National Guard trucks, fed hot meals from the lodge kitchen, then bedded down on cots or in sleeping bags wherever there was room for them.

The epicenter of the epicenter was the vast, two-story-high main room on the ground floor, which was ringed on three sides by the jutting second-floor balcony, rather like an old Elizabethan theater. Huge topographical maps, pale green and white, were spread out contiguously on trestle tables, and grids staked out on them with string and thumbtacks. Pender, wearing a plaid sport coat that made him look like the backseat of a '57 Chevy, walked up to a man wearing a Civil Aviation Authority baseball cap and a navy blue windbreaker with SEARCH AND RESCUE across the back, who seemed to be giving the most orders and receiving the most deference.

"Ed Pender, FBI," he said, sticking out his hand. "I got here as soon as I could."

The man looked down at Pender's hand like he'd never seen one before. "I'll be with you when I get a second. In the meantime, why don't you get on the horn to your people, see if you can find out where the hell is that chopper they promised me three hours ago."

Before Pender could respond, a man in a khaki uniform bustled around from the far side of the map table. "Agent Pender, thanks for coming," he said, grasping Pender's outstretched hand and pumping it vigorously while simultaneously steering him aside with a smooth, politic pressure of his left hand on Pender's elbow. "I'm Sheriff Ajanian. Sorry about the confusion—actually, I'm the one who sent for you."

Medium height, tailored uniform that couldn't disguise a hard little volleyball belly. Toothbrush mustache, probably a comb-over under the peaked cap. Nervous, darting eyes.

"What can I do for you, Sheriff?"

"I understand you interviewed young Sweet last week?"

"For half an hour or so, till he lawyered up." Jonesing for a cigarette, Pender glanced around the room, but nobody else was smoking.

"That half an hour, Agent Pender, makes you the nation's number one law enforcement expert on Luke Sweet, Jr. Here's our situation: The Mountain Project is one of these Outward Bound operations. The last session started last Friday night, the seventeenth, with five kids, one of whom was Sweet. Last night around midnight, one of the counselors did a bed check, and Sweet and a fifteen-year-old girl by the name of Dusty Walker came up missing.

"The search kicked off at first light. The other Mountain Project kids joined the search party—one of them, a sixteen-year-old from San Diego named Brent Perry, failed to return to his rendezvous point this afternoon. The search dogs found him lying by the side of the trail a few hours ago with his skull cracked open. They medevaced him over to Eureka General—as far as I know, he still hasn't recovered consciousness.

"Now, as sheriff of this county, my chief concern of course is the public welfare. So what I'm trying to ascertain here, given the attack on Perry, and Sweet's history, is whether the boy should be considered a danger to public safety. Trying to get a straight answer out of the shrink over there"—Ajanian nodded toward a dazed-looking post-preppy in the far corner of the room. Wearing a corduroy jacket with elbow patches, a button-down shirt and loosely knotted tie, chinos, and penny loafers, he was getting a pep talk from a younger woman with cropped hair—"is like pulling hens' teeth. But you're familiar with the situation down in Marshall County, you've talked to the kid, what's your opinion?"

That clears that *up,* thought Pender, who'd been wondering why he'd been sent for ever since Pool gave him his marching orders. The county sheriff, he now understood, was less interested in his actual opinion than he was in simply getting Pender to *give* him an

opinion. That way, Ajanian's ass was covered if things went bad.
The FBI assured us . . . , he would say at the press conference.

As chief Bureau liaison dealing with multivictim, multijurisdic-
tional homicides (read: traveling serial killers), Pender had played
this game before. "Good question," he said. "Frankly, I'd like to
poke around a little, get a better feel for the situation up here, before I make up my mind one way or the other."

Just then, Ajanian was interrupted by one of his deputies, who
drew him aside and whispered into his ear. They conferred earnestly for a moment, then Ajanian returned to Pender. "A CDF
chopper just spotted something that might help you make up your
mind. My search-and-rescue boys are going to take a flyover. Care
to ride along?"

"Wouldn't miss it for the world," said Pender.

2

A big old rambling wooden house built out over a river you could
spit into from the back porch. Indians coming and going all evening, watching TV, playing cards, teenagers playing Nintendo,
kids in pajamas just hanging out past their bedtimes, trying not to
be noticed. In the kitchen an old Indian woman was making tor-
tillas in a cast-iron press and cooking rice and beans over a huge
black cast-iron stove.

I was sitting at the round, scar-topped kitchen table eating Indian pizza (flatbread crust, bean topping) with a couple of Rudy's
cousins when Rudy returned. Black hair pulled back in a braid,
black hooded eyes, right-angled nose, skin the color of black-
raspberry fruit rolls. His faded denim jacket and jeans fit him like
they'd been tailored. He shooed his cousins away, sat down, tilted
his chair back on two legs, tipped his straw cowboy hat down

over his eyebrows, and folded his arms. "Now suppose you tell me why you shouldn't be lyin' dead at the bottom of the canyon," he said.

The thought of making stuff up or holding stuff back never even occurred to me. I gave Rudy the whole story, from the phone call in the trailer to the ride in the Buzzard-mobile. He listened impassively with his chair tipped back and his arms folded. No comments, no questions, nothing in his expression to reveal how he felt or what he was thinking. Every so often, somebody would come into the kitchen and whisper something to him, like in *The Godfather*. He'd hold up his hand for me to stop talking, whisper something back or nod or shake his head, then gesture for me to go on.

When I finished, Rudy told me to wait there, that he'd be right back, and left the kitchen. I knew without being told that my life was in his hands, like he was some old Roman emperor. I also knew I ought to be working on some kind of an escape plan in the event of a thumbs-down, even if it was only making a break for the back door or saying I had to use the bathroom and climbing out the window.

But I stayed put, even with nobody watching, for the simple reason that I had nowhere to escape *to*.

3

A patrol car shuttled Ajanian and Pender down to the Little League field being used as a helipad. The Humboldt County search-and-rescue helicopter was behind second base, ready to take off. Running in a crouched trot, holding on to his hat with one hand and holding the unfashionably wide lapels of his sport coat closed with the other, Pender followed Ajanian into the chopper. The sheriff introduced him to his two young, flight-suited deputies, Gabel and Garner. Seconds after they lifted off, the sun, which had set a few minutes earlier, was briefly and gloriously resurrected, streaking the dark gray horizon with crimson and yellow bands. Then it disappeared again as the helicopter tilted dizzyingly, wheeled eastward, and continued to climb.

Mountainous terrain rushed by beneath them; rolling hills gave way to bristling ravines and rocky crags. When they reached the designated coordinates, they saw the CDF helicopter circling over the body, shining its bobbing searchlight on a brave white scrap of cloth suspended in the evergreen canopy. The two pilots exchanged thumbs-up through their Plexiglas canopies, then the forestry chopper wheeled away into the darkness. Ajanian duckwalked up to the front of the cabin, removed his cap (Pender had been right about the comb-over), put on a headset with a microphone, conferred briefly with whoever was at the other end, then put his hat back on and duckwalked back to his deputies.

"THE CONSENSUS IS, WE'D JUST AS SOON BRING HER OUT TONIGHT," he shouted over the noise of the rotors. "YOU GUYS GET THE FINAL SAY, THOUGH. IF YOU THINK IT'S TOO DANGEROUS TO BRING HER UP IN THE DARK . . ."

The consensus? *Ajanian's got to be the king of buck passing,* thought Pender. Asking a search-and-rescue daredevil whether something was too dangerous was like asking a three-year-old whether candy was too sweet.

The rescue operation commenced smoothly. While the pilot maneuvered them into position, Gabel attached a safety harness to the cable holding the body basket, basically a stretcher with side rails and straps, and when they were directly above the body, he lowered himself over the side, with Ajanian aiming the searchlight, Pender operating the electric winch, and Garner spotting his partner.

"LOWER, LOWER," Garner called to Pender, who was trying not to notice how close they were to the cliff.

"SLOW IT DOWN . . . SLOWER! OKAY, A LITTLE LOWER . . . AAAND . . . STOP! STOP IT AND LOCK IT."

It took Gabel only a few minutes of midair ballet to free the body from the trees and strap it into the basket. But *only* is a relative concept when at any moment a capricious up-, down-, or cross-draft might have dashed the dangling deputy against the side of the cliff or sent the helicopter spiraling into the ravine.

Working the winch again, Pender didn't get a look at the dead girl until the other three had finished wrestling the basket into the chopper, which rose vertically to gain clearance the second the grisly cargo was aboard, then veered away from the mountainside.

The supine corpse, Pender noted, was in full rigor, arched drastically, with the head and heels touching the stretcher and the pelvis upthrust in a ghastly parody of sexual ecstasy. The girl's outspread arms were curved gracefully, as if she had been flash-frozen in the middle of a swan dive. Rather than risk further damage to the body by trying to work it free, Gabel had sawn off the branch upon which she'd been impaled, so the front of her T-shirt, stiff with dried blood, was poked up above her heart.

Pender's gaze traveled upward to the girl's neck. With the upper surface of the body pale from postmortem lividity, the dark bruises on either side of the throat were clearly visible even in the dim light of the helicopter. As for her eyes, well, they were gone. One socket gaped raw red; the lid of the other had collapsed inward, giving the socket a shrunken appearance. Pender's stomach churned; he tasted the bile rising in his throat, clamped his lips together, swallowed it back down. *You've seen worse than this,* he told himself. *Get a goddamn grip.*

Ajanian, who wasn't looking all that chipper himself, agreed with Pender that the degree of rigor mortis and the absence of blanching meant the girl had been dead at least twelve hours. He had noticed the bruised throat, too, but agreed that the amount of blood on the T-shirt meant she had to have been alive when she was impaled, which ruled out strangulation as the immediate cause of death.

But whatever had ultimately killed the girl—presumably they'd know more after the autopsy—Ajanian was adamant that if nothing else, the presence of the bruises on her throat meant Luke Sweet would now have to be considered a danger to public safety. This would alter the character of the search considerably. No more all-volunteer or one-person search parties, to begin with. And the public would have to be alerted along with law enforcement.

The sheriff was all but licking his mustache at the thought of a well-attended press conference, with TV lights blazing and microphones bristling, but he still wanted Pender's help in covering his ass. "WE'RE IN AGREEMENT, RIGHT?" he shouted, as the lights of the ball field came into view.

"YES AND NO."

Ajanian, incredulous: "EXCUSE ME?"

"YES, HE COULD BE DANGEROUS. NO, I DON'T THINK YOU SHOULD ANNOUNCE IT."

On the ground, while the deputies and paramedics were transferring the now blanket-covered body from the basket to a gurney, Pender explained his reasoning to the sheriff. There were too many people with too many guns out there, he said—it would be like painting a bull's-eye on the kid's back. And since Pender also had the impression that the more threatened the boy felt, the more dangerous he'd become, declaring him a threat to the public would only increase the danger to both himself *and* the public.

"So what am I supposed to tell *them,* then?" Ajanian said testily, adjusting his cap as the men and women with the cameras and microphones closed in on them.

"As little as possible," suggested Pender.

"Thanks for nothing," Ajanian whispered out of the side of his mouth as the flashbulbs started popping.

"The Bureau is always happy to be of assistance to local law enforcement agencies," replied Pender.

4

"Hi. You must be Luke." Dark-haired Indian girl, around my age and height, soft-spoken, pretty cute.

"If I must, I must." I hadn't seen Rudy since he'd left the kitchen twenty minutes ago.

"I'm Shawnee. Uncle Rudy says you're gonna be staying with us awhile, and I should find you a room."

"Okay by me," I told her. But in that rambling old house by the river, "finding" a room had a double meaning. Because of the way it had been built and altered and added on to over the years, the place was like a three-dimensional maze, with forked, rambling corridors, secret rooms, and staircases that led up, down, sideways, and in some cases, to nowhere.

So I followed Shawnee up, down, and sideways, to a room on the second-and-a-half floor. It wasn't much bigger than a closet, with a low, slanting ceiling and barely enough space for a twin bed and a small chest of drawers. Even so, I was a lot better off than I'd have been being lost in the mountains, or dead, both of which had already loomed as strong possibilities that night.

Lying in bed, through the tiny, open window I listened to the running river, which sounded like a hundred people whispering in a foreign language, and heard an owl hooting in the darkness. It must have been around midnight by then. Beat as I was, I thought for sure I'd fall asleep the second my head hit the pillow, but then I realized I had to take a piss.

On the way up, Shawnee had showed me the bathroom I was supposed to use. I pulled on my jeans, opened the door, and climbed down the short, steep staircase, but when I reached the hallway, I couldn't remember to save my life which way I'd come, from the left or the right.

You probably should have left a trail of bread crumbs, I told myself.

Then I eeny-meeny-miny-moed which way to go, and picked wrong. The door I chose opened on a rickety wooden staircase built along the side of the house. The *outside* of the house. But when you gotta go, you gotta go, and the great outdoors seemed like as good a place as any, so down the steep wooden stairs I went.

The grass was damp under my bare feet. The river smelled fresh and new, and the night sky was amazing, with the stars scattered like diamonds across black velvet. I took a mighty whiz into the flower bed alongside the house. Just as I had finished and was shaking off, I heard a car or truck climbing the driveway and saw the beam from its headlights sweeping toward me across the lawn.

I moved a few feet up from where I had pissed, flattened myself against the side of the house, and held my breath. The light kept coming and coming, stopping just short of my toes. It was so bright I could see the individual blades of grass casting shadows. Then it went out. Car doors slammed. I heard men's voices. "Take him into the barn," said one of them. I was pretty sure it was Rudy.

From where I stood, I was staring straight at the barn in question, only fifteen or twenty yards across the lawn. I started edging my way around to the back of the house. Out of the corner of my eye I saw a cluster of dark figures crossing the lawn, and quickly crouched behind the nearest bush.

A light went on in the barn. Rudy was standing under a swinging lamp hanging from the underside of the loft. The cluster of figures on the lawn resolved itself into two men half-dragging a third man by the arms. They hauled him into the barn and slung him onto the floor, and in the instant before Rudy slid the barn doors closed, I recognized the fallen man by the white feathers in his headband. It was Buzzard John.

I crossed the lawn quietly on my bare feet and peeked through the slit between the two sliding doors. *"My . . . fucking . . . house,"* Rudy was saying, accenting each word as he stood over Buzzard John, whose headband had slipped down over one bleeding eyebrow. The other eye was all puffy and purple, and his thin blade of a nose was mashed sideways. "You bring a stranger to *my . . . fucking . . . house!*"

"It was a kid," Buzzard John said through swollen lips. "He didn't have nowhere else to go."

"Then you take him to *your* house, you call me on the telephone. But you don't bring a stranger to *my . . . fucking . . . house!*"

I swear to god, part of me wanted to bust in and rescue Buzzard John. After all, where would I have been if he hadn't stopped for me, or brought me here? But Rudy definitely had a point. My dad would have agreed with him. Big Luke had an under-the-counter business, too, and I wasn't even allowed to bring any *friends* home with me (not that there was anybody especially clamoring for the honor), much less strangers.

Anyway, what could I have said that would have made a difference? It wasn't like Rudy owed *me* any favors. No, all I was likely to accomplish by sticking my two cents in was to get myself beat up and kicked out. *They were probably almost finished with him anyway,* I told myself as I turned away from the barn and headed back across the lawn to the house.

5

Pender ducked out of Sheriff Ajanian's press conference and caught a ride back to the lodge with a freelance photographer. The search-and-rescue effort had been suspended for the night, the lights were dimmed, and the sound of snoring emanated from the cots set up around the periphery of the main room.

Pender's intention had been to look for a motel in which to spend the night, but the Bu-car was blocked in by a fire truck. He decided he was too exhausted to drive, anyway, and wandered off in search of a spare cot to crash on. It was hard to believe that he'd gone swimming in the Kern River only that morning; the idyll with Amy already felt like ancient history.

The beds and cots were all taken, but there was an unoccupied sofa in a darkened office on the second floor that looked like it would do in a pinch. Pender took off his shoes and curled up on his side, fully clothed, using the arm of the couch for a pillow. But as soon as he closed his eyes, the dead girl's ravaged face appeared to him out of the darkness, eyeless and accusatory, and suddenly he was wide awake again.

He swung his feet off the couch and sat up, his elbows on his knees and his head in his hands, wondering if there was anything he could have done differently last week. Maybe if he'd questioned the boy a little more skillfully that night in Santa Cruz, Little Luke would still be behind bars, and little Dusty would still have her eyes. "I *had* him," he said aloud. "I had the little bastard in my goddamn hands and I let him get away."

"Yeah, tell me about it," said a slurred male voice from across the room.

Startled, Pender looked up and saw a man sitting in the dark, with a bottle on the desk in front of him. "Who's that?"

"Owen Oliver. *Doctor* Owen Oliver, not that it matters anymore." The man switched on the gooseneck desk lamp, and Pender recognized the Mountain Project psychologist Sheriff Ajanian had pointed out earlier. Gone were the corduroy jacket and the tie; his shirtsleeves were unbuttoned and turned back loosely, and his hair was a wispy mess.

"Sorry for busting in on you," said Pender, climbing wearily to his feet. "I was looking for a place to sleep—I didn't see you there."

"No, no, stay where you are." Grandly, his shirtsleeves flapping, Dr. Oliver waved him back down. "Care for a nightcap?"

"I'm not really supposed to . . ."

"Me neither." Oliver grabbed the bottle of Johnnie Walker Red by the neck, rose with difficulty, wobbled across the room, and perched unsteadily on the arm of the sofa. "Here. Hope you don't mind drinking out of the bottle. I had a glass, but it broke. Story of my life."

Pender wiped the top of the bottle with his palm, took a slash, and handed it back. "Thanks. I needed that."

"Me, too." Oliver took a slash in return, then wiped his mouth with his dangling sleeve. "He's a psychopath, you know. A flat-out, textbook psychopath."

"Little Luke, you mean?"

"Yeah. Little Luke." A harsh laugh. "Antisocial personality disorder, we're supposed to call it nowadays. DSM says the kid has to be at least eighteen for you to make a diagnosis, but I say, why wait? Act now and beat the crowd. Because it's all there. In spades. Superficial charm, failure to conform to societal norms, deceit, aggression, pervasive disregard for the rights of others. And family history—did I mention family history?" He took another slug. "I knew it, too. By the second day. Should've sent him back then and there," Oliver continued. "Know why I didn't?"

Pender shook his head.

"Money." Oliver made the universal sign, rubbing his thumb against the tips of his first two fingers. "Moola. The almighty dollar. See, the fifth kid's the profit margin. Less than five, we're scarcely breaking even." He offered the bottle to Pender, who took another slash and handed it back. "Now that poor little girl is dead, the other boy's in a coma, and the Mountain Project is history. Along with my reputation. And for what? A few thousand bucks? If I had the guts of a flea, I'd . . ." His voice trailed off; he looked down at Pender as if he'd just remembered he was there. "Say, I don't suppose you have a gun on you?"

"Can't help you there," said Pender, casually buttoning his sport jacket over his shoulder holster. "But you know what they say: in most cases, suicide is a permanent solution to a temporary problem."

No reply from Oliver, who was starting to topple off the arm of the couch, still clutching the bottle. Reacting with an agility that belied his bulk, Pender caught the psychologist with one hand and snatched up Johnnie Walker with the other. The former he laid out on the sofa, on his side lest he vomit in his sleep; the latter he took with him as he set off in search of a place to lie down for the night.

6

Pender awoke at dawn on Thursday in an Adirondack chair on the back porch of the lodge, damp and chilled, with his right arm temporarily paralyzed from being leaned on. Feeling returned gradually to the arm, starting with agonizing pins and needles, but the shoulder remained sore all day.

Although there had been no official announcement, it was obvious to Pender that a new paradigm had been established. Search parties were now deployed in groups of no less than three, with at least one of the three being an armed sheriff's deputy. This had the effect of reducing by almost two thirds the area that could be covered in a day. The search parameters were further reduced later that morning when the California Department of Forestry pulled its helicopters in order to fight a catastrophic wildfire raging in the southern portion of the state.

By then, however, the search for Luke Sweet was no longer Pender's concern. When he called in to Liaison Support, Pool told him he'd been ordered back to Washington. First, though, he had to return the Bu-car to the field office in Sacramento, along with the detailed mileage log he was supposed to have been keeping all along.

Oops.

But a veteran agent like Pender was not without coping strategies. Stopping for lunch at a Denny's near Sacramento, he filled in the blanks in dense black squiggles, with actual place names and legible numbers interspersed throughout, spilled black coffee on the little booklet while the ink was still wet, and dried it out under the hot-air blower in the men's room.

Booked to Dulles by way of Phoenix, Pender used the long layover to catch up on his expense report, concerning which he was more meticulous; the pockets of his clamorous sport coat were stuffed with crumpled receipts. On the night flight out of Phoenix, as sometimes happened when he showed his badge and Department of Justice photo ID in order to carry his weapon aboard, he was upgraded, this time to business class. The extra legroom was greatly appreciated, as were the cute little whiskey bottles given him on the sly by the cute little flight attendant.

Losing another two hours to time zone changes, Pender arrived at Dulles a little after 2:00 A.M., eastern time. Pam wasn't waiting at the gate for him, but then, he wasn't really expecting her, though he had left a message on their machine before leaving Sacramento. The airport was mostly deserted except for the floor waxers, but there was one taxi waiting at the curbside stand. Pender woke the driver, who reminded him of little Billy Fish, from the movie version of *The Man Who Would Be King*.

"Where can I take you, sah?"

"You know where Potomac is?"

"You are meaning the river?"

"No, the town in Maryland. Across the river."

"Ah, yes, of course. Now I've got you."

They drove east on 267, then turned north on the nearly empty Beltway. Pender rolled down his window as they crossed the river into Maryland, and inhaled gratefully; swampy and miasmal as the air might have seemed to some, to Pender it smelled like home.

At Bethesda, the cab left the Beltway, traveling northwest up River Road to the newly built subdivision halfway between Potomac and Seneca where Ed and Pam Pender had lived since early spring of that year. The lawns were so new you could still make out the sod lines, and there wasn't a tree taller than Pender in the whole development, but the two- and three-bedroom Virginia Colonials were solidly built on rolling half-acre lots. According to the Realtor, they were all but guaranteed to appreciate in value as the Washington exurbs continued their northward creep.

Pender paid Billy Fish, who rewarded his generous tip with a blank receipt for his expense report. As the headlights of the retreating taxi swept across the front of the house, Pender noticed that the living room curtains were drawn. No lights inside or out. *The least she could have done was leave the porch light on,* thought Pender, stumbling blindly up the walk leading from the driveway to the front door.

By the flickering light of his old Zippo, he managed to insert his key into the lock. The key turned easily enough, but Pender had to lean his shoulder against the door to shove it open. When he switched on the foyer light, he discovered why: the pile of letters and circulars under the mail slot in the door was a good three or four inches high. And where was the dog? he asked himself. Purvis worshiped Pender—the young German shepherd should have been all over him by now.

Not surprisingly, considering his occupation, Pender's first thought was of mayhem. He dropped his suitcase and raced upstairs, taking the steps two at a time, picturing his wife lying in a pool of blood. He rushed into the bedroom, flicked on the light, and found the room empty, the big bed neatly made. Also empty were the bathroom and spare bedroom, which Pam, who was studying for her Realtor's license, had turned into an office.

Puzzled and drained of adrenaline, Pender plodded back downstairs to check out the living room. A layer of dust had settled on the brown baize side table next to his recliner, and on top of the television. He made his way down the hall, past the seldom-used dining room, and into the kitchen. His mind was working furiously, trying to manufacture plausible explanations for Pam's extended absence. One of her parents was sick; she was staying at a friend's because she didn't like being alone in the new house; or maybe . . .

Aah, fuck it. He knew. Even before he found the envelope with his name on it propped up against the salt and pepper shakers on the kitchen table, he knew. Which was why he took his time before opening it. He got down a glass from the cupboard, filled it with ice from the refrigerator's built-in dispenser, and took a new bottle of Jim Beam out of the case in the back of the duck-in pantry.

Sitting at the yellow maple table they'd bought only a few months ago, Pender slit the bottle's seal with his thumbnail and twisted off the cap. He could hear the ice crackling as he filled the glass to the rim. He took a sip, smacked his lips, then opened the envelope. The note inside was dated a full week ago. "Dear Ed," it began, "It's over . . ."

Before reading on, Pender went back upstairs, took off his shoulder holster, and locked it and his gun in the combination safe bolted to the floor of the bedroom closet. That way, he figured, if he got so drunk he turned suicidal, he'd also be too drunk to re-member the combination.

CHAPTER EIGHT

I

Back in the Buzzard-mobile, zooming down a long dark tunnel of a highway, I was trying to explain to Buzzard John why I hadn't stepped in to stop him from being beaten up.

"But sssee . . . *hunh* . . . what they done . . . *hunh* . . . to me," he was saying, in this weird, thin voice, hissing on the *s* sounds and grunting between words. "Just sssee . . . *hunh, hunh* . . . what they done."

I didn't want to look, but I couldn't help myself. I turned and saw a vulture's horrible red head bobbing and weaving at the end of the long snaky neck sticking up out of the collar of Buzzard John's shirt. It fixed its beady little eyes on me and opened its beak. "Sssee what they done," it hissed at me, its stubby crimson tongue wiggling in the back of its throat. Then it grunted again, *hunh,* and its head darted toward me. I scrabbled around for the door handle and couldn't find it, pounded the window with my fists and couldn't break it, threw my shoulder against the door and couldn't budge it.

Now it had me by the shoulder with its vulture's claw, three scaly, crooked fingers ending in horrible sharp nails. I made a desperate, backward lunge, throwing myself against the door, which for some reason was no longer there. Screaming silently, I fell out of the moving truck, and just before I hit the ground . . .

You guessed it: I woke up. Shawnee was kneeling by the edge of my mattress, her hand outstretched, looking startled. "Rudy told me to wake you for breakfast."

I felt so relieved, it was like getting a second lease on life. But in a way that's what was really happening. However the thing with Buzzard John had been resolved, Rudy had made up his mind to take me in. He didn't care that I wasn't a Hatchapec, or that the police were looking for me. That might even have helped, because Rudy had done time himself. No, all that mattered was that I was an orphan who'd showed up on his doorstep, and according to Indian notions of hospitality and responsibility, he wouldn't have been much of a man if he'd turned me away.

There was, of course, another reason why Rudy might have wanted to take in a fifteen-year-old boy, but back then, it never even crossed my mind. All I knew was that for the first time in a long time, things were looking up.

I located the bathroom all by myself this time, then joined Shawnee down in the kitchen, which I found with only a couple of wrong turns. There was an old woman (she might have been the same one as last night or not, I wasn't sure) making Indian toast, which was like French toast, only thicker and heavier. I met some people I hadn't seen the night before, most of whom Shawnee seemed to be related to. It was kind of neat, seeing all those generations together. And educational: I noticed, for instance, that old

Indian women were mostly pretty fat and old Indian men were so shriveled and skinny you'd think the old women were feeding off them. Best of all, nobody seemed to hold it against me that I was white, and a stranger.

After breakfast, I followed Shawnee outside, and she began showing me the ropes. Growing Humboldt sinsemilla, I learned, was a surprisingly labor-intensive affair. There were always chores to be done, from potting and sexing the plants over the winter, to planting them in spring (females only), to tending the drip lines, hand-watering and fertilizing the isolated patches, weeding, and mending deer fences throughout the summer.

In addition to all that work, this time of year was considered prime raiding season. An armed watch had to be kept over the crop twenty-four hours a day, seven days a week, to protect it from the pot pirates. (Because they were on a reservation, the Hatchapecs weren't supposed to be subject to raids by state or federal authorities, but they did have to keep the palms of the rez police greased.)

With the grown men patrolling the fields, the edge of the property, and even the back roads leading in and out of the reservation, the rest of us had to take up the slack. Shawnee and I were assigned to tend the isolated plants hidden in the woods. All that first day, I tagged along after her, learning where the various plants were hidden, how to pinch back the dead leaves, and how to spot boughs that might be turning hermaphrodite in a desperate effort to reproduce. (The whole idea behind sinsemilla, which means "without seeds" in Spanish, is that without exposure to male plants, instead of throwing seeds, the females put all their energy into growing big, sticky, THC-laden buds.)

Naturally, hearing the word *hermaphrodite* reminded me of my stepmother. As we worked, I started to tell Shawnee about Teddy, but her reaction was entirely opposite from Dusty's: she did *not* want to hear the details.

All morning, we worked our way up the mountain from secret plant to secret plant. For lunch, Shawnee had packed peanut-butter-

and-jelly sandwiches that we washed down with warm Mountain
Dew. Sitting with our backs against the trunk of a red-barked madrone at the edge of a high, grassy meadow dotted with white puffs
of clover, we watched a pair of hawks riding the thermals, swooping and gliding so lightly and gracefully they looked like they were
made out of paper.

After lunch we worked our way down the other side of the
mountain, where the plants with southern exposure got so much
more sun we had to tie up the nodding branches so they wouldn't
break off from the weight of the buds. When I took out the clasp
knife with the buzzard head carved into the handle to cut twine for
Shawnee, my nightmare, which I'd almost managed to forget, came
rushing back so vividly that my knees went weak.

The best part of the day came after we'd finished our circuit,
when Shawnee took me swimming in the river. It was still pretty
hot out, and the current was slow. We floated on our backs, looking up through the feathery branches of the river willows to the
powder blue sky. Shawnee had worn her swimsuit under her
clothes; it was a white two-piece that made her bronze skin glow.
Peeking sideways at her, I got a hard-on pushing up the underpants I was using for a bathing suit. Peeking sideways at me peeking sideways at her, she must have noticed it. She rolled over onto
her stomach and swam away, then ducked under the water and
popped up next to me. We exchanged long watery kisses floating
in the shallows, then made out standing up, with the waist-high
water pushing and tugging at us. I slid her top up over her breasts
and pushed them together with both hands, sucking and nuzzling
while she reached under my briefs and grabbed me tight, maybe
a little too tight, working my joystick in a serious, goal-oriented
manner.

The test of wills, with me trying to put off coming and her trying to make me come as quickly as possible, didn't last very long.
She was victorious, of course, but if any contest ever had a win-win
outcome, it was that one. "There," she said, laughing deep in her

throat, then dove away upstream to get away from my hardy little swimmers.

Half an hour later we were trudging homeward along the dusty rutted track that followed the riverbank. Rudy drove up alongside us in his big red Dodge Ram pickup. "You kids want a ride?"

"Thanks, Uncle Rudy." Shawnee went around back, put her foot on the bumper hitch, and climbed over the tailgate, but I was still kind of frozen in place by the side of the road, staring up at Rudy's old straw cowboy hat, which now had three long white eagle feathers stuck into the side of the crown, sweeping backward at a rakish angle.

Time did one of those weird double-clutch, theory-of-relativity moves, slowing to a crawl on the outside, zipping along at light speed on the inside. All these visuals of Buzzard John started flashing through my mind like an ultrahigh-speed slide show. Behind the wheel of the Buzzard-mobile, fussily arranging the eagle feathers in his sweatband; driving with his head thrown back and laughing, wreathed in a cloud of pot smoke; on his knees in the stark light of the barn; behind the wheel in my nightmare, the vulture's naked head darting cobralike at the end of his long scaly neck.

Then time snapped back like a rubber band. "What are *you* starin' at?" Rudy was saying, leaning out the window of the pickup.

"Sorry." I shook my head sharply to clear it. "Guess I must've spaced out or something."

"You probably got too much sun," said Rudy. "Here." He took off his hat and handed it to me through the window.

"I can't take your hat, Rudy," I told him.

"You can't not take it," he insisted. So I did, and as I climbed over the side of the truck to join Shawnee, it occurred to me that I now had Buzzard John's knife *and* the eagle feathers.

Lucky me.

2

A week after I got to the rez, we began the backbreaking work of harvesting the crop, tying up the plants, and hanging them upside down from the ceilings of the barn and drying sheds. Then came a monthlong lull, with little to do but grow my hair out. Having a Mohawk didn't seem so cool when you were living with Indians.

It took a month for the plants to dry. Shawnee and I did a lot of hiking, some swimming until the river got too cold. I don't know if any of the grown-ups knew we were having sex. If they did, they didn't say anything. Then when the plants were ready, Shawnee and I joined the trimming crews working day and night at long plywood tables in the barn. She taught me how to clip away all but the tiny hip leaves from the sticky, skunky, purplish green buds, and how to shape and manicure them. I got pretty good at it, too. I could clip as fast as any of the Indians, and never once ruined a bud.

It makes me happy now to think back on those stony, fuzzy weeks, the haze of pot smoke drifting under the high roof, the spooky, snaky sound of R. Carlos Nakai's wooden flute music over the sound system, and the constant *snip, snip, snip* of the special scissors Rudy ordered by the case from a hardware store in San Francisco's Japantown.

By mid-October the product was dried, trimmed, and ready to ship. Because at that time of year a single man driving a van didn't have much chance of getting out of Humboldt County without being pulled over and searched, Rudy told me I'd be going with him on his business trip.

And off we went the very next day, in a customized white Dodge Tradesman van, with false interior walls and raised floor filled with vacuum-sealed one- to ten-kilo bags of bud. Sorry as I was to be separated from Shawnee, but mindful of my status as a charity case, I looked at this as a tremendous opportunity to prove to Rudy how useful I could be. My job, as we worked our way down the coast to San Diego, then north up the Central Valley, was mostly to sit high in the passenger seat, always visible, when we were on the road, to roll joints while Rudy drove, and to guard the van while Rudy took care of business. At night we shared a motel room, but only in motels where we could park the van right outside our room.

Our last stop was Stockton, where Rudy sold the last of the weed, except for a few kilos he'd held back for personal use, to some other California Indians, some Pomos, I believe. The van's false floor and walls were stuffed with cash and I was more than ready to go home, which already meant the big house by the side of the river for me, though I'd lived there only two months. I especially wanted to get back in time for the big Halloween party the following night.

But Rudy wanted to celebrate first. We took a motel room with two queen-size beds and got good and stoned. Rudy treated us to a prime rib dinner, then went out partying with his Indian friends while I watched TV in bed with the room curtains open so I could keep an eye on the van. I must have fallen asleep, though, because the next thing I knew it was dark, and Rudy was climbing into bed with me.

I knew right away he was drunk. His movements were clumsy and his speech was slurry and he didn't seem to understand when I tried to tell him that he had the wrong bed. He just kept pawing at me, patting me roughly on the head like I was a big sheepdog or something, and saying things like "You're a good kid, c'mon, you know what to do."

But I didn't. I didn't even know what was going on yet. I still thought Rudy just had the wrong bed, so I got up and moved over to the other one, farther away from the window. But Rudy climbed in after me, buck-ass naked with a hard-on, and started slobbering against my neck, saying shit like "Give it to me, short stuff, c'mon, give it to me," and shoving his dick at me.

By now it was pretty obvious what was going on, but I still didn't completely get it. I told myself Rudy was so drunk he thought I was a girl. So I pushed him away and turned on the light. "Quit it," I kept saying. "Cut it out. It's me, Rudy, it's Luke."

Rudy's eyes were all piggy and bloodshot, his dark skin was all splotchy, and his face with its bent-down nose was all twisted around like a devil mask. "No shit, white meat," he said, looking right into my eyes. "Now roll the fuck over."

"I'm gonna go sleep in the van," I told him, trying to climb out of bed. Rudy grabbed me around the neck with one hand and started punching me in the back of the head with the other, short hard jabs with his fist. I scrambled free, half-stunned, and dove off the bed. I was scrabbling around on the floor, snatching up my clothes, trying to get dressed and get away at the same time, while Rudy was riding my back, trying to force me down.

Punch after punch rained down on me. I was trying to get my pants on when my fingers closed around something hard in the pocket of my jeans. It was Buzzard John's knife. Still crawling around with Rudy on top of me, punching and grabbing at me, I fumbled it open, started jabbing backward with it, just poking it at Rudy, trying to get him off my back. Then I heard a gasp, lost my hold on the knife, and collapsed underneath Rudy's weight, feeling a hot wetness soaking the back of my T-shirt.

I rolled out from under Rudy. He was lying on his back, grabbing his neck with both hands, blood oozing out between his fingers. Buzzard John's's knife lay on the floor, the blade coated with a coppery sheen. I watched in disbelief as Rudy started convulsing, his back arching and his heels drumming the floor. After a few endless seconds of that, he went limp.

"Rudy?" I said, my voice a horrified whisper. "It was an accident, dude. I swear, it was an accident."

But Rudy, whose eyes were still open, bugged out and staring at the ceiling, was beyond forgiving anybody anything. And in the end, of course, it didn't really matter whether I had meant to do it or not. Once again, through no fault of my own, my life had been torn apart. I couldn't very well go back to Hatchapec now. My new friends, my adoptive family, and especially Shawnee, were lost to me, so lost it was like they'd never even existed.

Then through the open curtains I caught a glimpse of the white van parked in the blacktop lot in the rear of the motel, and was reminded that things could have been a whole lot worse.

3

One of the truer things I learned from Rudy was that in spite of what most people thought, a person is less conspicuous driving during the daytime, when there are lots of cars on the road, than he is late at night. I left Stockton at dawn in my customized Dodge van with a shitload of cash, a few kilos of high-quality sinsemilla, and three mottoes to guide me on my path. Trust nobody, look out for number one, do unto others as others have done unto Luke.

Not that I was looking for trouble or anything. All I wanted was not to be fucked with anymore, to be left alone to figure out what I was going to do with the rest of my life. But where? I needed someplace safe, off the beaten path, where nobody would think to look for me.

I'd been working on the problem all night, but it wasn't until I was on the road that I thought of the old homestead in Marshall County. That'd be the last place anybody would look for me, I figured. And I knew the area. I could drive around the back way, scope things out, make sure there were no cops still poking around. If the coast was clear, I could move back into my old bus.

If not, I knew a few places in the hills where I could hide out until it was safe.

I crossed the Marshall County line late in the afternoon. Traffic slowed to a crawl where the state highway merged with Marshall Street, running through the heart of Marshall City. The main drag had stoplights every few blocks, the better to snag the summer tourists. I couldn't help thinking that the last time I'd seen these buildings was from the back of a squad car. Who *was* that kid who'd sat up half the night in a segregation cell in Juvie, waiting for his milk and cookies?

Normally it was about a forty-five-minute drive from the city to what was now my place. For it was just beginning to sink in for me that with Big Luke having owned the property free and clear, and me being his only child, it probably belonged to me now. Still, I knew better than to just waltz up to the front door. Instead I cut off the county road half a mile before our driveway and circled around, coming in from the north, via a neighboring parcel known as Murphy's farm, despite the fact that there hadn't been a Murphy there, or a farm, for nobody knew how long.

Murphy's house had collapsed long before my time, but the barn still stood. When I was younger, I'd spent hours swinging from the rope swing attached to the rafter over the hayloft. Grab the rope, jump off, swing out into thin air, try not to smash into the side of the barn on the return swing. What a rush!

Leaving the van hidden in the barn, I walked the rest of the way home, through the woods. It was nearly dark when I reached the northern edge of the property. I wanted to cry when I saw what the cops had done to the place. My bus was torn up like it had been hit by a tornado. My clothes and belongings were scattered all over the place, they'd unraveled my cassettes and taken my priceless vinyl records out of their sleeves and tossed them around like Frisbees, and slit my mattress and all my pillows. What a fucking mess!

Down the hill things were even worse. The shed and the trailer were completely trashed, the trailer jacked off its moorings and the ground dug up underneath it, and the yard looked as if they'd gone over it with a rototiller or something. They'd dug up the fire circle, too, but at least Teddy was gone, trunk and all. Which made sense. It was only my subconscious that had half-expected to find her still there, rotting away along with the turkey vultures I'd shot.

I returned to my bus feeling kind of raw and sad. I restuffed my mattress as best I could, dragged it up to the roof, and spread out my sleeping bag on top of it. Dinner was a warm can of Mountain Dew and a package of cheese-and-peanut-butter crackers from a vending machine at a highway rest stop, dessert was a spliff-size joint, and on my last night as a free man, the night sky framed by graceful pine boughs was my bedroom ceiling.

4

I woke in the middle of the night, chilled and wet. The sleeping bag was damp and the flashlight batteries were dead. By moonlight, I climbed down from the roof and cleared a space at the front of the bus. I dragged the mattress inside, unzipped the sleeping bag, and covered myself with the half that was still dry.

After a few hits off the roach from my bedtime joint, I had no trouble falling asleep. When I awoke again it was daylight. I was lying on my right side with my head pillowed on my arm. Opening my eyes, I saw a skinny guy with fading reddish brown hair grinning down at me from the bus driver's seat.

"He lives, he wakes—'tis Death is dead, not he!"

I started to sit up, but my right arm, the one I was lying on, jerked me back down. The guy, it seemed, had handcuffed my wrist to the railing above the front stairwell. "Sorry about that," he said. "You were snoring away so peacefully I didn't have the heart to wake you." He stuck out his hand like he expected me to shake it. "Skip Epstein."

I rattled my handcuff. Epstein, who was wearing shorts and an old green T-shirt, chuckled at himself, then changed hands and we shook lefty.

"You a cop?" I asked him.

"Bounty hunter." I could tell from the way he said it how much he liked saying it. "Like Steve McQueen in *Wanted: Dead or Alive.* Your grandfather hired me to find you before the cops did."

I knew who Steve McQueen was from *The Great Escape,* but I'd never heard of *Wanted: Dead or Alive.* The title did fit in with what Big Luke had told me about bounty hunters. They worked for bail bondsmen, he'd said, and actually had more powers than real cops did. They didn't need warrants, they didn't have to read you your rights, and they didn't have to face a review board if they shot you.

Epstein, though, didn't look nearly as tough and mean as the bounty hunters Big Luke had described. "How much is my grandfather paying you?" I asked him.

"Enough."

"I'll give you twice as much to let me go."

Epstein shook his head slowly, like he really regretted having to turn me down, then reached for the gun in his belt holster, and racked the slide to jack a round into the chamber.

I thought he was going to shoot me then and there, but he only used the gun to cover me while he removed the handcuffs so I could take a piss and get dressed. After recuffing my hands behind my back, Epstein marched me down the hill. That's when I realized he was a cripple, with a withered left leg, a built-up shoe, and a head that bobbed up and down like a yo-yo with every step.

Epstein had parked his car, a black Camry, at the bottom of the driveway, in the blazing sun. By the time we reached it, the interior was so hot you could have baked bread on the dashboard, then toasted it on the vinyl upholstery. I got in first. It wasn't so bad for me because I was wearing jeans, but Epstein, in his cheap cotton shorts, would have seared his ass good if I hadn't warned him. I wasn't going to at first, but I guess I felt kind of sorry for the guy.

Once the air-conditioning kicked in, we had a pretty nice ride, considering the circumstances. We bopped along shooting the breeze, admiring the scenery, stopping at fast-food drive-thrus when we were hungry. You know, just two buddies cruising the Golden State, except that one of us was wearing handcuffs.

Epstein never did say where he was taking me. All he told me was that I was blind-ass lucky that he had found me before the cops did. When I asked him *how* he'd found me, he said that in order to catch the prey, Grasshopper, one must think like the prey. I laughed and told him he was full of shit, then he laughed and admitted that he'd just gotten lucky. It turned out he was a private investigator from San Francisco who'd been hired to find me by my grandparents. He'd driven up to the old homestead this morning just to take a look around, hoping to find some clue as to where I might have gone. Instead, lo and behold, there I was, snoozing away like a complete idiot.

We crossed over Pacheco Pass late in the afternoon, continued north and west on 152, then north on Highway 1. When it became obvious that we were heading toward Santa Cruz, I found myself indulging in a pitiful fantasy. I imagined that Fred and Evelyn had hired Epstein to bring me back to live with them. Internally, I made a shitload of promises. I'd get clean and stay clean, find a way to get along with my grandfather, work hard in school, make them glad they'd changed their minds.

After which world peace would be declared and everybody would shit ice cream in their favorite flavor. Because instead of heading into town when we reached the infamous Highway 1 fish-hook, Epstein swung around to Graham Hill Road, and on into the growing darkness we drove, onward and upward until the Santa Cruz Mountains closed around us, swallowing me up like a haunted forest in a fairy tale.

5

You know how people are always joking about the men in the white coats? Guess what—sometimes it's not a joke. Somewhere around Bonny Doon, Epstein pulled up to a pair of high wrought-iron gates set into a stone wall that stretched off into the deep, dark woods in either direction as far as the eye could see. MEADOWS ROAD, read the sign affixed to the wall.

Next to the gate was a square stone cottage. A uniformed guard leaned out the window, Epstein gave him our names, and the gates swung open. We followed a winding driveway uphill to an ivy-covered three-story brick building with green awnings and a white portico.

From the front it looked like a very nice retirement home, the kind rich folks wouldn't feel bad about sending their aged parents to. But we didn't go in through the front, we drove around to the back of the building, where the windows had security grilles an anorexic hamster couldn't have crawled through, except on the third floor, where they were bricked up entirely.

That was when I made the acquaintance of the men in the white coats. Two of them. One white, one black, both big. They came around to the passenger door. Epstein leaned over and unlocked my handcuffs. It felt strange, having my hands free. The door opened. I unhooked my own seat belt, but somehow I couldn't bring myself to step out of the car. I think I must have been waiting for Epstein to say something. Nice meeting you, good luck, something like that. But he said nothing, just gave me a big phony wink. Then one of the orderlies, the white one, grabbed me by the arm, and yanked me roughly out of the car, sending me sprawling across the hard concrete.

I went absolutely apeshit, so apeshit I don't know how long it lasted, or what happened in what order. My memory of that time is more like a shoe box full of random, black-and-white snapshots. Some are blurred and some are dark and some are shot from crazy angles. This one was taken from the ground, looking up, and that one from above, looking down. Another one's kind of surreal. Is it a trench? Is it a . . . canyon? No, it's an extreme close-up of the nose of the white man in the white coat, which was split wide open down the middle. Then there's a picture, kind of streaky and overexposed around the edges like it's from the end of the roll, of a hypodermic syringe sticking out of a blue-jeaned thigh. My blue-jeaned thigh.

And at the bottom of the imaginary shoe box there's one last, dim snapshot of the traitor Epstein waving good-bye as they drag me away. On his face is a sickly grin; in his waving hand is a sheet of paper he had one of the whitecoats sign. It's a receipt for the delivery of yours truly. A receipt he can bring back to show my grandparents in order to claim his thirty pieces of silver. A receipt that earns him a privileged spot on my all-time fantasy revenge list.

Oh, and one more thing. The date on the receipt? It would have been October 31, 1985. Halloween, of course.

CHAPTER NINE

1

Darkness. Dreams. Teddy, burning. Dusty, falling. Rudy, staring. A round bed afloat in a black sea, jagged flashes of lightning on the horizon. Big balloon faces, bending low to mine. Voices, inhuman voices like running water. And terrible creatures, obscene, impossible creatures, turkey vultures with human faces, humans with feathered arms and long curved talons instead of hands . . .

A windowless room. A nurse holding a syringe to the light, tapping it delicately a few times with her finger. We both watch the bubble rise to the light. "I want to go home now," I whisper hoarsely, through dry, cracked lips.

"Sure thing," she says. "Home you go." A prick, a sting, a falling away . . .

Sometimes darkness and dreams, sometimes the windowless room. Sometimes a tray of food is in front of me, sometimes pills in a tiny paper cup. And sometimes a whitecoat with a bandage on his nose takes me into the bathroom and twists my arm behind my back and hurts me and I pray for the darkness to swallow me up again . . .

There comes a time when, instead of the whitecoat with the bandaged nose, it's a whitecoat with a long scar down his nose who takes me into the bathroom and twists my arm behind my back and hurts me, but then one day another man in a longer white coat and one of those things with black tubing and a silver disk around his neck rushes in yelling at him to stop, and after that I never see either the man with the bandage or the man with the scar again . . .

Over time, the darkness and the dreams begin to fade, until one morning I awake to find myself in a new room, one with a window. And when I look out the window I can see a small garden with flowers, pink flowers and red flowers and yellow flowers, and sometimes I see a bird, one of those blue birds, the name is on the tip of my tongue but I can't quite remember it.

Slowly my world opens up. Now there are other rooms, other people. I learn to braid shiny plastic strands into something called a lanyard, I have no idea what it's for. And sometimes a new, different whitecoat, a much nicer one, leads me out into a garden that

I think is the same one I can see from my new window, and I see that blue bird flying by again, and I discover that I know its name now, it's a jay. A *blue* jay. Duh!

Not long after that, maybe even that same afternoon, I'm back in my room, washing up in the bathroom after using the toilet, when I notice an oddly familiar-looking fellow in the mirror over the sink. He has dark brown hair and dark brown eyes, and a little brown mole next to his eye, just like me. But he also has hair on his face, like he's growing a beard, which I'd never been old enough to do.

As we stare into each other's eyes, a confused look comes over his face. He reaches up and rubs his chin wonderingly, with his fingertips, like he's wondering why it's all stubbly. And when I realize that I'm rubbing my chin, too, and feeling the stubble, the other man's eyes fill with tears. "Luke," he says, with the tears rolling down his cheeks now. "Your name is Luke."

2

Chemical restraint. That's the official term, in case you're wondering. A marvelous thing, really, at least for jailers. Couple bucks a day worth of medications, sedatives, antipsychotics, combinations thereof, and lo and behold, there's no need for bars, armed guards, straitjackets, or razor wire. Why, just think of all the money the state could save if only CR were adopted throughout the correctional system. No need for a supermax prison like Pelican Bay—a little chemical restraint and you could house them bad boys in pup tents and guard them with Cub Scouts.

But that's never going to happen. Can you imagine the outcry? The lawyers, the ACLU, they'd be all over it like stink on shit. And why? Because it's INHUMANE! It robs an individual of the very things our society claims to value: his personality, his individuality. His humanity, for God's sake, his simple humanity.

Unless, like me, he's been deemed mentally ill by a competent, or at least licensed, mental health professional. Then he can expect to spend the rest his life in darkness and dreams, serenaded by a babble of inhuman voices and visited by a bestiary of obscene, impossible creatures.

I was approaching my twenty-fifth birthday when the boy I had been looked in the bathroom mirror and saw the man I had become. While I'd like to say it was due to my willpower or strength of character that I was able to overcome the effects of the powerful drugs they had been pouring into me all those years, the truth, I suspect, is that I probably had something much simpler to thank: my weight.

I'd been around five-six, maybe a hundred and thirty pounds when I entered Meadows Road, but after a late growth spurt I was closer to six feet tall, and weighed somewhere around one sixty-five, one seventy. They were probably still medicating me as if I were forty pounds lighter, though. And while my higher faculties were as yet nonexistent (I couldn't have spelled *fuck* if you'd spotted me the *uck*), something deeper and more basic was starting to surface inside me. You can call it my personality or my identity if you want to, but I prefer to think of it as my soul.

Whatever it was, it told me not to swallow the pills in the little white cup that the nurse brought me that night. Instead I stashed them between cheek and molar. I guess I'd been a good boy for so long that she didn't bother, on that night or any other night, to make sure I'd swallowed them down. All I had to do was keep my head turned until she left, then spit them out and flush them down the toilet.

I suspect it was that long slow detox that saved me from going into withdrawal when I stopped taking my medications. But since the meds I was spurning also included a nightly sleeping pill, I found myself lying awake hour after hour, night after night, trying to force my poor, benumbed mind to think, to reason, and most agonizingly of all, to remember.

My childhood memories were still there. But they weren't the problem. I could remember most of the stuff that had happened to me up until the day my father called from Marshall City to say the FBI had him surrounded. Everything after that, except for a few wispy fragments of sense-memory, like walking through a field of pot plants seven feet high, lacy green light filtering through the leaves, was either blank, or so confused and conflated with my CR hallucinations and nightmares that I couldn't separate the real from the fantastic.

Somehow, though, after a few nights of struggling, I managed to stumble upon a solution to my problem. Write it down, something told me, you have to write it down. Which led to the next problem: how to obtain writing implements without giving away my secret?

Pens were easy, there were plenty of them lying around the nursing station desks. All I could find to write in, though, was this 1995 Pocket Pal notebook-calendar. I found it in a drawer in the nurses' station. It's one of those pocket-sized drug company giveaways with the name and address of the local Pfizer sales rep printed in fake gold leaf on the fake leather cover. Not a lot of room for writing, obviously. But by printing in microscopically tiny letters, jamming the lines infinitesimally close together, and making use of every available inch of space including the margins around the "Useful Information" pages (first aid instructions, a metric conversion chart, zip and area code listings, etc.), I have managed to squeeze ten full years of my life into these cramped and no doubt barely legible pages.

It worked, too! My marbles and my memories, they are back. I know who I am, and I know what happened to me. And thanks to my psychiatrist, who left me alone in his office with my records and charts the other day while he went off to attend to some emergency, I even know how they got away with doing what they did.

It all started with a diagnosis of antisocial personality disorder. In other words, according to the shrinks I am a total psychopath. That's why, they say, I helped Big Luke and Teddy rape and kill at least three women. No mention of the fact that Judge Higuera dismissed all the charges against me.

Then I strangled Dusty and threw her over the cliff, snuck up on Brent and attacked him from behind, and stabbed Rudy to death for good measure. Never mind that I was never convicted, or even brought to trial, for any of those terrible deeds. Apparently that bit in the Constitution about how you're innocent until proven guilty doesn't apply to psychos.

Next they brought me to Meadows Road, where I started attacking orderlies indiscriminately, willy-nilly, no mention of how it was the *whitecoats* who jumped *me* the second I arrived. And as for how that whitecoat used to take me into the bathroom and beat me up when I was drugged and helpless, somehow none of that ever made it into the records, even though one of the doctors caught him in the act.

I realize now that in a way, it would have been better if I *had* been convicted of something. At least then I'd have a lawyer and I could appeal. Instead, I'm serving life without parole and I can't even argue my own case, because if they so much as suspect that I've got my marbles back, they'll have me back under chemical restraint before you can say phenothiazine.

So come to think of it, yeah, maybe I am a little crazy by now. But can you blame me? I'm only twenty-five years old, but I've already been lied to and betrayed by everyone I've ever trusted, robbed of my freedom and robbed of my mind, then locked up for life in this shithole they call Meadows Road. And I don't even know why.

My grandparents do, though. And thanks to some information one of the inmates gave me yesterday morning, I may get a chance to ask them about it any day now, face-to-face, live and in person.

And when I've finished discussing matters with Fred and Evelyn, there are a few other people I'd like to have a word or two with.

I know, I know, everybody says that living well is the best revenge. But for me, living well is probably an unrealistic goal, even if I do manage to make it out of here. So I guess I'm going to have to settle for second best: seeing every single one of the treacherous, backstabbing bastards on my list die slow and painful deaths, and maybe even sticking around long enough to watch the turkey vultures munch-munch-munching on their remains.

3

Thanks to a sudden April shower, there were only two patients in the little garden courtyard yesterday morning. There was me, wearing a raincoat over my pajamas and robe, carrying an umbrella, and shuffling along in the flat-footed walk I'd copied off the other chemically restrained droolers I saw every day. Then there was a tall, stooped old lunatic with luxurious sorcerer's eyebrows, who was wearing a transparent poncho over a shapeless, egg-stained brown cardigan.

"Spitting out the old meds again, eh?" he said, when we were out of earshot of the whitecoat assigned to the garden, who had taken refuge on a bench under the eaves.

"Hibbing owza wha?" I replied in a drooler slur: the trick was to pretend your tongue was as thick as a sirloin steak.

"You can fool *them*," he said, "but you can't fool me. I've been here forever. I know where the bodies are buried." He delivered the words in machine-gun bursts: *ratta-ta-tat.*

Oh great, busted by a full-blown loony. I decided my best bet was to play along with him. "How'd I give myself away?"

"Aura. Your sulfur black has turned to primrose pink."

"You can see auras?"

"I see everything. That's why I'm here. Too much input, not enough filter. I used to think it was the antennas." Pointing toward his upper molars. "Delusional behavior: *they* don't need no stinkin' antennas."

"I'm C.R. myself," I told him.

He nodded knowingly. "If I was you, sonny, I'd get the hell out of here. Before your next blood workup. Which will tell them you've been spitting out your meds. Which they'll then start injecting."

"But . . . but they took blood from me just the other day."

"Then my advice to you is make like a banana and split. Decamp, posthaste before the results come back."

"I can't: I'm not a voluntary commit."

"But you are on the third floor, right?" he said with a wink. Or it might have been a tic.

I nodded.

"Spend much time in the lounge?" A huge, dark, high-ceilinged room, oppressively overfurnished with high-backed leather chairs, carved oaken side tables, tasseled lamps, and sofas with deedle-ball trim. Even the television set, encased in a heavy walnut credenza, looked kind of Victorian.

"Of course." What else was there to do? A guy can only take so many naps and so many walks.

"Ever looked behind the curtains?"

Dusty drapes of eggplant-colored velvet were drawn across the back wall; I'd never seen them opened. "No, but I saw the windows from the outside when they first brought me here. They're all bricked up."

"Windows? What windows? Forget the windows. Who said anything about windows?"

"Sorry." The rain worsened; I angled the umbrella to shield him as well. "Go ahead, I'm listening."

"Here's the tale, boy. Once upon a time, I was lounging in the dayroom when the fire alarm went off. The whitecoat opened the curtains. Voila, a fire door opened onto an enclosed stairwell. Shoo, shoo, down we went. One flight, two flights, three flights. Then the all clear. Shoo, shoo, back up we came. But there must have been an egress down there somewhere. Either that," the old loon added confidentially, "or they were leading us to our deaths."

After lunch, I made my way to the lounge. Dressed in drab pajamas, a shapeless robe, and paper slippers, I took a seat at the chess table, and while moving the pieces aimlessly around the inlaid squares of walnut and maple, I discreetly surveyed the room's inhabitants.

Standing in one corner, staring intently at something no one else could see, was Chuckles, the inmate whose bearing and behavior I had studiously observed and copied in order to perfect my ongoing imitation of a drugged-out drooler.

A few feet away from Chuckles, the saddest-looking man I'd ever seen rocked back and forth in a squeaky red leather armchair that was not made for rocking. Two more inmates, one man, one woman, were sitting together on an overstuffed sofa, watching soap operas on the antique TV, while in the far corner, a female lunatic was braiding a lanyard out of those shiny, linguine-shaped, vomity-smelling plastic strands they give you in occupational therapy.

As my eyes traveled around the big room, my glance inadvertently met that of the whitecoat sitting by the door, who had just looked up from his magazine. I let my eyes glaze over, then formed a spit bubble in my mouth and pushed it out onto my lower lip. The whitecoat's interest faded instantly, and he broke off eye contact.

A few minutes later, when the lanyard braider, a middle-aged woman wearing a pleated skirt, drab blouse, and fingerless gloves, put down her basket and left the room, I glanced over at the whitecoat, who hadn't seemed to notice. Nor did he look up from his magazine when she returned, which suggested to me that keeping track of comings and goings in the lounge might not be part of the man's job description.

To test my theory, I spent the rest of the afternoon wandering in and out of the lounge at random intervals. Each time I left, I stayed away a few minutes longer, and each time I returned I sat in a different part of the room. When I was as sure as I could be that my absence would not be noted by the whitecoat, I returned to the chess table in the corner of the room, which was close enough to the curtains that I could smell the dust and see the faint, slightly lighter stripes where the old purple velvet had faded lengthwise along the pleats.

And there I waited, still as a mime, poised on the edge of my chair, until the lanyard lady broke into tears. When the whitecoat got up to see to her, I slipped behind the curtain and flattened myself against the wall.

There were scarcely eighteen inches of clearance between the wall and the back of the curtains. I sidled along until I reached a wide steel door with a safety-yellow sign above the breaker bar, barely readable in the dusty gloom: EMERGENCY EXIT!!! TO BE LEFT UNLOCKED AT ALL HOURS!!!

I gave the bar a gentle shove. It opened with a click that sounded deafening to my ears, but apparently went unnoticed on the other side of the curtain.

Closing the door quietly behind me, I found myself at the top of an enclosed, dimly lighted stairwell with concrete walls and iron steps. Moving noiselessly in my paper slippers, I descended three flights to the basement, then followed a trail of Day-Glo orange chevrons and illuminated exit signs down a long corridor with cinder-block walls, passing storage rooms, file rooms, branching corridors, and a boiler room with a yellow hazard triangle marked DANGER!!! NATURAL GAS!!! NO OPEN FLAMES!!! on the door. Either the sign painter at Meadows Road was paid by the exclamation mark, I decided, or else they had some manic-phase bipolar making signs in occupational therapy.

The trail of chevrons and exit signs continued on for thirty or forty feet, ending at another steel-plated, breaker-barred door marked EMERGENCY EXIT!!! TO BE LEFT UNLOCKED AT ALL HOURS!!! But on this door there was a second sign that read: TO BE OPENED ONLY IN EVENT OF EMERGENCY!!! ALARM WILL SOUND!!!

Shit. I must have been crazy to let that old nutcase get my hopes up, I told myself as I began retracing my steps, following the yellow chevrons backward through the basement maze. There *was* no easy way out of here. The second that alarm went off, the whitecoats would be all over me.

But when I passed the boiler room on my way back, the warning signs stopped me dead in my tracks. Danger, natural gas, no open flames!!!! What if there were some way to create a diversion, to set off some kind of explosion *before* I opened the exit door? I asked myself. The whitecoats would be so busy dealing with that, they might not even notice the alarm, or maybe they'd decide that it was the explosion that had blown it open, or maybe the alarm wouldn't even work. Whatever happened, at the very worst I'd have a running start on them.

It's a long shot, I know. And I may very well blow myself up in the process. But compared to the prospect of spending the rest of my life in this shithole, that doesn't sound all that bad. So wish me luck, Pocket Pal: by this time tomorrow, I'll either be free or I'll be dead.

Part Two

CHAPTER ONE

1

Pandemonium in the wake of a bank robbery interrupted. Alarm bells clamoring, sirens shrieking. On one side of the plywood and veneer tellers' cages, hostages wept and prayed. On the other side, bodies lay motionless on the carpeted floor of the bank lobby, while a baby-faced young man in a blue FBI windbreaker shouted himself hoarse from the doorway. "You're surrounded, give yourself up, come out with your hands on your heads," and so on.

"Here we go again," Special Agent E. L. Pender whispered to the man crouched next to him.

The man clapped Pender on the shoulder. "Courage, *mon ami,* nobody lives forever."

They stood up. Pender crooked his arm around the smaller

man's neck from behind, and together, in lockstep, they shuffled out from behind the counter and through the waist-high swinging gate into the lobby, where the other man ducked out of Pender's grasp.

"Freeze," shouted the kid in the blue windbreaker as Pender's right hand moved toward the inside pocket of his rumpled plaid sport jacket; the other man, wearing respectable banker's pin-stripes, backed away obediently, his hands half-raised. Without hesitating, the baby-faced Bureau trainee dropped to a bent-kneed crouch and fired two rounds at Pender, who grabbed his chest with his free hand (the other was still inside his jacket), lowered himself carefully to the floor, and flopped over onto his side.

The trainee crossed the room holding his nine-millimeter automatic at the ready. "Are you all right, sir?" he asked the man in the suit, without taking his eyes off the recumbent Pender.

"Just fine. You, on the other hand, are in deep, deep shit."

The trainee looked up from Pender and saw the man in pin-stripes pointing a Glock .40 at his chest. "What—what's going on?"

"Bang," the man replied, rather than fire off a blank cartridge—everybody's ears were still ringing from the earlier shots.

"Congratulations, son." Pender hauled himself to his feet and flipped his leather badge case open to show the kid his DOJ shield. "You shot your inside man, then got yourself killed."

He returned the badge case to the inside pocket of his sport coat, then reached down to offer a helping hand to a healthy-looking brunette corpse lying on the floor with her skirt rucked up high on her shapely thigh. All over the lobby, dead bodies were springing up and brushing themselves off, while freed hostages strolled out from behind the counter, discussing their performances in low, excited tones. (All the participants, save Pender, were professional or semiprofessional actors from a D.C. casting agency under contract to the FBI; having a real, if un-likely looking, special agent playing the undercover inside man, it was believed, helped drive home the point of the exercise more forcefully.)

"Ed." Mick Lawler, an instructor at the FBI Academy, bustled into the bank with his hand outstretched. "Thanks so much, I really appreciate your help." He pumped Pender's hand a few times, then turned to the crestfallen trainee, standing alone by the tellers' cages, gun in hand. "Remember what we said about making assumptions, Mr. Kincheloe?"

After shaking hands all around, Pender exited the phony bank through the plywood front door and stepped out into the sunshine of Hogan's Alley, the simulated small town constructed for training purposes on the grounds of the FBI Academy, which was located within the borders of the U.S. Marine base in Quantico, Virginia. He fired up a Marlboro as he strolled down the center of a deserted street lined with false-front stores, a street that ended disconcertingly as always, morphing into what might have been a rolling, landscaped college campus.

A meandering walkway bordered with flower beds climbed a grassy knoll to a recently completed minimalist office building with photographs of President William Jefferson Clinton and FBI Director Louis J. Freeh gracing the lobby wall. Pender stubbed out his cigarette in an urn filled with white sand and rode a silent elevator to the fourth floor, where the suite of offices housing the Liaison Support Unit was guarded by the fiercely protective Miss Pool.

"From your ex," she announced, handing Pender an envelope.

"I trust you took the liberty of having it sniffed for explosive residue," said Pender. The acrimonious divorce proceedings, initiated by Pam in August of '85, while Pender was still out in California watching snuff videos, had been finalized on the first of May 1986—nine years ago yesterday—with Pam getting the house, the car, a monthly alimony check for the next five years, and Purvis the dog—she even got the goddamn dog.

Pender's new office had a low acoustic ceiling and fluorescent light panels. Three walls were decorated to his specifications with corkboards and whiteboards; horizontal windows set into the fourth wall looked out over the manicured grounds. Seating himself at the scarred oak-veneer desk he'd brought over from Liaison Support's old basement offices next door to Behavioral Science, Pender could see all the way to the defensive driving course in the hazy blue distance.

After settling into a creaky, wide-bottomed oak swivel chair that had also accompanied him from the old office, Pender donned his half-moon drugstore reading glasses and opened the square, cream-colored envelope from the former Pam Pender. Glossy black letters on heavy card stock informed him that Pamela Jardine (her maiden name), formerly of Blatty and Broom Realty, had opened her own office, Jardine & Associates, and was available to assist him with all his real estate needs, residential or commercial.

Pender's real estate needs, however, were currently nonexistent—not long after the divorce, he had signed a National Park Service Heritage Lease for a ramshackle cabin overlooking the C & O Canal. So after running Pam's card and envelope through his personal shredder, he turned his attention to the daily printout of stranger homicides compiled for him by Thom Davies, a database manager working out of the CJIS headquarters in Clarksburg, West Virginia.

The computer printout, arranged chronologically on perforated, vertically accordioned computer paper, included all newly reported homicides, or attempted homicides, believed to have been committed by a person or persons unknown to the victim. (Fortunately for Pender's workload, in America the average murder victim was three times more likely to be killed by a family member or acquaintance than by a stranger.) Pender read it carefully as always, relying on his prodigious memory to alert him to telltale patterns, such as victims with descriptions similar to those in previous stranger homicides, or killers with similar m.o.'s.

Today, it was the location of a week-old double murder on the printout that caught Pender's eye. Santa Cruz, California, once known to the FBI's monster hunters as the serial killer capital of the United States, with three separate multiple murderers operating simultaneously during the early seventies.

For Pender, however, the words *Santa Cruz* brought to mind a quick succession of images from the summer of 1985: the stakeout in the post office, the skull in the tomato patch, the fifteen-year-old boy who'd dropped out of a second-story window. Suddenly he realized he had no idea how any of it had come out. How many bodies had been dug up? Had anyone else ever been arrested for the snuff films? And what about Little Luke? Had he ever been found, alive or dead, and if alive, what had become of him?

But that was life in Liaison Support for you. Rarely did Pender find himself involved in either the beginning or the end of an investigation, and although during his travels he was often called upon to interview imprisoned serial offenders for ViCAP, the Violent Criminal Apprehension Program, since he'd never interviewed a criminal he'd helped apprehend, there was no sense of closure there, either.

So Pender wouldn't have wasted any of his precious time wondering what had become of Luke Sweet if the identities of the victims in that double homicide in Santa Cruz—Frederick and Evelyn Harris; married couple; ages seventy-three and seventy, respectively—hadn't rung a bell.

Pender put down the printout, picked up his phone, speed-dialed Thom Davies in Clarksburg, got his British-accented voice mail. "CJIS, Thom Davies. Leave your message at the tone, and please bear in mind: a lack of foresight on your part does not constitute an emergency on my part."

"Hey, Thom, it's Ed Pender. Could you take a look in your magic box, see what you can come up with on one Luke Sweet, Jr.? That's Luke as in the third book of the New Testament, Sweet as in, please sweetheart, do this for me ASAP. I think we might have a live one."

2

The old man's golf game was a zigzag journey of short increments; a diagram of his progress from tee to green would have resembled a map of a honeybee's pollen dance. His putting was nothing to write home about, either, but he dressed a good game, from his fawn-colored Ben Hogan cap to his tasseled FootJoys, and never cheated, never improved a lie or took a mulligan even when he was playing alone.

Early morning was the old man's favorite time of day. The tattered wisps of fog scudding across the emerald fairways, the smell of the dew-damp grass, the hoarse barking of the sea lions conspired to awaken even his age-dimmed senses. "It doesn't get much better than this, does it, Willis?" he said to his favorite caddy, as the two stood alone on the fourth tee, waiting for a doe and her white-spotted, wobbly-legged fawn to cross the misty fairway.

"Lord, no," said Willis Jones, who'd had to drag himself out of a warm bed while it was still dark out, then ride two buses and a company shuttle. As he knelt to tee up the rich old white man's ball for him, he spied a shiny green golf cart bucketing along at top speed down the cart path, heading toward them from the fourth green, with the driver leaning out the side, steering with one hand and waving with the other.

"Now what does that fool think he's doin'?" the caddy muttered when the cart left the path to cut diagonally across the fairway toward them, tracing dark stripes against the grain.

"Stop, stop," called the old man, waving his arms over his head. "Wait there, I'll come to you."

His caddy followed him, leaving the old man's bag behind but carrying the three-wood he'd been about to hand him.

"Mr. Brobauer?" Dressed in a worn denim jacket and jeans

with the cuffs turned up, the man climbing down from the cart was of medium height, round-shouldered, and barrel-chested, with close-cropped hair and an almost simian brow.

"Yes, I'm Judge Brobauer." Although it had been many years since he'd served as a Superior Court justice, the old man had retained the customary honorific.

"You have to come with me right away. There was an accident." The words came out flat and underinflected, like an over-rehearsed speech in an elementary school play.

"To whom?" asked the old man, a widower with two grown children and no grandchildren.

"I . . . don't know. But you have to come with me right away."

Willis Jones shook his head firmly. "Somp'ns not right, Judge," he said, interposing himself between the other two, with his back to the newcomer. "I don't know this fella from Adam, I never even *seen* him around here before. So how 'bout you let *me* give you a lift back to the clubhouse, just to—"

Brobauer heard a flat, anechoic popping sound. Jones crumpled violently to the ground like a hundred-and-sixty-pound marionette with all its strings cut simultaneously. It happened so quickly and bloodlessly that Judge Brobauer half-expected Jones to scramble to his feet, grinning, as if he were performing in a *Candid Camera* stunt. Instead, the hulking newcomer waved a smoking pistol in the direction of the cart he'd arrived in. "Get in," he said matter-of-factly.

Brobauer glanced from the man with the gun to the man on the ground, then back to the man with the gun. "We can still work this out," he said. "I could say your gun went off accidentally. You could plead involuntary manslaughter."

The gunman shook his head slowly but firmly. "If you don't get in the cart I'll have to kill you here."

"No, wait, listen to—"

"I am going . . . to count . . . to three."

"Please, you have to—"

"One."

"let me—"

"Two."

"Just listen to—"

"Three."

3

"Quitting time," said Pool, standing in the doorway of Pender's office, holding her purse.

"Already?" Pender glanced at his watch, widened his eyes comically. "Oh well. Like the frog said, time's fun when you're having flies."

"Are you working late?"

Pender nodded. "One thing I've learned about the Beltway at rush hour: you can spend it sitting in traffic or you can spend it sitting in your office—either way, you spend it sitting."

"Good night, then."

"G'night, Pool." Pender waited with his great bald head cocked, listening for the civilized little *ding* of the elevator bell and the *whoosh* of the elevator doors, then unlocked the bottom left drawer of his desk, took out a shot glass and a bottle of Jim Beam, and poured himself his first drink of the day.

To demonstrate his mastery over the booze (as if holding off your first drink until after 5:00 weren't proof enough), Pender took only the smallest of sips, savoring it appreciatively and at length before knocking back the rest of the shot. He sighed as the whiskey hit his stomach and began to spread its amber warmth outward.

After his second drink, Pender had mellowed enough to think about telephoning Pam to congratulate her on opening her own agency. Then he remembered how badly their last conversation—it had to have been at least a year ago—had gone, and had just about decided to send her a congratulatory telegram instead, when his desk phone rang.

"Pender here."

"Ed, it's Thom Davies." Pronounced *Davis*—the database wizard was an expatriate Shropshire lad.

Pender grabbed a pad and pencil. "What've you got for me, Tommy boy?"

"The greatest of admiration, along with the following information regarding your alleged live one."

"Shoot."

"All righty, then: Mistah Sweet, he dead."

"Dead," Pender echoed weakly. He'd been so sure of the scenario he'd constructed in his mind that he'd forgotten it was only a scenario.

"Dead. Deceased. 'E's a stiff. Bereft of life. Pushing up daisies. Kicked the bucket. Joined the bleedin' choir invis—"

"I got it, I got it." Pender cut him off before he could run through the rest of the dead parrot sketch. "This *is* Luke Sweet *Junior* we're talking about?"

"It is indeed. Do you remember that California mental hospital that went up in blazes a couple of weeks ago?"

"Vaguely."

"That's probably because Oklahoma City knocked it clean off the front pages two days later. At any rate, according to the San Jose *Mercury News,* your man was one of the inmates presumed to have died in the fire."

"Presumed?" Pender pronounced it with the same distaste most people reserve for words like *smegma*.

"I gather there was some difficulty sorting out the remains."

"Yeah, well, speaking of remains, I see by today's stranger homicides list that somebody murdered Sweet's maternal grandparents last week."

"So you think the reports of his death may be exaggerated?"

"Considerably. Would you mind faxing over those newspaper articles?"

"Or I could teach you how to run a search on your computer. You know, that white box thingie on your desk, looks a little like a television set?"

"I was wondering what that was," said Pender.

4

"He lives, he wakes," says a voice somewhere above and behind Ellis Brobauer. "'Tis Death is dead, not he."

Brobauer takes stock: he is lying on his back on a grassy, gently sloping hillside, his arms outstretched. Ache in his neck, wrenching pain in his shoulders, fingers numb. Eyelids glued together, crusty with gunk; lips dry and cracked with deep, painful fissures. The North African sun beating down—somehow Rommel must have flanked the column, cut off his unit. Brobauer can't remember his tank being captured; he wonders how badly he was injured, and how his crew had fared.

"Water," he croaks. His throat is raw, as though he's been screaming for hours. When there's no response, he tries again, in his rudimentary, phrase-book German. *"Wasser, bitte."*

Glug-glug-glug. Waves of warm water cascade down, pounding against Brobauer's upturned face as he spits and sputters and gasps for air, tossing his head from side to side, trying to evade the deluge.

Then it's over. Brobauer licks his lips, then opens his eyes a slit, squinting against the glaring sky. Suddenly it all comes back to him: the solo morning round, the stranger who shot Willis Jones, the jouncing, stiflingly hot ride in the trunk of the stranger's

BMW. "Who are you? What do you want? If it's money, I assure you I can— What are you doing? Wait, stop!"

The denim-clad man pauses with the wooden mallet raised. In his other hand he holds a metal tent stake with a sharp, serrated tip poised above and between the third and fourth metacarpals of Ellis Brobauer's outstretched right hand. His eyes are oddly out of focus, as if he were seeing things that weren't there, or not seeing things that were. "What?"

His mind momentarily blank, Judge Brobauer blurts out the first thing that pops into his head—anything to keep that mallet from beginning its downward arc. "Why—why are you doing this?"

The other man lowers the mallet and closes his eyes; while he speaks, in an uninflected monotone, his eyeballs shuttle back and forth behind the closed lids, as if he were reading a teleprompter. "I'm only twenty-five years old, but I've already been lied to and betrayed by everyone I've ever trusted, robbed of my freedom and robbed of my mind, then locked up for life in this shithole they call Meadows Road."

Brobauer's abductor opens his eyes again; the unfocused look returns. "Wish me luck, Pocket Pal," he adds, raising the mallet, and with a series of forceful taps he drives the leading edge of the stake through Ellis's palm, neatly parting the metacarpals without breaking them, and pinning the back of the old man's hand against the grassy hillside.

5

Just before six o'clock, the fax machine in Pool's outer office/command center dinged and began spitting out pages. Pender gathered them up, brought them back to his office, and locked the door be-

hind him. Then he poured himself another shot, put his feet up
on the desk, tilted his creaky old behemoth of a chair back, back,
back until his head was level with his chocolate brown Hush Puppies, and began reading.

BONNY DOON MENTAL HOSPITAL DESTROYED BY EXPLOSION, FIRE,
shouted the large-type, front-page headline in the morning edition
of the San Jose *Mercury News* on April 18. DEATH TOLL COULD REACH
20 was the subhead. Pender had to put on his half-moon reading
glasses to make out the text, which had been further reduced in
size by the faxing process.

Somewhere between two and three o'clock on the afternoon of
the seventeenth, exact time still to be determined, there'd been an
explosion in a private mental hospital known as Meadows Road,
presumably in the basement boiler room, presumably caused
by natural gas. It felt as if the entire building had been lifted off
its foundations, reported one survivor. The subsequent fire had
greatly complicated efforts to evacuate the confused mental patients, according to the chief of the Bonny Doon Volunteer Fire
Department. Not long afterward (exact time again to be determined), the three-story building had suffered a "catastrophic structural failure."

On the following day, *The Mercury News* again headlined the
story. The number of injured had risen to thirty-seven, seventeen
dead bodies had been identified, and a third category had been
added: eleven persons "missing or unaccounted for." At the end
of the article, in smaller type (reduced to ant tracks on the fax), the
newspaper printed the lists of casualties and m.o.u.f.'s for the first
time.

Pender squinted over the small print long enough to realize the
names were not in alphabetical order, then put the pages down,
took off his half-moon reading glasses, and rubbed his eyes. He
could feel a headache coming on—probably those damn drugstore
glasses. One of these days, he told himself, he'd have to break
down and visit an optometrist, get some real eyeglasses. The only

thing holding him back was sheer vanity, not over his looks (that train left the station when he began losing his hair at the age of nineteen) but over his eyesight. Having boasted about his twenty-twenty vision too often to too many colleagues over the years, he knew he'd be eating mucho crow the day he showed up at the office wearing specs.

Back to work, this time bending over the fax with the magnifying glass, skimming down, down . . . And there it was, toward the bottom of the list of persons missing or unaccounted for: "Sweet, Luke Jr., 25, Santa Cruz."

But missing ain't dead, thought Pender. He skimmed past the text of the next day's article to check out the appended, updated casualty list. Whoops: "Sweet, Luke Jr." was now one of four names listed as missing, presumed dead.

Presumed—there was that word again. But why the change? Pender asked himself. How had four bodies gone from being unaccounted for to being presumed dead after only two days? It couldn't have been through DNA identification—at that time, a one-week window was the best-case scenario for industry-standard RFLP testing, and then only if the samples were of good quality and high molecular weight. If they'd had to use the newer PCR technique to amplify the smaller or more damaged samples, the identification would have taken even longer.

So maybe they'd identified all four bodies through dental records, Pender told himself. Or maybe the Santa Cruz authorities had just assumed that no one could have survived an explosion of that magnitude. But Pender's gut told him that someone had, and in the absence of high-molecular-weight evidence to the contrary, Pender always followed his gut.

6

The sun is low over the ocean when the old man's surprisingly robust old heart finally ceases to beat. Asmador (he used to have another name, a human name he can no longer remember) presses his ear against Brobauer's chest to be sure he's dead, then gathers up his things and hides behind an elephantine live oak at the edge of the clearing to wait for the vultures.

And wait, and wait. The problem is that the corpse is too fresh, the process of putrefaction not advanced enough to attract the attention even of a *Cathartes aura,* which is able to detect the presence of a single molecule of cadaverine within a ten-mile radius. However, leaving the body to ripen into carrion on this hillside overnight is not an option. Vultures rarely scavenge after dark, and he hasn't gone to all this trouble just to feed some mangy coyotes.

But the wind begins to shift as the sun sinks lower, swinging around to the south and carrying with it the faint, sickly sweet scent of decay. Asmador's low forehead furrows, his nostrils twitch, and his unhandsome face takes on an expression of sheer animal cunning. Legs bowed, arms swinging, he snuffles along through the woods, bent double with his nose nearly to the ground, until he's traced the odor to its source: a dead opossum hidden in a tangled thicket.

Its lips are drawn back in a snarl, revealing worn and yellowed fangs; its pelt writhes with oat-colored maggots. Asmador picks up the reeking carcass by the tail and carries it back to the clearing, lays it atop the dead lawyer's chest. Retreating behind the live oak again, he sniffs his fingers—there's something about the smell of carrion that he finds calming.

The sky is on fire to the west, and the sun has flattened itself against the vast, blue-gray horizon like a crimson-yoked egg sizzling on a griddle when the first turkey vulture comes swooping in low over the hillside. Its wings are raised in a shallow, dihedral V, and its body tilts unevenly from one side to the other. It lands clumsily, its powerful black wings beating backward, and takes a compensating hop, looking for all the world like a gymnast trying to stick the landing at the end of a vault.

Instead of rushing in, the vulture circles the funereal offering unhurriedly, with a mincing, high-stepping gait, its red head cocked suspiciously to the side. Then the arrival of a second vulture galvanizes the first one into action. Interposing itself between rival and prize, hissing and grunting angrily, it spreads its wings to make itself appear larger as it backs slowly toward its intended supper.

That's right, thinks Asmador, peering out from behind the tree, his cheek pressed against the rough, elephant-hide bark—*you chase dat dirty baldhead out of de town.*

7

There were advantages and disadvantages to living in a National Historical Park. Nights were quiet, and the view from the raised back porch of the lockkeeper's cabin was a knockout—the flat, silvery-smooth ribbon of the C & O Canal at the bottom of the hill, the swampy Potomac winding through the midground, the verdant Virginia countryside on the horizon. On the other hand, Pender's lease required that all new exterior renovations be period, the period being the 1850s, and if you needed to borrow a cup of sugar, forget it: there were no neighbors within a mile of Tinsman's Lock in any direction.

The term *cabin* was actually a misnomer. Chez Pender was sprawling and ramshackle, jerry-built by the lock's first keeper on a wooded hillside overlooking the canal. It had six tiny, low-ceilinged bedrooms lining either side of a corridor off the living room; the living room itself featured a peaked roof and grandfathered non-period sliding glass doors leading out to the back porch. Due to the severe slope of the terrain, the front entrance of the house was at ground level, while the porch was raised on stilts.

Only one bedroom had been habitable when Pender first moved in. On a forced leave of absence from the Bureau—which is to say, while he was drying out after his divorce—he had restored the others one at a time, refloored the living room, replaced the plumbing, rewired the house, propped up the sagging porch, and in his remaining spare time had rebuilt the engine of his vintage Barracuda. Amazing what a man can accomplish with no job and no booze.

After nuking a Hungry-Man Salisbury steak dinner and pouring himself a Thirsty-Man tumblerful of Jim Beam on the rocks, Pender set up a TV tray in the living room, intending to watch the Orioles game while he ate. Instead he found himself thinking about Little Luke. A flat-out, textbook psychopath, the Mountain Project shrink had labeled him—no wonder he'd ended up in a mental hospital. But had the boy ever been convicted of any murders? Or even been tried? Pender decided to ask Thom Davies to search the CJIS records first thing in the morning.

He also made up his mind to get in touch with the Santa Cruz coroner to find out whether Luke Sweet, Jr., was maybe dead, really dead, or really, really dead. And while he was at it, he decided to contact the homicide detectives investigating the Harris double murder to let them know it might not be a stranger killing after all.

Looking up at the television, Pender realized that although the Orioles game was in the third inning, he hadn't seen a single play. Nor did he recall eating, although he must have, because the plastic tray had been cleaned out, right down to the dessert brownie.

Feeling cheated, he nuked another dinner, refilled his tumbler, and set up a second TV tray for the sheaf of faxed newspaper articles he'd brought home with him. Then he donned his half-moon specs and read through the articles while he ate, glancing up at the television only when he heard a loud crack of the bat, or when the home crowd roared loudly enough to attract his attention.

The last clipping was dated April 25. Twenty-one confirmed dead was the final body count, which included Little Luke. No one left missing or unaccounted for. The initial explosion was held to be the result of arson at the hands of person or persons unknown, said person or persons believed to have perished either in the initial explosion or in the subsequent fire.

That last item, Pender realized, would explain why the investigation might not be vigorously pursued: the locals were assuming the perp was deceased. But then again, they were also assuming that Luke Sweet was deceased, and Pender's gut continued to insist that they were dead wrong about that.

CHAPTER TWO

I

6:00 A.M., Pacific daylight time. The pain in his hips and lower back awoke Skip Epstein as surely and promptly as any alarm clock or telephone wake-up service. Rolling over onto his side, he fumbled around for the bottle of Norco tablets on the bedside table, and washed two of them down with a swig of bottled water.

6:40 A.M. For the first and probably last time that day, nothing hurt. Skip might even have been a little buzzed—sometimes it was difficult for chronic pain sufferers to distinguish between a drug high and the euphoria that came with being temporarily pain free. *Five minutes,* he told himself: *you can have five minutes to enjoy it.*

6:45 A.M. *Okay, five more minutes.*

7:30 A.M. The thump of the *Chronicle* hitting the front door of Skip's two-bedroom flat on Francisco Street—he lived on the ground floor and rented out the top to a family of Russian immigrants—finally lured him out of bed. Even in San Francisco's prosperous Marina district, there were people who saw a newspaper lying on the sidewalk as fair game. But the walk from the bed to the door reawakened the pain in his hips; bending stiffly from the waist to pick up the paper reaggravated the ache in his back.

One glance at the front page and the pain was momentarily forgotten. PROMINENT SF ATTORNEY MISSING, BELIEVED KIDNAPPED, read the headline. CADDY FOUND SHOT TO DEATH was the subhead, which seemed like kind of an ass-backward priority to Skip, but not particularly surprising.

Accompanying the article was a photograph of Ellis Brobauer shaking hands with Assembly Speaker Willie Brown at a black-tie charity event. Skip skimmed the story on the stoop, in his bathrobe. As he reentered the apartment, he heard the telephone ringing and hurried down the hall to the kitchen—you couldn't say *ran,* though he did employ the awkward, hopping gait that had earned little David Epstein the nickname Skip in grade school.

Skip managed to snatch the wall phone out of the cradle just before the answering machine intercepted the call. He was glad he had, because it was his father on the line, and Leon J. Epstein, Esq., took machine-answered calls as personal affronts. "Did you see, Davey?"

"I saw."

"What do you think?"

"I think somebody wanted that corner office of his real bad." Though largely retired and spending most of his time at his second home in Pebble Beach, the Chairman Emeritus of Wengert & Brobauer had refused to give up his twenty-third-floor office with its power view of the bay from Alcatraz to Treasure Island.

"Not funny, sonny. You know how much our family owes that man?" With Ellis's backing, Leon Epstein had become the first member of his faith ever to make full partner at Wengert & Brobauer.

"I know, Dad." When Skip first struck out on his own, folks weren't exactly knocking each other down for the privilege of hiring a gimpy P.I. Jobs and referrals from W & B had kept him afloat that first year, and the law firm was still one of Epstein Investigative Services's most important clients.

"So what *do* you think?"

"Professionally?"

"No, as a baseball fan." Leon J. rolled his eyes—yes, over the phone. "Of course, professionally."

"Unless there was some contact they're not telling us about, this was no kidnapping for ransom."

"Which you know because . . . ?"

"Kidnappers who're hoping for ransom almost always contact the family within the first few hours to tell them not to call the cops."

"So if not ransom, then what?"

Skip shrugged—if his father could roll his eyes over the phone, Skip could shrug. "Who knows? Listen, I gotta go, Dad. If I hear anything over the grapevine, I'll let you know."

The Buchanan Street headquarters of Epstein Investigative Services were a vast improvement over the old digs, in a derelict warehouse south of Market that had been condemned after the '89 quake. In the new offices, the receptionist sat behind a swooping art deco counter that looked like it belonged in an airport terminal, while the heart of the business, the bull pen, was situated in an airy, well-lighted room that took up over half the floor. There, skip tracers in soundproofed carrels employed telephones and personal computers in an ongoing campaign to threaten, cajole, hoodwink, and bamboozle bureaucrats, contacts, and functionaries into disclosing the whereabouts of debtors, deadbeat dads, repossessable vehicles, and white-collar criminals.

Although the Marina district location was only a few blocks from his apartment on Francisco Street, Skip drove to work as always, parking his Buick in a reserved space in the basement garage. He took the elevator up to the second floor, stopping off at the reception desk long enough to admire Tanya's latest piercing and pick up his messages, one of which was from Warren Brobauer, Ellis's son, currently the managing partner of Wengert & Brobauer.

Skip returned the call from his corner office. "Warren. Skip." In San Francisco, business etiquette required the use of first names for everyone below the rank of mayor.

"Thanks for getting back to me, Skip. Are you aware of what's going on vis-à-vis my father?"

"Just what I read in the *Chron* this morning. Do the cops have any leads yet?"

"Cops! Hah! You can stuff what they know in the proverbial gnat's ass and still have room for a set of matched luggage. I spoke with Lil this morning"—Warren's older sister was named Lillian, although as Herb Caen had once remarked in his column, most newspaper readers thought her first two names were Prominent Socialite—"and we both agreed we want you to look into this on behalf of the family."

"I have to tell you, Warren, police departments do not generally appreciate P.I.'s getting involved with ongoing homicide investigations."

"And I have to tell you, Skip, I'm so frustrated with the lack of motivation on the part of the Monterey Sheriff's Department that at this point I could give a proverbial rat's proverbial ass what any police department does or does not appreciate."

Skip punched the air in silent triumph, then sighed audibly into the phone like a man coming to a hard decision. "Okay, Warren, let me see what I can find out."

"Thank you. We—we'd be grateful." For the first time in the conversation, there was a catch in Warren's voice. Suddenly Skip realized that the poor bastard was hurting, that his *father* had just been kidnapped, for shit's sake. *Protestants,* thought Skip: *if it was my dad, I'd have been a basket case by now.*

"*De nada,*" said Skip, a little more gently. "I'll get back to you as soon as I know anything."

2

9:00 A.M., Eastern time. Just another morning at the office for Pender. Coffee, a couple Danish, the sports section of *The Washington Post.* Not a bad life if you can stand the excitement.

As always, Pender saved Shirley Povich's column for last, then brushed the crumbs from his desk blotter, and with a yellow legal pad and a coffee mug full of sharpened pencils at hand, he began placing calls and returning phone messages in geographical order, working from east to west according to time zone.

Normally he would have postponed his West Coast calls until after lunch, but today he was so antsy about this Luke Sweet business that he postponed lunch instead. Long-distance directory assistance gave him the number for the Santa Cruz County Coroner's Office, a division of the sheriff's department. The deputy who answered the phone connected him with Sergeant Bagley, the ranking officer, and Bagley referred him to the forensic pathologist Dr. Alicia Gallagher.

"Good morning, Dr. Gallagher. This is Special Agent E. L. Pender, with the Federal Bureau of Investigation. I understand you were in charge of identifying the victims in the Meadows Road fire?"

"That's correct," she said, with what may have been a sigh.

But sighs were more than okay with Pender. He loved to hear them when he was conducting an interview: they almost always meant *ask me more.* "It must have been one unholy mess," he prompted.

"That's a bit of an understatement."

"How so?"

"Oh, let me count the ways. To begin with, the building was a brick structure, which may have worked for the third little pig, but is a very bad idea in California. How it survived the '89 quake is anybody's guess. Then there was the initial explosion of a few thousand cubic feet of natural gas, causing a partial structural failure and triggering an absolute holocaust of a fire. At its peak, over seventy-five percent of the building was engulfed. Then, as the fire grew hotter, what was left of the building underwent a catastrophic structural collapse—in layman's terms, the place completely pancaked."

Pender gave her a little *whew*—just enough to let her know he was paying attention without interrupting the flow.

"Exactly. And do you know how you identify a human body after it's been blown up, smashed, incinerated, then crushed again under a few thousand tons of brick and rubble, Agent Pender? Well, neither do I."

"And yet you had to," Pender prompted gently.

"Precisely. We had to. And of course they weren't all as bad as that worst-case scenario I gave you. We managed to identify all but four of the bodies through dental records."

She sounded reluctant to go on. Pender prodded her gently. "And the rest?"

A deep breath, an unmistakable suck-it-up sigh. "By the time we reached the bottommost strata, there were four names unaccounted for out of the list of all those known to have been present at the hospital at the time of the explosion. Two patients, two orderlies. So what we did was—ultimately, it was Sergeant Bagley's call, but I believe the sheriff signed off on it as well—we took the organic matter we found at the bottom of the pile—enough to fill a shoe box, none of it with viable DNA—and declared it mixed remains. We gave a portion to the families of any of the remaining unaccounted-fors who requested it. We didn't fudge the identification, mind you—they knew what they were getting."

"I don't doubt it for a moment," said Pender. "And please understand that nobody's second-guessing you here. But now comes
the sixty-four-thousand-dollar question, if that doesn't date me
too badly. Those two unaccounted-for patients—would one of
them have been Luke Sweet?"

Long pause, troubled pause. Then: "Yes. Yes, that's correct.
How did you know?"

Pender felt like whooping in triumph, but he settled for drawing a series of exclamation points on his legal pad—he didn't
want her to think he was gloating. "Somebody murdered Sweet's
grandparents last week—a real hack job, from what I understand.
Seeing as how that's only a week after their psychopathic grandson
disappeared in a suspicious fire, it just seemed like too much of a
coincidence."

"Oh. Oh I see," said the doctor. "And now *I* have a sixty-four
thousand-dollar question for *you,* Agent Pender: Are we talking
about the Harris murders?"

"We are."

"And Luke Sweet was their grandson?"

"He was."

"Holy moly," said Dr. Gallagher.

"I take it you're familiar with their case?"

"I caught it. Another unholy mess. The bodies had been de-
capitated, dismembered, and strewn all over the Santa Cruz Mountains. We never did find the heads."

"Holy moly back atcha."

"Of course, it could still be a coincidence."

"Absolutely," said Pender—but they both knew he didn't
mean it.

3

The crust of the Blasted Land is coal black, porous, and brittle, with burrs that look sharp enough to slice through tender human flesh, but crumble like volcanic ash beneath Asmador's feet. Jets of steam vent upward from bottomless cracks in the broken ground; the air smells foul and scorched, as though someone, somewhere, were burning a gigantic omelet made with rotten eggs.

Above the jagged horizon, the sky is a smoky, bloodshot gray. The light is diffuse, directionless. Slumped beneath the weight of the dead human he carries on his shoulders, Asmador trudges listlessly through a landscape devoid of shadow, toward the crumbling ruins of an ancient amphitheater. He passes beneath an arched entryway, its portcullis raised, and strides down a dank, dirt-floored tunnel that dips beneath the coliseum walls, then rises gradually, opening out onto a bullring circled by tier upon tier of stone benches.

There are no spectators at this meeting of the Concilium Infernalis—just Asmador and the Council members themselves, who have convened at the far end of the arena floor, twisting and squirming in high-backed, thronelike chairs framed from human bones and upholstered in leather tanned from human skins.

Because many of them are shape-shifters, lacking in repose, and others sport multiple heads (Asmodeus the Dandy, for instance, has three, a bull, a ram, and a human male, all symbolic of lechery, while Azazel the Armorer wears seven serpent heads, each of which has two faces), it's difficult for Asmador to be sure how many of them are present as he shuffles forward to lay his burden, the bloodied, partially consumed corpse of an old man, at their feet. "Three down, three to go," he announces.

Sammael the Red, also known as the Poison Angel (in Hebrew, *sam* means poison, *el* means angel), steps forward in his human guise: youthful, handsome, and redheaded, with a sneer that always makes Asmador want to check to make sure his fly is closed. "Three down, my feathered ass! The first two hardly suffered, and this one died of a heart attack."

This seems a little unfair to Asmador—but perhaps fairness isn't a quality one should expect of a high-ranking demon. "I'll do better next time, I promise. Just tell me which of them it should be."

"The answer is in the Book," hisses Sammael, disconcertingly transmogrifying into his other aspect—half-human, half-vulture. Even more disconcertingly, the Blasted Land begins to shimmer and fade like a soap bubble around him. "The answer is always in the Book," he adds, his form so faint Asmador can see right through him. He laughs, and then he's gone, and the others with him. But his laughter lingers. That's one of the Poison Angel's more annoying traits, Asmador remembers: that mocking, disembodied laughter.

4

Infantile Paralysis, the gift that keeps on giving, thought Skip, washing down two more Norco tablets with the dregs of his third cup of coffee. Polio was a rotten enough deal; post-polio syndrome, with a median onset of over thirty years after the initial course of the disease, felt a little like piling on to Skip.

Still, all things considered, he'd gotten off relatively lightly, and he knew it. Having a withered left leg inches shorter than the right and fused at the ankle for good measure may not have been a picnic, but it beat the crap out of dying in an iron lung, like some of the kids he'd known in the hospital. And he couldn't blame PPS for the damage his bobbing, skipping gait had done to his hips and spine—it was his own child-self's fault for insisting on wearing

Keds or PF Flyers like the other kids, instead of the built-up shoe his orthopedist had prescribed.

While waiting for the pain pills to kick in, Skip worked the Brobauer case in his mind. No ransom demands had been received yet—Warren or Lillian would have been notified. But if money wasn't the motive, what was? Ellis Brobauer had no known surviving enemies, and there'd been no family squabbles or romantic/sexual entanglements that Warren or Lillian were aware of—or would admit to, anyway. Nor had there been any work-related problems. According to Warren, except for a little rainmaking and a little estate work for his oldest clients, Ellis Brobauer had more or less retired from the law firm that bore his name.

But along with that coveted corner office, Judge Brobauer had retained the services of his secretary, the unforgettably named Doris Dragon. If the old man had been involved in some risky business that had led to his kidnapping and/or murder, Ms. Dragon, who'd been with him since the Ford administration, might know something about it.

It was worth a shot, anyway. Skip hauled the phone book down from the shelf and found a listing for Dragon, D., at 1000 Mason Street, which he guessed would be somewhere up on Nob Hill. She recognized his name—"Leon's boy, of course"—and agreed to meet with him, although she doubted she could be of much help.

It took Skip five minutes to get to the car, ten minutes to reach Nob Hill, and another ten for a handicapped parking space to open up across the street from 1000 Mason, which turned out to be the grand old wedding cake of an apartment house known as the Brocklebank, where James Stewart had stalked Kim Novak in *Vertigo*.

Ms. Dragon met Skip at the door of her seventh-floor apartment dressed in a fitted pantsuit of cobalt blue accessorized with a turquoise scarf. With her apricot-colored hair teased up into a hollow-looking pouf and her eyelids red beneath a hasty application of mascara, she might have been Margaret Thatcher's slightly slutty older sister.

"I've been wracking my brain all morning," she told Skip as she led him down a dark hallway to a living room cluttered with enough Oriental rugs, hangings, furniture, and tchotchkes to stock a good-size antiques store. "But I honestly can't think of any reason anyone would want to harm Judge Brobauer."

"Has he been working on any contentious cases lately?"

"As far as I'm aware, the only case he's involved in directly is an estate matter. An elderly couple had been planning to leave everything in a trust for their grandson, who's been institutionalized for several years. They had to rewrite their wills after the boy was killed in that terrible fire last month—surely you must have seen it in the news?"

But Skip had spent the last two weeks of April vacationing on Maui with his on-again, off-again lady friend—no newspapers, no television.

"It was a place called Meadows Road? North of Santa Cruz?"

Meadows Road! Meadows fucking Road. "Excuse me, Ms. Dragon? This grandson—was that Luke Sweet, by any chance?"

"It was. His grandparents were Fred and Evelyn Harris. They'd been clients of Mr. Brobauer for thirty years. When he told me they'd been murdered last week, you could have knocked me over with a feather."

"I know what you mean," Skip murmured.

"But I can't see how that would have anything to do with his abduction—it wasn't as if the wills were being contested. I believe most of the estate is going to be divided up among charities, now that the grandson is deceased."

But Skip's thoughts were already tending in the same direction as those of a certain overweight FBI agent in Quantico, Virginia, 2,843 miles to the east. "Excuse me, Ms. Dragon. Do you happen to know whether the authorities are absolutely *sure* Luke Sweet is dead?"

"I certainly hope so," she replied. "As I recall, the young man was a rather nasty piece of work."

5

"Oh, gawd," said Steven P. McDougal, the head of the FBI's Liaison Support Unit.

"What?" Pender was dressed for spring in a green-and-yellow madras sport jacket over a short-sleeved cotton-poly pink dress shirt that had been white until he'd laundered it with a pair of red socks a few months ago; his too-short, too-wide necktie might have been hand-painted by Jackson Pollock on a bad peyote trip.

"It looks like the Easter Bunny threw up on you."

"That's a good one, chief. Not new, but good." Pender and McDougal went back a long way together. They'd shared an apartment as recruits, and after graduation they'd both been posted to the Arkansas field office in Little Rock, where during their rookie year, Pender had taken a bullet meant for McDougal. True, it was only in the buttocks, but a grateful McDougal had saved Pender's job at least twice in the intervening decades, and he still ran interference between Pender and the Bureau-cracy on a regular basis.

Of course, even with Steve McDougal running interference, there was a price to be paid for individualism in the buttoned-down, black-Florsheimed world of the FBI. Pender would never make AD, SAC, or even ASAC, and after twenty-three years on the job, he had gone as high on the GS pay scale as a special agent could go. But he doubted he'd have been any happier in management, or that any bump in salary could possibly equal the satisfaction that came with getting serial killers off the street. And besides, Pender sometimes argued, when you were as bald and homely as he was, having people make fun of your clothes was something of an improvement.

Their minimum daily banter requirement fulfilled, McDougal leaned back in his desk chair and laced his hands behind his head. He was in shirtsleeves; the diagonal silver stripes of his navy blue necktie matched his thick, brush-cut hair to perfection. "What's up?"

"I think we've got a live one out in California. Kid from Santa Cruz—"

McDougal groaned.

"—name of Luke Sweet, Junior. Luke Senior was the perp in that snuff porn case in Marshall County, back in '85. You loaned me out to Izzo in Organized Crime for the stakeout, remember?"

"Refresh me."

"There were two filmed, or I guess I should say videotaped murders, but they dug up three female bodies altogether. Luke, Jr.—Little Luke, we called him—was implicated in one of the snuff films. He also strangled his girlfriend and threw her body over a cliff, nearly killed another boy, and according to the records Thom Davies pulled for me today, he was also a suspect in the murder of an Indian pot dealer in Stockton. But his grandparents managed to pull some strings, got him declared non compos, and committed him to a private mental hospital. Place called Meadows Road. Which burned down last month, allegedly with him in it."

"Whose *allegedly* is that—yours or the locals'?"

"Mine," replied Pender, unapologetically. "My gut tells me there's a good chance it was Little Luke who torched it, and an even better one that he survived the fire."

"Does your gut have any . . . What's that word? Oh yes: *evidence*?"

"A week after the fire, somebody killed both of Little Luke's grandparents. *Overkilled* them and scattered the pieces. And when I talked to the forensic pathologist who identified Sweet's remains, she admitted they had no body—the ID was based on a process of elimination."

"And our jurisdiction?" McDougal said dubiously. "Last time I checked, this was still the *Federal* Bureau of Investigation."

"So was the original case, the snuff video. And we were called in to consult by both the Marshall County and Humboldt County sheriff's departments."

"That's a tad thin, don't you think?"

"Steve, please, don't go all Bureau on me now. I have one of my bad feelings about this one. I think this kid's alive, I think he's out for revenge, and I think more people are going to die unless we catch him soon. The way I see it, either we pursue this aggressively *before* he kills again or we sit around with our thumbs up our asses as per usual, waiting for the next corpse to turn up."

McDougal said nothing; neither did he break off eye contact. "Put me in, coach," pleaded Pender. "This is what I *do,* this is what Liaison Support is *for.*"

His boss sighed, shook his head like a mark who'd just made his choice as to which shell the pea was under, and wasn't at all sure he'd gotten it right. "I'll give you a provisional okay. Here are the provisions. First of all, what with the manpower drain from Oklahoma City, the Bureau is seriously understaffed. So I want this handled expeditiously. I'll give you two, three days, then I want you back at your desk. Secondly, it's only May and our budget's already shot to shit, so you're going to have to fly coach, rent a compact car, and stay at a Motel Six or the equivalent. And third, you are not to step on any toes, local or Bureau."

"Three days, on the cheap, no toes," said Pender, who was already halfway out the door. "I read you five by five, and I guarantee you, you will not regret this."

He closed McDougal's door behind him. Pool beckoned him over to her command station/front desk.

"I hear and obey," muttered Pender, veering toward her. "Yes, ma'am?"

"Here, this is for you." She handed him a small gray rectangular object with a plastic faceplate, telescoping antenna, and rounded corners.

"What is it, a new pager?"

"No, it's a cell phone."

"Kind of small, isn't it?"

"That's how they're making them nowadays. I've put my number on speed-dial and set the ring tone for 'Moon River,' if that's all right with you."

"Peachy."

"And here, this device is to charge the battery, and this one is for charging it when you're in your car. So from now on, no excuses, no road trip disappearances. You can reach us twenty-four hours a day, seven days a week, and we can reach you."

"Oh, swell," said Pender.

6

Without the magic words *Federal Bureau of Investigation* after his name, it took Skip a little longer to track down Dr. Gallagher than it had Pender. But what he lacked in official standing he more than made up for by his refusal to take no for an answer. Or yes, for that matter. Even after Sergeant Bagley of the Santa Cruz County Coroner's Office finally agreed to pass on his request for information to the appropriate forensic pathologist, Skip continued to pester him. After his second follow-up call, he received a chewing-out from the beleaguered sergeant. "What the hell's your problem, Epstein? I gave her the message. If she wants to get back to you, she will, so don't call me again."

Skip apologized as meekly as you can when you're grinning from ear to ear, then popped into the bull pen, waved a twenty in the air like Captain Ahab holding up the golden doubloon, and offered it to the first man or woman who could come up with a name and contact number for a female forensic pathologist who worked with the Santa Cruz coroner. His operatives, an independent-minded bunch who would have bitched about, forestalled, or even ignored a direct order, dropped everything they were working on and threw themselves into the challenge.

The winner was Sandy Pollock, a tiny, T-shirted, jeans-wearing single mother in her mid-thirties whose forearms were blue to the elbows with tattoos. "There's only the one," she said, handing him a slip of paper with one hand and snatching the twenty from Skip's fingers with the other. "Dr. Alicia Gallagher. Contract pathologist. The first number's her office at U.C. Santa Cruz, the second's her cell."

"Fine work," said Skip, to a chorus of grumbling. "Thank you, one and all."

He made the call from his office, spinning his chair around to face the picture window overlooking the Marina Safeway parking lot. "Hello, Dr. Gallagher. This is David Epstein, Epstein Investigative Services in San Francisco. I've just been talking to Sergeant Bagley. I believe you were the lead pathologist on the Meadows Road investigation?" All true statements—just not connected.

"And . . . ?"

"I'd like to ask you about your identification of one victim in particular, name of Luke Sweet."

Long pause. Long, long pause.

"Dr. Gallagher? You still there, Dr. Gallagher?"

"I'm here."

"Well?"

"Well, what?"

"Luke Sweet—is there a possibility he's still alive?"

"That's, um, currently under review."

"Which means there *is* a possibility he's still alive."

"Which means precisely what it says."

That was all Skip could get out of her, but more than he'd expected. Obviously there was now some official doubt as to whether Luke Sweet had perished in the Meadows Road fire. This didn't necessarily mean he'd killed his grandparents or kidnapped Judge Brobauer, thought Skip—just that, alive, he'd be the number one suspect. And at the moment, there was no number two.

7

The answer is in the Book.

Asmador opens his eyes. The light in the tumbledown barn is dim and fawn-colored; dust motes dance in columns of sunlight shining through holes in the riddled roof. He unzips his sleeping bag to the waist, then reaches in and feels around at the bottom of the bag until his fingers brush the familiar, nubbly-textured faux-leather cover. He opens the Book at random on his lap, positioning his magnifying glass between the page and a pencil-thin shaft of sunlight. Even with the glass, the microscopic text is difficult to decipher—Asmador's low forehead is furrowed in concentration—but luckily he only needs to make out a few words to fill in the rest from memory.

And at the bottom of the imaginary shoe box, reads the illuminated paragraph, *there's one last, dim snapshot of the traitor Epstein waving good-bye as they drag me away . . .*

Epstein! A younger man than Brobauer, presumably with a stronger heart. Maybe this time the vultures can be tricked or persuaded to tear off a hunk of some living flesh—that's a little wrinkle Asmador came up with all on his own, for extra credit with the Infernal Council, as it were; just thinking about it energizes him, motivates him out of his sleeping bag.

He stumbles outside, his joints still stiff from sleeping on the dirty wooden floor, and relieves himself against the side of the barn, then hurries back inside to get dressed: denim shirt, jeans, denim jacket. He peels a dozen or so bills off a brick of twenties from under the floorboard of the abandoned van to replenish his roll, checks to make sure the .38 is loaded and ready in the glove compartment of the BMW.

It takes half an hour to drive to the Marshall City Public Library. The librarian behind the checkout desk glances at Asmador disinterestedly as he enters, then turns away. His senses on full alert, he heads directly for the wall of yellow-and-black California telephone directories in the back. Having neglected to bring the Book along with him, he closes his eyes to visualize it, then mentally flips through the pages until he finds the part he's looking for.

. . . a skinny guy with fading reddish brown hair . . . two buddies cruising the Golden State . . . a private investigator from San Francisco.

San Francisco it is, then. Taking the appropriate directories down from the shelf, Asmador checks out the white pages first. There are dozens upon dozens of listings for Epsteins, but no Skip. So he flips to *I* for *Investigators* in the yellow pages, and hot damn if there isn't a quarter-page advertisement for Epstein Investigative Services, featuring a photograph of the proprietor, captioned "David 'Skip' Epstein, Licensed Private Investigator."

Asmador quickly memorizes the address on Buchanan Street, then turns back to the residential listings. There he finds an entry for one Epstein, David, on Francisco Street, which he also commits to memory. Then he flips to the map section of the directory, traces out a route with his fingertip.

Good job! thinks Asmador triumphantly as he reshelves the directories. *And what's more, you did it all by yourself.*

"Oh, did you?" whispers a voice in his ear. "Did you really?"

Asmador whirls around, but there's no one there. Just a faint whiff of demon—they smell like burned matches, in case you're interested—and the echo of Sammael the Red's mocking, sac-shriveling laughter.

CHAPTER THREE

1

The flying dream again. The school yard—Skip's old elementary school. The usual chaos: a game of tag, kids running, dodging, shrieking in pretend fear. Skip stumbling, limping, ducking, hiding, making up in stealth what he lacks in speed. But the crowd of kids keeps thinning out and thinning out, until there are only two of them, Skip and the big kid who's *it*. The sky is growing darker, the big kid is closing in on him, and Skip is clumping along as best as he can, pushing off on his good leg, *ka-thump, ka-thump*. The school yard is deserted except for Skip and his pursuer when Skip suddenly realizes this is no longer a game and starts running for his life. He's running fast, faster than he's ever run, and smoother, too, zooming along, picking up more and more speed, until the next thing he knows he's airborne, with the ground rushing along beneath him and his pursuer falling behind, growing smaller and smaller. And just as Skip is beginning to understand that he's fly- ing, really flying—

Most of the covers were on the floor when Skip awoke. The exhilaration of dream flying had given way to a pervasive feel- ing of loss and longing. But that was the way that particular dream always went: as soon as he realized he was flying, it was over.

Leaving his bedclothes and pajamas on the floor—today was Thursday, the maid's day—Skip downed two Norco tablets, then took a hard-won dump (opioids'll shut you down faster than see- ing a highway patrol car in the rearview mirror), and a long hot shower.

On his way out, he paused to inspect his appearance in the hall mirror. Straw-colored sport jacket, open-necked shirt of royal blue oxford cloth, navy slacks; curly hair moussed and shiny. He patted through his pockets to make sure he had his keys, money clip, wallet, and cell phone. As he reached for the doorknob, his eyes were drawn to the lacquered, mushroom-shaped umbrella stand, where the cane his chiropractor had given him two months ago stood gathering dust.

No, not today, he told himself. Because to Skip's way of think- ing, using a crutch when he could still manage without one would be like, well, like using a crutch.

The morning *Chronicle* was still on the doormat. PROMINENT ATTORNEY STILL MISSING had been relegated to the local news sec- tion. "Caddy still dead," muttered Skip—he couldn't get over how quickly the poorer and darker of the two victims had become a nonperson.

There were no new developments detailed in the *Chron* article, but around ten o'clock Warren Brobauer called to tell Skip that the judge's body had been discovered by a pair of backpackers earlier that morning, on a hillside just south of Big Sur.

"Oh, God, I'm so sorry, Warren. Is there anything I can do?"

"As a matter of fact, there is. I'm up to my ass in alligators here, and Lil's under sedation. I was wondering, would you mind terribly going down to Monterey to make a formal identification of the body? Seems they need one before they can perform the autopsy."

"Of course."

"Thanks so much. And, Skip?"

"Warren."

"Lil and I want whoever did this caught and punished. Have you made any progress on your end of the investigation?"

"Matter of fact, I have." He told Warren what he'd learned so far.

"Stay with it, then, if you don't mind. Because quite frankly, Skip, I've spent half the morning on the telephone with the lead homicide detective down there, and just between us, I'm neither thrilled by his attitude nor overwhelmed with his intelligence. In fact, I'm not sure he could find his ass with both hands if he were sitting on them, something at which he appears to have a good deal of practice."

"Okay, Warren, I'm on it. I'll give you a call as soon as I have anything to report. And once again, I'm so, *so* sorry about your dad."

"Thank you. 'Preciate it."

Skip clicked off, then hit the intercom button. "Tanya, would you get me the address of the Monterey County morgue? I think it's part of the sheriff's department. I also need directions to Meadows Road, that mental asylum that blew up a few weeks ago. I was there ten years ago, but all I seem to remember is that it's somewhere north of Santa Cruz."

"So is half the state of California," the receptionist pointed out. "Could you be more specific?"

"Remind me again why I put up with your crap?"

"Because nobody else is willing to work for this pitiful salary."

"Oh, right. Never mind."

2

Asmador had arrived in San Francisco around two o'clock in the morning and parked the Beemer just down the street from Epstein's building. He'd climbed in back to catch a few hours of sleep, which was all he really needed, and awoke with the sun. Pissed into a plastic milk jug. Broke his fast with a Snickers bar. Waited and watched Epstein's door from the front seat, absentmindedly fingering the gun in his pocket.

Gradually the street had come to life. Female human walking a dog. *Chronicle* truck spitting out rolled-up newspapers that thud and thump against doors, onto walkways, into hedges. Garage doors opening, disgorging single-occupant vehicles. Little humans skipping or plodding off to school by twos and threes.

Epstein's building was two stories high, beige stucco with dark brown trim. Asmador's attention had been focused on the front door, waiting, watching, willing it to move, when someone tapped on the car window. Startled, Asmador had pressed his nose against the tinted glass and seen a meter maid rapping the window with her summons book, then pointing to the alternate side of the street parking sign, and giving him the thumb—g'wan, get outta here.

And of course, no sooner had Asmador pulled away from the curb than he spotted a white Buick backing out of the garage of Epstein's building and driving away. With an oath, he'd started up the BMW, pulled out without signaling, and tromped down on the accelerator. At the end of the block he'd almost plowed into the back of the Buick, which had stopped for a light, and had to slam on the brakes.

Asmador had to wait a few seconds for Epstein's car to pull away, then followed it at a discreet distance until it disappeared into the maw of a basement parking garage on Buchanan Street, with a sign that read PARKING BY PERMIT ONLY. Seeing no empty parking spots on either side of Buchanan, Asmador turned right into the Safeway lot and parked the Beemer head-on in an angled stall directly across the street from the underground ramp. Then he settled back to watch and wait, his hands folded across his chest and his eyes half-closed.

One hour later, almost to the minute, spotting the white-on-white grille of the Buick emerging from the darkness of the exit ramp across the street, Asmador starts up his engine, throws the Beemer into reverse—and nearly backs into some old beater of a Chevy that's blocking him in. He jams on the brakes, hits the horn, sticks his head out the window. "Out of my way! Get out of my way!"

The driver, a forty-something female, smiles and holds up a polite wait-a-sec finger, points to the car backing out in front of her. Meanwhile the Buick is turning left on Buchanan, heading toward the bay. Asmador sounds the horn. The woman gives him a helpless what-can-I-do? shrug. Asmador pounds the steering wheel in frustration as the Buick turns left again onto Marina Boulevard.

When the way finally clears, Asmador burns rubber backing out. But when he reaches the Marina Green, the Buick is nowhere in sight, so he buys a Croissan'wich and coffee at the drive-thru window of the Burger King on Bay Street, then returns to Francisco, parks across the street from Epstein's building, and settles in for what he expects will be another long wait.

But only a few minutes later, a Hispanic-looking woman in a green maid's uniform shows up on Epstein's doorstep and lets herself in with a key. Asmador gobbles down the rest of his Croissan'wich, then slips the gun, with the safety off and a round in the firing chamber, into the back of his jeans before crossing the street and ringing Epstein's doorbell.

"Jess?" says the cleaning woman, opening the door.

Only nine days ago, Asmador had found himself stammering

helplessly at the grandparents' door, unable to remember the little speech he'd memorized. When the old man tried to slam the door in his face, he'd had to bull his way in and kill them both immediately to keep them from calling for help. And even though the vultures *had* eventually feasted, or at least snacked, on their bodies, all in all, the Council had *not* been pleased.

And only two days ago, although Asmador had successfully memorized the speech he'd prepared for his meeting with Judge Brobauer, his delivery had been so awkward it had alerted both the old man and his caddy.

But somehow, in the intervening forty-eight hours, Asmador's communication skills have improved exponentially. "Hello there. Hola! I'm an old friend of Mr. Epstein—he said it'd be okay if I wait for him here until he gets back." Without waiting for an answer, he shoulders his way past her into the hallway, baring his teeth in what is intended to be a reassuring smile. "It'll be all right, I promise. I'll take full responsibility."

"Hokay, but joo wait here. I call Mr. Skeep, tell heeng joo here."

"Actually, I was hoping to surprise him."

"Surprise heeng?" the woman parrots uncomprehendingly.

"Yeah, you know, like this." Asmador draws the .38 from behind his back and shoots her twice, once in the chest as she backs away with both hands raised, and again in the head as her body lies twitching on the hardwood floor.

3

Pender's early morning flight from Dulles to San Francisco was three-quarters empty, so flying coach was not the ordeal it might have been, and the landing went smoothly enough. The rent-a-car, however, turned out to be a generic white Toyota with all the legroom and power of a bumper car, and there wasn't much in the way of scenery at first—Highway 101 was mostly industrial parks and shopping malls all the way from San Francisco to San Jose.

It wasn't until he'd turned off onto Highway 17, a dappled, winding, two-lane mountain road lined with sharp-smelling eucalyptus and towering redwoods, that Pender felt he was really back in California. From 17, he followed a succession of narrow, winding roads that plunged deeper and deeper into the Santa Cruz Mountains, and as brightest noon turned to dusk in the canyons, Pender was forcibly reminded that it was in these dark and brooding hills that Kemper, Mullin, and Frazier had plied their bloody trade.

As it turned out, Pender could have saved himself the trip. There was nothing left of Meadows Road but a gatehouse at the bottom of the steep, narrow driveway and a vast, debris-filled hole in the ground at the top, currently being excavated by two scurrying backhoes and a queue of patient dump trucks.

But having come this far, Pender was determined to make the best of it. After parking the Toyota on the far side of the hole, next to a makeshift chainlink construction fence, he loosened his tie, took off his tomato-soup–colored sport jacket, and draped it across the back of the front passenger seat, then set out to explore the periphery of the blast, dime-store pocket notebook and tooth-marked pencil stub in hand.

The first thing he noticed was that the trees on the edge of the woods, some twenty yards from the edge of the building's footprint, had either been stripped and scorched on the side facing the blast, or leveled entirely. Hard to believe anyone could have lived through *that* son of a bitch.

Yet many had. Was Little Luke one of them? If so, how had he managed to get away without anyone noticing? Of course, it must have been a real clusterfuck here after the explosion . . .

While Pender's mind nattered on, his Hush Puppies carried him into the woods. Nearly two and a half weeks after the fire, there was still a light dusting of ash on some of the bushes. Behind this tame woodland loomed a forbidding-looking stone fence some ten feet high, topped with electrified wire. Pender jotted down a note, "Elec. fence: juice?" to remind himself to inquire whether the power had been knocked out immediately after the explosion, thereby making the fence, if not inviting, at least climbable.

Unless of course the juice was supplied at the gatehouse, and the gatehouse juice was on a separate line from the hospital. "Pwr source?" he wrote. Then, "Auto theft?" meaning that if Little Luke *had* gotten over the wall, it would be nice to know if any cars had been stolen within hiking distance of the hospital that day.

And so question led to question until Pender had filled a page of the notebook with one- or two-word entries. When he got back to his car, there was a late-model, white-on-white Buick parked next to it. A lanky guy with faded reddish brown hair leaned against the side of the Buick, surveying the ruins.

"Hey, how's it going?" called Pender.

The guy gave him a wary nod. Suddenly Pender realized that with his jacket off, his shoulder holster was in plain sight. *So much for staying undercover,* he thought, sticking out his hand and smiling unthreateningly as he approached the other man.

"Ed Pender, FBI."

"Epstein. Skip Epstein."

Epstein waited for Pender to reach him, rather than coming forward to meet him halfway. Glancing downward as they shook hands, Pender noted the mismatched legs and built-up shoe. "Quite a mess," he said, gesturing to the obscenely empty hole.

"No shit," said Epstein.

"You here on business, or just having a look-see?"

"Little of both."

"Meaning . . . ?"

Epstein sighed. "I'm a licensed private investigator," he said wearily, as if he were gearing up for a hassle.

But a hassle was the last thing Pender, who taught a daylong course in the art of affective interviewing at the Academy every year, had in mind. "Cool," he said, in the vernacular of the natives. "Are you on a case?"

"A client asked me to look into a recent kidnapping in Pebble Beach."

Pender's turn to sigh. "Pebble Beach!" he said, in the same tone of voice Homer Simpson reserved for the word *doughnuts*.

"Golfer, eh?"

"I try," said Pender. "Who got kidnapped?"

"Actually, it's a homicide now. Some backpackers found the body early this morning, down in Big Sur."

"So what are you doing all the way up here?"

"The victim was an attorney. His last case involved rewriting the will of an old couple whose grandson had been a patient here. He was supposed to have been killed in the explosion, this grandson."

"Only you're not all that sure he was," said Pender, trying not to sound smug.

Epstein looked surprised. "That's right. And neither is the coroner. Because just last week—"

"The grandparents were both murdered," Pender broke in. "I know—that's why I'm here, too."

Epstein raised an eyebrow. "Luke Sweet?" he said carefully.

"Luke Sweet."

"Well, fuuuuck me," Skip muttered.

"How 'bout if I just buy you lunch," suggested Pender, "and we'll see how it goes from there."

4

Pender followed Epstein's Buick down out of the mountains to a retro-style diner on Ocean Street in Santa Cruz. They sat in a red vinyl booth with its own Seeburg jukebox outlet and ordered from a laminated menu featuring fifties-style comfort food at mid-nineties prices. Skip had a tuna melt, side slaw, and fries; Pender made his selection in accordance with the set of road rules he'd worked out over many years of traveling, which he was more than happy to share with Skip.

"One, it's not cheating if you're at least a day's travel from home. Two, always memorize where the bathroom is before you go to bed, in case you have to get up in the middle of the night to piss. Three, when in doubt, order the club sandwich. It's hard to screw up a club sandwich."

"I'll keep it in mind."

"So how long have you been a P.I.?"

"A little over ten years."

"Do you like it?"

"It's okay. When I was a kid, though, adults'd ask me what I wanted to be when I grew up—I'd tell 'em a G-man."

Pender chuckled. "Now, there's a term you don't hear much anymore."

"The thing is, I'd always get this weird look back. It wasn't until I was ten or twelve that I realized you never see an FBI agent with a limp on TV or in the movies."

Pender gave him a whaddaya-gonna-do? shrug. Then after a vaguely uncomfortable pause in the conversation: "You know, I wasn't going to ask. But since you brought it up . . . ?"

"Polio. I was one of the control subjects in the first trials of the Salk vaccine—you know, one of the kids who got an injection of saline solution instead of the vaccine. We were all supposed to get

the real thing after the trials, of course, only by then it was too late.
Which makes me one of the last, possibly *the* last, polio case in the
USA. So to quote Abe Lincoln quoting the guy who got tarred,
feathered, and ridden out of town on a rail: 'if it wasn't for the
honor of the thing . . . '"

"Well, shit, buddy!" Pender sounded impressed.

"Don't get me wrong, I'm not complaining." Skip added hurriedly. "I like being a P.I. I have my own agency now, with a dozen
operatives, I set my own hours, I'm making a decent living. But
compared to what you do, going after serial killers and shit, it
makes tracking down deadbeats and repoing cars look kind of, I
don't know, kind of . . . *blah.*"

"Trust me, it's not that exciting. I spend a third of my time on
the phone, another third going over computer printouts, and most
of what's left dealing with Bureau-crats and bullshit."

By the time the waitress arrived with their orders, the conversation had turned to business. Since Pender had an appointment
with a Detective Klug from the Santa Cruz PD at two o'clock, while
Skip had promised to show up in Salinas to identify Brobauer's
corpse no later than three, they had to talk while they ate—never a
good idea when scarfing American comfort food.

"Luke and I actually got along pretty well, once he got over the
idea he could con me into cutting him loose." Skip was fighting a
losing battle trying to keep the overstuffed filling of his tuna melt
from squishing out the other side every time he took a bite. "But
the second I handed him over, he went bananas. Split this one or-
derly's nose wide open with a head butt, knocked another one on
his ass before they got a needle into him."

Pender's triple-decker sandwich was presenting him with the
usual dilemma: take out the toothpicks and have the sandwich
fall apart, or leave them in and risk spearing his palate. He com-
promised by moving the toothpicks outward in increments, which
only postponed the inevitable structural failure. "I've seen the
bananas act. He tried to get to me after I interviewed him at his

172   Jonathan Nasaw

grandparents' house—it took two big Santa Cruz cops to bring him down."

"Yeah, he told me about that," said Skip. "Then he said they sent him to some wilderness training school, and he and his girl-friend escaped, then she fell over a cliff."

"Thrown over, more likely," said Pender, picturing the eyeless corpse in the rescue basket. But like many sewer workers, Pender had long ago erected a fire wall between his job and his appetite; he ate on as he talked. "I went through her autopsy report on the plane this morning. The M.E. determined she died from the fall, but her body also showed signs consistent with rape—abrasions on the hoo-ha and so on—and there were bruises on her neck. My guess is that he probably strangled her until she was unconscious, raped her either before or after or both, then tossed her over the cliff, either thinking she was dead or making sure of it."

"Well, he sure fooled my ass," said Skip. "I totally bought it."

"Oh, he's convincing, all right. Most psychopaths are. But I'll bet you anything he didn't tell you about his pal Brent."

"Who?"

"Yeah, I didn't think so." Pender used the side of his pinkie nail to work a scrap of toothpick cellophane from between two teeth, then flicked it away. "Brent Perry was one of the other Mountain Project kids. Our boy Luke clubbed him over the head, left him by the side of the trail with his brains leaking out. Then there was this Indian pot dealer up in Humboldt whose family took the Lukester in after he ran away from the Mountain Project. *He* was found stabbed to death in a motel room near Stockton, and guess whose fingerprints were all over the room?"

"The Lukester's?"

"You got it."

Pender plucked a scrap of bacon off his napkin, popped it into his mouth, then looked up slyly. "So what do you say, Magnum, P.I.? You want to work with me on this, find out whether catching serial killers for the FBI really beats repoing cars? I can't promise to pay you anything, but I can probably score you an FBI sweatshirt or a cap or something."

Skip briefly considered whether Pender might be making the offer out of . . . well, out of the P word. But Pender didn't strike him as the pitying type. And besides, since he was already involved on behalf of a client, who was to say it wasn't a matter of the *FBI* helping *him*? "Man, I'd be honored," he told Pender.

When they'd finished eating, Pender grabbed the check and Skip left the tip. Skip took a toothpick from the dispenser at the cashier's counter; Pender pocketed a handful of mints. They left the diner together, and shook hands out in the parking lot. "It's a lucky thing we happened to run into each other back there," said Pender.

"As we say in California, there are no accidents," Skip told him.

Pender laughed. "That must make your insurance companies awfully happy."

5

Detective Lloyd Klug was a scrappy old-timer with gray hair cut *en brosse* and the flattened nose of a pugilist. Pender figured him for a welterweight, the kind of brawler who'd gladly take two shots to land one. He met Pender in the lobby of the Santa Cruz Police Department headquarters, a mission-style structure on Center Street with arched doorways and a red-tiled roof. His first question, after they'd shaken hands, was, "Mind if I smoke?"

By way of answer, Pender flashed his Marlboro hard pack. They adjourned the meeting to the courtyard, which had as a centerpiece a circular fountain with a sculpture of what looked like two elongated shark's fins sticking up from its center. Klug fired up a Camel straight and apologized for his sketchy grasp of the Harris case.

He'd only been assigned to it the day before, he told Pender, when the Santa Cruz municipal police department took over jurisdiction from the county sheriff. It had been one of those jurisdictional pissing contests: two headless bodies had been discovered up in the unincorporated hills, and it wasn't until after they'd been identified that a search of their home indicated they had been murdered inside the city limits.

"And even then, the sheriff's department held on to it until yesterday, probably on the off chance they'd be able to solve it. When that didn't turn out to be so easy, lo and behold: 'Sorry, our mistake—I guess it was you guys's case all along.'"

You guys's. "Am I right in guessing you're not from around here?"

"Philly. I came out here twenty years ago. Smartest move I ever made."

"You're going to look even smarter when this is over," said Pender.

Klug worked a shred of tobacco from between his teeth, spat it out cleanly, expertly, just beyond the toes of his Bates Uniform oxford-style cop shoes. "Oh?"

Pender laid it all out for him: the psychopathic grandson who would have been everybody's prime suspect if he weren't already deceased; the coroner who now admitted he might not be all that deceased after all; the possibly related kidnap-murder down in Monterey County just the other day.

"So listen," Klug said when Pender had finished. "I don't want you to take this the wrong way, but I've dealt with the Bureau before, so I gotta ask: Is there some quid pro involved here?"

"What?"

"You looking to put the cuffs on him, hold a press conference? Or maybe there's a federal warrant out for him someplace?"

Pender sighed. "Let's make a deal. You don't assume I'm a

face-time-hungry Bureau asshole, I won't assume you're a local yokel who couldn't find a turd in a bag of marshmallows."

"At least until proven otherwise," said Klug.

"You bet," said Pender.

6

As a private investigator, Skip Epstein had encountered no shortage of cheating spouses, insurance fakers, and runaway debtors. What he hadn't seen many of were dead bodies, so for a moment there, when the jumpsuited morgue attendant had lowered the rubber sheet to reveal the face of the corpse underneath, Skip saw stars, heard a roaring in his ears, and retasted the tuna melt rising in his gorge. When he came back to full consciousness after a brief temporal discontinuity, Sergeant Darrien, the sheriff's deputy who'd walked him down to the morgue, was holding him by the elbow to steady him while the morgue attendant held out a barf basin.

"I'm okay now," Skip protested unconvincingly.

Darrien led him over to a folding chair. "Is that Mr. Brobauer?"

"Judge Brobauer—no question about it. But what in God's name happened to his eyes?"

"Turkey vulture, we think. There were some feathers scattered around where we found the body."

"Really? And where was that?" Skip put a little extra gee whiz in his voice, trying to draw Darrien out without seeming to be grilling him.

"On a ridge just south of Big Sur. Sickest crime scene I've ever seen."

"No shit?"

"Swear to God. The victim was staked to the ground with metal tent stakes, and there was a dead animal placed on his chest—a *very* dead animal. I can't tell you what kind—that's a control variable." Control variables were clues the police held back in order to weed out the nut jobs who came out of the woodwork to confess every time a juicy murder hit the news.

Just then the phone on the wall started ringing. The sergeant excused himself to answer it, then turned back to Skip after a brief conversation. "I'm supposed to bring you back upstairs," he said tersely. "Lieutenant Farley wants to talk to you."

Farley, Skip soon discovered, was a compact, khaki-uniformed forty-something with a square face and a Julius Caesar haircut. He greeted Skip coldly, nodded toward an uncushioned, decidedly un-ergonomic wooden chair next to his desk, then turned back to his computer and ignored Skip for the next few minutes.

Sitting down provided Skip with momentary relief—he'd done more walking in the last few hours than he normally did in a week. But after a few minutes in the hard-bottomed chair, his pain returned with a vengeance, and brought a gang of friends along for company. Skip dry-popped two Norco that left a not-unwelcome bitter taste at the back of his throat.

Finally the lieutenant looked up at him. "Epstein, eh?"

He'd pronounced it as if it rhymed with *mean* instead of *fine;* Skip let it go. "Yes, sir."

"David Epstein?"

Skip nodded, not sure where this was going, but not much liking the ride.

"Friend of the victim's family, eh?"

Another nod.

"Any reason why you didn't happen to mention to anybody down here that you were a private investigator?"

Oh, crap. "It didn't seem relevant—I only came down to ID the body."

"I see. And you've done that?"

"Yes, sir."

"It's Brobauer?"

"No question."

"Good. Now get the hell out of here."

"I beg your pardon?"

"They're all one-syllable words, they shouldn't be that difficult to understand."

"But—"

"And when you get back to San Francisco"—enunciated with extreme distaste, if not full-out loathing—"please inform Warren Brobauer that if and when the Monterey County Sheriff's Department requires the assistance of a private investigator, rest assured we will send for one. Until then, if I catch you sticking your nose into one of my cases without permission, I'll have your license pulled so fast your head'll spin like that girl in *The Exorcist*."

Afterward, Skip would admit to Pender that he knew his response was childish. In the interest of public safety, he should have given Luke Sweet's name to the detective, hurt feelings or no hurt feelings. Instead, he'd turned in the doorway on his way out and called, "Chuck you, Farley!"

It sure had seemed like a good idea at the time, though, he told Pender.

"Say what? You're breaking up."

"I SAID: IT SEEMED LIKE A GOOD IDEA AT THE TIME!" Skip shouted into his cell. Driving north up the peninsula on 101, he had just cleared San Jose and was hoping to reach San Francisco before the rush-hour traffic closed in.

"No harm done," said Pender, speaking from a slightly mildewed room in the least expensive motel in Santa Cruz, the Bide-A-Nite on Soquel Avenue. "I told Klug about Brobauer, so if he hasn't already hooked up with Farley on that, he will soon."

"And Klug likes Sweet for the Harris murders?"

"Adores him." A snick and a hiss—Pender had fired up a Marlboro with his venerable Zippo. "You know, I was thinking, as long as the locals down here seem to be getting their shit together, how about you and me taking a run up to Sweet's old place to poke around? That's where he tried to hole up the last time he was on the run."

"Sure, why not?" said Skip. "Maybe I'll get lucky twice."

They agreed to meet at Skip's apartment around nine o'clock the following morning. After giving Pender directions and signing off, Skip noticed that his cell phone battery was getting low. He switched the phone off, hooked it up to the car charger, and spent the rest of the ride listening to drive-time sports talk on KNBR. A particularly evocative beer commercial started him thinking about the icy green bottle of Heineken currently chilling in his refrigerator—he was all but salivating by the time he pulled into the single-car garage attached to his apartment.

The phone was fully charged by then. Skip unplugged it from the charger and slipped it into the right front pocket of his slacks. He used the remote device clipped to the sun visor to close the garage door behind him, and entered the apartment through a connecting door that led directly from the garage into the kitchen.

Still thinking about that beer, he tossed his jacket over the back of a kitchen chair, then headed straight for the refrigerator. Opened the door. Stooped to reach for the bottle of Heineken on the bottom shelf. Sensed movement behind him. Started to turn. Felt a blow on the back of the head and saw the universe explode into jagged spears of white light against a black velvet backdrop.

CHAPTER FOUR

1

Whoever wrote that song wasn't kidding about the morning fog filling the air, thought Pender, when he reached San Francisco early the next morning. Even with the headlights and windshield wipers on, he couldn't see much farther than the end of the Toyota's hood. Somehow he found his way to Francisco Street, though, and pulled into a convenient parking spot directly across the street from Epstein's building.

A mist of silver droplets hung suspended in the air like a stop-motion rainstorm, muffling the *thud* of the car door. The city smelled of the ocean, sharp tang and faint rot; the pavement gleamed wet and gray. A rolled-up newspaper in a thin plastic bag lay on Epstein's doormat. Pender picked it up and pressed the doorbell, heard chimes bing-bonging inside. *Excuse me, I'm look-ing for Tony Bennett's heart,* he was planning to say when Epstein answered the door, only Epstein never answered the door. Pender rang the bell again and pressed his ear against the door. No foot-steps, no sounds of life inside.

Puzzled, he took out his notebook to make sure he had the street number right, then tried the doorknob. To his surprise, it wasn't locked. He shoved the door open and stuck his head inside. "Anybody home?" he called down the dimly lighted hallway. "It's me, Pender."

He closed the door behind him, put the paper down on the whatnot table next to the umbrella stand, then stooped to check out the mail that had fallen through the slot. It all had Epstein's name on it—either that or "Occupant."

But everything else was wrong, wrong, wrong, from the door that had not been locked to the dangling chain that had not been latched to the dual dead bolts that had not been thrown. Why would anybody so lax about security have installed redundant dead bolts in the first place?

Then there were those reddish brown flecks on the baseboard and the faint, roughly circular stain where the gloss had been rubbed off the hardwood floor of the hallway. *Mark well,* said Pender's gut—after chasing serial killers for almost twenty years, he didn't need phenolphthalein or luminol to tell him he was looking at blood spatter and a clumsy cleanup job.

Pender took a giant step over the stain and walked on down the hall, checking out the rooms on either side. In the living room, an upright vacuum cleaner stood abandoned, its power cord still plugged into the socket. In the kitchen, a full bottle of Heineken lay on the floor next to the refrigerator.

By now, Pender was in full don't-fuck-up-the-crime-scene mode. Touching nothing, planting his feet wide so as not to step where footprints were most likely to be found, he used his hand-kerchief to turn the doorknob by the base when he opened the door of the bedroom at the end of the hall. The bed was unmade, with a duvet and a pair of pajamas on the floor, and the door of the adjoining bathroom was open. Backing out, Pender grabbed the edge of the door rather than the knob, and yanked the door closed behind him.

The door to the left of that one was slightly ajar. Pender edged it open, glanced around. Originally a guest bedroom, judging by the single bed and narrow dresser, the room was currently being used for storage. An old TV console minus the TV, an upended rowing machine leaning against the wall, boxes of old clothes, books, cassettes, LPs, board games, rolled-up posters, and small appliances, including a radio with a cracked Bakelite case and a toaster oven with a frayed cord.

It all looked random enough at first glance, but a closer inspection revealed to Pender's trained eye a story written in the dust. A pattern of scrapes, drag marks, and rectangular depressions in the nap-worn carpet told him that someone had recently cleared a path diagonally across the room, shoving cartons aside to drag something heavy from the doorway to the closet.

In order to avoid disturbing the marks on the floor, Pender delicately picked his way around the edge of the room. When he reached the closet door, he took a deep, deliberate breath—slow the breath, slow the painful pounding of the heart—then used his handkerchief to turn the knob.

Sometimes you know what you're going to see before you see it; sometimes you're wrong. Pender had himself so convinced he was going to find Epstein's body in the closet that after the door swung open, releasing the sickly sweet odor of day-old death, it took him a few seconds to realize that it was *not* Skip Epstein in drag he saw lying crumpled in the back of the cluttered, junk-filled closet, but a brown-skinned woman with her head wrapped in a bloody turban of paper towels.

2

When Skip regained consciousness the previous night, he'd been lying on his kitchen floor with his hands tied behind his back, a throbbing at the base of his skull, and a rubbery-smelling sack covering his head. An inner voice had tried to convince him that he was having a nightmare, that if only he could wake up, it would all be over, but he wasn't buying it. *Face it, man,* he'd told himself: *Luke Sweet's got you now. Same as he got his grandparents, same as he got Judge Bro——*

Oh, God! A wave of sheer animal terror had overwhelmed Skip when he pictured the old man's eyeless corpse. He'd fought against the panic and mastered it to a degree, but had still been trembling when a firm hand gripped his arm just above the elbow and steered him through an open door. Unable to see or smell anything through the rubber sack, he hadn't realized he was in the garage until he heard the clank and whine of the electric door rising above him.

Sweet's car must have been parked directly outside the garage, backed up with its rear bumper nearly flush with the garage entrance and the trunk lid raised, Skip had realized, because the door was still rising overhead when a hard shove on the back sent him tumbling blindly into the trunk. Turning as he fell, he'd landed hard and curled up instinctively on his left side, with his knees almost to his chest; the trunk lid had slammed closed only inches above him.

Skip had spent the next several hours being tossed around, half-asphyxiated, in the trunk of the moving car. Eventually, mercifully, he'd passed out, and when he'd come to again, he'd found himself lying on a hard floor somewhere so deep in the boondocks that all he could hear were crickets and a lonesome hooting that even a city boy like Skip was able to identify as an owl.

Stiff-jointed, bruised, and sore, his hips and head aching and his bladder all but bursting, Skip had to beg his captor to let him take a piss. The man—presumably Luke Sweet—had untied Skip's wrists and ankles but left the rubber sack covering his head, then led him outside to pee against what Skip guessed, from the hollow spattering sound, was probably the side of a wooden building.

Back inside, lying on his left side with his wrists and ankles bound again, Skip had heard the rasp of a disposable cigarette lighter; seconds later, the funky, leafy scent of pot smoke had been so strong he could smell it through the rubber sack. "Listen, Luke," he'd said, raising his unsupported head, "you've got this all wrong. I'm on *your* side, Luke."

"My name," the other man had replied, "is Asmador."

"Okay, Luke, Asmador, whatever you want to call yourself, all I'm saying is, your grandparents asked me to find you before the cops did, and bring you to Meadows Road so you could get some treatment. Otherwise you'd have gotten thrown into Juvie, or maybe even done hard time if they decided to try you as an adult. I thought I was doing you a favor—I had no way of knowing they were going to keep you there all those years."

The only response had been the hiss of a deep, long toke, followed by a spate of coughing. Skip's instinct, or compulsion, had been to talk on despite the absence of feedback, if only to keep the darkness at bay. And the withdrawal symptoms: going from eight Norco tablets a day down to zero without tapering off first was going to be like hitting the brakes at a hundred miles an hour without a seat belt—helloooo, windshield! "I swear, Luke—"

"Asmador," the other man had hissed again, between tokes.

"Sorry, Asmador. I swear, even if you did blow the place up, your secret's safe with me. I mean, I saw them beat you up when you first got there, and God knows what they've put you through since. In my book, they deserved whatever they got."

No answer. Skip had tried another approach. "Hey, what do you say you take this bag off my head? Just for a couple minutes—I promise I won't peek. It's just that it's getting kind of hard to breathe under here. Okay, Luke? I mean, Asmador?"

But by then Sweet had been snoring stertorously—he'd either fallen asleep or was feigning it. Skip had sighed, rolled onto his back, and closed his eyes, intending to rest for a few minutes and let his head clear while he worked out his next move.

The next thing he knew, it was morning. Birds were singing, a faint glow of daylight had crept in under the neck of the rubber sack, Skip's head was pounding, and the old familiar pain in his lower back and hips had turned feral, like a family pet gone rabid. Rolling onto his right side for relief, Skip felt something in his right front pants pocket digging painfully into his right thigh.

Something hard.

Something like a cell phone.

3

Pender used his cell phone to call 911. He was waiting outside Epstein's door with his badge case clipped to the breast pocket of his sport jacket and his badge hanging in plain sight when the first cruiser arrived. The rest was attitude—he treated the responding officers as if they'd been dispatched to *his* crime scene, directing them to stand guard outside Epstein's door and make sure nobody touched the doorknob until it had been dusted.

Pender maintained control of the scene until a pair of veteran SFPD homicide detectives arrived in an unmarked car. Their initial assumption was that the missing man had shot his cleaning lady and fled; it took Pender a good deal of effort to convince the locals that they were dealing instead with a homicide-kidnapping case involving a serial offender.

Pender's next move was to give the San Francisco detectives the names of their counterparts in Santa Cruz and Monterey. When he'd finished doing that, his job as liaison support was over. Or so Steve McDougal informed him via his cell phone a few minutes later.

"You don't understand, Steve," said Pender, who had stepped off the curb and was now performing a primitive cell phone reception dance in the middle of Francisco Street, shuffling around in circles holding the phone to one ear and sticking his forefinger in the other. "Epstein was *working* with us—we can't just turn our backs on him."

"What's this *we* stuff, kemo sabe?"

"All right, *I* was working with him. So there's—"

"Ed."

"No way I'm—"

"Ed?"

"Walking away from—"

"Ed!"

"What?"

"I want you on the next available commercial flight home. You're a fifty-year-old liaison support specialist, not a case agent, not a field agent. If field assistance is requested, the Bureau has field offices and resident agencies from one end of California to the other, and if any liaising needs to be done, you can do it from here as easily as you can from there, with considerably less damage to my budget."

"What if I pay my own expenses? It's already Friday—what do you care where I spend the weekend?"

There was no immediate response. Pender wasn't sure whether McDougal had been struck dumb, or if they'd lost the connection—either way, he decided to take the silence for permission. "Thanks, Steve, you won't regret it," he said, and hurriedly pushed the End Call button.

4

"Luke?" you call. "You there, Luke?"

No response. You lie still, holding your breath and listening intently for the faintest rustle to betray the other man's presence. Then when you're sure you're alone—or as sure as you can be: there's always the possibility Sweet is also lying still and holding *his* breath—you roll onto your stomach, wriggling and squirming, squirming and wriggling, until you've twisted your pants around on your hips far enough to bring the pocket with the phone in it within reach of your hands, which are still tied together behind your back, palms facing.

Somehow you manage to slide both hands into your pocket, but not far enough to reach the phone, which is jammed into the very bottom of the pocket, just out of reach of your yearning fingertips. So you stretch and strain and arch your spine backward and your shoulder blades downward, fighting for one . . . last . . . crucial . . . mini . . . micro . . . millimeter . . .

There! Got it!

Now bring your thumbs into play . . . trying to flip the phone open . . . can't quite . . . almost there—*Ouch, ouch, cramp, thumb cramp, sonofa*——

Calm down, wait for the cramp to pass, try again. Work your thumbs up, up . . . force them into the gap . . . try to leverage the—

Sonofabitch! It can't be done. You can't open the phone without taking it out of the pocket, any more than you could open a sandwich without taking it out of the Baggie.

Okay, okay, don't panic. Slight adjustment necessary. Plan B: instead of working the trousers *sideways* any farther, work them *downward,* down over your hips. One of those if-you-can't-raise-the-bridge-lower-the-water deals. Or in this case, if you can't raise the phone, lower the pocket by lowering the pants. It doesn't have to be far . . . just far enough . . . an inch, another inch . . .

Ta-daaaaa! The phone is out. Now work your thumbs between the gap again, pry the halves apart . . . a little farther . . .

Ta-daaaa again: the phone is open.

Now visualize the faceplate. Small buttons numbered like a telephone dial. Larger buttons above them marked with little telephone icons—the one on the left is for placing or answering calls. But first you have to turn it on—that's the larger button on the right, that's the one you need to press and hold first.

Problem: the buttons are set nearly flush with the base—you can't tell which is which just by touch.

Solution: just keep pressing buttons and holding them down, one after the other, until you find the one that goes *beep.*

Okay, pressing buttons now. Trial and error: no beep . . . no beep . . . no beep . . .

Beep.

5

Lacking permission to request support from the Bureau's San Francisco field office, Pender decided to try a different approach. Before leaving for Marshall County, he dropped by the Buchanan Street offices of Epstein Investigative Services. The receptionist, Tanya, an otherwise attractive young lady with Smurf blue hair, was bristling with rings, studs, and so many piercings it looked as though someone had taken a riveting gun to her face. Even before Pender tinned her, he could tell that she was as yet unaware that Epstein had been kidnapped only a few blocks away.

He broke the news gently, stressing that there was every reason to believe Skip was still alive. Tears sprang to Tanya's eyes never-theless. *Don't cry,* Pender wanted to tell her, *you'll rust.*

Minutes later, he was addressing the assembled staff in a small conference room behind the bull pen—you could tell by the ping-pong table that it was seldom used for conferences. A motley crew, casually dressed for the most part in T-shirts, bowling shirts, jeans, and cross-trainers, they sat in stunned silence after Pender finished talking.

"Come on," he urged them. "You guys are all pros, you find people every day of your lives. If you've got any ideas, now's the time to speak up."

A tiny woman wearing a softball jersey raised her hand tenta-tively, revealing a heavily tattooed forearm.

"Yes, what's your name, dear?" said Pender.

"Sandy Pollock—and don't call me dear."

"Sorry, no disrespect intended. What've you got?"

"Do you know if Skip had his cell phone with him when he was taken?"

"I believe so. I know he had it with him yesterday—he called me from it while he was driving home from Salinas, and I didn't see it anywhere around the apartment."

"Great. Far out. Tanya, would you get me Skip's cell number and his service provider so I can get hold of their security people? Then assuming he has his phone turned on, if he makes a call or takes a call, it doesn't matter how short or long it is, they can still get the GPS coordinates by triangulating from the location of the microwave relay towers."

"Sandy, Sandy!" Short guy, big head, tragic acne, trifocals. "Give me the number. I've got an automatic dialer rigged up back in my cubicle—you know, for radio call-in contests and stuff. I can set it to continuous calling."

"And let's hook it up to a tape recorder," the office manager suggested. Older than the others, sideburned and pudgy, he was the only necktie wearer in the room apart from Pender. "Even if he can't *say* anything, they might be able to narrow down the search parameters based on ambient sounds, stuff like birdcalls, traffic noises, railroad crossings. I saw that on *Tales of the FBI*," he added, with a friendly nod in Pender's direction.

Twenty minutes later, Pender was still trying to process this new information about cellular call tracking. The implications for law enforcement in general were staggering. But then again, so were the implications for a special agent who had been thinking about calling his boss to report that he was at the San Francisco airport but couldn't get a flight out until Monday, when he was actually calling from a rent-a-car on the road to Marshall County, because his gut told him that's where Sweet was holed up with his latest captive— assuming, of course, that he hadn't already killed him.

6

It should have been easier to call 911—wasn't the 9 button at the bottom right and the 1 at the top left? But Skip's fingertips were so numb and clumsy and the buttons set so flush and close together he could hardly differentiate them from the faceplate, much less from each other.

After several failed attempts, it finally occurred to Skip that he didn't actually have to call 911. Any number would do. Even better, somewhere toward the top of the faceplate there was a redial button that would reconnect him with the last number he'd called. And as far as he could remember, the last number he'd called was . . . Pender! Pender of the Eff Bee Fucking Eye.

Of course, finding the redial button with both hands tied behind your back was no walk in the park. He had to switch the phone on, try a button, switch it off, try another. Trial and error, trial and error, story of my life. If at first you don't succeed—

Suddenly Skip heard the *skreee* of the rusty, off-track sliding door. Quickly he folded up the phone and hid it between his palms. He heard footsteps coming toward him.

"On your feet, Epstein."

Skip sat up, the cell phone concealed between his bound hands. Luke, or Asmador, or whatever he was calling himself, untied Skip's ankles. Skip got his feet under him and tried unsuccessfully to stand up; his legs felt like fat water balloons.

"I think I'm going to puke," he said between clenched teeth, when suddenly the Clash started playing "Rock the Casbah" behind his back—it was, of course, the ring tone of his cell phone.

"What's that?" The phone was snatched from Skip's hands. He heard "Sorry, dude, you got the wrong number," followed by a rending noise, followed by two hollow thuds he took to be the sound of his cell phone being snapped in half and thrown against a wooden wall a few feet away.

CHAPTER FIVE

1

Lieutenant J. B. Sperry, in command of the Marshall County Sheriff Department's tactical response squad, jabbed with his pointer at a tiny red-penciled cross on the topographical map spread out across Sheriff Mike Lisle's desk.

"*X* marks the spot where Epstein's cell phone was triangulated," he explained to the recently arrived Pender. "Access is via either the county road *here*"—jabbing the map with his pointer again—"or this old fire trail coming in from the south"—jab—"which is going to be slower and rougher, but should provide better cover."

"The problem is, we don't have any information on the site itself, such as how many buildings are still standing, if any," said

Sheriff Lisle, who had graying temples and a Batman jaw. "That's
why I want to wait for the satellite photos before we mount an
assault."

"But while we're waiting, Sweet could be on the move," argued
Sperry, a beefy Joe Montana type, dimpled chin and all. He had,
he'd been sure to let Pender know, done his tac squad training
at Quantico. "In which case, every minute we delay increases his
chances of getting away."

"Whereas going in blind increases our chances of sustaining
casualties," Lisle said wearily—obviously, they'd been over this
ground before. "What do you think, Agent Pender?"

"I think we need to move as quickly as possible. If Sweet hasn't
killed Epstein already, it's only because he's still torturing him.
And since we're only going up against one man, I can't see how
deploying sooner rather than later is going to put your people in
any additional jeopardy."

After mulling it over, or giving the appearance of having mulled
it over, Lisle nodded decisively. "Okay, let's do it."

In the muster room, the tac squad was buddying up, each team
member double-checking his or her partner's weapons, armor,
and communication gear, and being double-checked in return.
The tense mood, the nervous banter, and the clatter of equipment
reminded Pender of his old high school football team suiting up
before a game. All that was missing was the *click-clack* of spikes on
the locker room floor.

Pender didn't stick around for the coach's pep talk. Instead,
operating on the Hopper principle—it's more effective to ask for-
giveness than to ask permission—he slipped out the back door
while Sperry was still addressing his squad, and climbed into the
back of the shiny black Lenco BEAR, the multiuse, ballistic engi-
neered armored response vehicle that was to ferry the tac squad up
into the foothills.

Air-conditioned for stakeouts, armored for assaults, with run-
flat tires, bulletproof portholes, shielded gunports, a rotating turret,

and a sniper's platform on the roof, the BEAR had padded benches running the full length of the cabin on either side. Pender hunched his shoulders and tried to make himself inconspicuous as the squad began belting themselves in around him. But somehow the sharp-eyed Lieutenant Sperry, sitting in the swiveling command seat next to the driver, managed to pick the six-four, two-hundred-and-fifty-pound federal agent in the houndstooth-checked hat and tomato-soup-colored sport coat out of a dozen armored, helmeted deputies in paratrooper boots and desert camo. They locked eyes. *You need me,* Pender vibed him. *You know you need me. I'm the only guy you've got who knows Sweet and Epstein both, you'd be crazy not to—*

Sperry broke eye contact first. "Somebody get that man a vest and a helmet," he barked.

2

Skip was marched stumbling out of the barn. He could tell he was outside even with the rubber sack over his head.

Dull as his mind had grown from the ordeal and the unrelenting fear, he was still capable of forming coherent thoughts. *Schmuck,* he told himself, *you're letting him walk you to your death.*

For like many American Jews of his generation, Skip Epstein had at one time or another blithely measured himself against the victims of the Holocaust, and had convinced himself, however naïvely, that if it ever happened here, he wouldn't allow himself to be led like a lamb to the slaughter the way they had. No way they take *me* without a fight, he'd always promised himself—and yet here he was, letting himself be marched along by a single psychopath with a gun.

When the path, if it was a path, turned uphill, Skip found the ankle-high grass tough going. At times only his captor's firm grasp

on his bound wrists kept him upright. Both hips were screaming as he stumbled along, and beneath the stifling hood the sweat
pouring into his eyes stung like liniment. *Do something,* Skip told
himself. *For God's sake, do—*

"Down you go," said the other man, swiping Skip's legs out
from under him. Unable to break his fall, he landed hard on his
side, on his elbow, knocking the air out of his lungs.

When you can't breathe, everything else is irrelevant. It wasn't
until his diaphragm had begun functioning again and he'd managed a few exploratory sips of air that Skip became aware of the
stench creeping in under the hood—it smelled as if he were lying
next to an open cesspool filled with roadkill.

Distracted first by the struggle to breathe, then by the terrible
odor, Skip was only vaguely conscious of the way his body was
being manhandled, rocked and shoved, lifted and dropped. Eventually, though, he managed to piece it all together, and concluded
that he was being tied up again—and this time he was not alone.
His captor had knocked him down alongside some other poor bastard and was now lashing the two of them together, back to back,
with coils of rope.

Once he was securely bound, Skip's hood was removed. After
being blinded by darkness for so long, he was suddenly blinded
by the light. He quickly shut his eyes, but not before the hulking,
round-shouldered silhouette of his departing captor was imprinted
in negative behind his eyelids.

"Hey," Skip whispered after a few minutes of silence. "Hey, I
think he's gone."

No response from whomever he was tied to.

"Man, what a stink. You know where it's coming from?"

No answer.

"Say something, man. Grunt if you can't talk."

Nothing.

One last try: "Can you hear me?"

Apparently not. Skip opened his eyes again. The terrain ahead of him was pretty much what he'd expected—a sideways view of a grassy, green-gold hillside that could have been almost anywhere in Northern California. Leaning back, Skip wiggled his shoulders, trying to jostle his new companion awake. "Hey, wake up—maybe we can untie each other."

Still no response. "C'mon, man," he said, more urgently. But when he closed his fingers around his fellow captive's wrists and began rubbing and chafing them to bring him around, the flesh—the dead man's rotting flesh—had the texture of crackling pig at a luau, and slid loosely over the bone.

At least now you know where that god-awful smell is coming from, Skip told himself, when his diaphragm finally stopped spasming. By then, however, the vultures were already circling overhead, so the realization was far from comforting.

3

The Sierra foothills were greener than they'd been during Pender's last visit, and the streams ran higher. A few miles out of town, Pender heard "Third Rate Romance" playing quietly on his mental jukebox. A moment later he caught a glimpse, through the inch-thick acrylic of the view port, of a familiar-looking old roadhouse, its doors and windows boarded up and a FOR SALE OR LEASE sign on the lawn.

"Hey, didn't that used to be the Nugget?" he asked.

"Sure did," said one of the tac squad deputies. "Me and my wife used to go dancing there almost every weekend."

"I don't suppose you'd happen to know what became of the gal that owned it?"

"Amy, you mean? She passed away, oh, two, three years ago. Cancer, I think it was. She fought the good fight, though. Couldn't have weighed more than seventy-five, eighty pounds, but she kept on dancing right up until the end."

I bet she did, thought Pender, feeling like somebody'd hit him in the chest with a medicine ball. *I just bet she did.*

But there was no time to dwell on the past, no time for grief or even tenderness. *Gut it out, you big sissy,* Pender ordered himself, as the BEAR swung off the county road onto a deeply rutted, unpaved fire trail. *You can mourn her later.*

For the moment, job one was grabbing a strap and hanging on for dear life as the BEAR lurched up the steep, narrow fire trail in four-wheel drive, tires spinning, branches scraping at its roof and sides. For a while the driver was able to use the vehicle's bluntly sloping armored nose to plow down the brush and saplings that sprang up in its path, but as they climbed, the saplings turned into full-grown trees.

"End of the line," called Lieutenant Sperry. "We'll hike in from here."

The squad piled out. Pender, who'd exchanged his sport jacket for a too-small Kevlar vest, flipped down the darkened visor of his borrowed, ill-fitting helmet and slipped into line. Again Sperry gave him the ol' skunk eye; again he permitted him to remain. "Just keep your eye on me and follow my hand signals. This"—palms down—"means get down, this"—finger to lips—"means maintain silence . . ."

Yeah, I think I could have figured that out, thought Pender.

"And when I do this"—slapped one, then two fingers against his forearm, then with bladed hands perpendicular to the ground, made veering motions to the left or right—"I'm signaling to teams one and two which way to go. Which has nothing to do with you— if we have to split up, I want you to stay behind and cover our rear. If I need you to come up, I'll do this." He clicked the tin cricket in his hand twice. "Got all that?"

"Got it."

"Okay, team. Cell phones off, let's move out."

4

It's been a long, hard day for Asmador. Digging up the decomposing corpse he'd buried last week along with Fred and Evelyn's rapidly decaying heads, dragging it half a mile to the top of the highest grassy hill to serve as vulture bait, hiking back down to get Epstein, walking the gimp up to where he'd left the corpse, and finally lashing the two of them, the live man and the dead one, together—that was a lot of walking and a lot of work under a broiling sun.

And with no guarantee of success. Asmador hasn't the slightest idea whether a week-old, disinterred corpse will serve to whet the appetite of a *Cathartes aura*. And even if the scent does manage to attract the vultures, there is always the possibility that the presence of a live human, no matter how firmly bound, will scare them away. Even if it doesn't, it's still anybody's guess whether, having been attracted initially to the corpse, the birds will move on to the fresh—

Wait, wait—there they are, right on time! Asmador, crouched behind a patch of creosote bushes on the very crest of the hill, some twenty yards above Epstein and the corpse, can feel the hairs on the back of his neck rising. Watching the birds swoop and glide in ever-narrowing circles, he is reminded of that sweet pastoral passage in the Book: *Sitting with our backs against the trunk of a red-barked madrone at the edge of a high, grassy meadow dotted with white puffs of clover, we watched a pair of hawks riding the thermals, swooping and gliding so lightly and gracefully they looked like they were made out of paper.*

Surely these vultures are no less graceful—maybe even more so, thanks to their greater wingspan. But why aren't they landing? They circle and circle, but they don't land. Is it because of all that squirming and screaming Epstein's doing? *The vultures are no more used to their meals moving around or making noise than you are,* Asmador reminds himself.

But just then, the larger of the two birds flattens out its orbit and dives. Half-rising from his crouch to get a better view, Asmador spots a sudden glint of sunlight bouncing off something shiny in the wooded hillside directly across the valley. It's there and gone like a firefly, then there and gone again, a little farther to Asmador's right. The longer he watches, the more certain he becomes that there are several humans in the woods across the valley, moving from Asmador's left to his right, in the general direction of the barn.

But who are they? If they're cops, there's no time to waste. He has to get to the barn first. That's where the car's parked—he can't take a chance on being cut off from it. So the only question that remains is whether or not to kill Epstein first. If he doesn't, and those *are* cops over there, there's a good chance Epstein will wind up being rescued. But if he does kill Epstein, and the interlopers are only kids or hunters, he'll not only have spared Epstein the greater part of the suffering he had in mind for him, he'll have disappointed the Infernal Council once again.

To kill or not to kill? For once, the answer is not in the Book, so Asmador digs into his jeans pocket, feels around for loose change, comes up with a quarter. *Heads you kill him, tails you don't,* he tells himself, and with a flick of his thumb Asmador sends the coin spinning into the air.

5

Like the Eskimos say, unless you're the lead dog, the view never changes. Drenched in sweat beneath the bulky Kevlar vest, with more sweat dripping down his face from under the too-small helmet, Pender followed the camouflaged back of the deputy in front of him through a sun-dappled second-growth forest, pickin' 'em up and layin' 'em down to a medley of unlikely march-time oldies playing on his internal jukebox: "Ballad of the Green Berets," "The Battle of New Orleans," and "Fifty Ways to Leave Your Lover."

The column halted at the edge of a wooded ridge looking out over a wedge-shaped valley that fanned west to east, with a range of grassy hills, greenish gold in the spring, forming the opposite rise. Below and to the squad's right, on the broad side of the wedge, lay a flat patchwork of abandoned fields, subsumed now by scrub brush and man-high weeds, with only a few discontinuous stretches of three-rail wooden fencing still standing to demarcate the borders.

Below to the left, at the narrow end of the valley, the front end of a weathered gray barn protruded from a steep scree of dirt and rocks. At first it appeared to Pender as if the barn had been constructed half underground, but a closer look through borrowed binoculars spoke instead of a monumental landslide that had buried the rear half of the barn but left the front half miraculously standing.

The lieutenant showed Pender the readout on his handheld GPS device—the first one Pender had ever seen. "The cell phone was picked up in or near that structure," Sperry whispered, pointing to the barn. "We're going to circle around the back, then split into two teams to flank the barn. I need you to stay up here and watch our backs—I'll leave you the glasses along with a walkie-talkie and a cricket. If it looks like we're heading into any shit, key Talk and click the cricket twice, but do not, repeat not, speak into it for any reason until I give you the go-ahead. Otherwise you might accidentally give our position away. Got all that?"

"Got it."

"Good." Sperry turned to the squad. "Okay, let's move out. I'll take the point. And maintain mission silence, everybody—we want the element of surprise on our side."

Although he'd never have admitted it, not even to himself, Pender was more than a little relieved at no longer having to keep up with the younger, fitter tac squadders. After taking a slug of water from a plastic bottle one of them had loaned him, he removed his helmet and sluiced the rest of the water over his steaming dome. Then he dropped to a prone position at the edge of the tree line and began scanning the barn, left to right, top to bottom, with the binoculars.

The sliding front door was wide open, askew on its hinges. No signs of life inside or out—but of course Sweet could be hiding almost anywhere in there. Or he could be lying in wait behind the building, or around the side, or somewhere out there in the weeds, or in the hills directly across the way, Pender realized. Expanding the parameters of his scan accordingly, he began sweeping the binoculars the length and breadth of the valley.

But the only thing moving on this hot, windless spring afternoon was a pair of turkey vultures circling the grassy hill to the north, directly across the valley from Pender's position. Pender watched them soar, following them through the glasses as they swooped and glided, then resumed his visual sweep of the valley. But the cop part of his brain, the area where law enforcement professionals store information like the mug shots of the FBI's Ten Most Wanted criminals and the license plate numbers of stolen cars, had already begun flashing the red lights and sounding the awooga horn to remind Pender that turkey vultures were an integral part of Luke Sweet's m.o. lately.

So he turned the glasses back to the vultures, and when one of them suddenly peeled away from the other and swooped downward, Pender followed its flight all the way to the ground. It touched down with a skidding hop and darted up to a struggling, heaving mass that Pender first took to be a dying calf. But when he adjusted the focus and zeroed in again, he realized that there were in fact *two* bodies lying there, roped back-to-back. One of them looked like a corpse in an advanced state of decay; the other appeared to be . . . yes, it was Epstein—no mistaking that built-up shoe.

Pender swung the glasses back around to the west, past the barn, just as the squad's point man emerged from the woods. Urgently he thumbed the Talk key on the walkie-talkie and clicked the cricket twice.

6

You'd think there'd be some kind of shutdown mechanism that would kick in, some threshold of horror beyond which consciousness would glaze over and self-awareness cease.

You'd be wrong. The only part of Skip's neurosystem that seemed to be affected by being lashed to a decaying corpse was the olfactory sense, which rather than shutting down completely, merely shifted its baseline. When stench is all, stench is the norm: a fish doesn't know it's wet.

Then the first vulture landed. Skip had never seen one close up before. Its face was shiny crimson, its short, sharp beak curved and ivory-colored. It stalked toward him at an oblique angle, moving with a ducking, bobbing gait. "Shoo!" he shouted, his voice cracking plaintively. "G'wan, get out of here."

The vulture hissed and hopped backward, confusion in its oval-shaped, oddly pensive eyes. It took another tentative hop toward Skip, who yelled at it again. But this time the bird took only a single backward hop before resuming its oblique approach, and the third time Skip shouted, it ignored him entirely.

This is not happening, this is not happening, this is not happening was Skip's mantra as the creature closed the ground between them. Lying motionless, holding his breath, he waited until it was only a few feet away, then shrieked and threw his body against the ropes.

Startled, the vulture jumped backward, hissing and clacking. *You're going to wake up any second now,* Skip assured himself as the bird spread its wings and launched itself at him. *Any second now . . .*

The vulture landed heavily on Skip's left shoulder and upper arm and dug its sharp talons into his flesh to anchor itself. The red head darted downward. Skip shut his eyes and braced himself, but instead of striking him, the vulture tore a chunk of rotting meat from the carrion hulk to which Skip was lashed, and gulped it down whole like a cormorant swallowing a fish.

Skip felt an immense upwelling of relief that quickly died away when a second vulture skidded to a landing in the tracks of the first. An image from a Discovery Channel documentary flashed through his mind: on a wide, grassy plain, the body of an antelope or wildebeest or something is all but obscured beneath a writhing black mound of feathered scavengers. *You are so fucked,* Skip told himself. *You are so fucking—*

Crack! A distant gunshot. *Crack!* A second shot. With a heavy, sullen beating of its wings, the vulture atop him released its claw hold on his shoulder and took flight. Skip opened his eyes, saw what looked like half a dozen helmeted, camo-clad soldiers charging up the hill at a fast trot. *Holy crap,* he thought, with a rush of gratitude so intense he could scarcely breathe, *they called out the National Guard.*

A moment later, Pender was kneeling in front of him, wearing an armored vest and holding a handkerchief over his nose and mouth. "Hang in there," he said soothingly, his voice muffled by the handkerchief as he sawed at Skip's ropes with a wicked-looking commando knife. "You're safe now, it's all over. Just hang in there, we'll have you loose in a second."

The last rope parted. Strong hands lifted Skip by his arms and legs, rushed him unceremoniously down the hill with his ass sagging, and lowered him gently to the grass. For Skip, it was one of those eye-of-the-hurricane moments. He lay motionless on his back, staring up dazedly into the bluest, most beneficent sky he'd ever seen, and thinking how sweet and strange it was to still be alive. Then Pender's face floated above him, big and pale as a harvest moon—funny how he didn't look half so homely now, thought Skip.

"You okay, Magnum?"

"No major damage," said Skip. "Did you get him?"

"Missed him by a couple minutes. Do you have any idea who our fragrant friend is?" Pender jerked a thumb behind him, in the direction of the corpse.

"Not a clue." Skip sat up slowly. The body was fifteen yards up the hill, lying on its side with its back to him. He could almost *see* the stink coming off it in little, wavy cartoon lines. But in his current adrenaline-filled, endorphin-drenched condition, Skip found his heart going out to whoever it was lying there all curled up and lonesome, and he experienced the weirdest urge to go back and sit with it, to keep it company until the meat wagon arrived.

The tac squad paramedic had other ideas. Learning that a vulture's talons had inflicted the shallow, parallel cuts on Skip's shoulder while he was tied to a rotting corpse, she administered a field lavage, a heavy dose of wide-spectrum antibiotics, and a syrette of morphine, then insisted on calling in a helicopter to medevac Skip to the trauma center at Marshall County General.

There was a minor holdup just as they were about to load Skip into the chopper. Due to the residual corpse-stink, the pilot demanded that Skip first be stripped of what was left of his clothes, which were relegated to a sealed, hard-plastic biohazard bin.

At County General, the E.R. doctor was adamant that Skip remain overnight for observation. "Purely as a precaution," he told Skip, who was feeling so nauseated by the antibiotics that he gave in without an argument, despite a near-phobic aversion to hospitals not uncommon in polio survivors.

Skip slept fitfully, despite or because of all the drugs they were pumping into him—Demerol for pain, Donnatal for nausea, diazepam for anxiety. At one point during the long night, he fell into a troubled, hallucinatory doze and dreamed that they'd moved the dead body from the hillside into his room to keep him company. Curious to get a look at it, Skip's dream-self climbed out of bed, padded noiselessly across the room, lifted the sheet covering its face, and recognized the corpse immediately, in spite of the horrific damage done to it by the process of decay.

"I—I don't understand," said Skip. "If you're dead, then who kidnapped me?"

But the only answer from the corpse of Luke Sweet, Jr., was a merry wink of his only remaining eyelid.

Part Three

CHAPTER ONE

I

April 17

I did it. I actually did it. Blew the joint to kingdom come, got away clean, and now I only have one question: Who's crazy now, ladies and gentlemen? Who's fucking crazy now?

I have to admit, for a while there, things weren't exactly looking rosy. Maybe I overestimated how long it would take for the gas to fill the boiler room once the shutoff valve had been bypassed. (And by the way, whoever had the bright idea of posting the printed instructions for bypassing the valve right there on the wall next to the boiler: thanks a bunch.) Or maybe I underestimated the speed at which the trail of paint thinner would burn its way from the fire exit to the boiler room door. Either way, the last thing I remember is touching the match to the paint thinner and watching the blue flame sizzling down the corridor and around the corner.

Next thing I know, I'm lying on my back, looking up into a heat-wavy blue sky streaked with oily brown smoke. Scorched flakes spin dizzily through the superheated air, and ashes pile in scalloped mounds atop the fence posts and the bushes and the domed roofs of the cars in the parking lot, transforming the landscape into a mute, gray statuary garden.

It's not so bad at first, this snowstorm from hell. A peaceful silence reigns momentarily. Then suddenly, as on that long-ago summer morning, my hearing returns. Crackling flames, clanging bells, ululating car alarms, anguished screams. It occurs to me that I'd better get the hell out of there before the whole fucking building comes crashing down on top of me. But when I try to crawl away, I realize my left ankle is firmly pinned beneath the heavy, steel-plated Alarm Will Sound fire door, which had been blown clear off its hinges.

"Help! Somebody help me! Somebody get this thing offa me!" Another voice joins the trapped and panicked chorus: mine. I've never been so scared or screamed so loud in my entire life, and yet I can barely hear myself. Sitting up, I see that I'm lying only a few feet from the burning building. A brick wall rises straight over me, blocking out half the sky. The ashes are falling thick and fast. I can feel the heat coming through the bricks. I grab my trapped leg in both hands and try to yank it out from under the un-budgeable weight. The pain is so intense that I lose consciousness momentarily.

When I come to again, a shambling figure looms over me, his face in shadow, his round-shouldered trunk silhouetted against the ash gray sky. I recognize him after a second or two: it's Chuckles, the drooler whose mannerisms I copied when I was first coming out from under chemical restraint.

"Help me, please?" I plead.

His long arms swing loosely at his sides as he hunkers down beside me. "Heh?"

Fortunately, I am fluent in the thick-tongued dialect of the chemically restrained. "That's right, help. I need you to help me lift this door off my leg."

His eyes are deep-set, dark, and puzzled. Then comprehension dawns and they light up with an almost animal intelligence. Squatting low like a weight lifter, he grabs the edge of the door in both hands. Straining upward with his arms extended on either side of his thighs, he manages to raise the bulky slab high enough for me to haul my leg out from under. Quite a feat for a drooler.

After setting the door down again, Chuckles hunkers next to me, slings my left arm over his shoulder, and helps me to my feet. Leaning together with our arms draped across one another's shoulders, half-blinded by falling ash, the two of us join the procession of scorched and bleeding stragglers staggering away from the doomed building, past the staff parking lot, and into the uncertain shelter of the trees.

Just as we reach the woods there's a deafening roar behind us, loud as a jetliner. A concussive blast of air smacks into us with the force of a monster wave breaking, and knocks us apart. I hit the ground and lie there stunned for a few seconds. When I look back, the hospital is no longer there. In its place is a roiling pillar of smoke and ash three stories high.

Chuckles is nowhere to be seen. Using a broken tree branch to push myself up, I climb to my feet just in time to see a burning figure emerge from the smoking ruins, lurching drunkenly, arms outstretched, hair and clothes engulfed. Whoever it is gets a lot farther than I'd have predicted he would, making it almost to the tree line before he collapses.

Maybe I'm still in shock, maybe I'm not. All I know is how I feel, and how I feel is sharp and focused, like the calm at the center of the storm. I limp forward, leaning on the forked branch to keep the weight off my injured ankle. I kneel by the side of the fallen man, who's now a smoldering corpse, and scoop loose dirt on top of him until the little dancing fairy-flames have died down. Then I start going through his pockets, taking care not to scorch my fingers. The lightly charred wallet in the inside jacket pocket belongs to Bernard J. Ruhr; it says "Staff Psychologist" on his hospital ID card. In another pocket is a roll of bills in a gold, paper-clip-shaped money clip, and a set of car keys for a BMW.

I'm starting to hear sirens now. Someone is shouting garbled commands through what sounds like a megaphone. Quickly I pocket the wallet and keys. *Limping like Long John Silver on my crooked crutch, under the cover of the hovering cloud of ash and smoke, I head straight for the staff parking lot, where I spy a smoke-and-ash-begrimed dark blue BMW parked in front of a sign reading* MD PARKING ONLY!!! ALL OTHERS WILL BE TOWED!!!

The key fits; the engine turns over smoothly. With the headlights and windshield wipers turned on, I drive slowly through the murky parking lot, feeling a little like a character in one of those postapocalypse science fiction movies.

And what happens next won't surprise anybody who's ever seen one of those movies: just as I'm driving out of the parking lot, a shambling figure emerges suddenly from the gloom and steps in front of the car, waving its arms.

I jam on the brakes, and the sloping hood of the Beemer shudders to a stop only inches from my recent savior, Chuckles. His pleading monkey eyes meet mine through the dingy, ash-smeared windshield. Please, *they seem to be saying,* please take me with you, *and for some reason I'll never understand, I find myself leaning across the front seat and throwing open the passenger door.*

"Climb in," I shout, over the crackling of the flames, the howling of the sirens, and the terrible shrieking of the burned and dying.

2

HIC LOCUS EST UBI MORS GAUDET SUCCERRERE VITAE, read the sign above the door to the autopsy room of the Marshall County morgue: Here is where death rejoices to help the living.

Pender, having intentionally skipped breakfast, arrived shortly after 6:00 A.M. and rapped on the frosted glass pane. The diener, a tall black man in surgical greens, hurried over to intercept him—the autopsy was already under way. "It's a nasty one," he warned Pender. "You might want to wait outside."

"Hey, this isn't my first rodeo," Pender assured him, buttoning his sport jacket to the neck and turning up his collar against the arctic chill of the Marshall County morgue.

"If you say so. Here, put this under your nose—a little dab'll do ya." He unscrewed the top of a jar of Vicks VapoRub. Pender smeared a little across his upper lip. His eyes were watering as he approached the slab upon which the dreadful corpse had been laid out. Its skin was greenish black, but that was a function of decay—it could have been any race or ethnicity. The chest had already been opened with a Y-shaped incision, the heart and lungs removed.

"Dr. Flemm?"

"Yes?" The Marshall County medical examiner was short and round. Above his surgical mask he wore thick-lensed spectacles with heavy black frames. Beneath his green paper cap he was as bald as Pender.

"Special Agent Pender, FBI. I spoke to you this morning about the fingerprints."

"Ah yes, the fingerprints." Flemm turned the corpse's right hand palm up. Pender, who was on the opposite side of the table, started to lean across the corpse, which turned out to be a mistake—not even the pungent odor of the Vicks could mask the stench. He walked around to Flemm's side of the table. Supporting the corpse's forearm and elbow, Flemm raised the arm to give Pender a closer look. "What do you think? Not bad after a week or two in damp ground, eh?"

The fingertips were the same greenish black as the rest of the body, but the ridges and whorls were still discernible. "Can they be lifted?" asked Pender.

"If we glove him." Flemm selected a simple surgical scalpel from the tray of medieval-looking instruments, scissors, needles, chisels, forceps, and saws, on the cloth-draped table next to him. He cut a circular incision around the right wrist, then carefully worked the skin free until it slipped off the hand as neatly as if it had been a glove.

Pender's stomach lurched as Flemm laid the ghastly "glove" on a drawerlike extension he'd pulled out from the side of the table, and severed each of the fingertips neatly at the first joint. Then he sprayed the fingertips with a drying agent while his diener filled a shallow glass saucer with black ink, viscous from the cold of the autopsy room, and microwaved it for several seconds.

When the fingertip skin was dry enough and the ink fluid enough, Flemm removed his surgical gloves and fit a small latex finger-cot over his forefinger, then slipped the skin fingertips over the latex. Meanwhile the diener had laid out a fingerprint card on the stainless-steel counter. Gingerly, Flemm dipped his forefinger into the saucer, shook off the excess ink, then gently pressed his double-gloved fingertip against the card and rocked it delicately from side to side.

Peering over Flemm's shoulder, Pender whistled low in appreciation. "Perfect," he exclaimed. "Absolutely perfect."

"And only nine more to go," said Dr. Flemm, beaming.

3

April 18

To tell the truth (and why would I lie to you, my own brand-new, full-sized dear diary), I could have thought this thing out a little better. Or maybe I didn't really believe I was going to make it. I wouldn't have, if I hadn't come up lucky on a couple of counts, the first of which was that it had been my left ankle that was injured, so driving a car with an automatic was not a major problem.

The most crucial piece of luck was that Murphy's barn was still standing. Or at least leaning. Half of it, anyway. A landslide had taken out the rear half of the building, hayloft and all, but the front was still intact, jutting out from the base of the landslide.

More luck: Rudy's untouched van was parked right where I'd left it ten years ago, inside the barn, facing the rear, with the front bumper only inches from the edge of the landslide. The money was still there, too, stuffed behind the false walls and floor along with two kilos of vacuum-sealed Humboldt County wacky weed.

Unfortunately, dear diary, you can't live on money and weed alone. So after I'd cleaned the two of us up as best I could without water, and exchanged our ash-smeared clothes for clean but creased and musty-smelling jeans and shirts from Rudy's suitcase, we drove back to the giant Wal-Mart outside Marshall City to stock up. I figured it would be safe enough, that no one would be looking for us so soon after the fire, and I was right.

We did get some curious stares, what with me tootling around in the electric scooter (I couldn't put any weight on my left ankle) and Chuckles lumbering along beside me pushing two shopping carts. But by the time we left, with the trunk and backseat of the Beemer stuffed with food, clothing, medical supplies, including a pair of crutches for yours truly, camping equipment, etc., etc., all paid for in cash, we were provisioned for a good long siege.

It was full dark by the time we got back to Murphy's farm. Chuckles got out and opened the sliding barn door. I drove the Beemer inside and parked it next to the van, which left us a living space around fifteen feet wide and twenty feet deep. For supper we ate bologna sandwiches by lantern light, then crawled into our new sleeping bags. Chuckles dropped off while I was writing yesterday's entry, and I followed him into dreamland an hour or so later.

And that, dire deary, was about the extent of my good luck. When I woke up this morning, my left ankle resembled an eggplant in both size and color, and was throbbing painfully. With the aid of my new crutches I went outside to take a leak, and when I got back Chuckles was sitting up in his sleeping bag, hugging his knees and rocking back and forth while muttering unintelligibly under his breath.

That was twelve hours ago, and guess what, he's still there, rocking and muttering. The only thing that's changed is that now he seems to be aware of my presence: every once in a while he looks over at me and glowers. So *even though I'm pretty sure that he's only detoxing, I'm glad I've got Rudy's .38 automatic in my sleeping bag with me. My plan, as soon as I finish this entry, is to turn off the flashlight and pretend to close my eyes. If he makes a move toward me, I'll shoot him dead. If not, I'll try to get some sleep, and hope my ankle will start to show some improvement in the morning.*

Because I didn't go to all this trouble just to sit around here watching Chuckles drool. I've got more important things to do, like driving back down to Santa Cruz to pay a little call on my grandparents. And won't they be surprised to see me! I can hardly wait to see the expression on their dear old faces.

4

Pender found Skip sitting on the edge of his hospital bed dressed in a paper-thin seersucker robe over an open-arsed hospital gown. "Hey there, Magnum, P.I.! How's it going?"

"Not bad, G-man, not bad at all. I just talked the doctor into cutting me loose. The problem is, they seem to have burned everything but my wallet and my shoes."

Pender winked. "Wait here, I'll be right back."

Twenty minutes later, Skip left the hospital wearing a pair of ludicrously oversize blue-and-green plaid golf pants, a loosely draped, periwinkle-colored polo shirt, and a pair of ankle-high pink socks. "I don't want to seem ungrateful," he told Pender as they drove away in Pender's dusty rental car, "but would you mind stopping off at the first clothing store we come to?"

"Right after I get this to the sheriff's station," said Pender, waving the card with the dead man's fingerprints. "Cal-ID's promised to give it crash priority." Cal-ID was the computer network that linked population centers all over the state with the main fingerprint database in Sacramento.

Skip told Pender he'd wait in the car while Pender dropped off the card and conferred briefly with Sheriff Lisle. But when they drove off again, instead of heading back into town to find a clothing or department store, Pender aimed the Toyota in the opposite direction. "They found something out at the site that the crime scene tech thinks might interest us."

"No way," Skip protested. "I'm not going anywhere dressed like this."

"Are you kidding?" said Pender. "You look great in periwinkle. It brings out your eyes."

5

April 19

Dear Diary: Other than sleeping, smoking weed is the only thing that even comes close to fighting the pain in my leg. The worst part is the throbbing—it feels kind of like there's a balloon in my ankle that somebody keeps blowing up to just short of bursting, then letting the air out, then blowing it up again.

When I'm stoned, though, it feels more like the pain is coming in waves, long, slow rollers an old Steamer Lane boogie boarder like myself can ride all the way in to shore.

The dope is doing wonders for Chuckles, too. His first few turns I had to hold the joint to his lips, but he got the hang of it pretty quickly, and it must really be helping him with his detox, because oh, man, is he ever grateful. I've never owned a dog myself, but when I first moved in with my father he had a chocolate Lab named Toots that absolutely doted on him, and the look Chuckles gives me when I roll a joint for him is the exact same look Toots used to give my dad when Big Luke tossed him a piece of bacon.

The downside is that now Chuckles wants to stay stoned all the time.

He keeps waking me up to ask me to roll him another doobie, as he calls them, doobie being one of the few words he can pronounce intelligibly. I finally got smart and prerolled half a dozen fatties for him, which ought to hold him long enough for me to get some uninterrupted shut-eye.

April 20

Well, I slept, dear Di. Not that it did me any good. When I woke up this morning I was so weak I could hardly get up on my crutches, and had to piss into an empty plastic water jug. My leg isn't hurting quite as much as yesterday, but my left ankle is still swollen double its size, plus my left foot is now the color of a plum, and the toenails are blueish purple, which I'm pretty sure is not a good sign.

My mind is as sharp as ever, though, and focused in like a laser on the problem at hand, which is that while I'm lying in a crumbling barn in Marshall County, rotting from the bottom up, my grandparents are living happily ever after down in Santa Cruz.

THIS CANNOT STAND.

But neither can I.

April 21

At least I think it's the 21st. It's easy to lose track when you're spending most of your time stoned or sleeping.

Whatever day it is, dire deary, my condition continues to deteriorate. The whole foot is now blueish purple, while the toenails are almost black. Chuckles, however, is doing much, much better. The drugs they gave him in the hospital seem to be wearing off. No more drooling, hardly any jerky movements, and as for his mental functioning, when I woke up this morning (I'm pretty sure it was this morning) he was sitting up cross-legged with his nose buried in the BMW owner's manual, turning the pages rapidly and apparently reading with intense concentration.

"So how'd it come out?" I quipped, when he finally closed the booklet.

To my surprise, he shut his eyes for a few seconds. I saw his eyeballs tracking left to right behind the flickering eyelids, then he opened them again. "Windshield Wipers, 71, 159," he said, clearly and intelligibly. "Wiper Blade Replacement, 159. Wipers, intermittent, 72."

Which proved to be the last three entries on the last page of the booklet, word for word. Far fucking out, as Big Luke used to say. A few days ago the guy's a babbling idiot, now he can recite a 200-page car manual by heart. That's got to be a jump of at least a hundred IQ points, which means he must have been some kind of major genius before they started drugging him. Either that, or he's one of those, what do they call them, idiot savants.

Still April 21?

It's dark out, dear Di, so unless I just slept something like 36 hours, I'm assuming it's still the same day. And since I can't seem to get back to sleep, I might as well get you caught up on recent events.

To begin with, Chuckles, or rather Asmador, as he now prefers to be called, woke me up a little while ago, dragging his Wal-Mart sleeping bag over next to mine and asking me, with a haunted look in his deep-shadowed eyes, to roll him a doobie. By the hissing light of the Coleman I twisted up a bomber, and after we'd each had a couple tokes, I asked him what was bothering him.

I was lying on my side and he was sitting up in his sleeping bag. With the lantern throwing our flickering shadows across the sloping mountain of dirt that formed the back wall of the barn, it felt like we were a couple of old-time western outlaws holed up in a cave. "It's the Council," he said cautiously. "The Infernal Council."

I gave him a knowing nod. "Oh, them."

"Yes! Them!" He leaned forward earnestly, so relieved and grateful to be taken seriously that I almost felt guilty for putting him on like that.

"What about them?"

With his mind moving faster than his tongue, it took him a few tries *to explain it. The gist, I gathered, was that something called the Concilium Infernalis, or Infernal Council, which was basically hell's board of directors, had some kind of task or mission he was supposed to complete in order to become a Council member, as opposed to (and here he'd shuddered so hard he shook the ash right off the joint), being consigned for all eternity to the ranks of the damned souls in hell. "I know I have to prove myself to them," he repeated firmly. "But the thing is, they won't tell me what they want me to do." He toked up, passed the joint back to me. "They won't even . . . (cough, choke) . . . give me a . . . (cough, choke) . . . hint."*

I took a prodigious toke, and suddenly it was like one of those astronomy or astrology deals where all the planets line up in a row. I saw clearly how our lives intersected, how our strengths and weaknesses, our needs and our abilities, meshed, and all at once I understood why fate had brought us together and led us out of Meadows Road, Asmador with his need for a mission, me with my need to have one carried out.

"Oh, but they will, my friend," I assured him, the words streaming out of my mouth in a cloud of milky white smoke that curled upward through the stark light of the lantern like Aladdin's genie trying to take shape. "I guarantee you, they will."

6

Murphy's farm was crawling with crime scene techs dusting for fingerprints, taking plaster tire impressions, probing the shallow grave from which they'd exhumed two decaying heads, and searching the grass at the bottom of the hill for ejected cartridges left by the warning shots Pender had fired to scare away the vultures yesterday.

Skip and Pender followed Laurel Baldinger, the sheriff's crime scene analyst, out of the glaring daylight into the barn, where the dim light was pierced by glowing shafts of morning sunlight angling in through pinholes in the roof. Having been blindfolded during his entire stay, Skip had never actually *seen* the inside of the barn, but it felt eerily familiar to him all the same, as if he'd seen it in a dream.

"Do you have any idea how long Sweet might have been holed up in here?" Pender asked the CSA.

"We found a receipt from a Seven-Eleven near Marshall City dated April seventeenth."

"That was the day the hospital blew up. He must have come directly here."

"You mean *they,* plural," she corrected him. "Almost everywhere we're dusting, we're finding two distinct sets of latents."

"Couldn't the second set have been the other victim's, the one Skip here was tied to?"

Baldinger shook her head. "Both sets of prints are all over the barn and the van, inside and out. So whoever it was obviously had free run of the entire place. To me, that says accomplice, not victim."

Pender turned to Skip. "Looks like we need to have another chat with Dr. Gallagher," he said, then turned back to the analyst. "I was told you'd found something you wanted me to take a look at."

"Yes, sir." She handed Pender a small black pocket diary. "The reason I called you is, we found your name in it."

Pender read the cover aloud. "1995 Pocket Pal, courtesy of your Pfizer Sales Representative, Robert F. Peterson, 2500 Mission Street, Santa Cruz, California." He opened the book, squinted exaggeratedly, brought it up to within an inch of his nose, then held it out at arm's length before giving up. "If you can read this, your eyes are better than mine."

"Oh, sorry. Here." Baldinger handed him her own round, thick-lensed magnifying glass, which had a raised rectangular inset of even higher magnifying power. It took a little experimenting, but after a few tries, he was able to make out the first sentence. *"On the morning my father telephoned from Marshall City to announce that the FBI was closing in, I was in the trailer watching Teddy, my stepmother, getting dressed. . . ."*

7

Apr 22

It took me half the night, but when Asmador woke up this morning, he found my old Pocket Pal next to his sleeping bag, along with the little magnifying glass Rudy used to bring out in order to show his customers the THC crystals sparkling atop the sinsemilla buds.

The effort damn near killed me, but Asmador, whose condition has continued to improve almost hourly, was like a kid on Christmas morning. Obviously not one to look a gift horse in the mouth, he tore into the new reading material with the same intensity with which he'd devoured the BMW owner's manual, sitting up cross-legged with the book in one hand and the magnifying glass and a joint in the other, not stopping to eat or piss, his head wreathed in a cloud of pot smoke.

When he got to the final entry, where I'd added a crucial postscript last night, his eyes widened and his mouth fell open, like he was a ham silent movie actor miming astonishment.

"What's up?" I called over to him. "You look all excited."

He looked up from the book and asked me if I could keep a secret.

"To the grave and beyond," I told him.

"My mission from the Council," he said, his brown eyes sparkling like a kid's on Christmas morning. "I know what it is."

"That's terrific," I told him. "If there's anything I can do to help you, just say the word."

"Okay, I will," he said solemnly. Then he lowered his head to the book in his lap, turned back to the first page, and started all over again.

Apr 23

Asmador spent all day yesterday reading and rereading my Pocket Pal from cover to cover with the aid of the magnifying glass, then was up half the night flipping through the pages at random, the way born-again Christians page through their Bibles, looking for inspiration and guidance. I can tell he has it memorized already: when I awoke this morning, he raised his forefinger in the air like Abe Lincoln giving the Gettysburg Address, and proclaimed, "He lives, he wakes—'tis Death is dead, not he!"

For a while there, I was worried that at some point he might get suspicious of my role in this whole affair. I certainly would have if I were him. But it doesn't seem to have occurred to him to question who I am or what I'm doing here. He's never called me by my name. I don't think he even knows I have a name, much less that it's Luke. As for the possibility that I'm the guy featured in the Pocket Pal, I'm pretty sure that's never crossed his mind.

Of course, it helps that he doesn't seem to remember anything that happened in the real world while he was under the influence of chemical restraint. As far as Asmador is concerned, he was sent here by the Infernal Council to carry out his mission, and nothing else matters. And when you look at the situation from his point of view, it only makes sense that there'd be a guy here whose entire function in life (other than rolling doobies for him) was to help him with that mission. He probably thinks the Infernal Council sent me to him for precisely that reason, and I sure don't plan to disabuse him on that score.

At least not intentionally. I did come close to screwing it up this afternoon, however, while I was explaining how to get to Fred and Evelyn's house, and accidentally referred to them as "my" grandparents instead of the grandparents. Luckily, he didn't seem to notice.

Apr 24

Asmador was like a new man this morning. He emptied my piss jug, made instant coffee, and even twisted up a sloppy but serviceable breakfast doobie for us to share. Then he hunkered down next to me, glanced to his left, then to his right, and whispered, "Tonight's the night."

Turns out he'd visited the Council last night and received his marching orders. Me, I wasn't all that convinced he was ready yet, but when we went through the plan for about the zillionth time, I had to admit he had it down cold.

Of course, that's no guarantee he'll be able to perform under pressure, or improvise successfully if things go wrong. But I can't let myself worry about stuff like that. I'll just have to be contented with knowing that I've done everything I can, and hope I live long enough to find out how it all comes out.

Apr 25

It's not so bad, this dying. I thought it'd be scarier. Instead it's kind of peaceful. My leg doesn't even hurt anymore. Not because it's better, but because it's numb. I can't feel anything below midcalf. Which is lucky, because my foot sure looks *painful, all black and swollen and getting ready to split open like an overripe tomato. Plus there's this sweetish-sour rotting smell hovering around my corner of the barn. Can you say* gangrene, *boys and girls?*

Of course, I could probably still save my life (though probably not my foot) by hopping into the old Beemer when Asmador gets back and driving straight to the nearest emergency room. But then what? I get to spend the rest of my life either in prison (I imagine some people are still pretty pissed off about that whole blowing up Meadows Road deal) or in some state-run maximum-security nut farm. And I've already done enough time in Meadows Road to know that that's not really living, it's only slower dying.

No, better to let it end here. But not quite yet, not until I get to see my grandparents again.

Asmador should be back with their heads any time now.

8

Tapocketa tapocketa ka-chunk.

Open lid, turn page of book, place book facedown on glass, push down lid to flatten book, press big green button.

Tapocketa tapocketa ka-chunk.

Open lid, turn page . . . place book . . . flatten book . . . green button.

Tapocketa tapocketa ka-chunk . . .

Pender and Epstein were in a rhythm now, slaving over a hot photocopier in the windowless room in the back of the Marshall County sheriff's station, where they kept the office equipment. Laura Baldinger had agreed to let Pender enlarge Luke Sweet's Pocket Pal diary for the purposes of the investigation, on the condition that he return it to her at the crime scene as soon as they'd finished.

"Here's you," Pender exclaimed, reading from a floppy, still-warm sheet of copier paper. *"A skinny guy with fading reddish brown hair. . . . Skip Epstein. . . . Bounty hunter."* Pender glanced up at him. "Bounty hunter?"

Skip reddened—with his fair complexion, he'd always blushed easily—then flipped back through his copy of the sheets. "And here's *you. A huge fat guy wearing a loud sport coat and one of those stupid little checked hats with feathers in the brim."*

Pender took off his trusty hat and turned it around a few times. "Looks fine to me," he said, just as his cell phone began playing "Moon River" in his pants pocket.

A practiced hand by now, Pender flipped the phone open with a flourish while Skip continued to work the copier. "Pender here. . . . Uh-huh. . . . Uh-huh. . . . That didn't take long. . . . Yeah, I understand. Okay, shoot. . . . Really? . . . That explains the smell. . . . Thanks, Doc, I—No, nothing from Cal-ID yet. I'll let you know the minute I hear anything. . . . You bet. Thanks again. . . . Bye."

He keyed the End Call button, snapped the phone closed, turned to Skip. "That was Dr. Flemm, the M.E. He's reasonably convinced he's got the cause of death for our deceased friend—provisional of course, pending blood work and toxicology, but he says so far, everything points to gangrene from a crushed ankle."

The phone, still in his hand, went off again. Pender, who was heartily sick of "Moon River" by this time, gave Skip the upraised, sorry-gotta-take-this forefinger. "Pender here. . . . Oh, hi. . . . Tell me you have good news for— No kidding? Out-*standing*! Fast work! Hold on just a second. . . . Okay, shoot," he said, notebook at the ready, pencil stub poised, cell phone jammed between his shoulder and his ear. But a puzzled look crossed his face at what must have been the caller's first words, and the pencil didn't move.

"Wait a minute, there must be some kind of mistake. Are we talking about a match from the card *I* sent you, or are we talking about the latent prints from the barn? . . . Oh, you haven't? How good is the match? . . . That good . . . ? Thanks, I guess." He snapped the phone shut, then dropped it back into the side pocket of his jacket.

"What is it?" said Skip. "What's going on?"

Dazedly: "That was Cal-ID. They got a ten-by-ten match on the dead guy."

"And?"

"It was him, it was Sweet."

Stunned didn't quite cover Skip's response; flabbergasted was closer. "Luke Sweet?" he said, his mind flashing back to last night's dream.

"Little Luke himself, dead and in person. Ten-point match on all ten fingers—that makes the probability somewhere around ninety-nine point nine percent."

"What's the point one percent?" was all Skip's muddled brain could come up with.

"Clerical error," said Pender, as his phone began chirping yet again. "Pender here. . . . Oh, hi, Laurel. We're just about finished with— You did? Can we— Okay, yeah, sure." He checked his watch: it was straight-up noon. "See you in about half an hour."

"What now?" Skip asked.

"One of the CS techs found a second journal buried in the dirt in the back of the barn. Luke again, but the new one's only ten pages or so, in regular-size handwriting. Laurel says we can look it over as soon as they're done dusting it."

"I can hardly wait," murmured Skip, glancing over the last page of the Pocket Pal. "Maybe it'll help us make some sense out of this," he added, then read the final entry, which was hand-printed in capital letters, aloud to Pender:

"To Asmador: Your mission, by order of the Infernal Council, is to exact revenge for all slights and injustices visited upon Luke Sweet, Jr., by the traitors named herein. You will know neither peace nor rest until vultures have feasted on their remains."

"What the fuck?" said Pender.

"My sentiments exactly," said Skip.

9

April . . . something. Who knows, who cares. This is probably my last entry. I can't feel my leg below the knee anymore, and every time I drop off to sleep, I sink a little deeper, stay a little longer, and come back a little weaker than the time before.

Don't get me wrong, I'm not complaining. I have some good memories. Eating Marianne's ice cream with my mother. Riding the Giant Dipper 67 times in a row. Making love with Shawnee, waist-deep in the sparkling river.

And at least I'm at peace, which is more than you can say for Fred and Evelyn. Asmador brought their heads back yesterday in plastic grocery bags and set them up on a plank so I can see them from where I'm lying. Judging by the expression on their faces, their mouths wide open and screaming and their eyes practically popping out of their heads, those two were anything but peaceful at the end.

Serves 'em right: they should have treated me better when they had the chance. They all should have treated me better. And now, thanks to Asmador, who just left for the Marshall City library to research the current whereabouts of Judge Brobauer, they're all going to pay.

How's that for a happy ending?

Yours truly, Luke Sweet, Jr., Murphy's Farm, Marshall County, California, USA, North America, Western Hemisphere, Earth, the Galaxy, the Universe, and whatever lies beyond.

CHAPTER TWO

I

A little more than an hour after losing their prime suspect, whose death had provided him with the most unimpeachable alibi of all, the ad hoc investigative duo of Pender and Epstein left Marshall County in Pender's dust-covered, dirt-spattered rental car, with Skip behind the wheel and Pender working the cell phone.

"Dr. Gallagher, it's Ed Pender from the FBI, I spoke to you Wednesday? Sorry to bother you at home, but it's urgent. . . . Oh, please, don't give it another thought. We all made assumptions. You assumed Luke Sweet was dead, I assumed he was our killer. Turns out we were both wrong. . . . No, according to this new journal he didn't even kill his grandparents. . . . I was hoping *you'd* be able tell *us*. You said there were four people unaccounted for, two orderlies, two inmates. . . . Right, the other inmate. . . . Sure, I'll wait."

"She's looking it up in her computer," he had time to whisper to Skip before Dr. Gallagher came back on the line. "That was quick," he told her, notebook at the ready. "Okay, shoot. . . . Is that *M* for Mike or *N* for November? Right, got it. Do you have any other information about him? Relatives, home address. . . . Okay, I'll be here."

Pender closed the phone, glanced over at Skip. "We've got a name. Charles Mesker. With an *M*. She's going to get back to me with the address where they shipped the so-called remains."

He leaned over and turned the radio back up. Driving with Pender, Skip had already learned, involved a heavy dose of sing-along oldies. Pender rocked around the clock, got his thrill on Blueberry Hill, and was wakin' up little Susie just outside Vacaville when his cell phone began chirping yet again. He reached over and turned down the radio, then out came the notebook and half-chewed pencil stub. "Okay, shoot. . . . Right, right." Scribbling busily. "Got it. Thank you, Dr. Gallagher. I imagine we'll be in touch."

He closed the phone and turned to Skip. "Mesker's next of kin were his parents. They still live in Santa Cruz. We should probably go check them out."

"Tonight?"

"Yes, tonight. You know, just in case."

"Just in case what?" asked Skip, as he pulled out of the slow lane to overtake a little old lady from Pasadena on a long straightaway.

"Just in case son Charles is holed up there. He wouldn't be the first fugitive in history to run home to Mommy and Daddy."

Even with the accelerator pedal floored, it took the Toyota half a mile to put Granny in the rearview mirror. "Okay, you're on," Skip told Pender. "But first I want to stop by my apartment to change my clothes and pick up the Buick. I'm also thinking maybe we ought to call your friend Klug and arrange for backup."

Pender laughed and clapped Skip encouragingly on his uninjured shoulder. "What do we need backup for?" he said. "We've already got him outnumbered two to one."

2

There'd been no time to pack Friday afternoon, no time to plan, barely time for Asmador to toss the money and what was left of the weed into the trunk of the BMW and haul ass before the cops showed up at Murphy's farm. Luckily the dirt road leading from the barn to the county road curved behind the hills to the north, blocking the view of the retreating Beemer from the deputies, so Asmador had gotten away clean, and was well into the next county by the time the cops finished setting up their roadblocks behind him.

"That was a close one," he'd muttered, talking aloud to keep himself company.

"You think?" A voice from the backseat.

Startled, Asmador had glanced up at the rearview mirror, where he saw the reflection of a handsome, redheaded youth grinning at him mischievously. "Eyes front," Sammael had remarked as a car horn blared. Asmador had turned back again, discovered he'd drifted into the lane of oncoming traffic, and jerked the wheel to the right just in time to avoid a head-on collision with a black Jetta. He'd caught a glimpse of the chalk white face of the other driver as the Jetta shot by.

"That was close," the Poison Angel had said calmly; somehow he'd magically transported himself into the front passenger seat.

"What are you doing here?"

"The Council sent me. They are mightily p.o.'d."

"The Book! I left the Book in the barn!"

Sammael had winked broadly. "Lucky for you, you have friends in low places. Bear in mind, though: this is a one-time only deal. You fuck up again, you're on your own. Oh, and by the way, you stink to high heaven, as the saying goes. Better get out of those clothes before they arrest you as a health hazard."

Then he was gone, and in his place, lying on the bucket seat, had been a perfect copy of the Book, identical to it in every aspect but one. This simulacrum was perpetually on fire, bathed in lambent blue flames that flickered and danced like heat lightning across its surface, but like the flames of the burning bush in Exodus, failed to consume it, or even scorch the leather upholstery on which it lay.

3

There were several messages on the answering machine in Skip's kitchen. The last was from Warren Brobauer, thanking Skip for his work and sacrifice on the family's behalf, hoping he was recovering from his ordeal, and notifying him that, insofar as the authorities finally seemed to have the situation in hand, his professional services were no longer required.

The apartment, meanwhile, was a wreck. Yellow tape, fingerprint powder, overturned furniture, chalk marks, evidence flags. Maybe the maid could come in a few days early next week, Skip started to tell himself, then remembered suddenly that she was dead—that was *her* blood in the hallway. And she wasn't just a maid, anyway—she was *Anna*. Anna of the warm brown eyes and the thousand-watt smile and the valiant broken English; Anna who'd washed his underpants and scrubbed his toilet for five years; Anna who'd been gunned down and stuffed into a closet like a sack of old clothes. So to hell with Warren and his money and his good wishes, thought Skip—Epstein Investigative Services was in this one for the duration, client or no client.

"I'm going to change my clothes," he told Pender. "Feel free to help yourself to the good Scotch. It'll go to waste otherwise."

"You don't drink?"

"I can't," Skip called over his shoulder as he limped down the hallway. "It's all the acetaminophen in the Norco I take. My doctor says if I have one drink, even a beer, my poor liver will go belly-up like a dead salmon."

After washing down two of the aforementioned Norco with a slug of tap water, Skip changed into a clean pair of chinos and a freshly laundered (by Anna!) blue oxford-cloth shirt, and retrieved the kidney holster containing his 9mm Beretta Parabellum from the shoe box on the top shelf of his closet before returning to the kitchen.

"You have a license for that thing?" Pender wanted to know.

"Sure do," said Skip, clipping the holster to the back of his belt.

"Any good with it?"

"Pretty good. How about you?"

"As far as the Bureau's concerned, I'm range-qualified," said Pender. "But you remember those two shots I fired to scare away the buzzards yesterday?"

"Uh-huh."

"I missed the sky. Twice."

4

Leaving Marshall County one step ahead of the law, Asmador had driven north, for no particular reason, and after stopping at the Wal-Mart to purchase a complete change of clothes—another denim shirt, another pair of jeans, another denim jacket—he'd spent Friday night in a rustic, trailer court–style motel with detached bungalows just outside of Red Bluff.

The square, low-ceilinged, wood-paneled room had been furnished with twin beds covered with musty old striped blankets, and had smelled of Pine-Sol and mold. Asmador had smelled of sweat and corpse until he treated himself to a long, hot shower. He'd slept poorly, dreaming of soaring vultures outlined against a scarlet sky, and had awakened in the dark. The only light in the room issued from the television, where the image of the Poison Angel grinned out at him from behind what looked like a news anchor's desk.

"And in news of the Underworld," Sammael had reported "authorities in the Blasted Land tonight revealed the identity of *your* next victim."

Asmador had sat up, openmouthed with astonishment, as the redheaded demon jerked a thumb in the direction of a rectangular inset in the upper-left corner of the screen, where one of the names from Luke Sweet's fantasy revenge list was written in letters of fire.

"And bear in mind," Sammael had added, forming an imaginary pistol with his hand and aiming the forefinger–gun barrel directly at Asmador, "if you fuck up again, things are gonna get mighty hot for you."

Then he'd pulled the imaginary trigger with his middle finger, and *ka-whoooosh!* a ball of fire had shot out of his fingertip and through the television screen, heading straight for Asmador, who'd shrieked and thrown up his forearm to shield his eyes.

But the fireball had never arrived, and when he'd uncovered his eyes, the room had been dark again, save for the ghostly afterglow of the television screen, and relatively quiet, save for one last peal of demonic laughter.

5

Charles Mesker's parents lived on the second floor of a converted motel in a blighted neighborhood only a few blocks from the Boardwalk. Suspicious looking characters loitered under shattered streetlights; a strung-out looking hooker tottered on high heels toward the Buick as it pulled up to the curb, then turned away without explanation.

Skip rang the bell and announced himself as Special Agent Pender, FBI, while the real Pender went around behind the building to make sure Charles didn't try to sneak out the back way, over one of the second-story balconies. After a minute or two, he rejoined Skip in the entrance lobby, which had the thinnest, drabbest, unhappiest-looking carpet either of them had ever seen. They took the stairs up to the second floor, where Gerald Mesker, white-haired and professorial-looking in a shawl-necked cardigan, met them at the door and asked to see their credentials.

Pender tinned him, introducing Skip as his colleague, Mr. Epstein. Mesker, who'd taught mathematics at UC Santa Cruz from its founding in 1965 to his retirement a few years earlier, ushered them into a low-ceilinged studio apartment and seated them in cheap matching side chairs with low arms and scratchy upholstery. His wife, Helwidge, a round-faced, apple-cheeked Santa's wife in loose-bottomed granny jeans and a high-necked blouse buttoned to her chin, served them coffee in delicate blue willow china cups and saucers that looked sadly out of place in the sparsely furnished room.

"When did you last see your son Charles?" asked Pender, after some minimal small talk.

"We visited Charlie three weeks before he died," said Gerald Mesker, seated next to his wife on the convertible sofa that doubled as their marital bed.

"It's hard to say whether he recognized us or not," Helwidge Mesker confided in a hoarse whisper. "But I prefer to think he did, and that he knew we still loved him and cared for him."

"I'm sure he did," said Pender, taking out his pocket notebook and well-gnawed pencil stub. "By the way, who was his psychiatrist?"

"Dr. Hillovi," said the professor. "Fredu Hillovi."

"Do you happen to know how I can get in touch with him?"

Mesker shook his head. "I don't even know if he survived the fire—I'd read he was badly burned."

"I'm sorry to hear that." Pender's homely mug was radiant with sympathy as he glanced around the dismal little room. There were two framed photographs of son Charles on the sofa side table. One was of a teenager in a Boy Scout uniform; he had an archer's bow in one hand and was holding up a blue ribbon in the other. The other was a candid snapshot of a hulking, middle-aged man with a low forehead and a thousand-yard stare. "It must have been quite a strain, financially, keeping Charles in a private facility."

"Any parent would have done the same," the professor replied. "We tried caring for him at home, but . . ." He glanced over at his wife, who shook her head almost imperceptibly. "Let's just say it didn't work out. And if you've ever seen the facilities the state of California provides, Agent Pender, you'd understand why we made the choices we did." Choices, he went on to explain, that included heavily mortgaging their home, then renting it out, furnished, to help pay the bills from Meadows Road.

"But you must understand, we don't regret any of the sacrifices we made for Charlie," Helwidge added, in a barely audible voice. "In a way, it's a comfort, knowing that we did everything we could for him. And now that Charlie is finally at peace . . ." Overcome with emotion, she slumped sideways against her husband, took his hand, and pressed it movingly against her cheek.

"What Helwidge was going to say is, she and I will be moving back into our house on the first of June," Gerald concluded brusquely. "And now it's getting rather late, so if you don't mind, can we please get this over with as quickly as possible?"

"Of course," said Pender, setting down his cup and saucer. "Could I speak to you alone?"

"I don't think—"

"Please."

Gerald took his wife's cup and saucer from her and returned them to the tray along with his own. He patted her knee and started to rise, but she seized his hand again and would not relinquish it. "No, I want to hear," she told Pender. "Whatever you have to say to my husband, you can say in front of me."

Pender leaned forward. "There is every reason to believe that your son was *not* killed at Meadows Road," he said gently. "We have some very convincing evidence that he escaped with another inmate after the fire. We believe he's still at large, but highly delusional, and I'm sorry to say, very dangerous." He gave it a moment to sink in before adding, "So if Charles should happen to show up here, I beg you, for your own safety as well as his and everybody else's, please call 911."

Helwidge turned to her husband. "What does he mean, Gerry? Is he saying that Charlie's . . . alive? He's alive?"

Judging by the strained, distracted smile Gerald gave his wife, the irony of their situation had not escaped him. "Apparently," he said, patting his wife's hand.

"I'm so . . . happy," Helwidge managed to say, the color blanching from her cheeks. Then her eyes rolled back in her head and she toppled sideways off the sofa onto the shag-carpeted floor before her husband could catch her.

6

It had never occurred to Asmador that there were libraries with telephone directories in almost every town in America. The library in Marshall City was the one he'd used before, so regardless of the danger, that's where he'd headed after checking out of the trailer court early Saturday morning.

Asmador had reached the library at 3:45 P.M., just before closing time, and headed immediately for the shelves of yellow-and-black telephone books in the back of the main room. After striking out in the Humboldt County directory, the last known address of his next intended victim, he'd been in the process of going through the directories in alphabetical order when the reference librarian called to him from her nearby desk. "Excuse me, sir?"

He'd turned, remembering at the last second to smile at the lady. Humans respond well to smiles, he was learning. "Who, me?"

Yeah, him. She couldn't help noticing . . . wondered whether he was aware . . . internet . . . happy to be of assistance . . .

"If it's not too much trouble." He'd graced her with another smile, and given her the name of the old friend he was trying to locate. She'd tapped a few keys . . . waited . . . waited . . . waited . . . and there it was. She'd jotted down the number on an index card and handed it across the desk.

"Great, thanks," he'd said, as the overhead lights winked off and on twice, signaling five minutes to closing. "Do you know where that area code is?"

"No, but I can . . ." Her fingers had played lightly across the keys again. "That's Mendocino County."

"Far out." Asmador had thanked her again, with all the warmth he could summon, then added sincerely, "I sure wish I'd've known about this Internet thing earlier—imagine all the time and trouble I could have saved."

When he'd returned to the car, though, Sammael had been waiting for him in the backseat, and the Poison Angel had not been a happy councilor. "What do you think's going to happen when you finish carrying out your mission and that librarian sees your victim's name in the newspaper? You think she's not going to remember you, and give the cops your description? Then the next thing you know, there's one of those, what do they call them, composite sketches of your ugly puss on the front page of every newspaper and the wall of every police station in the country."

"Okay, okay, I'll take care of it."

"See that you do."

"I will."

"You'd better." With a wink, Sammael had vanished again.

Asmador had sighed. *Just try and get the last word in with a demon,* he'd told himself, opening the glove compartment and taking out the pistol he'd been using to eliminate ancillary problems on the order of caddies and housemaids. A few minutes later, the reference librarian, a wide-hipped female in a frilly-bosomed white blouse, a taut gray skirt, and sensible heels, had emerged from the library, accompanied by an older, bespectacled female librarian pushing a book cart. Asmador had slouched down behind the wheel as the women opened the back of the book drop at the curb, transferred the books to the cart, and wrestled it back inside.

After double-checking to make sure he had a round chambered, Asmador had dropped the pistol into the left inside pocket of his stiff new denim jacket. Leaving the car unlocked in case he needed to make a quick getaway, he'd strolled back to the library entrance and rapped on the automatic glass door, now locked. A few seconds later, he'd seen the reference librarian crossing the darkened room toward the door, shading her eyes to peer through the glass.

"Hi, it's me," Asmador had called, waving cheerfully.

Coming closer, she'd recognized him, and smiled apologetically. "We're closed."

He'd cupped a hand to his ear to indicate he couldn't hear, then silently mouthed, "I think I left something" and pointed to the back of the library.

The ruse had worked. Convinced the door was preventing them from hearing each other, the woman had opened it. "What is it, I'll get it for you."

"That's okay, I'll get it." Asmador had brushed past her into the dark quiet room. The older woman had been behind the desk, using what looked like a laser gun to check in the books from the outside bin. Asmador had drawn his gun and pointed it at the first librarian. "Is there anybody else here?"

Her eyes had widened, going all soft and round with fear. "No. I mean, yes, there's—"

He'd put a bullet through the center of her chest, but for some reason it hadn't dropped her right away. She'd just stood there for a few seconds with a red stain blossoming across the white bosom of her blouse. When she'd finally crumpled, Asmador had strolled over to the checkout desk and leaned across the counter. The other librarian had been on her hands and knees, scuttling toward the telephone at the other end of the desk. Her long gray hair, he'd noticed, was done up in a thick braid coiled into a bun at the back of her head, which had made a tempting bull's-eye.

But the library was, after all, in the middle of a small city, so instead of risking a second shot, Asmador had vaulted over the counter, grabbed her by the ankles, and yanked her away from the telephone.

"Please don't shoot me," she'd begged him, in a shaky, old lady's voice.

"I won't," Asmador had told her—and to her great misfortune he was as good as his word.

7.

"That went well, don't you think," Pender observed drily, as he and Skip left the motel. Gerald Mesker had chased them out of the apartment before Pender had a chance to ask them about their son's mental history.

"At least they can still move back into their house," Skip pointed out. "Because where Charlie's going, they don't charge for room, board, or psychiatric care."

"Assuming he lets himself be taken alive."

Skip shrugged. "Either way, he won't have to pay any rent," he said. "So what do you want to do next, track down this Dr. Hillovi?"

"We need to bring Klug up to speed first," said Pender, who was well aware that by not informing the Santa Cruz detective earlier about the change of suspects, he had probably violated Steve McDougal's prohibition against stepping on local toes. Still, if Charles Mesker *had* been at his parents' house, and Pender had made the pop himself, to the greater glory of the Bureau, not only would he *not* have been reprimanded, he'd have been a hero. In the FBI, as elsewhere, Pender understood, you pays your money and you takes your chances.

With the aid of his handy cell phone, Pender tracked down Klug to a bar on the municipal wharf. Skip drove the Buick all the way to the end of the wharf, angle-parked in a handicapped zone, and hung his blue placard from the rearview mirror.

Klug was outside the bar, leaning against the board fence surrounding the noisy, noisome sea lion corral, wearing a Popeye Doyle porkpie hat with the brim turned up, and smoking one of his Camel straights. Pender introduced Skip, half-shouting over the grumbling and baying of the sea lions, and mispronouncing the name as *Ep-steen.*

"That's *Epstein,* rhymes with *fine.*" Skip gave them the short-form correction; the long form included a speech about how you didn't say Albert Einsteen or Gertrude Steen or drink a steen of beer.

The homicide detective stuck out his hand. "Lloyd Klug, rhymes with *bug, mug, drug,* and *hug.*" He'd obviously had a few drinks but sobered up fast when Pender handed him the small, framed snapshot of Charles Mesker—the grown-up, not the Boy Scout—which he'd pocketed on his way out of the Meskers' apartment.

"Let me get this straight," said Klug, when Pender had finished telling him about their new suspect. "This guy Mesker is going around killing people named in Sweet's journal because Sweet told him to?"

"You got it," said Pender. "I suspect we'll have a more detailed answer after we track down his psychiatrist, but we wanted to bring you up to date first."

Klug's eyes narrowed. "And am I?" He took a last lung-charring drag off the Camel, then flicked it over the side of the pier.

"Are you what?"

"Up to date. Because I've got the distinct feeling you're holding out on me."

"Hey, what I got, you got." Pender was the picture of injured innocence. He sounded so sincere that even Skip might have believed him, if he hadn't already known about the list of potential victims in Luke's journal. Skip also noticed that during the course of the conversation, Pender had gradually adopted an unobtrusive version of Klug's Philadelphia accent.

After the meeting with Klug, Pender used the magic cell phone to track down Dr. Fredu Hillovi, Charles Mesker's staff psychiatrist at Meadows Road, to the regional burn center at Valley Medical in San Jose, where he was still a patient. To Pender's surprise, when he spoke with the night charge nurse to find out when he and his colleague could interview Dr. Hillovi, she asked him how soon they could get there.

"You mean, like tonight?" Pender's plans had been tending more toward a few drinks, a motel room, and beddy-bye.

"Yes, tonight. As soon as possible, in fact. He's having a terrible time, pain-wise, and doesn't want to be left alone. Meanwhile I'm short-staffed beyond belief, so you'd be doing us both a favor."

"In that case, keep a light in the window," said Pender. "We're on our way."

8

When Lorraine Neely had failed to pick up her four-year-old daughter at her mother's house by 4:30 Saturday afternoon, as arranged, her mother had tried calling the library but reached the answering machine. By six o'clock she'd been worried enough to call her husband and ask him to stop by the library on his way home from work. Irv Neely, who owned the hardware store on John Marshall Avenue, thought it was a waste of time, but he'd rapped on the locked library door anyway.

When no one responded, he'd turned to leave, and spied a bloody shoe print on the cement walk to his left, just outside the exit door, pointing away from the building. Stooping, he'd seen a second, lighter print a little farther on, and the faint trace of a third. He'd immediately called 911 from the pay phone on the cantilevered fieldstone wall to the right of the library entrance.

Officer William Baer, responding for the Marshall City Police Department, had agreed with Irv that the waffle-soled shoe prints might have resulted from someone stepping in blood, but he'd also thought they could have been left by wood stain, paint, or sealant. So rather than break in, he'd asked the dispatcher to notify the head librarian, who'd arrived with a key fifteen minutes later. Officer Baer had asked the other two to wait outside and entered the hushed, dimly lighted building alone.

The trail of waffle-soled prints, right shoe only, had led backward into the room, growing more distinct as it skirted past the crumpled body of the first victim and continued on around behind the checkout desk. The young officer, recognizing that the first victim did not appear to have lost enough blood to supply all those prints, had circled the enclosure apprehensively, his right hand resting on the butt of his holstered weapon for reassurance, and had discovered the second victim lying facedown behind the desk.

Although the body'd had that rag doll look that came with multiple broken bones, most of the blood, which had fanned out in a pool around her head, was later determined to have come from a broken nose, one of her lesser injuries. Following procedure, Officer Baer had secured the premises by herding Irv Neely and the head librarian away from the entrance before he called in the double homicide.

The hamsterlike county medical examiner, Dr. Flemm, had arrived half an hour later, his mustache quivering busily. "Everybody got their photos?" he'd asked briskly, donning his dust-free, latex-free rubber gloves and stooping beside the first victim. After checking for morbidity and lividity, and taking a rectal temperature to establish the time of death, he'd rolled the victim onto her back. "Oh, I know her," he'd said, as if he were pleasantly surprised. Then, over his shoulder to the homicide detective, as more flashbulbs glared: "Heart shot—looks like about a thirty-eight."

"And how long would you say she's been dead?"

"Around three hours."

"Yeah, that fits." The library closed at four on Saturdays, and the other victim's analog wristwatch, having been stomped to death along with its owner, still read 4:17.

After changing gloves, Dr. Flemm had taken his time examining the second woman, kneeling beside her behind the checkout desk and running his plump hands up and down her body, feeling for broken bones. Her rib cage he'd seemed to find particularly fascinating. In twenty years, he'd never encountered a torso so thoroughly crushed, he'd told the detective, with the possible exception of an artichoke grower in Castroville who'd been run over by his own thresher.

"The only possible way anyone could have done that much damage," Dr. Flemm had added, "was to climb on top of this desk here, jump down and land on her with both feet, then climb back up and do it again—maybe ten, fifteen times."

"Oh, Christ." The homicide detective had sounded almost awed.

9

Highway 17 was somewhat intimidating in the dark. Skip was glad they'd taken the Buick, especially when the truck drivers decided to make up on the narrow, twisting downhill stretches the time they'd lost on the uphill climbs. But the highway leveled out on the other side of the mountains, and they reached the medical center, which appeared to have been built with giant see-through Legos, around eleven-thirty on Saturday night.

Once again Skip used his blue placard to claim a prime parking space. They took the elevator up to the burn unit, where the restive quiet was accentuated by the muted wheezing of respirators, the soft beeping of monitors, the whispered conversations of nurses padding about on rubber-soled shoes.

The charge nurse was waiting for them with sterile caps, gowns, gloves, and masks. "Infection is the burn patient's most dangerous enemy," she explained, sounding like she was quoting from a manual. She even subjected Pender's badge case, notebook, and half-chewed pencil stub to a UV-ray decontamination before allowing him to enter Dr. Hillovi's room.

The patient lay on his right side, swaddled fore and aft with ointment-stained dressings, and covered by a sheet supported by a frame to keep it from touching his skin. "Pardon me if I don't get up," he said, in an urbane, British-inflected Czech accent. Dr. Hillovi had colorless, quarter-inch stubble for hair and a long, narrow face anchored by an aristocratically aquiline nose.

"We'll give you a pass, considering the circumstances." Pender, mountainous in green, his face masked, held his badge in front of the doctor's eyes. "I'm Special Agent Pender, this is Mr. Ep-*stine*."

"Fredu Hillovi. What can I do for you gentlemen?"

"We were wondering if we could ask you a few questions about one of your former patients at Meadows Road," said Pender.

"Within the bounds of confidentiality, of course."

"Of course."

"And the patient's name?"

"Charles Mesker."

"Charles Mesker?" Hillovi appeared to have been taken by surprise but recovered quickly. "Ah, yes, poor Charles. I remember that, when I saw his name listed among the casualties, I was almost, well, not exactly *happy* about it, but I thought, at least he's finally at peace."

"Not exactly," said Pender.

"Oh?"

"Charles Mesker and another patient appear to have escaped from the facility after the fire." Skip noticed that Pender was now echoing Hillovi's choice of words and relatively formal diction. "The other patient, the man whom we believe was actually responsible for setting the initial explosion in the boiler room, later died of injuries sustained in the explosion. Mesker, though, is still very much at large."

Hillovi closed his eyes. Thirty seconds or so—an eternity in burn unit time—wheezed and beeped and whispered by before he opened them again. "This other patient, the one who caused the fire—it was Luke Sweet, wasn't it?"

Pender was startled; his eyebrows bobbed upward, momentarily wrinkling the prodigious expanse of brow between themselves and the green surgical cap perched like a beanie atop his big bald head. "How did you know?"

"There's an old Czech saying, my friend: if you want to find the truth, look for it among your fears." The psychiatrist's eyes were still open, but his gaze had turned inward. "First, do no harm," he muttered softly, more to himself than to his visitors. "Ha!"

Another eternity ticked by. Skip, sitting on the molded plastic chair by the head of the bed, was exhausted and wanted to hurry the interview along. But when he glanced over his shoulder at Pender, who was standing behind him, Pender shook his head almost imperceptibly. There were two kinds of silence employed by reluctant subjects, he explained to the Academy recruits every year when he gave his lecture on the art of affective interviewing. One meant *make me talk,* and required more aggressive questioning; the other meant *let me talk,* and required only patience.

Clearly, Dr. Hillovi belonged to the let-me-talk camp. It took him another minute to get started, but once he got going, there was no stopping him until he'd finished unburdening.

"On some level, I think I must have known all along," he began quietly, speaking with a sort of bemused intensity. "I just didn't want to admit it—not even to myself." He looked from Skip to Pender and back; his eyes were gray, Skip noticed, and the pupils so dilated he could see his reflection in their curved, black mirrors.

"When I took charge of his psychiatric care two years ago, I was dismayed to learn that Luke Sweet had been under continuous chemical restraint since his admission over seven years earlier.

"To some extent, this was understandable. Young Sweet, who'd scored an impressive thirty-nine on the Psychopathy Checklist, seemed to have a penchant for unprovoked attacks on nurses and orderlies. And since no one's ever developed an even remotely successful treatment protocol for psychopathy, chemical restraint certainly had to be considered as a viable alternative to a straitjacket and a padded cell.

"But not *continuous* chemical restraint. Because while there is no known treatment for psychopathy, there *is* a kind of self-correcting mechanism that sometimes comes into play with maturity.

"Most psychopaths, you see, are highly intelligent, testing out at ten to twenty points higher than the norm. This enables some of them, in the fullness of time, to reason out intellectually what most of us learned and internalized in early childhood: how to moderate one's behavior in order to achieve rewards and avoid punishments.

"In life, if he learns it early enough (I say *he* because almost all psychopaths are male), he becomes a so-called *successful* psychopath: a politician, a captain of industry, or yes, even a doctor. Or if he figures it out after he's already in prison, which is where the majority of psychopathy diagnoses are made, he might very well transform himself into a model inmate, even a mentor for other prisoners.

"But under continuous high-dosage chemical restraint, Sweet would never have had the opportunity to mature intellectually, nor would we have known it if he had. This means that, along with the opportunity of injuring others, he'd also been deprived of any chance he'd ever have to help himself.

"So my first decision when I was assigned the case was to cut back on the number of medications and reduce the dosages of the drugs we continued to administer. And when there was no immediate amelioration of the side effects, which included lethargy, emotional dullness, and most alarmingly, moderate to severe tardive dyskinesia—facial tics, uncontrollable grimacing, loss of motor control—I ordered further cutbacks.

"By mid-April, after two years of the new drug regimen, Luke Sweet was to all intents and purposes drug-free. Yet still the side effects, including the dyskinesia, continued unabated. I was of course concerned that my patient had suffered permanent damage to his nervous system as a result of extended chemical restraint, and scheduled him for a complete neurological workup in May.

"And yes, I did realize there was a possibility he might be feigning the symptoms in order to avoid whatever criminal charges he would have faced if he were ever declared compos mentis. But it never occurred to me he might be planning to blow the entire hospital to kingdom come."

Hillovi's voice had by then degenerated into a painful rasp. "Please," he said, gesturing toward the glass of water on the bedside table. Skip held the glass to his mouth and placed the straw between his lips. Hillovi took a sip, thanked Skip, then lowered his cheek to the pillow and closed his eyes.

But Pender was by no means through with him. "Excuse me, Doctor, there's something I don't understand. When I asked you how you'd guessed that it was Sweet who'd set the explosion, you said something about that being one of your worst fears. But a moment ago you said it never occurred to you that Sweet might be planning to blow up the hospital. So when did you first begin to suspect that—"

"From the moment I saw your badge," Hillovi interrupted. "It wasn't a question of *suspecting*, either. I *knew* it—I knew it in my bones, to put it unscientifically. That's why I was so surprised when you told me you wanted to talk about Charles Mesker instead."

"I still do," said Pender. "And in case you have any qualms about breaching doctor-patient confidentiality, let me assure you that by almost any reasonable standard of judgment, Charles Mesker represents an immediate and serious threat to public safety."

"I don't doubt that for a moment—not if he's at large and off his meds. What do you want to know?"

"Let's start with the diagnosis," said Pender, irradiated notebook and pencil stub in hand.

"Substance-induced psychotic disorder."

Pender jotted that down. "And the substance?"

"The—" The doctor broke into another coughing fit. Skip refilled the glass with ice water from a plastic carafe and gave him another sip. Hillovi nodded his thanks. "I'm sorry, what was the question?"

"You were about to tell us the name of the substance that induced Charles Mesker's psychotic disorder."

"Yes, yes, of course. The substance was Asmador."

10

A dark green 1994 Jeep Cherokee with New Jersey plates pulled into an isolated rest stop off Highway 101 North between Geyserville and Cloverdale around 10:00 P.M. Saturday. Asmador, who'd nodded off in the driver's seat of the BMW, was awakened by Sammael in time to see two humans climbing wearily out of the Cherokee, groaning and stretching. The male of the couple tweaked his crotch to relieve a wedgie, then they departed, bound for separate restrooms.

"You really think he looks like me?" Asmador said doubtfully.

"Near enough," replied Sammael. "Nobody examines those driver's license pictures closely anyway."

"If you say so."

"I just did." Once again, the snarky Poison Angel got in the last word before vanishing.

Asmador climbed out of the BMW carrying the suitcase with the remainder of his cash and weed, leaving the Beemer unlocked behind him in the hope that someone would steal it. The male of the couple returned first and resumed his seat behind the wheel of the Cherokee. Asmador waited for the female to return and climb up into the passenger's seat, then strode toward her with the suitcase in his left hand. "Excuse me," he called, in a generic foreign accent. "Could you answer for me a qvestion?"

As he'd hoped, the woman rolled down her window, whereupon he drew his gun from inside his denim jacket and jammed it against the side of her head. "Don't try anything stupid," he told her husband. "All I need is a ride."

Asmador was never sure whether they believed him or not, but in the end it didn't matter. They followed orders with alacrity and died together, kneeling and holding hands, in a dark redwood grove three hundred yards off the side of Highway 128, somewhere between Boonville and Philo.

11

"Asmador?" Pender and Epstein exchanged baffled glances.

"Asmador," said Hillovi.

"But that's what he calls himself."

"Yes, that's his alter ego whenever his delusions get the better of him—which is to say, when he's not sedated to the point of near-catatonia. Originally, however, Dr. Shiffman's Asmador was the commercial name for a popular over-the-counter asthma remedy. Its major active ingredient was belladonna. I don't recall what else was in it, but I remember it came in a powdered form, and was intended to be burned in a smudge fire or smoked in a cigarette to alleviate severe asthma symptoms.

"There was a period of time, however, back in the late sixties and early seventies, when certain poor souls decided it would be a good idea to ingest the stuff. Those that vomited immediately survived with relatively minor damage. Those with stronger stomachs fared less well. They became highly delusional, were unable to differentiate between reality and hallucination, and exhibited behavior patterns that ranged from unusual to downright bizarre.

"Some mistook human beings for objects and vice versa, another saw a solid floor as a piranha-infested lagoon, and still another passed most of his time watching Technicolor movies on his thumbnail. One patient died as a result of banging his head against a wall, trying to turn off a radio only he could hear. Another was run over by an automobile while trying to dig a hole in the middle of a busy street to free the people he believed were trapped beneath the pavement."

"And how did this stuff affect Mesker?" Pender asked, kneeling next to Skip's chair so Hillovi, lying on his side, could see him without having to raise his head from the pillow.

Profoundly, was Hillovi's reply. Charles Mesker, he explained, had been seventeen years old, an insatiable reader possessed of a brilliant mind and an eidetic (more commonly known as a photographic) memory, but long-haired and rebellious, with a disturbingly intense interest in demonology. He was also already an inveterate and indiscriminate drug user by the summer of 1972, when Santa Cruz experienced a temporary drug drought.

No one seemed to have any pot for sale, and what few psychedelics were available were of poor quality, or heavily boosted with methedrine, so Charles and a friend decided to experiment with the friend's grandmother's asthma remedy. Someone had told them that eating the stuff, as opposed to smoking it, would result in an intense psychedelic experience, during which they would be able to contact their cosmic archetypes. Neither boy was sure exactly what that meant, but they each managed to choke down several teaspoonfuls of the noxious green powder.

Charles never saw the other boy again—whatever his friend's archetype was, it was evidently airborne, because a few hours into the trip, the young man did a Linkletter off the roof. In some ways, he might have been the more fortunate of the two.

Charles's trip, perhaps due to his interest in demonology, took on a dark cast. Leaving his friend's house, he found himself wandering through a hellish world in which features of the familiar Santa Cruz landscape were conflated with visions of what he would later come to call the Blasted Land.

Gargoyles cavorted on rooftops and swung from the hands of the Santa Cruz town clock. At the Boardwalk, where the shrieking of the damned souls all but deafened him, Charles saw hideous demons cavorting among the crowd. Some masqueraded as vendors, serving up scoops of steaming shit in ice cream cones and severed penises in hot dog buns.

As day gave way to night, the ocean turned into desert dunes and the beach into red-hot coals. Fleeing the Boardwalk, Charles trudged westward along the sand, castellated cliffs towering above him like battlements, blocking out the stars.

The next morning the authorities, alerted by alarmed beachgoers, found Charles dancing and waving atop the rock formation known as Natural Bridges, naked as the day he was born and completely out of touch with reality. Still, he cooperated wholeheartedly with the officers, referring to them as his loyal minions and graciously allowing himself to be led through the knee-high surf to a waiting ambulance.

Although they had never treated a case of Asmador ingestion before, staffers at the Dominican Hospital emergency room were not unfamiliar with handling psychedelic overdoses. Their basic approach was to administer Thorazine until the patient quieted down or fell asleep. Twelve to twenty-four hours later, most patients were generally as good as new.

But not Charles Mesker. As soon as the Thorazine wore off, Charles's delusions and hallucinations—the Blasted Land, the demons, the Infernal Council, and so on—returned unabated. So the E.R. doctors knocked him out for another twenty-four hours, and once again, when consciousness returned, so did the effects of the Asmador.

After a short stay in the psych unit at Dominican Hospital,

Charles was transferred to the Meadows Road facility, where the most effective treatment they managed to come up with was to keep the boy so heavily tranquilized that he was unable to respond to his hallucinations or act upon his delusions. In other words, chemical restraint.

The side effects were predictably devastating, said Dr. Hillovi, who was by then exhausted and in growing pain. Charles suffered a loss of motor control, was wracked by tardive dyskinesia, and worst of all, from Charles's point of view, he lost the ability to read, which had once been his chief consolation. So every few years, his doctors tried weaning Charles off his meds long enough to see if the effects of the Asmador might have worn off on their own.

But the hallucinations and delusions inevitably returned, said Hillovi—that is, up until their most recent attempt to withdraw Charles from chemical restraint, a little over four years ago. "To our delight and surprise, within two weeks Charles was giving every indication of having recovered from his disorder. He appeared to be cooperative, rational, and high-functioning on an intellectual and emotional level—he even began reading again.

"After three months without any sign of a relapse, Charles was deemed an appropriate candidate for supervised release into the care of his parents. For six months he slept in his own room, read everything he could get his hands on, and even applied for his driver's license. Then one December night, he crept into his parents' bedroom and cut his mother's throat with a steak knife."

Just then, the light on the front of the machine that timed the automatic release of morphine sulfate into Hillovi's bloodstream switched from steady red to blinking green. He sighed gratefully and closed his eyes for a moment; when he opened them again, his pupils had already begun to contract. "When Charles was arrested, he gave his name as Asmador, and told the police that he'd cut the old lady's throat on orders from the Infernal Council.

"Mrs. Mesker refused to press charges, of course, so Charles was returned to Meadows Road." By now, Hillovi's pupils were mere pinpoints, and his affect disconcertingly jocular. "And so, my jolly green giant," he told Pender with a crooked grin, "if you have any further questions, I suggest you ask them soon, or forever hold your peas."

Pender, who had a million of 'em, winnowed them down to two with immediate and practical applications. "What do you think's going to happen as the effects of the chemical restraint continue to wear off?"

"Based on past history, I'd expect Charles's hallucinations to grow more vivid, yet also better integrated, as time passes. In other words, his two worlds should begin to merge again, and continue to merge until they become as one to him."

"Last question: Do you have any suggestions as to the best way to handle Charles when he's in that condition?"

"From a great distance, with a tranquilizer dart," said Hillovi, with a stoned wink and a laugh that sounded more like the barking of a phthisic sea lion.

12

Returning alone to the Cherokee, Asmador took inventory of the luggage and gear under the tarpaulin in the cargo area. And a most unusual inventory it was: two hunting bows, two target bows, dozens of arrows, spare bowstrings, calibrated sights, scopes, binoculars, night-vision goggles, day and night camouflage outfits, backpacks with built-in quivers, archery gloves and leather wrist guards, face black, hunting and field-dressing knives, trail mix, freeze-dried rations.

Moving like a man in a trance, Asmador picked up the larger hunting bow and assumed a sideways stance with his left arm extended, the elbow locked, the wrist cocked, the hand wrapped firmly around the leather-padded grip. Dazedly, he hooked the fingertips of his right hand around an imaginary string and drew it back until it was tucked in against his right cheek.

Suddenly he found himself transported by a combination of muscle-memory and sense-memory to a sunbaked field where stuffed targets were lined up on three-legged wooden stands, with straw bales stacked to provide a backstop. He smelled sweat and leather and straw, heard the *snap* of the bowstring, the sizzling sound of an arrow zipping past his ear, the solid *thunk* of the arrowhead striking home.

Obviously, this current humanoid incarnation was no stranger to the sport of archery, Asmador realized, snapping out of his trancelike state. And a lucky thing it was, too, he told himself— surely using a bow and arrow would be more satisfying and rewarding than firing a gun. So impersonal, guns. Of course, a knife would be even better, but you have to get really close to your victims to use a knife. Either that, or have them already hog-tied. But something told Asmador it might not be all that easy to sneak up on the traitor Epstein a second time. Nor was the FBI man, Pender, likely to let himself be taken without a fight. So if they did have to be ambushed from a distance, using a bow would be a most satisfactory compromise.

But you're getting ahead of yourself again, thought Asmador, tossing the bow back into the Cherokee and snapping the tarpaulin down to cover it. The first thing he needed to do was get a room for the night. Then tomorrow morning, he'd try to obtain an address to go along with the phone number that helpful, regrettably deceased librarian had given him this afternoon.

CHAPTER THREE

1

Pender dragged himself out of bed around eight o'clock on Sunday morning, still logy after only five hours of sleep. Donning the shapeless old corduroy bathrobe Skip had loaned him, he padded barefoot down the quiet, dawn gray hallway to the kitchen. Skip was sitting at the kitchen table in a T-shirt and pajama bottoms, poring over the photocopied enlargements of Luke Sweet's Pocket Pal and making notes on a legal pad.

Blessedly, there was fresh coffee on the stove. "What are you doing?" Pender carried a mug imprinted with a Far Side cartoon of the Boneless Chicken Ranch over to the table, where Skip was working by the yellow light of an overhead lamp with a stained-glass shade shaped like a mushroom.

"I'm compiling the late Mr. Sweet's so-called fantasy revenge list, which I'm presuming Asmador is using as his guide."

As much as he hated the 'suming words, *ass* and *pre,* Pender told Skip, he had to agree that sounded likely enough.

"He never actually *makes* the list," Skip pointed out, "he just adds to it. But here's what I've come up with." He tilted the legal pad toward Pender. There were six names on it: F. Harris, E. Harris, Pender, Brobauer, Oliver, Epstein; Skip had drawn a line through the first two and the fourth. "From what I can tell, there was no particular order to the first three attacks. Or at least nothing obvious or chronological that would give us a hint as to who's next."

Pender took a thoughtful slurp of coffee. "I can think of a set of circumstances under which the question of who comes next is irrelevant, no 'suming required," he announced. "Care to take a guess?"

Skip, an only child who unconsciously tended to assign older males the role of surrogate big brother, really wanted to get this one right. Stalling, he took a sip of the now lukewarm coffee in his mustard yellow mug. And another, and another, until it came to him: "If we're all three in the same place at the same time!"

"Bingo!" Pender raised the Far Side cup in a mock toast to Skip, who gave him a strained smile. "You know, you don't have to do this," Pender told him. "You have no client—nobody's going to think less of you if you decide to take a pass."

"No, it's not that. It's just . . ." Skip picked up the photocopied pages and riffled idly through them. "I've been through this two or three times since yesterday, and I can't help wondering—don't laugh now—but I can't help wondering, what if Little Luke was telling the truth?" He absentmindedly jogged the pages until the edges were lined up, then carefully put them back down on the table. "I mean, taken as a whole, his story kind of holds up in a way, doesn't it? So what are the chances he was just some poor kid who had a shitload of hard luck, and got railroaded all the way to the funny farm? With our help, I might add."

Pender blew a blubbery raspberry and blithely waved away the possibility with his free hand. "Remember how Hillovi said the kid racked up a thirty-nine on the Psychopathy Checklist when he was admitted?"

"Vaguely. Why?"

"The PCL scale only goes as high as forty. Charlie Manson barely made thirty-eight."

"No shit?" said Skip, brightening visibly.

"Scout's honor," said Pender, who had of course pulled the Manson number out of his enormous ass. "And now that we've got that out of the way, do you think you can locate Dr. Oliver's whereabouts for us? If not, I could try contacting a friend of mine at the CJIS, but I'm not sure—"

Skip cut him off. "Let me put it this way: if I can't find him, neither can Asmador."

2

Awakened early Sunday morning by the mournful bleat of a foghorn, Asmador throws back the quilted counterpane, rolls out of bed, and pads barefoot out onto the balcony of an overpriced hotel room in Fort Bragg, overlooking the mouth of the Noyo River, where a squat, weather-beaten fishing trawler is just putting out to sea.

The sky is ablaze to the east, casting a fiery glow over the estuary; bare-masted sailboats rock and creak in the tidal swell. Leaning out over the wooden railing of the balcony, Asmador is startled at first to see a grotesquely naked, hunchbacked, rat-tailed demon capering on the raised bridge of the trawler, cupping its misshapen genitals in one hand and gesturing lewdly toward the oblivious crewmen with the other. But along with the shock comes a strong sense of familiarity, even homecoming. This was how it had been in the time before, when the Blasted Land resembled Santa Cruz, and demons danced on the Boardwalk and swung from the hands of the town clock.

After rolling a joint and brewing a cup of complimentary coffee in the little machine on the counter outside the bathroom, Asmador tries calling the number the librarian had given him. He reaches an answering machine, which refers him to a second number, where a second answering machine informs him that although the Oliver Institute will be closed through May 15 for its annual two-week residential training at Braxton Hot Springs, Dr. Oliver will be checking his messages from time to time. So if you'd care to leave a message . . .

Asmador does not care to leave a message. Instead he calls the front desk. "This is Mr. Daniel in room 230." Peter Daniel was the name on the dead archer's driver's license and credit cards. "Do you know where Braxton Hot Springs is?"

"I believe it's in Lake County. If you give me a few minutes, I could probably find out for sure."

"Would you?" says Asmador, scratching absentmindedly at his pubic hair. "That would be terrif."

3

Pender and Epstein reached Braxton Hot Springs, a New Age retreat center in the heart of Lake County, shortly after one o'clock on Sunday afternoon. ABSOLUTELY NO MOTOR VEHICLES BEYOND THIS POINT, declared the hand-painted wooden sign on the gate at the end of the winding, two-and-a-half-mile-long driveway. A half dozen vehicles, ranging from a handsome new Lexus to a rusted-out VW bus with a psychedelic paint job, were parked in a dirt lot by the side of the road.

ELDERS, DELIVERIES, DIFFERENTLY ABLED, USE FOR ASSISTANCE, read a second, smaller sign nailed to the last telephone pole. Skip opened the rusty metal cabinet mounted beneath the sign, picked up the handset inside it, and clicked the hook with his forefinger like a character in an old-timey movie—Hello, Operator, give me Central!

Figuring that the chances of smoking being permitted beyond the gate were slim, Pender fired up a Marlboro while Skip talked to somebody at the other end. He only managed to sneak a few puffs before a lovely, fresh-faced, wet-haired young woman in a damp caftan arrived in a four-seater golf cart. "Are you here for the ceremony tonight?" she asked, looking them over dubiously.

"Could be," said Pender, buttoning his tomato soup sport coat to hide the Smith & Wesson Model 10 in his shoulder holster.

"You never know," added Skip—he was wearing a tan, zipper-front working man's jacket long enough to cover the Beretta in his kidney holster.

The young woman dropped them off in front of the Center, a two-story, wood-and-glass building with a cantilevered roof. "O's probably out on the deck," she called over her shoulder, casually stripping off her caftan as she trotted up the dusty road in the direction of the hot springs.

"Welcome to California," said Skip, smugly.

Pender rapped on the aluminum-framed screen door.

"Come on up!"

An open-treaded spiral staircase led to a carpeted, glass-enclosed room as sparsely furnished as a dance studio. Sliding glass doors opened onto a hardwood deck where an overweight, middle-aged man with a shaved head and a bushy, gray-blond beard was standing on one foot. The sole of his other foot was pressed flat against the inside of the opposite knee, and both hands were raised over his head, palms together like a football referee signaling a safety. "Can I help you?"

"I'm sorry," called Pender, who remembered Dr. O as a slender, beardless preppy with sandy hair. "We were looking for Dr. Oliver."

"You found him." Oliver, who was wearing a pair of white cotton meditation pajamas, abandoned his yoga posture. "What can I do for you?"

Obviously, Dr. O had failed to recognize Pender from their previous meeting, which meant Skip was free to launch into the cover story he and Pender had agreed to try first. They were, he told Oliver, two freelance writers working on a book about the evolution of the spiritual movement in the West from *Be Here Now* to, well, *now*. Skip apologized for not having contacted Dr. Oliver in advance, explaining that they had only heard about his institute a few days ago and had been trying to track him down since then.

Ten minutes later, seated at a trestle table in the rustic dining hall downstairs, sipping some surprisingly kick-ass chai in lieu of coffee, Dr. Oliver described the sequence of events that had transformed him from a jacket-and-tie psychologist to a pajama-wearing guru. It included a pilgrimage to the East (no mention of the Mountain Project debacle), a blinding flash of enlightenment, and subsequent years of study and meditation at the bare or sandaled feet of various spiritual teachers, the last of whom ordered him to return to the West to pass on the wisdom he had gained.

He then gave them a brief outline of the two-week training currently under way. The first week had consisted largely of breaking down the trainees' baseline assumptions and ego structures. This evening's ceremony marked the turning point, then the second week would be concerned with building up healthier, spiritually oriented human beings.

And no, he told them in response to their request, he would not give them permission to *observe* the ceremony tonight—dramatic pause—but he would be willing to let them *participate* in the ceremony, if they agreed to sign waivers and let him vet anything they might write about himself or the institute or the training.

Skip jumped at the offer so eagerly that Pender was afraid he might have given them away. No real journalist would have even considered allowing a subject the equivalent of a filmmaker's final cut.

But Oliver didn't appear to have noticed anything amiss. He would have one of his assistants draw up an interim agreement and prepare the requisite waivers for them to sign before the ceremony, he told them. "Until then, feel free to explore our beautiful surroundings, have a soak in the world-famous hot springs. Myself, I'm going back to my cabin for my midafternoon 'horizontal meditation,'" he added, winking broadly and bracketing the last two words with two-finger quotation marks, in case they hadn't figured out that he was going down for a nap.

4

"Braxton is a little over a hundred miles southeast of here, in Lake County," says the desk clerk. "I jotted down the directions for you. If you'd like a map, I could print you—Mr. Daniel? Is everything okay, Mr. Daniel?"

"What? Oh, everything's just fine." Except for the smirking, leathery-faced imp perched like a pet monkey on the clerk's shoulder, making washing motions with its clever little paws. "You were saying?"

"Do you need me to print you out a map to Braxton Hot Springs?"

"That won't be necessary."

"Here you go, then. And if you could sign here?"

"Sure thing." Asmador closes his eyes long enough to access

his eidetic recall, and visualizes the signature on the late Peter Daniel's Mastercard before forging it on the receipt.

The route, all state highways save for a fifteen-mile stretch of U.S. 101, is straightforward enough; the driving is anything but. The hardest part isn't so much staying on the road as it is ignoring the distractions—the blazing fields, the writhing trees, the mocking demons. For now that his system has managed to cleanse itself after three chemical restraint–free weeks, as Dr. Hillovi predicted, Asmador's two worlds are beginning to merge at a disconcerting pace.

But Asmador perseveres. By tucking in behind another car and copying its movements, he learns to tell the difference between the things you have to brake for—cows, stop signs, and railroad crossings—and the things you don't, the things the other cars drive through—capering demons, smoking geysers, and heaps of offal.

A few hours after leaving Fort Bragg, Asmador spots the turnoff for Braxton Springs Road. A blacktop driveway winds for another two and a half miles, to an unpaved lot with seven parked vehicles and no attendant. Asmador jockeys the dark green Cherokee into an empty space between an old hippie bus and a white . . . Hot damn! Could it be? Yes, it could. Out of all the vehicles in either of his worlds, Asmador has stumbled upon the same Buick he tailed and lost in San Francisco a few days ago. Epstein's Buick.

Scarcely able to believe his eyes or his luck, Asmador has to get out and run his hands wonderingly over the smooth metal curves of the car to convince himself it's real. But it is—and the hood is still warm.

5

Steve Stahl, Oliver's dour, crew-cut factotum, entered the dining hall just as Pender and Epstein were leaving. Shirtless and shoeless, wearing a terry-cloth robe over a pair of baggy surfer shorts, he held the screen door open for them, then performed an exaggerated, head-swiveling double take behind their departing backs. "Who in the name of all that's holy was that?"

"Writers. They're doing a book on the movement. They want to observe the ceremony tonight."

"You turned them down, right?" said Stahl, a retired Marine captain who also functioned as Oliver's chief son of a bitch. (Every spiritual leader has one.)

"Partially—I told them that if they wanted to stick around, they'd have to participate like everyone else."

"You're kidding! Did you *look* at them, O—there's a pair of walking buzzkills if I ever saw one."

"I'm quite aware of that, Steven. But this could be a major opportunity for the institute—the big break that moves us from the backwaters to the forefront of the movement."

Oliver lifted his cup of chai to his lips, discovered it was empty, and handed it wordlessly to Stahl, who refilled it from the gleaming stainless-steel urn on the table by the wall and brought it back to him. The guru, who preferred to be called a spiritual adviser, took a sip, nodded appreciatively, then closed his eyes. He inhaled slowly and deliberately through his nostrils, then exhaled a gentle stream of air from between his pursed lips. "So rather than send them away," he continued after a few more calming breaths, "what we need to work on is how to maximize their experience tonight while minimizing the, ah, 'buzzkill' effect, as you put it."

"How much do they actually know about the ceremony?"

"Very little."

"The sacrament?"

"I shouldn't think so."

"But you want them to take the sacrament, same as everybody else?"

The boss nodded ever so slightly. The icy blue eyes of the designated s.o.b. took on a hint of a sparkle. "Leave it to me, O."

Oliver put down his cup. "That's all I wanted to hear," he told his aide. "But, Steven?"

"Sir?"

"Be sly. I have the distinct impression that neither of them is as stupid as he looks—particularly the stupid-looking one."

"Understood," said Stahl.

"Good man," said Oliver.

6

After leaving the dining hall, Skip and Pender commandeered the golf cart for a tour of the grounds and soon discovered that Pender's cell phone was useless even at the higher elevations. They also learned that there was no practical way of securing any of the buildings, much less the surrounding wilderness area. "Instead of flanking Oliver," said Pender on their way back, "one of us'll have to keep watch on the other two at all times, from concealment, if possible."

"It should be me—I'm the better shot," Skip pointed out.

"Only if there's a good stationary vantage point—if not, it'll have to be me."

"Fair enough," said Skip, casting a longing glance at the bathhouses coming up on their left.

Pender either caught Skip's glance out of the corner of his eye or read his mind. "You want to take a dip while there's still time? I can keep an eye on Oliver."

"Why don't we take turns?"

"I'm not that big on hot tubs or saunas," Pender confessed. "They make me feel all watery in the knees. And to tell you the truth, I've never been all that comfortable taking my clothes off in mixed company."

"What's the matter, you afraid you'll get a hard-on? That hardly ever happens."

"To you, maybe," said Pender proudly.

Up the road from the Center, on the other side of the dirt lane, there were four volcanically heated springs housed in ascending order of temperature in dim, echoey, half-timbered fieldstone bathhouses the size of one-car garages. After a mandatory shower and a dip in the lower pool, Skip worked his way up to the hottest spring, where he lay alone, submerged to his chin in steaming 113°F water, listening to the plangent echoes, watching the Tinker Bells of light dancing off the azure-tiled walls, and feeling the tension and soreness of the last forty-eight hours gradually beginning to ooze out of his aching—

Skip awoke with a gasp from a half-conscious dream in which he was being attacked by a vulture, and inhaled a mouthful of sulfury-tasting water. Splashing, floundering, coughing, windmilling his arms like a drowning man, he had just succeeded in struggling to his feet when Dr. Oliver's statuesque assistant Candace appeared out of nowhere, naked as a jaybird, and began slapping him between the shoulder blades with one hand while guiding him toward the side of the pool with the other. "Just try to breathe normally."

"I'm okay, really I'm okay," protested Skip, lowering himself onto the submerged ledge that ran the circumference of the pool and patting the bandage covering the talon marks on his shoulder back into place.

Candace eased down next to him. Out of the corner of his eye, he caught a glimpse of her magnificent young breasts bobbing on the dimly sparkling, silvery gray surface of the water. "I don't want to interfere in your process," she said in her soft, imaginary-gum-chewing California accent, "and no offense intended, but you seem to be wired rilly tight for some reason."

"No, I'm fine. Just a little PTSD flashback, is all." Post-traumatic stress disorder. "I can handle it."

"Oh." Candace nodded knowingly—the Oliver Institute had held a sliding-scale retreat for troubled veterans a year earlier. "Were you in Vietnam? Is that where you hurt your leg? If you don't mind my asking."

I'd—I'd rather not talk about the war, if that's all right with you, Skip wanted to say, haltingly and humbly. Instead he told her the unglamorous truth, then quickly changed the subject. "About this thing tonight," he said. "You know, I'm not really all that clear on exactly what's supposed to happen."

She smiled and touched his forearm lightly. "Lucky you," she said. "You get to be surprised."

7

For his preliminary recon, Asmador changes into a light-colored, green-and-tan camo jumpsuit. Loping silently up the path through the woods, he refuses to be distracted by the way the forest keeps bursting into flames on either side of the path, the fresh young spring leaves dancing with pale green fire, the shafts of sunlight burning like golden pillars.

Eventually the path widens out into a one-lane dirt road with a two-story, wood-and-glass building on the left and a steaming, open-air pool farther ahead on the right. Coming directly toward him down that road is a golf cart with a striped canopy. A cart being driven by—and here an eidetic image of a blown-up fragment of text from the Book flashes through Asmador's mind as he ducks into the bushes by the side of the path—*a huge fat guy wear-ing a loud sport coat and one of those stupid little checked hats with feathers in the brim.*

Fat guy, loud jacket, checked hat—the realization scarcely has time to register before the driver pulls the cart off the road and hurries into the two-story building with the slanting roof.

Asmador can scarcely believe his luck. All three of his surviv-ing enemies—Dr. O, Epstein, Pender—gathered in one place for his convenience. It couldn't possibly be a coincidence, he tells himself—surely all hell must have been brought to bear to bring this about. And why? For the same reason he and the husband-and-wife team of bow hunters had converged on that lonely rest stop last night: to ensure that his mission will be carried out.

Asmador's first inclination is to wait for Pender to emerge again, then put an arrow through him. But crouching in the bushes with his laminated bow drawn and a carbon-shafted arrow nocked, Asmador has time to mull over the probable consequences. Sure, he could kill Pender easily enough from here (unless he misses his shot: there is always that possibility). But that would put the other two on alert, and soon the place would be crawling with cops. Maybe he'd get a second shot from cover at either Epstein or Dr. O during the confusion, maybe he wouldn't; maybe he'd have time to make it back to the Cherokee, maybe he wouldn't.

But the powers below haven't gone to all the trouble of arrang-ing this miraculous confluence in order to have him pick off one victim at the cost of losing the other two, Asmador decides. No, it would be better to—

A scratching, scurrying sound breaks Asmador's train of thought. He wheels, draws back the bowstring, aims downward at a forty-degree angle, and releases the arrow in one smooth, continuous motion. It sizzles through the shimmering, green-and-gold-dappled air and with a solid *thwack!* pins something furry, a large chipmunk or a small squirrel, to the base of a tree with mossy gray bark a good ten or fifteen yards away.

Or maybe missing *isn't* always a possibility, Asmador tells himself as he approaches the still twitching critter. By the time he reaches it, the light has drained from its eyes. The little body looks like an empty sack of fur—the arrow, rated for a much larger mammal, has done an astounding amount of damage.

"Ouch," Asmador squeaks aloud, as if speaking for the tiny creature—for him, that's about as close to empathy as it gets.

8

After dropping off Skip, Pender continued on to the Center and parked the cart where he'd found it. He hopped down and buttoned his sport coat to cover his shoulder holster before entering.

The dining hall was cool and dim; the paneled walls and varnished trestle tables gave off a buttery, honey-brown glow. "Anybody home?" called Pender.

"Back here in the kitchen."

The crew-cut, bathrobe-clad man Pender had passed in the doorway earlier was standing with his back to the room, washing a bunch of dusky red grapes in the big industrial sink. "Hi. Where's Dr. Oliver?"

"In his cabin. Why?"

"I, uh, I just wanted to ask him a few questions about tonight's ceremony."

Leaving the grapes in a colander to drain, Steve dried his hands on a dish towel, then turned and extended his hand to Pender. "You're Ed, right?"

"Right as rain."

They shook hands. Stahl, who stood a sturdy-looking five-ten, with a weathered complexion that accentuated the arctic blue of his eyes, had a firm grip, but his hand was lost in Pender's huge paw. "I'm Steve. I can answer any questions you may have."

"Okay, sure," said Pender. "How about a quick summary of what's going to go down tonight?"

"We're going to meet upstairs at five o'clock. O's going to introduce you to everybody, then lead a breathing exercise. After that, we'll hike up into the hills, to a clearing known as the Omphalos, where O will lead everybody in a Bodhisattva vow. Then comes the, uh, sacrament, then everybody chants for a while, then we head up to the bluff to watch the sunset. Then more chanting and meditation, and around ten o'clock we come back here and usually everybody dances or meditates or whatever until dawn."

Pender had not missed the quick sideways flicker of Stahl's eyes or the hesitation that preceded the word *sacrament*. "Tell me more about this sacrament," he prompted. "What exactly does it involve?"

"A single grape, a crouton, and a drink of springwater," said Stahl, without making eye contact.

Is he that bad a liar, Pender wondered, *or is he trying to give me a heads-up here?* "I see. And of those three items, which one is spiked?"

Stahl's frosty eyes narrowed and his thin lips tightened. Then he sighed an unmistakable I-guess-you-got-me sigh. "Everybody else knows about it, so I guess there's no reason you shouldn't. But just to cover my ass, let's make it a hypothetical, okay?"

"That'll work."

"Okay, let's say there was a group of people doing a ceremony that involved taking a substance that might not be technically legal but in the proper setting, under the proper guidance, would help them reach a higher state of consciousness—you know, kind of open the doors of perception, as Huxley put it. Are you with me so far?"

Pender nodded—he could always ask Skip who this Huxley was, if it turned out to be important.

"Excellent. Now let's say maybe one person was nervous about the substance-taking part of it, or just didn't feel like he or she was ready for that. Still with me?"

"Still with you."

"Okay, do you know what I'd advise that person?"

"I'm all ears."

"I'd say, Don't eat the crouton. Got it? Do not . . . eat . . . the crouton."

"Loud and clear," said Pender. "I appreciate the heads-up."

"Glad to help," said Stahl, who waited until Pender was gone before turning back to the wet grapes, which he now began to dry with a clean dish towel, one at a time, as carefully and painstakingly as if they were precious gems, or little baby eyeballs.

CHAPTER FOUR

1

Around five o'clock, Steve Stahl wrestled a six-foot-long didgeri-doo out the screen door of the Center, took a deep breath, puffed out his cheeks, and blew a series of long, deep-toned, peritoneum-tingling *hawaughhh*s that resounded the length and breadth of Braxton Hot Springs. Then he rejoined Skip, Pender, Dr. Oliver, and Candace, who were watching from the glass-enclosed second story as the trainees converged on the building, strolling down the dirt road or climbing the lightly wooded slope leading up from the campground in the woods behind the Center. They were all dressed in comfortable-looking cotton meditation outfits similar to those worn by Oliver and his aides, and carried coats and sweaters over their arms.

Laughing and chattering, the trainees climbed the open-treaded spiral staircase to the second floor, where sage and sandalwood incense burned in bowls and a small boom box played a CD of ethereal Steve Reich space music. Fat, round meditation pillows known as zafus were already arranged in a circle; the atmosphere was intense, charged with nervous energy as the trainees took their places.

"Namasté," said Dr. Oliver, seating himself cross-legged on a white zafu with an incense bowl and a small silver bell in front of it. His meditation pajamas were white, Steve and Candace wore royal blue, and the ten trainees were dressed in pale orange.

"Namasté," the others echoed, lightly pressing their palms and fingers together in a prayerful mudra.

"It's so good to see your shining faces. Let's take a few calming breaths, taking in peace through the nostrils, letting out ego through the mouth. Eyes shut? Here we go . . ."

Pender had seated himself next to Oliver. Skip was sitting directly across the circle, his good leg folded and his withered leg outstretched, with the toe of his built-up shoe pointing straight up. He opened his eyes after a few seconds, caught Pender looking back at him, and winked.

After the breathing exercise, Oliver introduced the newcomers to the group, then asked the trainees to introduce themselves. First up was Beryl, an elderly, bird-boned woman, her face as wrinkled as a dried apple. Juana was a buxom Argentinean in her mid-forties, with a round brown face and a toasty smile. Then came Michael, a pale, thirtyish commodities trader, and next to him was a man named Jonah, wearing dark-rimmed glasses he was constantly adjusting.

In addition to the four single trainees, there were three couples. George Speaks, a Native American college professor with a broad Eskimo-looking face and a long black braid, was seated next to his wife, Layla, who had sleepy eyes and a soft Southern accent. Elaine and Marty, both lawyers, had pronounced New York accents. Tom and Mitch were a fit and handsome gay couple in their mid-thirties.

When they'd finished, Oliver thanked the group. "*Good* job, everyone," he said, sounding a little like a kindergarten teacher. "And now, unless anybody has any last-minute questions or concerns . . . ?" His eyes traveled clockwise around the circle. "Yes, Beryl?"

"I'm not sure I can do this, Dr. O," she said, wringing her bony hands nervously. "I—I thought I could, but I'm . . . well, I'm scared. That's the plain truth of it: I'm scared."

"Okay, I get that," Oliver responded mildly. "And the first thing I need you to understand is that nobody here is going to force you to do anything you're not ready to do. But may I ask you a question?"

"Please."

"Which 'I' is it that's scared?" Air quotes around the pronoun. "Is it the 'I' that thinks it's still a helpless infant, dependent on others for its very survival? Or is it the 'I' who's a full-grown, capable, adult human being who for over seventy years has succeeded in handling anything and everything the universe has seen fit to throw at her with such admirable grace and courage?"

The answer came in the form of a shy, pleased schoolgirlish smile.

"Yeah, that's what I thought," said Oliver, beaming. "Now who's ready to let go and let God?"

A chorus of assent: "Me!" "Yay!" "I am!" "Ya-hoo!"

"Al-*hum*-dilly-la!" Oliver clapped his hands together sharply, then rose, picked up his zafu, crossed the circle, helped Beryl to her feet, and offered her his arm. Together they started down the spiral staircase, with the others following. Skip and Pender trailed behind.

"Locked and loaded?" whispered Pender.

"Locked and loaded," said Skip.

"And what don't we do?"

"We don't eat the crouton."

2

Asmador awakes from his short, marijuana-assisted nap in the back of the Cherokee. The razzle-dazzle of late afternoon sunlight glinting off the cars makes the little parking lot look as though it were ablaze with brightly colored stars.

Driving up from the county road earlier that day, Asmador had noticed that the line of telephone poles by the side of the winding driveway ended at the parking lot. The highest aerial wire, a power line with ceramic insulators, descended the last pole and burrowed itself into the earth; the lower wire led to a rusty, gray-painted metal box mounted on the pole beneath a sign instructing those in need to call for assistance.

Asmador opens the cabinet, which encloses a telephone handset wired into a single line that exits through a hole in the bottom of the cabinet before disappearing underground. He slices through the wire above the box with the serrated inner edge of Peter Daniel's hunting knife, then punctures all four tires on every vehicle save the Cherokee.

Having done what he can to buy himself time to complete the mission, Asmador changes into a night-camo jumpsuit, splotchy blacks and grays with elasticized waist and cuffs, blacks his face and white sneakers, jams all the gear that will fit, including the night-vision goggles, into the backpack, and fills the built-in, hard-walled quiver with an assortment of arrows.

"Wish me luck, Pocket Pal," he calls to the starlings perched on the telephone wire. From behind him comes the sound of mocking laughter. He turns to see Sammael sitting cross-legged on the roof of the Cherokee, jingling a set of car keys. Asmador reaches for them; the redhead pulls one of his vanishing acts. But to Asmador's considerable relief, when he peers through the window of the Cherokee, he sees the keys dangling from the ignition; the door, fortunately, is unlocked.

"Thank you," he calls sheepishly, locking the car and pocketing the keys; not surprisingly, the only response is a burst of disembodied laughter.

3

The little procession, with Dr. Oliver marching in front and Skip bringing up the rear in the golf cart, followed a dirt trail bordered with spring-green poison oak that led uphill through a transition forest of red aspens, mountain alders, graceful poplars, fragrant-leaved bay laurels, and mossy live oaks so gnarled and ancient they looked almost sentient.

After marching for half an hour, Oliver turned off the main trail at an arrow-shaped wooden signpost pointing the way to something called the Omphalos. The side trail was too narrow for the cart, so Skip abandoned it at the turnoff and limped after the others on foot, down a rocky path that hugged the base of a shaley cliff for a hundred yards or so. Then it took a sharp downhill right turn and opened out onto a perfectly round, enchanted-looking clearing surrounded by a grove of quaking aspens that whispered and shimmered in the faint breeze.

"Welcome to Omphalos, the navel of the world," Oliver boomed, in a voice that echoed around the clearing. "Let's see if we can form a circle as perfect as the one nature made here."

While the others arranged their zafus on the springy, cloverlike ground cover, Skip and Pender discussed the security arrangements. Because there was no vantage point from which Skip could keep a stationary watch, they agreed that he should stay as close to Oliver as possible while Pender kept an eye out for Charlie Mesker from the cover of the trees. "And remember," Pender added—

"Don't eat the crouton. Yeah, I know."

*   *   *

Circles within circles. The pellucid sky; the round earth; the magical clearing; the circle of seekers seated cross-legged, tailor fashion, or in half- or full lotuses as their joints permitted. Oliver jingled his little silver bell and instructed them to listen for the farthest sound. As the throbbing echo of the bell died away, Skip became aware of the papery rustling of aspen leaves, the harsh cawing of crows, and the melodic call of some unseen songbird.

Twice more, Oliver rang the bell; twice more they listened for the farthest sound. Then Oliver led them in the bodhisattva vow: "We dedicate this journey we are about to take . . ."

"We dedicate this journey we are about to take . . ."

"To the spiritual advancement . . ."

"To the spiritual advancement . . ."

"Of all humanity . . ."

"Of all humanity . . ."

"And we pledge never to rest . . ."

"And we pledge never to rest . . ."

"Until all sentient beings . . ."

"Until all sentient beings . . ."

"Have reached Nirvana . . ."

"Have reached Nirvana."

"*Svaha!*" Oliver clapped his hands together sharply.

"*Svaha!*" Fourteen sets of hands clapped in ragged, imperfect unison, like a firing squad.

After administering the vow, Oliver went around the inside of the circle from trainee to trainee, trailed closely by Steve, bearing a filigreed silver tray, and Candace, whose job it was to set out upon the salver a grape, a crouton, and a fluted paper cup the size of a shot glass, which she refilled at every stop with a draft of clear water from a purple thermos.

One by one, the celebrants ate of the fruit and the grain, then drank the water—except of course for Pender and Skip, who drank the water and popped down the grape, but surreptitiously palmed the crouton, then tossed it away when no one was looking.

After Oliver and his two acolytes had themselves partaken of the sacrament, the guru resumed his place in the circle and led the others in a chant, *"Gaté Gaté, Paragaté, Parasamgaté, Bodhi Svaha,"* providing his own simultaneous translation from the Sanskrit.

"Gaté Gaté: that means, go on, go on. *Paragaté:* go further. *Parasamgaté:* go even further. *Bodhi:* to enlightenment. *Svaha:* amen, so be it."

Over and over they chanted the ancient formula—*"Gaté Gaté, Paragaté, Parasamgaté, Bodhi Svaha"*—while dust motes danced in the dappled light, and the trees rustled, and the birds sang, and the sun cast its honeyed glow over the meadow, until eventually time lost meaning and the chant began chanting them. *Gaté Gaté,* whispered the aspen leaves. Go on, go on.

And awaayyy Skip went. After the first few dozen repetitions of the prayer, he began experiencing a euphoric sense of belonging. Looking around the circle, he felt as if he were seeing the others, really *seeing* each of them, or any human being, for that matter, for the first time. Then after a few dozen more repetitions, Skip began playing tricks with their faces. He discovered that if he stared hard enough he could, for instance, turn beaming Oliver, with his bushy beard and broad, benevolent visage, into Aslan, the golden-eyed lion from the Narnia books, or transform the head of the fey, elderly Beryl into one of those wrinkled old Pennsylvania Dutch apple dolls.

But messing around with faces proved to be a dangerous experiment. Somewhere between the zillionth *gaté* and *svaha,* Skip lost the ability to change them back. From then on he could only watch in horror as the features began to shift and change on their own, melting and blurring and eventually sloughing away entirely, until all that remained was the grinning armature of the skull beneath the perishable flesh.

And finally, much too late, it dawned on him that he'd been

dosed. Seriously. With acid, most likely, and plenty of it. Don't panic, he cautioned himself as the skull-headed creature that had once been Candace beamed across the circle at him. It's not like you've never tripped before.

But something's different this time . . . danger . . . something wicked . . . this way . . .

No! Don't do it, don't go there, Skip warned himself, closing his eyes and covering his face with his hands. It's only the acid. That's what you're supposed to tell yourself when you start freaking: it's only the acid.

But there's something out there!

No! You took some acid and in a few hours everything will be back to normal.

But—

No! Say it: I took some acid . . .

I took some acid . . .

And in a few hours . . .

And in a few hours . . .

Everything will be back to normal.

Everything will be back to—Aw, fuck it.

Because it didn't work. In the infinite darkness behind Skip's eyelids, concepts like *hours* and *normal* were equally meaningless. And there *was* something evil out there, some . . . some rough beast slouching—

Suddenly, with his eyes still firmly shut, he visualized Asmador, with the head of a vulture and the body of a man, loping through the forest, getting closer, closer . . .

Hearing someone moaning pitifully, Skip was nearly overcome with compassion. Somebody help him, he thought. Won't somebody *please* help that poor bastard.

4

It didn't take long for Pender to grow bored with the chanting. Nor could he shake the mounting sense of dread that came with sitting in an open clearing, surrounded by a dark forest, hearing God knows what all rustling in the underbrush. He felt like a sacrificial goat tethered to a stake, listening for the tiger's approach.

Opening his eyes to peek around the circle, he saw that everyone else had their eyes firmly closed, even Skip, whose eyelids were twitching like a dreaming dog's. He remembered an old joke about the moribund shopkeeper whose family had all gathered around his deathbed. *So who's watching the store?* was the punch line.

Special Agent E. L. Goddamn Pender, that's who, he told himself, climbing to his feet. Glancing downward while dusting off the seat of his slacks, he experienced a peculiar sort of Alice-in-Wonderland effect. His Hush Puppies appeared to be much smaller and farther away looking than he was accustomed to, as if his legs had grown absurdly elongated.

It only lasted a second; when he looked again, his lower extremities had resumed their customary proportions. But something still wasn't right. Time, or his memory, started missing beats, skipping like an old vinyl record. He had no memory, for instance, of leaving the circle or crossing the clearing. But here he was, hiding behind a tree at the edge of the woods.

Then out of the confusion, a burst of clarity. *Asmador,* Pender reminded himself with an effort, *don't forget Asmador.* From where he crouched in the underbrush, he could see clear across the field to the gap in the trees that marked the trailhead. But what were the odds Charlie "Asmador" Mesker would come waltzing down the path in plain sight? *Slim to none,* as Sheriff Hartung used to say, *and I don't see no nuns around here.*

No, if he'd been smart enough to escape capture thus far,

Mesker would certainly be smart enough to cut off the trail long before he came into sight of the clearing, then circle around and approach the clearing from clover—No, cover! From cover. They don't even rhyme, those words. *Cover* and *clover.* Lots more songs about clover though. *Roll me over in the clover do it again.* And *I'm looking over a four-leaf clover.* Or, as they used to sing when he was a kid, *I'm looking over my dead dog Rover, Who lies on the bathroom floor. One leg's broken, the other one's lame, Dah-dah-dah-dah, He got run over by a railroad train.*

Pender's mind wandered back to 1952 Cortland, he and his gang playing soldiers in the woods, wearing plastic G.I. helmets and gunning down Japs with their Daisy rifles. *Bang! I got you! No, I got you first. Lie down, you're dead. No, you lie down, you're—*

A crackling in the brush wrenched Pender back to the present. *What's the* matter *with you?* he asked himself. *Can't you concentrate on the job at hand for five goddamn minutes without . . . drifting . . .*

Looking around, he realized suddenly that he could no longer see the clearing. Everywhere he looked, every direction he turned, three hundred and sixty degrees of trees, trees, and more trees, stretching outward to infinity. Pender held his breath, listening, and heard the forest—or was it the universe?—breathing all around him, expanding with every inhale, shrinking with every exhale. When he looked down again, his feet were so tiny and far away he could hardly see them.

And that's when it occurred to him that he'd been drugged, involuntarily dosed with LSD. Suddenly he was afraid, more afraid than he'd ever been, except for when he'd nearly blinded himself with a firecracker when he was a kid. This was worse, though, because not only was he afraid, he was afraid of *being* afraid.

But you didn't eat the crouton, his mind protested. *You never even had it near your mouth.*

Which meant what? That Stahl had played him like a Stradivarius. Don't eat the crouton? Ha! The crouton was a straw man, a red herring. A red straw herring man. Because the LSD was in the grape or the water—that was the *how* of it. As for the *why,* Pender realized with a sad, sinking sensation that it didn't really matter. *Stahl, you stupid fuck,* he thought, more in sorrow than in anger. *You stupid, stupid fuck.*

5

The humans are gone. But they haven't passed him on his way up from the parking lot. Therefore, Asmador reasons, they must have gone in the other direction. And when he hunkers down outside the two-story building and squints up the dirt road, he notices that the surface is scuffed with sneaker and sandal prints, all pointing uphill. And cutting vertically down the center of the road are two lines of tire tracks too thick for bicycles but too close together for an automobile—they must have been left by the golf cart he'd seen Pender driving earlier.

Confident that he'll be able to hear or scent the humans long before they hear or scent him, Asmador makes no attempt to conceal his presence as he follows their trail up into the forest, his stiflingly hot night-camo jumpsuit unzipped to the waist. Occasionally he practices reaching behind his back, drawing an arrow from the quiver, nocking it, and drawing the bowstring back to his cheek in one slick, effortless motion, without slowing his pace.

He never lets a practice arrow fly, however, because based on the number of footprints he'd seen before the road narrowed and the tracks went single file, there appear to be a whole herd of humans shuffling along ahead of him. If they stay all bunched up, he realizes, he may have need of every arrow in his quiver. But oh, how happy the vultures would be—Asmador hasn't entirely forgotten about the vultures.

In fact, he is finding it increasingly easy to concentrate his

mind as the day progresses. He hasn't seen a demon all afternoon, and although things are still kind of squirmy out on the
edge of his vision, as if the tree limbs were hung with writhing
snakes and worms, when he swivels his head to look directly at
them, they turn back into ordinary trees just as meekly as you
please.

The first indication that he's caught up to the humans is a
glimpse of blue-and-yellow fabric winking into view on the far
side of a meander in the path. Asmador ducks behind a tree, peers
around the trunk, and recognizes the striped circus tent canopy of
Pender's abandoned golf cart.

The key, conveniently enough, is in the ignition. As Asmador
slips it into one of the jumpsuit's many pockets, his ears pick up
the eerie, inhuman sound of humans chanting. It seems to be
coming from the direction in which the arrow-shaped wooden sign
is pointing.

But instead of following the sound of the chanting, Asmador
edges past the cart and continues up the main trail, hoping that, as
the path climbs, it will lead him to a vantage point from which he
can look down upon the humans and, in the remaining daylight,
work out the best way to hunt them down and pick them off later,
when it's dark.

6

Feeling a tender hand stroking his forehead, Skip opened his
eyes and found himself lying on his back with his head in Anna's
lap, posing for the Pietà. But when she smiled down at him, light
streaming around her round, light brown face, he realized this
wasn't Anna, who was dead, but Juana, who was alive. Only there
wasn't really any difference, because they were all made of the

same . . . stuff. And death wasn't real, either—it couldn't be, because time wasn't real.

"Wow," he breathed reverently. He wanted to tell Anna/Juana so many things. How he felt as if he'd been away for eons, flying through other universes; how he'd seen terrible and wonderful sights; how he'd learned all these important lessons about life and death, time and eternity, fear and wonder, and why they call a trip a trip. He also wanted to tell her how great it felt to be back, but when he opened his mouth, all that came out was another, longer "Wow."

He looked past Juana and saw that Oliver, Steve, and Candace had gathered around and were looking down at him all relieved and happy like the farmhands at the end of *The Wizard of Oz*. Then he remembered how he'd seen Oliver turn into a lion. How mind-blowingly perfect and interconnected everything was.

But that's acid for you. Like existence, only more so. Skip spent the last hour of full daylight in a state of pure cosmic bliss. Colors were otherworldly bright in that sun-kissed clearing, and human contact profound. They took off their tops, even the women—even old Beryl—and worshiped the sun, whose light was everywhere broken into crystalline prisms and streaming rainbows; they turned druid and bowed to the whispering aspens; they found the keys to koans that had stumped generations of seekers. The answer to "What is the sound of one hand clapping?" was *Schwingggg!* The perfect answer to "What was your face before your mother was born?" was, for some obscure reason, *Larry*.

As the sun neared the treetops, Oliver asked everyone to join him on a hike up to a bluff where they could celebrate the sunset by performing something called a Bija ceremony. The others cheered, but Skip's heart sank. To him, *hike* was just a four-letter word. He'd tried hiking before, and it was hard to say which he hated more, the pain of struggling to keep up or the anxiety and sense of abandonment he experienced when he inevitably fell behind.

Maybe it would be different this time, though, with these people. And besides, it seemed to Skip that there was a reason he needed to go with them, needed to keep Oliver in sight. The same reason why the sky seemed to darken when he thought about staying behind, alone. Something about—

But his new friends had gathered up their zafus and flashlights and jackets to follow their teacher up the rocky, uneven path leading back to the marked trail. Skip found his tan jacket folded neatly on his zafu. He put it on and zipped it up, vaguely aware that *something* was missing but unable to remember what it was. Then a nice thing happened. George Speaks, the American Indian with the Eskimo features and the long black braid, doubled back to present Skip with an aspen-limb staff, its bark and leaves stripped away to make a stout, smooth-skinned walking stick that fit Skip's hand so perfectly it might have been cut to his measure.

Skip was so moved by the gesture that he clean forgot all about . . . whatever it was he'd been trying to remember. Leaning gratefully on the staff as he hurried to catch up with the procession, he heard someone behind him calling his name. He turned at the edge of the clearing, puzzled—how could anyone be behind him when everyone was in front of him?—and saw a big, bearlike figure in a little tweed hat emerging from the trees on the far side of the clearing. The sharply angled sunlight made his dark red sport coat look as if it were glowing.

It took another instant for the name to come—*Pender!* he thought. *You forgot all about Pender!*—and another few seconds for the larger implications to register. As soon as he remembered who Pender was and why the two of them were there, Skip reached behind his back for the Beretta in his holster. His empty holster.

So that's *what was missing before,* thought Skip, as Pender charged toward him through the clover, holding his hat with one hand and waving at him with the other. Halfway across the clearing, though, Pender stumbled, seemed to catch his balance, then collapsed heavily to the ground with a feather-tipped arrow shaft sticking out of his left rib cage.

Skip started toward him, then glimpsed a black-clad figure with a bow silhouetted in profile between two thin, now sunlit aspens on the far side of the clearing. He hit the deck as an arrow sizzled over his head, so close to his scalp that if his hair had been any longer, it would now be parted straight down the center.

7

One down, two to go, thinks Asmador. It should have been three down, none to go—he knows now that not waiting until dark was a mistake. And he'd meant to wait, he really had. But when Pender had come trotting out of the trees less than twenty yards away from where Asmador stood watching, bow in hand, it had felt to Asmador as if the bow had taken on a will of its own. It had shifted to the right, made allowances for yardage and windage, led the lumbering target by the width of the arrowhead. All Asmador had had to do was pull the bowstring and release it, and down went Pender with a steel-tipped, large-mammal-rated arrow sticking heart-high out of the left side of his sport jacket.

But to Asmador's dismay, his hurried second arrow had overshot the next target, Epstein, by a hairbreadth, and Epstein had disappeared into the underbrush before Asmador could nock a third.

But the odds are still in his favor, he reminds himself as he circles around the periphery of the clearing, heading for a gully he'd seen earlier from his vantage point on the cliff overlooking the aspen grove. By following the gully, which rejoined the main trail below the cutoff leading to the clearing, he can block the humans' avenue of retreat. Then it will only be a matter of keeping the herd in front of him while he singles out his targets. Which shouldn't be difficult—with his limp, Epstein is classic predator prey, and as for Dr. O in his white pajamas, Asmador doesn't think he'll even need the infrared goggles to spot *him* in the dark.

And then what? Stay and pick off as many of the others as there are arrows in his quiver, and leave them for the vultures to find tomorrow? Or perhaps he'll somehow be magically transported back to the Blasted Land the moment the mission is complete, to take up his seat on the Concilium Infernalis.

8

When Skip reached the junction where the rocky path rejoined the marked trail, Oliver and the others were nowhere in sight. Spotting the golf cart by the side of the path was like seeing an old friend—if only the key had been in the ignition. Skip vaguely remembered having left it there, but with five hundred mikes of windowpane short-circuiting his synapses, fine points like that were scarcely worth the energy it took to process them.

So he continued up the trail on foot, leaning proudly on his fine, stout staff, while the universe throbbed slowly and majestically around him, *gnong-gnong-gnong,* like somebody'd struck an invisible gong the size of the moon. Through breaks in the patchy overhead canopy, the sky took on a bubblegum pink glow. An exquisite hush fell over the forest. Listening for the farthest sound, Skip heard the distant, dying echoes of a silvery bell. *Ring it again,* he thought, leaning on his staff, cupping his ear, and turning like a radar dish. Obediently, the bell rang again, faintly. By the third ring, Skip had oriented his body in the direction of the ringing—say, two o'clock, if twelve o'clock was straight ahead—and veered off the trail to follow the sound through the woods.

The going was slow and difficult. *If only I had a machete,* Skip thought, clubbing back the hungry branches and hindering brush with his walking stick. Then he had to laugh at himself. *As long as you're wishing, why not wish for a backhoe?*

Skip almost turned back a few times. All that drove him on was his determination to find the others, warn them, somehow get them to safety. Or should he disperse them instead, send them scattering into the woods in a game of mortal hide-and-go-seek? *Pender would know what to do,* thought Skip—then he remembered that Pender was stretched out in the middle of the Omphalos with an arrow sticking out of his side.

"I'm sorry," he said aloud, tears blurring his vision as he stumbled onward through the sharp-shadowed, green-gold maze of the forest at sunset, stopping only to wipe the sweat from his eyes with the sleeve of his zippered jacket. "I'm sorry, I'm sorry, I'm *so* fucking— Oh. Wow. Far out."

In his blundering, Skip had finally intercepted a well-trodden path that led uphill toward the spooky chanting sound that he'd been listening to for some time without actually hearing it—or was it the other way around?

Didn't matter. All that mattered now was following the path until it opened out onto a rocky, arrowhead-shaped bluff where his new friends sat in a semicircle with their backs to him, chanting *"Vaj-ra, Vaj-ra, Vaj-ra"* as the sun sank behind a jagged, tree-lined ridge.

The western sky was streaked with every red, yellow, and orange color in the Crayola box—the big box—and the air was still and green as Skip crossed the bluff and knelt behind the massive, white-clad figure in the middle of the semicircle. "Glad you could make it," Oliver said over his shoulder as the others continued the chant. "Where's Ed?"

"Dead," Skip whispered urgently, his voice sounding slow and wobbly in his ears, like a half-melted audiotape. "Asmador shot him with an arrow. We need to get everybody out of here right now."

"Calm down, son," whispered Oliver. Then, louder, "It's all right, everybody. Just keep chanting while Skip and I have a chat." He rose so nimbly from his half-lotus position that he appeared to have levitated, took Skip firmly by the elbow, and led him away from the others. "Now listen to me, Skip," he said, gently, insistently. "You need to know that you've taken some LSD and you're probably having some hallucinations."

Oh lordy, thought Skip. *How do I make this real to him? Where do I even begin?* "I know I'm tripping. I'm tripping my freakin' brains out."

"Yes, that's right."

"*Please*, man, would you *please* stop treating me like I'm fucking retarded. There *is* danger. It's *real,* it's *really, really* real."

"I hear you, Skip," said Oliver. "I want you to know I hear you, and I understand the danger *seems* real, but—"

"Luke Sweet."

Under other circumstances, Oliver's jaw-dropping, eye-popping double take would have been comical. "Luke Sweet?"

And now that I've got your attention, thought Skip. "Listen up, here's the deal . . ."

However long it took for Skip to get the whole story out (by then the whole concept of time seemed like a bad joke the universe had decided to play upon the human race), when he'd finished, Oliver nodded decisively, turned on his sandaled heels, and hurried back to the semicircle of sunset chanters.

"*Svaha,*" he shouted, clapping his hands together loudly, then spreading them outward in benediction. "*Good* job, everybody. What I need all of you to do now, I need you to head back to the Center. Steve, if you wouldn't mind leading the way? And Candace, if you'd follow to make sure no one falls behind?"

"What about you, O?" Stahl seemed to realize that something was wrong—but then, he was tripping his freakin' brains out, too. They all were.

"Skip and I will catch up," Oliver said reassuringly.

"Catch up, we will?" whispered Skip, channeling Yoda for some reason. The color was beginning to drain from the sky; the trainees were wandering about, dazedly gathering up their things.

Oliver shrugged. "You did say we're the ones this Asmador is after, didn't you? No sense putting the others in jeopardy along with us."

Skip was impressed. "I hadn't thought of that."

"I know, that's my job." Oliver rested his smooth, pink hand on Skip's shoulder. "It's a shepherd thing."

By then, the two were alone on the bluff—Oliver's flock had disappeared into the woods, scampering blithely down the trail Skip had just come up, and singing "Row, Row, Row Your Boat" in a ragged round. Merrily, merrily, merrily, merrily, life is but a dream . . .

No shit, thought Skip. Then he must have spaced out for a while, because the next thing he knew, he was being jerked back to what passed for consciousness by a great commotion—stampeding footsteps, crackling brush, people shouting, sobbing. He turned in time to see the trainees boiling out of the woods in a panicky, tangled mass, looking back over their shoulders as they ran, stumbling and falling over one another, their orange clothes pale apricot in the fading light.

Last out were George and Candace; between them they were hauling Steve Stahl by the arms. His body was limp, his bare heels were scraped and bleeding from dragging the rocky ground, and sticking out from the chest of his royal blue shirt was an aluminum shaft with feathers on one end and blood on the other.

9

The shortcut, obviously, had been a success. Asmador had regained the marked trail a quarter mile below the sign pointing to the Omphalos, long before the humans could possibly have reached it. To make sure, he'd knelt to examine the tracks again, and had been pleased to discover that those few footprints that could still be distinguished in the trampled dirt all pointed uphill.

By then, the sun was working Technicolor wonders in the west. The sky in that direction, what little Asmador had been able to see of it through the leafy canopy, had turned pink, shot through with bloody streaks of crimson. Nearer the ground the air seemed to have taken on an eerie goblin green glow. He'd marched on, lightly tapping the ground with the springy, curved tip of the bow every few steps, while chanting the names of the Infernal Council:

> *Furcalor, Hornblas, Satan, Rosier,*
> *Lucifer, Xaphan, Succor, Dozier.*
> *Astaroth, Azazel, Abadon, Moloch,*
> *Paimon, Rimmon, Kobadon, Misroch.*
> *Exael—*

Hearing the sound of human voices a little farther up the trail, Asmador had ducked off the side of the path to count them off as they hiked by. There'd been twelve altogether, ten in orange bracketed by two in blue. But no Oliver and no Epstein. Turning his back on the trail, Asmador had plunged deeper into the woods, circling downhill in his stealthy half crouch until he'd cut ahead of the humans again. Then he'd showed himself, stepping into the middle of a straight, tunnel-like stretch of trail and assuming the classic archer's position.

The blue shirt in the lead had braked and spread his arms wide to shield the ones behind him with his body. "Let's turn around, troopers," he'd called calmly over his shoulder. "Candy, take them—"

Asmador still wasn't sure whether he had released the arrow or it had released itself. Either way, it had felt *so* right and *so* preordained, the twang of the bowstring, the *zzzzip* of the arrow, the dull thump of the arrowhead striking home, the faint, shivering vibration of the feathers at the end of the shaft. Then the target had collapsed backward, and all was chaos at the other end of the tunnel, and all was calm at Asmador's end. Coolly, he had reached behind his back for another arrow, but by then the humans had fled screaming up the trail, the last two dragging Blue Shirt's body between them.

And now it is nearly dark under the trees; the undersides of the leaves are black against the violet gray of the sky. Asmador shucks off his backpack, returns the unused arrow to the quiver, and rummages around for the night-vision goggles. It takes him a few minutes to figure out how to work them. There are two switches, one to activate the goggles and the other to turn on the narrow infrared beam mounted above the eyepieces, which focus like binoculars. He soon gets the hang of it, though, and sets off up the trail again, following the bobbing neon green shaft of light up the glowing neon green tunnel, and taking up the singsong chant where he'd left off earlier:

Exael, Mastema, Beliar, Carnivean,
Minos, Asmodeus, Belial, Leviathan.
Beleth, Beelzebub, Behemoth, Baal,
Adramelech, Gressil, Hauras, Rofocale . . .

1Ø

At first there is no *I.* No self, no other. No here, no there. Just: *is.* But what *is? It* is. And what *is* this *it* that *is?* It is: *green.*

And with that first concept, the concept of *green,* the words, the ideas, follow one upon the other. Green is a color. A field of color. A field of clover. *I* am in a field of clover. But what is *I? I* is . . . *seeing. I* is . . . *thinking. I* is . . . *I* am . . .

I am! Here! Now!

And so what if I can't remember my name, he thought, lying on his side in the damp, sweet-smelling clover, resting his head on his outstretched arm and gradually drifting back like a cosmic jellyfish into the warm, black, amniotic sea of no self, no other, and no problems, pal, no problems whatsoever.

CHAPTER FIVE

1

"Over here, everybody!" called Skip, hunkering down next to Oliver. Behind them Beryl, a retired nurse, was crouched over Steve, crooning at him to hang on, telling him everything was going to be okay, which Skip, hearing the breath bubbling in Steve's lungs, rather doubted.

"Gather round, kids, we haven't much time," Oliver began, when the trainees who were more or less functional had finished rounding up the ones who weren't. Of the once glorious sunset, there remained only a few streaks of pale yellow melting regretfully into the gray sky. "There is a sick man out there, an armed man with a troubled mind, who wants to do us harm."

He paused, glancing around at the others like a quarterback

in a huddle. They were all rapt—stoned and rapt. "So here's what we're going to do. We're going to play a game we all played when we were children. It's called hide-and-seek, and we're going to play it like our lives depended on it. We're going to split up, and we're going to hide in the woods, separately if possible. Don't bunch up, and most of all, stay off the trail—*off* the trail, because that's where the danger is. Everybody got that?"

There were a few murmured assents; the rest of the cosmic rangers were too stunned or too high to respond.

"Good, good. So let's go now, let's split up. Find the best hidey-hole you can, and *stay* in it, stay in it until you hear some-one calling—" And here he lowered his voice to a whisper, "until you hear someone calling 'Ollee ollee in free.' Even if it takes all night. No matter what you hear, no matter what you see, you stay in hiding until somebody calls 'Ollee ollee in free.' We can do this, people—I know we can do this. Now off you go."

Nobody moved.

"Please—go! Now!" Oliver rose from his squat and made shoo-ing motions, until at last the group began to disperse. By then the sky had faded from gray to starry black, the night wind had begun to rise, and the leaves were whispering and murmuring like the hungry ghosts of Buddhist mythology.

2

It was a little frightening, being unable to remember one's name. But it was also somehow liberating, like having been relieved of a heavy, lifelong burden. He foresaw that when his name did come back to him, he would regret the loss of this unaccustomed buoy-ancy, this lightness of being.

Unless of course he was dead. That seemed like a distinct possibility, since there seemed to be an arrow sticking out of his side. But there was no blood, and little pain beyond a mild soreness in his ribs and a slight aching in his head, probably from striking the ground when he fell. So he ripped open the sport jacket pinned to his side and discovered that the arrowhead penetrating the leather safety flap of his shoulder holster had lodged in the trigger guard of the pistol inside it with such force that the metal rim had deformed outward.

And that was all it took—seeing the shoulder holster immediately transported him back down to the plane of everyday existence, the plane where he had a name, Ed Pender, and carried a gun, a Smith & Wesson Model 10. Where he and a man named Skip were trying to catch a killer. Where somebody had slipped him a heavy dose of . . . of the dread El Ess Dee.

Lucy in the sky with diamonds, he thought—*that's a song.* Then he looked up at the sky and actually saw the aforementioned diamonds sparkling there, and suddenly another lyric fragment went fluttering through his mind: *something something the diamond sky . . .* Followed by another: *stars shining up abuuuuve you . . .* And yet another: *bewitched, bothered, and bewildered . . .* And now there was no stopping them: *abandoned and forsaken . . . no direction home . . . can't tell the forest for the trees . . . of greeeen, red roses, too—*

Enough! Enough! He squeezed his head between his palms, trying to slow the flow of lyrics so he could think . . . *think* . . . *think what you're tryin' to—*

No! Make it stop! . . . *in the naaame of love, before you—*

Please, God, somebody, help me make it . . . *through the night . . .*

"Fuuuuck!" shouted Pender. The cry bounced off the surrounding trees and echoed across the clearing. Then the night went dead quiet, probably because there weren't any oldies that started with *fuuuuck.*

He was still tripping, though. Soaring. Suddenly the night noise came flooding back, like somebody'd turned up a big volume knob in the sky. The clatter of the aspen leaves like a zillion casta-nets, the lugubrious *who-who-who* of a great horned owl.

"Special Agent E. L. Pender, that's who, who, who," he said aloud, and discovered that, for some reason, talking out loud seemed to help. "Special Agent E. L. Goddamn Pender, getting his shit together for your FBI in peace and war, from here to eternity, till death do us—Shut up, Pender! Yes sir, this is me shutting up, sir!"

Now what? Got to find those fine folks in the pajamas before *he* does. Make them safe. Because like you told McDougal a couple centuries ago, that's what you *do*. Even more significantly, that's who you *are*. So focus, pal, focus.

"Okay, this is me focusing. First thing I need to do is . . ." He snapped off the arrow just above the ferrule and tossed the shaft aside, leaving the arrowhead embedded in the bent trigger guard. "Okay, now all I have to do is find the trail."

Which turned out to be easier said than done. Because from the center of the perfectly round clearing, everything looked the same. There *were* no directions, and the twinkling stars, though bright enough to sugar-frost the round expanse of clover, were not twinkling brightly enough to light his way.

But if the clearing was perfectly round, Pender told himself, then he couldn't get lost in it, could he? All he had to do was walk around the whatchamacallit, the circumference of the circle. Pick a direction, clockwise or counter-, and stick to it, and sooner or later he was bound to strike the trailhead.

And that was how it worked out. Pender aimed himself to-ward the edge of the circle, kept going until he couldn't go any farther without leaving the clearing, then turned to his right and continued walking, with the clearing on his right and the trees on his left. Then all he had to do was not forget which was right and which was left—a challenge, in his condition, but not an insur-mountable one.

To keep the deluge of song lyrics at bay, Pender counted his steps as he marched, and had reached sixty-two when the trees to his left parted, revealing what looked like the mouth of a narrow, twisting tunnel. A rush of triumph, then a sudden wrench of panic—what if this wasn't *the* path? What if it was some other path? Or no path at all? How goddamn lost would he be then?

His momentum halted, Pender was on the brink of the condition known as paralysis by analysis when a voice that sounded suspiciously like his own growled, "Nothin' to it but to do it," and the next thing he knew, he was twelve, thirteen, fourteen paces up the tunnel, and counting.

The rocky, uneven path from the main trail to the Omphalos hadn't been easy to descend in daylight, without psychedelics; the ascent in the dark, alone, on acid, must have been nearly heroic. Or so Pender had to assume when he reached the top, because he had no memory of the climb whatsoever: his runaway mind had switched his body over to automatic pilot.

Coming upon the golf cart parked by the side of the marked trail, Pender felt as though he'd stumbled on a relic of a lost civilization. Just beyond it, the trail forked downhill into the darkness to the left, uphill into the darkness to the right. The left fork, Pender somehow recognized, would take him back the way they'd come this afternoon, back to the Center and the hot springs and a telephone he could use to call for the cavalry to come bail his ass out of this one, because he had definitely screwed the pooch trying to handle it with only a gimpy P.I. for a partner.

"Left fork it is, then," he said aloud.

On the other hand, said that little voice inside Pender's head, not the one that knew all the song lyrics, but the one that listened to them.

"On the other hand, what?"

On the other hand, if they all went that way, they're probably al-

ready back and they've already called in the cavalry, so what do they need you for?

"And if they went the other way?"

If they went the other way, and they're in the shit, then you are the cavalry.

"Okay, right fork it is."

Good thinking.

3

Acid trips ebb and flow. The roller-coaster car is slowing down, clanking back to the start-finish line; convinced the ride is coming to an end, you've just unsnapped your seat belt and are waiting for the safety bar to release, when *whooosh*—off you go again.

Skip lost his hold on reality not long after everybody split up. The going got progressively weirder. At one point in time (insofar as there was such a thing), he saw himself in a great open-air ballroom, listening to a distant orchestra playing schmaltzy waltz music. And not long after that, he found himself limping with the aid of his staff down what seemed to be a long, dark tunnel with writhing walls and a lacy ceiling made of flickering stars and whispering leaves.

With only a vague idea where he was or how he'd come to be there, Skip realized he might have been dreaming—either that or he had just awakened from a dream. He also had a strong sense that he was either lost himself or searching for somebody else who was lost. In his free hand, he held a slender flashlight pointing down at the ground. Fascinated by the way the bobbing oblong splash of light on the ground managed to stay the same distance in front of him, a few feet ahead of his feet no matter how fast or slow he went, Skip forgot to look up even after the oblong of light began to climb a tree trunk, and *splat!* he walked right into the tree.

He bounced off, embarrassed but uninjured. Shining the flashlight around, he discovered that the path had taken a ninety-degree turn.

"My mistake," he murmured politely to the tree, then corrected course. Rounding the bend, Skip raised the flashlight to direct the beam straight ahead, and suddenly the weirdness quotient soared to heights he was totally unprepared to deal with. For standing sideways in the middle of the trail, caught dead center in the beam of the flashlight, a humanoid-shaped archer with a black face and round, protruding insect eyes dropped the arrow it was aiming at Skip's heart and threw up its arm to shield its bug eyes from the glare of Skip's flashlight.

While Skip's mind was still trying to make sense of that, a towering, ursine figure loomed up out of the darkness and seized the insect man from behind in a bear hug. Skip stood there dumbfounded, watching helplessly as the struggle raged on, the insect man throwing himself from side to side in an attempt to free himself from the encircling arms, the bear man heaving and grunting in an attempt to lift the insect man off his feet.

And just when Skip had convinced himself that things couldn't possibly get any weirder, the bear spoke. To him. "Hey, Magnum!" it called. "I could use a little help here, if it's not too much goddamn trouble."

◁

"Ollee ollee in freeee! Ollee ollee in freeee!"

After subduing Charles Mesker, a.k.a. Asmador, and binding him hand and foot with his own bowstrings, Skip and Pender led, tugged, pushed, dragged, and half-carried their struggling captive all the way back to the bluff at the top of the hill, yelling Owen Oliver's version of "home free all" at the top of their lungs every few steps.

Dr. Oliver, carrying Steve Stahl in his arms, was the last of the hide-and-seekers to emerge from the forest, his white pajamas torn and stained, tear tracks cutting through the dirt on his cheeks, leaf crumbs in his bushy beard. Gently, he laid Stahl on the ground with the arrow still sticking out of his chest.

Beryl bustled over and gave Steve a cursory examination by flashlight, then lay down with her ear pressed against his chest, taking care not to disturb the embedded arrow. He'd definitely lost a lot of blood, she told Oliver, and his left lung had probably collapsed. While they desperately needed to get him to a hospital as soon as possible, she was also concerned that he might not survive much more jostling.

In the end, they decided to send the fastest runners to summon help. Tom, who'd run track in college, and George Speaks, a marathoner, volunteered. Pender, Skip, Oliver, and Beryl were to remain behind, two to keep an eye on Mesker, two to nurse the injured man.

As for the others, suggested a visibly chastened Dr. O, casting an uneasy glance in Pender's direction, it might be best if Candace led them back to their tents or cabins while they waited for the "sacrament" to wear off, rather than subject them to a grilling by the authorities in their present, vulnerable condition.

"What condition is that?" said Pender, pointedly. Humiliation was the best outcome he could hope for if the gang back at Liaison Support learned he'd gotten himself dosed on LSD; more likely, he'd end up on the couch of some Bureau psychiatrist, trying to prove he hadn't been rendered permanently unfit for duty. "How about you, Skip—you know what condition he's talking about?"

"Not a clue."

"Thank you." Oliver's entire being sagged with relief—he looked as though he'd just had a twelve-hour massage. But there was something in him that wouldn't let him let it go. "You know, if you two had leveled with me in the beginning . . ."

"Don't push it, sir," snapped Pender. "I don't know what the penalty is for dosing a federal officer with an illicit substance, but I'm guessing it's serious."

Somewhat startled, Oliver apologized, then nodded toward their wildly struggling captive, whom they'd tied to a tall, slender tree at the wider, landward end of the arrowhead-shaped bluff. "Would you mind if I had a chat with our friend there? Maybe I can help him calm down a little."

"Be my guest." Embarrassed now at how readily he'd reverted to his asshole FBI guy persona, Pender began patting self-consciously through the pockets of his ruined sport coat, looking for his cigarettes. He was relieved to find his smokes undamaged—thank God for the Marlboro hard pack. Nor had the battered pewter flask in his right jacket pocket lost a drop of his emergency ration of Jim Beam. "And hey, I'm sorry I overreacted there. I don't know what happened—it was like Bruce Banner turning into the Incredible Hulk."

"I understand," said Oliver. "Old habits and all that."

Since his capture, Charlie Mesker had been alternating between extended spells of near catatonia and raging tantrums that were short-lived but exhausting, in which he threw his body around as if he were his own rag doll, or slammed the back of his head against the slender tree to which he was tied. His hands were bound behind him, and someone had thoughtfully provided a zafu for him to sit on.

"Charlie," Oliver said softly, hunkering down next to Mesker and cupping the back of the man's head with his palm to cushion the contact between occiput and tree. He popped an orange capsule of Thorazine into Mesker's mouth when Charlie opened it to spew curses, then tilted a water bottle to his lips. (Though not a prescribing physician, Oliver always took a few Thorazine along on these acid training exercises just in case.)

Oliver watched Mesker's Adam's apple bob, then recapped the water bottle and eased himself to a sitting position on the damp, sloping ground at the base of the tree and began crooning to him. "Taaake it easy, Charlie. Caaalm and easy. You don't have to fight *any* more. No one's going to hurt youuu, and youuu're not going to hurt aaanyone . . . , so you can juuust relaaax, relaaax into your breathing . . . thaaat's right, thaaat's the boy, Charlie . . . iiin and ouuut, niiice and easy . . ."

Charlie? thinks Asmador. *Why does he keep calling me Charlie? I don't even know anybody named—*

No, wait, hold on a sec. There was *a Charlie once . . . once upon a time. A human Charlie, a boy from Santa Cruz with a mother and a father and . . . and a dog. A mangy-looking, flop-eared mutt named Newton who got run over by a car on West Cliff Drive. And young Charlie, the tears in his eyes making everything all blurry, had helped his father bury Newton in the backyard, in a cardboard carton, and when they filled in the hole, the dirt and pebbles made a hollow, rattling sound hitting the cardboard.*

"Boo-hoo, boo-hoo." A devilish voice, derisive, amused. Asmador opens his eyes and sees Sammael leaning in over Dr. O's shoulder. The scornful redhead is in his changeling guise, with his wings half-furled and one talon-like hand resting lightly on the human's shoulder for balance. He's wearing his human face, though, and when he speaks again, he sounds a lot like poor Luke Sweet.

"Well, aren't you going to finish the story, dude? About how little Charlie dug up ol' Newton a couple weeks later just to see what he looked like? And how instead of reburying what was left of his precious doggy, he

hid it in one of the heat ducts in the school basement. And how they had to shut the place down for the rest of the week?"

"How did you know about that?"

"I'm the Poison Angel—I know everything."

"Oh yeah? Then what's going to happen to me?"

"That depends."

"On what?"

"On how patient you are, and how clever. Because it's going to take a long time, and you're going to have to fool a lot of humans, doctors and nurses and lawyers and judges and just about every other variety, before they're going to let you *anywhere* near a boiler room ever again."

"But if I can do it? If I'm very patient and very clever? What then?"

"The answer is in the Book," whispers Sammael. "The answer is always in the Book."

5

Oliver, who had done more camping than Skip and Pender (no great feat: Stephen Hawking had probably done more camping than Skip and Pender), supervised the laying of the fire, with a little nest of dry grass and dead leaves in the center, an understory of twigs and smaller sticks, and a pyramidal superstructure of interwoven branches supporting the heavier logs.

Then a flick of Pender's reliable old Zippo, a puff of orange, and soon the flames were leaping merrily, a beacon to guide the rescue helicopter that wheeled out of the western sky like an evening star less than an hour later and alighted in the middle of the bluff, blowing Oliver's campfire all to flinders.

Unfortunately, the little medevac chopper had only enough room for the injured man and two others.

"We'll be back for you in no time," the pilot shouted to Skip and Pender as the chopper lifted off with Steve, Dr. O, and Beryl aboard.

Skip had to laugh at that. "What does he know about *no time*?" he called to Pender, who had finished stomping out sparks at the edge of the woods and was now gathering kindling to revive the fire.

"I second that emotion," said Pender. "There was one . . . time back there when I looked at my watch and it was actually melting. I'd always thought that was just a cliché, like in the movies when they want to show the characters are tripping."

"That's how things *get* to be clichés—because they happen a lot," Skip pointed out. "Hey, you know what I just realized? I haven't taken a Norco since this morning, and *nothing hurts*!" Then, after thinking it over: "Of course, they'll probably have to carry me home on a stretcher when the acid wears off."

When they had the fire going again, the two huddled under the blankets the paramedics had left behind for them, arranging their zafus so they could watch the fire and keep an eye on Mesker, who appeared to be asleep. Pender took out his flask and took a sip, started to offer it to Skip, then remembered. "Oh, right, you don't drink."

"Oh, I drink," Skip said sensibly. "I drink plenty. Just not alcohol." He turned and brushed off the ground behind him, pried out a few of the larger rocks and tossed them aside, then lay back, propped himself up on his elbows, and watched the fire for either a long moment or a short eon. It all felt so elemental—the darkness, the crackle of the fire, the sparks shooting heavenward. "All we need is some marshmallows," he told Pender.

"I always thought toasting marshmallows was overrated," said Pender. "Picking that black shit out of your teeth—yucch!"

"You don't *have* to burn them black, y'know."

"I'm a man of extremes." They watched the fire for, well, for however long they watched the fire, then Pender broke the silence again. "Hey, Magnum, you want to hear something amazing?"

"Sure," said Skip. "But I have to warn you, my definition of *amazing* is a lot different than it was, I don't know, six, seven hours ago."

"Is that how long we've been tripping?"

"Beats me," replied Skip.

"And vice versa," said Pender, confusing both of them.

"You were going to tell me something amazing?" Skip prompted, after what may have been a long pause.

"Oh, right. Here it is: if it wasn't for Big Luke—you know, Little Luke's father?"

Skip nodded.

"If it wasn't for Big Luke, I wouldn't be sitting here talking to you."

Skip waited a few whatevers, then asked Pender if there was an explanation that came with that.

"Oh, right. The thing is, ten years ago, after Big Luke outdrew me in the post office, I swore to myself I'd never wear a kidney holster again. So last year, when the Bureau in its wisdom ordered everybody who was still wearing shoulder holsters to switch to behind-the-backs, I didn't make a big fuss—that's not how you do it in the Bureau. Instead I just sort of pretended I never got the memo, and my boss, bless his heart, sort of pretended not to notice. And the kicker, of course . . ."

Pender opened his jacket to show Skip his calfskin holster, with an inch of shaft sticking out from the safety flap and the arrowhead embedded in the bent trigger guard of the Model 10. "The kicker is that if I'd been wearing a kidney holster instead of old faithful here, then instead of sitting here talking to you I'd be lying dead in the clover with an arrow sticking out of my ribs."

"That is pretty amazing," said Skip. "But you know what's really, *really* amazing?"

"What's that?" said Pender.

Skip waved his hand around in a grand gesture loosely encompassing himself, Pender, the slumbering Charles Mesker, the breathtaking view, the earth below and the sky above. "Everything," he said. "Just . . . everything."

Special Agent E. L. Pender raised his pewter flask to the shimmering stars. "I'll drink to that," he said.

And he did.